THE OTHER ASSASSIN

Hours after Jack Ruby shot and killed Lee Harvey Oswald, two reporters visited Ruby's apartment. Shortly after this visit, both reporters were dead—one murdered by an unknown assailant, the other killed in an "accidental" shooting.

What did these reporters find? Why were they killed? Pulitzer Prize nominee Bill Sloan attempts to answer these questions through the eyes of a fictional third reporter who escapes death and attempts to discover the truth behind the mysterious murders of his friends.

A reporter for the *Dallas Times Herald* at the time of the assassination of John F. Kennedy, Bill Sloan interviewed key figures in the ensuing investigation. In *The Other Assassin*, Sloan takes the well-documented but little-known story of the reporters and brings it to life in a suspenseful novel that raises new questions about one of the most tragic events in our century.

THE
OTHER ASSASSIN

BILL SLOAN

A division of Shapolsky Publishers, Inc.

S.P.I. BOOKS

A division of Shapolsky Publishers, Inc.

For any additional information, contact:
S.P.I. BOOKS/Shapolsky Publishers, Inc.
136 West 22nd Street
New York, NY 10011
(212) 633-2022
FAX (212) 633-2123

ISBN: 1-56171-156-7

10 9 8 7 6 5 4 3 2 1

Printed and bound in the United States of America

For Lana, my compatriot and dearest critic . . .

PROLOGUE

Outside the faceless gray building in the old city of Dresden, German Democratic Republic, a cold drizzle was falling that Saturday morning. As he sat impatiently behind the desk in a windowless interview room on the third floor, Colonel Georgi Volkov of Red Army intelligence smoked an English cigarette and awaited the arrival of agent Igor Kaminski of the KGB for their final briefing session before Kaminski's departure.

There was a soft knock at the door, and as Volkov rose to his feet, a man wearing the uniform of a staff sergeant in the U.S. Army and the insignia of the American Military Police entered the room. He saluted, then stood at ease.

"Good morning, Colonel Volkov," the man said in flawless English without the slightest trace of an accent. "Nice weather we're having, isn't it?"

"Greetings, Igor," Volkov said with a tight smile. "That sounds very good, a very authentic Midwestern American. You *are* from Ohio, I believe—even though you have never been west of Washington—are you not?"

"Yes," the other man replied. "Van Wert, Ohio, to be exact. Graduated from Van Wert High School in 1950, ranked fourteenth scholastically out of a graduating class of one hundred and fifteen, lettered three years in football as outside linebacker. Attended Ohio State University at Columbus for two years, enlisted in the Army in May, 1954, six months after my parents were killed in an automobile accident. Went through basic training at Fort Bliss, Texas, attended military police school at Fort Sam Houston in San Antonio, and arrived in Germany in March, 1955. How am I doing so far?"

"Excellent, excellent, Igor," the colonel said. "After only one week with the captured American sergeant you have managed to duplicate his mannerisms, language and personality extremely well, and, of course, you already *were* his identical physical double. But in slightly more than forty-eight hours, you must assume his total identity, comrade. You must do it well enough to fool his commanding officer, his fellow soldiers, and, once you are discharged in his place two months from now, his friends back home in Ohio. Are you ready for this, my friend?"

Kaminski shrugged. "As ready as I possibly can be, Comrade Colonel," he said. "The eight months I spent as a third assistant secretary in the Soviet Embassy in D.C. gives me confidence that I can pass as an American without any problem."

"You do understand the experimental nature of your mission, and the effect it may have on the future espionage efforts of the U.S.S.R., do you not?" the colonel asked with emphasis. "And you do understand its importance? Thousands of hours have been spent in research and surveillance over the past three years to find someone in the American military who looks enough like you to be your twin brother. I don't have to tell you that Comrade Khrushchev himself has expressed great interest in this experiment."

"I'm aware of that, sir. I'm deeply honored to have been selected."

"You've been told this many times before, comrade, but there must be no misunderstanding on these points. Once you enter Allied occupied territory, and especially once you are in the United States, you are entirely on your own. If something goes wrong, the Soviet government will disavow you in the most emphatic terms possible. And you must not allow yourself to be captured alive under any circumstances. Is that clear?''

"Perfectly clear, Comrade Colonel."

"Your only assignment is to infiltrate a civilian police agency, preferably in the Southwestern U.S., where there is a high concentration of armaments manufacturing and top-security military bases, and where Soviet citizens are banned from travel. Understood?''

"Yes, sir, I understand completely."

"You have your contacts," Volkov said. "Are there any further questions?''

"None that I can think of," Kaminski replied.

The colonel ground out his cigarette in a metal ashtray on the desk, then stood up slowly and extended his hand. "I wish you success, Igor,'' he said. "It may be many years before you are able to return to Mother Russia, and there is a good chance you will never get home to the Ukraine again, but you must know that your mission is worth whatever sacrifice is necessary. You have been given the best training and preparation that the Soviet Union can provide. Good luck, my friend."

"Thank you, Comrade Colonel," Kaminsky said. He saluted smartly and turned toward the door.

"Oh, by the way, comrade," the colonel said as the other man was on his way out, "I assume you have no further use for the American sergeant."

Kaminsky frowned momentarily, then shook his head. "No," he said decisively, "I've gotten everything I can from him."

"Very well then. Carry on."

As the door closed firmly behind Kaminski, Colonel Volkov lit another English cigarette and inhaled deeply. He hated what he was about to do, but there was no way out of it and utterly no sense in postponing it. The American sergeant seemed a decent enough young man and had behaved both correctly and courageously ever since he had been kidnapped in Frankfurt, but that made no difference. The American was merely a pawn in a much larger game. He took another puff on the cigarette, then picked up the telephone on the desk and waited momentarily until he heard the voice of his orderly on the other end of the line.

"Tell Major Borshilov to execute the prisoner," he said tersely. "Tell him to have the body transported immediately by Army ambulance to the cemetery at Freiberg, where a grave is open and waiting. A marker is already in place, showing that a Wehrmacht corporal is buried there. Once the interment is completed, Major Borshilov and all concerned are to forget that such a prisoner ever existed. That means you as well, Yuri."

"Yes, Comrade Colonel," the orderly said. "Consider the matter forgotten already."

CHAPTER ONE

October 20, 1987

Only a few days ago, it had been summer, but now it was suddenly and undeniably fall. The cold front of the previous week had dissipated, as cold fronts do in mid-October, and it had turned pleasantly warm and sunny again, but there was no doubt that autumn had officially arrived. It was also unusually dry for southeastern Arkansas at this time of year. This was good for the cotton farmers who were struggling to bring in their crop, but the dry weather also increased the danger of grass fires or even forest fires. A single spark in one of the innumerable pine thickets that dotted the landscape could touch off a holocaust under these conditions. Nevertheless, the end result was strikingly beautiful. Because of the dry weather and the frost of the week before, the leaves on the sweetgum trees that fringed Highway 81 were no longer deep green, but flaming shades of scarlet and vermillion—the most colorful in years, the natives said—as David East drove past them that afternoon, heading south from Little Rock.

In a way, David East always had relished fall. The cool evenings were ideal for a fireplace and a cup of hot cider, and the bright, crisp mornings were perfect for leaning against a tree trunk on the bank of the creek behind his house, cradling his old 20-gauge shotgun in his arms and waiting for the sun to come up and the squirrels to start moving. Fall made him glad to be back in the country after all those confining years in one city or another, but fall also had an eerie, disquieting effect on David East. The bad dreams that often haunted his nights always seemed to come more often in the fall, and the regrets and misgivings that marred his days also seemed to edge closer to the surface of his conscious mind. Many times in the fall, he caught himself literally glancing back over his shoulder, fearful lest the monsters from his past might finally be catching up to him. It was, however, something that he didn't waste a lot of mental energy worrying about. It had been that way for well over 20 years, since long before David East had been David East, and it would most likely continue to be that way for as long as he lived. Besides, he had too little mental energy these days to expend on anything that wasn't absolutely essential.

The divided stretch of U.S. 65 had ended just south of Pine Bluff, and a little later, Highway 81 had branched off to the right, still a good hour's drive to his destination, the old Victorian farmhouse three miles from Jefferson. The trip from the U.S. 65 junction to home had grown steadily longer in the more than four years he had been making this trip periodically. The reason was mainly the inordinate, and continually increasing, number of 18-wheel tractor-trailer rigs that used the route as a shortcut between Interstate 30 on the north and Interstate 20 on the south. Every trucker in the South was familiar with this shortcut by now, and most of them used it, despite the fact that the two-lane highway was narrow and curving and wound its way through numerous small towns and villages. It was a dangerous highway, and there was talk of widening it, talk that just might be approaching the serious stage. That was one reason he had gone to Little Rock to interview State Representative Sam Cravens, who was pushing for a new highway bill in the Legislature.

It was funny how things happened, he thought, cutting the speed of the old Mustang convertible and easing in behind an

18-wheeler with a big, red Safeway "S" on the back of it, as it struggled up a long hill. Whenever he went to Little Rock, he had a habit of stopping at a large downtown newsstand, not far from the state capitol, and picking up the latest edition of the *Dallas Times Herald*. Sometimes he purchased some other big-city papers, too, just to see how they were doing things these days, but he never failed to buy a *Times Herald* if one was available. Once upon a time, in another life and under another name, he had written and edited copy for the *Times Herald*, and he still felt an odd attachment to it, despite the fact that its ownership, editorial direction and physical appearance had changed markedly over the years.

But if it had not been for the highway problems and the highway bill, he probably would not have gone to Little Rock at all this month, he thought. If he had not gone, he obviously would not have visited the newsstand in question and might never have seen the headline on the front page of yesterday's *Times Herald*. And if he had not seen the headline, it might have been weeks, perhaps even months, before he had learned that his old drinking buddy, Tommy Van Zandt, was running for governor of Texas.

While he coasted along, waiting for the truck in front of him to reach the crest of the hill and speed up again as it started down, he glanced over at the paper in the empty passenger's seat beside him. And again he felt a twinge of disbelief and something akin to apprehension as he read the bold, 36-point headline aloud to himself for what must have been the fiftieth time:

Van Zandt Enters Governor's Race as Instant Front Runner

The man known in Jefferson, Arkansas, as David East, owner and publisher of the town's weekly newspaper, *The Jeffersonian*, shook his head. When he thought of Tommy Van Zandt, he could still picture the dapper young assistant district attorney Van Zandt had been in the early '60s, before he turned to other pursuits and got rich. He thought of long afternoons back in the good old days, when he and his best friend, police reporter Jamie Cade, would meet Tommy and detective lieutenant Alexander Sutton and various other journalists, lawyers and cops for endless rounds of beer at Bill Martin's TV Bar.

They had all been young and carefree and full of bull, and then, seemingly almost overnight, everything had changed. Tommy had gotten hooked up with D. Wingo Conlan, a jaded millionaire industrialist with a taste for illicit drugs, pornography and power. Before long, Tommy had quit the DA's office, and pretty soon he was making a fortune in retainers form Conlan and commissions for funneling conservative Texas money into numbered Swiss bank accounts and tax-proof foreign investments for Conlan and other super-wealthy people. And along about the same time, Tommy had started talking some really radical political trash about the "five-idiot majority" on the Supreme Court and certain high-level political figures who needed to be "eliminated."

As David East also remembered another bright, sunny autumn day—November 22, 1963—his thoughts were suddenly crowded with other images: Jackie Kennedy, smiling and waving in Abraham Zapruder's classic film as the open-topped presidential limousine turned slowly into Elm Street toward the Triple Underpass—Jamie Cade, grinning and gregarious, and now dead these 23 years, with his killer still unpunished, uncaptured and unknown—Pretty Hollie O'Connor, Jamie's girlfriend and a stripper who briefly brightened the stage at Jack Ruby's shabby Carousel Club, crushed under the wheels of a hit-and-run car—Mollie O'Connor, Hollie's identical twin and the other half of the "Sugar 'n' Spice Sisters," who vanished forever two days after President Kennedy was assassinated—Jack Ruby himself, materializing out of nowhere in the basement of the Dallas City Hall, with the snubnosed Colt Cobra in his fat little hand—Lee Harvey Oswald, the grimace of surprise and pain frozen on his bruised and sallow face as Ruby shot him down. . . .

In the space of a single instant, all these images flashed through David East's mind, as they had a thousand times before and no doubt would a thousand times to come. And within that instant, he realized why fall made him feel uneasy.

* * *

He pulled the Mustang to a halt in the shadowed driveway beside the 100-year-old house. In Naperville, Illinois, where he had lived with his wife and child slightly more than four years ago, a house of this size and vintage, in good condition, would have easily commanded a price of $90,000 or more. But here in the isolated economic backwater of southeastern Arkansas, it had cost just $18,500, and he was pretty sure the seller had laughed all the way to the bank when he had found a buyer willing to pay that price.

The man who called himself David East got out of the car, walked up the steps to the front porch and unlocked the front door. He glanced at his watch, noticed that it was almost 5 p.m. on a Tuesday afternoon, and thought guiltily that he really should have put in an appearance at the office, instead of going straight home. After all, he was the publisher and sole owner of the only newspaper in Jefferson, Arkansas (population 5,862), and if that newspaper was to come off the press as scheduled tomorrow evening over at the printing plant in Monticello, he had certain responsibilities to fulfill.

Still, he knew there was no cause to worry, and he didn't. Sarah would take care of the paper, just as she had been doing even before he arrived on the scene. With calm, characteristic efficiency, Sarah would take care of everything. He fervently thanked God for Sarah whenever he thought about her. With Sarah as its editor, even at the budget-straining salary of $185 per week, *The Jeffersonian* actually had no need for a publisher—least of all one with a drinking problem, recurring bouts of depression, and a price on his head.

Nevertheless, if only for appearance sake, he picked up the phone on the table in the foyer and dialed the familiar number.

"Jeffersonian. Good afternoon," the voice said. It was Julie Bliss, the high school girl who came in after class to answer the phone and perform other menial, mostly meaningless chores.

"Julie, this is David East," he said, deciding to spare the girl the embarrassment of not recognizing his voice. "I need to speak to Sarah Archer, please."

"Yes sir, Mr. East," she said. "Just one minute."

There was a vacant silence as she put him on hold. Then, after about 30 seconds, the line came alive again, and he heard Sarah's husky, slightly harried voice. "Hi, boss," she said. "Everything under control in the big city?"

"Oh sure, no problem. They're still stealing us blind at the state capitol, and not giving us anything to show for it. Just the same as always. What's going on down there?"

"Not a lot," she said, "but we'll get this front page filled up somehow or other. Sometimes I think it'd be nice to have a triple axe murder around this place."

"I can't help you there," he told her, "but I will have a highway story for you in the morning, based on what little I got out of Sam Cravens today. Do you need me for anything else? I can come on down if you do."

It was odd, he thought, in the split-second before she answered, but he almost hoped she would ask him to come down. It would be nice to feel needed at the office for once, but there was something more, too. He knew, without understanding why, that he really wanted to see her. He wanted to look into her clear, cornflower-blue eyes as they stared quizzically back at him through her glasses. He wanted to enjoy the funny way her mouth turned up at the corners when she smiled. He wanted to observe the unruly strands of dark-brown hair that inevitably escaped from her ponytail and formed a wispy halo around her face when she was hard at work. He wanted to watch her chewing on the end of her pencil as she struggled with the process of converting a thought into a typewritten line of copy. He wanted . . .

"Nah, you don't need to do that, boss," she said. "I can tell you're tired just by the sound of your voice. You stay home and relax. We'll handle things at this end."

"You're sure?"

"Positive," she said. "See you in the morning."

Despite his slight disappointment as he hung up the phone, he realized what a blessing it was to have somebody like Sarah working for him. He had discovered how indispensible she was the very first week after he arrived, and now he seriously doubted that he could make it without her. She was one of those people who do things so well that those around them keep wanting them to do more and more and more. He knew that his dependence on her had reached unseemly proportions and was still growing, but most of the time he tried not to think about it. If she ever decided to quit for any reason, he might just have to close the place up and forget it. He couldn't conceive of any way he could get *The Jeffersonian* out every Thursday without her.

He walked back to the old-fashioned, high-ceilinged kitchen, flipping on lights as he went, and frowned when he got there. The sink was still piled with unwashed dishes, and the same litter of crumbs he had left there that morning still adorned the round oak table, along with the inky dregs of a cup of coffee. He opened the door of the wall cabinet to the right of the sink and removed a clean glass, then crossed the room to the pantry, took out a quart bottle about a third full of bourbon and dumped a couple of ounces into the glass.

Just to the left of where the bourbon bottle had sat, his glance fell on the bottle of cyanide-laced amaretto as he closed the pantry door. The amaretto had been there for months, so long that he almost forgot about it sometimes. Yet it was grotesquely comforting to know that it was always available, always within easy reach, and that it would take only seconds for it to do its work when it became necessary. He had read enough to know that death from cyanide poisoning was almost instantaneous if the dose was strong enough—and he had made abundantly sure that it was. He had put it in the amaretto because he theorized that the sweet liqueur would mask the bitter-almond taste of the poison more efficiently than plain whiskey. If the depression finally became more than he could bear, the amaretto was his certain ticket out.

He sat down at the round oak table, brushed the crumbs aside, and took a long sip of the bourbon. Then he carefully unfolded the copy of the *Dallas Times Herald* that he had brought home from Little Rock and gazed down at the photograph of Tommy Van Zandt on the front page.

"Well, Tommy, you old cowchip," he said aloud, borrowing a term that he had not used in more than two decades from the dusty lexicon in the back of his mind, "I guess you finally got all the money you wanted, so now you're going after the power."

He thought idly about calling Tommy Van Zandt and kidding him about his candidacy. "Remember to stay out of open cars, Tommy," he might say. "You know what happened to John Connally." He laughed a little, although it wasn't very funny. It would be a kick, though, to see Tommy's face if a voice from the past suddenly did call him up and say, "Hi, Tommy, this is David East. Remember me? Well, of course you don't, because my name was Matthew Eastman when you and I used to drink beer together and talk about what we were going to do when we grew up."

But, hell, he thought as he refilled his glass, guys that ran for governor had ways of avoiding voices from the past, ways like unlisted home telephone numbers and protective cordons of receptionists and secretaries and maybe even bodyguards. As a matter of fact, he actually had tried to call Tommy once several years ago during a Christmas party in Chicago, but had gotten no further than an impersonal secretary at Conlan Universal Aerospace in Dallas, who informed him that "Mr. Van Zandt is in a meeting and cannot be disturbed." Although he had been pretty drunk at the time, he had wisely declined her invitation to leave his name and number. Instead, he had asked for the company mailing address and sent Tommy a Christmas card. He had written something clever inside (he couldn't remember what) and signed it simply "Matt." He hadn't bothered to put a return address on the envelope.

About five months later, while David East had been out of town on business, his wife, Colleen, and their six-year-old daughter, Diana, had been blown to bits in an explosion at his house in Naperville. The police said it was an accident caused by a natural gas leak. Since then, David East had scarcely thought about Tommy Van Zandt, and he had also tried very hard not to think about Jamie Cade or Alex Sutton or Hollie and Mollie O'Connor or any of the godawful 24-year-old mess in Dallas—until today, when the story in the *Times Herald* had brought it all flooding back.

He folded the paper so that he could no longer see the headline about Tommy Van Zandt and tossed it to the far end of the table. He thought about going outside for a little while and puttering around in the warm sunshine among the color-splashed trees. He even thought of getting out the shotgun and a few shells and taking Hobo, his shaggy old dog, for a walk through the fields behind the house. They might even jump a rabbit if they were lucky.

He thought about all this, but in the end he did nothing except sit at the table and drink. He emptied the glass again and refilled it, fairly certain that he would not stop until the bottle was bone-dry.

CHAPTER TWO

October 24, 1987

He awoke that Saturday morning with what he had come to classify over the years as a "Class C Misdemeanor" hangover. It was a little worse than a "Fender-Bender" or "Disturbing the Peace" hangover, but not nearly as painful or long-lasting as a "First-Degree Felony"—much less a "Capital Offense." In certain acute cases, he was convinced that the latter variety could actually prove fatal, and it always made you *wish* you were dead. So he took comfort in the knowledge that the slight headache and rumbly, fluttery innards that were the main symptoms of a "Class C Misdemeanor" would ease off within a couple of hours. By early afternoon, David East reasoned, he would probably feel relatively normal again—as normal as he ever felt, at any rate.

The hangover might not have been nearly as bad if it hadn't been for what Sarah had told him after dinner the night before. The dinners were something they had been doing on Friday nights for close to a year now, ever since Sarah had decided not to marry the stodgy young school administrator she had been engaged to. They had happened just occasionally at first, but with gradually increasing frequency until they were now an established part of their weekly routine. He told himself that buying Sarah's dinner at the end of the week was merely his way of offering her a small reward for the hard work and long hours she endured in his employ, but the fact was, their dinner dates had become the high points of his existence.

They had eaten, as they often did, at the Catfish Cottage, one of the two or three "nice" restaurants in Jefferson. Since the town was legally dry, the Catfish Cottage didn't serve alcoholic beverages, and by the time he had eaten a half-dozen catfish steaks with hushpuppies, fries, coleslaw and green tomato relish, he had almost been out of the mood to drink. Not wanting to give up Sarah's company so early, however, and sensing that she wanted to say something to him, he had suggested driving the dozen miles out to Leon's Place on the El Dorado Highway for a beer. He had been delighted when she said yes. Sarah wasn't much of a drinker, and a couple of beers or a solitary glass of wine was usually her evening's limit, but on this occasion, it was soon apparent that she was thirstier than usual. In just over two hours at Leon's, she had finished off three bottles of Lite while he was drinking six (or was it seven?) Buds.

From the time they left the office a little after 6 p.m. that Friday, with another week and another issue of *The Jeffersonian* now safely behind them, it was pretty clear that something was weighing on Sarah's mind, but they had been at Leon's for almost an hour before she finally got around to telling him what it was.

He had just made one of his routine self-disparaging remarks about how boring it must be for an attractive girl in her 20s to spend her Friday evenings with an old dullard who was crowding 50 and never talked about anything but small-town journalism and "the good old days."

At that point, she wrinkled her nose at him and said, "Just knock it off, boss. You're probably the most interesting man in this town, and you know I think so. You also know I always have a good time with you. That's why I hate to go and spoil the evening. Fact is, though, there's something I need to tell you.'' Her tone was slightly ominous.

''I'm listening,'' he said, trying to sound casual, but suddenly feeling tight and tense inside.

''I got offered a job this week,'' she said with characteristic bluntness, ''and I'm thinking about taking it.''

He took a long pull from his beer, the tense feeling turning to sick dread inside him. He should have been prepared for this, but he wasn't, and the jarring realization that he might be about to lose her hit him like a punch in the stomach. ''Where?'' he asked. ''What kind of job?''

''Doing general assignments at the *Pine Bluff Commercial*,'' she said. ''It's strictly entry-level stuff. You know, obits and weather and rinky-dink features, but I'll probably never get offered anything better, and at least it's a chance to get out of the boonies and see if I can make it on a real daily.''

''Hey, if that's all you want to know, I can tell you right now you'll make it just fine. You'd be an asset to any paper in the country. What kind of money are they offering?''

''Two-thirty a week to start and a salary review in six months.''

He shook his head and stared into his beer. ''I wish I could match it, Sarah,'' he said, ''but I don't see how I can. I might be able to go a couple hundred, maybe as much as two-ten, but the old budget's just about stretched to the limit already.''

He looked up when he felt her hand on his arm. ''The money's not really that important, boss,'' she said. ''God, if I take the job, I'll probably end up netting less than I do now, with moving expenses and higher apartment rent and all that. But I think maybe I need to move up to a bigger paper pretty soon if I'm ever going to. I mean, Jefferson's a great little town, but I've already spent over twenty-seven years of my life around here, and sometimes I feel like I want to see some new scenery and do some new things. I want to feel, you know, like I'm somewhere for once.''

He raised his head and tried to smile at her, although his heart wasn't in it. ''Sounds to me like you're asking an awful lot from poor old Pine Bluff, Arkansas,'' he said lightly. "I was through there earlier this week, you know, and it still looked like the same down-at-the-heels cotton town to me. I didn't see anybody dancing in the streets, or anything that even resembled the Great White Way.''

Sarah laughed. "Give me credit for having a little sense, boss,'' she said. "I know it's not Manhattan, but it *is* a step. After a couple of years, maybe I could move on to Little Rock or Memphis or even Dallas, but we both know I'll never be able to make the jump to a metro paper from here.''

He thought about Dallas, tried to picture her working there, and it made him shudder. "I'd do just about anything to keep you from ever starting that jumping process," he said, "but I know I'm just being selfish. If that's what you really want, Sarah, then I guess you ought to do it.''

Her hand tightened on his arm. "You know I don't want to go," she said, "but try to understand how I feel. I was born in these pine thickets. I grew up here and went to college here and so far I've worked here for over six years. I've never been anywhere else except for a few days. I've never even been close to anything significant or important, and sometimes it depresses me to think about being stuck here for the rest of my life.''

"Worse things have happened to people,'' he said. He knew how stupid it must sound to her, but he wasn't really thinking about Sarah when he said it. He was thinking about a couple of ex-high school cheerleaders from Sweetwater, Texas, who were drawn to Dallas by the lure of bigger, more important things. They convinced themselves they were just stopping over at the Carousel Club enroute to New York and Broadway, but they ended up in oblivion instead.

"Oh, sure, I guess so,'' she said, "but look who's talking, boss. You've been in just about every interesting place there is, and I'd like to see some of those places, too.'' She smiled and lowered her voice. "Surely you can understand how I feel—can't you, David?''

It was the first time he could remember her calling him by the given name he had used for the past 18 years, and the word sounded strange on her lips, as if it belonged to somebody else. At first, she had addressed him very correctly as "Mr. East," but he let her know that it made him feel old and he hated it. So she had compromised by calling him "boss" ever since.

"Certainly I can," he said. "I don't blame you for wanting to spread your wings a little. I'm just not sure I can make it without you, that's all."

She laughed again. "Don't worry, boss," she said. "If I do leave—and I honestly haven't made up my mind yet—I promise you won't have any trouble replacing me."

"You want to bet a week's pay on that?" he asked sourly. He tried to smile then, but he felt like crying.

They had left Leon's Place a few minutes later, with him in a desolate mood, and Sarah obviously uneasy about upsetting him. They made the trip back to town in almost total silence, then exchanged quiet goodnights at the parking lot beside the newspaper office, where Sarah climbed into her aging Volkswagen Bug. He followed along behind her in the Mustang, as he customarily did, until she pulled up in front of the hulking old house on Poplar Street, where she rented an upstairs room and bath for $22.50 per week.

She jumped out of her car and motioned to him to wait as he started to drive away, and he rolled down the window and watched her run across the street toward the Mustang, thinking how pretty she looked with her dark hair blowing around her face in the autumn breeze. She leaned down and looked in the window at him and smiled. Then she reached inside, found his hand with hers and squeezed it.

"Don't be mad at me, David," she said softly. "Please."

He shook his head. "I'm not," he told her, holding her small hand in both of his. "You do whatever you think is right for you. That's the main thing."

"I know everything will work out fine for both of us," she said. "I just know it will."

For an instant he wanted to open the door, pull her into his arms and kiss her. He wanted to kiss her until both their lips were numb. He wanted to take her home with him and kiss her all night, and maybe all the next day, too. He felt like he could kiss her for a week and never get tired of kissing her.

He wanted to kiss her more than he could ever remember wanting to do anything—but he didn't.

All he did was say, "Sure, I know it will, too," and feel her hand slip from his grasp as she turned away.

Once, halfway up the walk to the porch, she had turned again and waved. He had waved back, and then he had gone home to open a fresh bottle of bourbon and finish getting drunk.

And now, with the effects of the hangover flooding over him along with the bright rays of the Saturday morning sun, he found the prospect of being without her—not only as the editor of *The Jeffersonian*, but also as his most vital personal support system—as demoralizing as ever. It was almost more than he could bear.

It was 8:50 a.m. by the clock on the nightstand as he shoved back the sheet and blanket and threw his legs over the edge of the bed. He stood up heavily, stepped into his pants and lurched down the gloomy hallway toward the bathroom to wash his face.

In the semidarkness, he tripped over something furry and bulky, something precisely the same muddy, chocolate color as the unfashionable shag carpet on the hall floor. He heard a muffled grunt of discomfort and dimly glimpsed a small flurry of movement in front of him. When he reached the bathroom door and flipped on the light, he found himself confronted by Hobo's sad, brown, accusatory eyes.

"Damn you, Hobo," he said, "why do you insist on sleeping in the hall, you camouflaged sonofabitch?" It had happened innumerable times before and would undoubtedly continue to happen, unless he fatally wounded Hobo in the process of tripping over him. For reasons only a dog understood, Hobo's favorite sleeping place was the one spot in the house where he was practically invisible.

"You not only stepped on me; you also forgot to feed me again last night, you inconsiderate rumpot," Hobo's eyes scolded in silent, straightforward body language.

"I apologize, old man," he said as washed his face. Back in the bedroom, he forced his reluctant feet into a worn pair of Hushpuppies and thrust his arms into the same soiled, slightly smelly shirt he had worn the day before. "Come on, let's go outside. Then I'll see what I can find for you."

The long-suffering mutt followed him down the hall to the kitchen, where he opened the back door and let Hobo out into the yard. Then he filled the kettle with water for instant coffee, turned on a burner on the range until a circle of blue flame sprang up under it, and went to the pantry for a can of dogfood. He was spooning the last of the sticky reddish-brown mass into Hobo's dish when the telephone rang.

He frowned and started not to answer it. He could think of at least 50 people who might be calling the publisher of *The Jeffersonian* on a Saturday morning, from the mayor or the county judge right on down to the lowliest subscriber, and he had no desire to talk to any of them. But then again, he thought, it might be Sarah. Maybe she had decided not to take the job in Pine Bluff after all. Maybe she wanted to come over and soothe his feelings, hold his hand and stroke his fevered brow. Maybe she wanted to spend the weekend with him. Maybe . . .

On the fifth ring, he went to the wall phone that hung beside the door to the hallway and lifted the receiver. "Hello," he said in a voice like sandpaper.

There was no sound for a moment, and he thought the caller must have already hung up. "Hello," he said again.

Then he heard a faraway female voice coming faintly over the line, and the first words it spoke sent an avalanche of ice-cold fear crashing down through him, from just behind his rib cage to the tips of his toes.

"Matt?" the voice asked furtively. "Matthew Eastman, is that you?"

His eyes darted to the open back door and the shaggy figure of Hobo sniffing the grass at the edge of the yard. He saw the steam beginning to rise from the spout of the kettle on the stove, the perpetual stack of dirty dishes in the sink, the table with its crumbs and sticky spots of spilled liquid. Down the hall, through the open door of the bedroom, he could see the unmade bed and a jumble of dirty clothes hanging over the back of a chair. Everything in his small, untidy world looked exactly as it had a few seconds before, but in reality nothing was the same. In the twinkling of an eye and the whispering of a name, everything had changed.

There was a giddy sensation in his head and his knees were rubbery. His heart was pounding like a bass drum in his ears. "You must have the wrong number," he managed to say. "There's nobody . . ."

"Please, Matt," the thin, urgent voice implored. "Please don't hang up. You've got to help me, Matt. You're the only one I can trust. This is Mollie O'Connor."

He felt the room spin around, and he clutched at the wall to keep from losing his balance and falling. The headache and the distress in his abdomen were suddenly much worse.

"I don't know what you're talking about, lady," he said miserably. "My name is David East. You must have the wrong number."

"I'm truly sorry, Matty," she said. "I know you don't want to talk to me, but I had to call you. There's nobody else left."

He heard her start to cry then, and it broke his heart, because he could visualize her as she had been the last time he saw her. She had been so incredibly beautiful and so incredibly frightened. Up until that day, he had always envied Alex Sutton for having a girlfriend like Mollie. But after that day, he had stopped envying Alex and started fearing him.

"How do I know you're who you say you are?" he heard himself asking in a surprisingly calm voice.

"Remember the night we got you that blind date with Jack's new Mexican stripper?" she asked. "There was Hollie and Jamie and Alex and me, and we all went to Sivil's Drive-In, remember? You kept wondering why we called her 'Chiquita Banana' until she started grabbing your banana right there in the back seat . . ." She laughed and almost choked at the same time, and he knew it was really her. "Oh, God," she added sorrowfully, "what happened to all of us, Matty? What happened to those crazy kids?"

His heart slowed down a little and he felt himself blushing again, even after all this time. "Some of them got old and some of them died," he said grimly. "It happens all the time."

"I desperately need you to meet me someplace, Matty. If you will, I promise I'll make it as safe for you as I can. You can pick any spot in the state of Arkansas and I'll be there, but it's got to be soon—real soon."

"It's no use, Mollie," he said. "What good will it do?" He had to get hold of himself, he thought. He had to have a little time to figure out what to do. If he just threw a few things in the Mustang and started driving right now, he could be hundreds of miles away by tomorrow.

"Please, Matt," she repeated softly.

He had the distinct feeling that he was about to vomit. "Where are you now?" he asked.

"Not too far from Little Rock," she said. "I'd better not pin it down any closer than that."

He knew what she meant; the phone might be tapped. He tried to think. "We could meet somewhere about halfway," he said.

"All you have to do is name the place."

"Did you ever hear of Star City?"

"No, but if it's on the map I can find it."

"It's a little over an hour's drive south of Little Rock," he said. "You take U.S. 65 through Pine Bluff, then veer right on Highway 81 and go about twenty miles. It's a very small place, but you can't miss it. I'll meet you in front of the post office."

"When?"

"How's seven o'clock tomorrow night?"

"I wish it could be sooner, but I'll be there," she said. "What kind of car will you be in?"

He hesitated and she knew immediately why. "It's all right," she told him. "I'll let you find me. I'll be in a light gray Lincoln Town Car with Arkansas tags—GKF-692. Okay?"

"Yes," he said, "I'll be there."

"Can you give me a signal so I'll recognize you?" she asked.

He shrugged. "There won't be that many people around," he said. "I'll pull in beside you and give you a short beep on the horn. But let's not keep each other waiting, Mollie. If we haven't made contact by 7:15, we'll have to call it off."

"All right," she said. "Thank you, Matt."

He hung up the telephone and went to the back door to let Hobo in. Then he turned off the burner under the kettle, as the old dog ravenously attacked the food in his dish. David East/Matthew Eastman had decided he didn't want any coffee, after all. On second thought, he told himself, looking down at his shaking hands and heading toward the pantry where he kept the bourbon, a little "hair of the dog" was precisely what the doctor ordered on this particular morning.

CHAPTER THREE

The drought ended pretty decisively that Sunday night, as it turned out. The rain started as a light drizzle while he was still a good 20 miles from Star City, and by the time he turned off Highway 81 into the center of the town, it was coming down in buckets with water running curb-deep in the gutters. It was two minutes after seven when he came in sight of the post office, and through the downpour his headlights illuminated the bulky shape of the gray Lincoln Town Car parked in front. He even managed to make out the GKF-692 on the license plate. Mollie was not only true to her word, but very punctual as well.

On his first pass, he kept his hand on the .22 revolver under his jacket and drifted by the parked Lincoln without slowing down. He had always kept the gun fully loaded ever since the day he bought it at an East Dallas pawn shop in 1969. Yet it had never been fired and had, in fact, rarely been outside the bureau drawer where it normally reposed beneath the innocuous white bulk of his shorts and T-shirts. He had once been a fairly decent pistol shot though and bringing the

.22 along tonight had given him some small measure of reassurance.

A block further on, he turned left and circled back, checking out the neighborhood as he did. He didn't encounter a single car along this route however, and by the time he reapproached the post office he was fairly sure that (a) no one was following him, and (b) there was no obvious nearby stake-out keeping the Lincoln under surveillance. So he pulled the old convertible into the parking space on the right side of the Lincoln and stopped. This way, he reasoned, the occupant of the other car—whether it was Mollie or someone else— would have to come all the way around the Lincoln to reach the Mustang, thereby giving him some time to look that person over.

He tapped the horn lightly once, and almost immediately the front door on the driver's side of the Lincoln swung open and a female shape in a tan trenchcoat emerged and ran toward the Mustang. He pushed open the door on the passenger's side and waited, his hands jammed tightly into his coat pockets, one of them gripping the .22 and the other a flashlight, as she approached.

"Hello, Matt," she said softly, as she leaned down and slipped into the seat beside him. "You'll never know how much I appreciate this."

Before he answered, he flipped on the flashlight and flicked the beam quickly across her face. An electric shock of emotion crackled through him at seeing her again after all these years. He was amazed at how attractive she still was, but her eyes were the eyes of a trapped animal caught in a snare. He reached out wordlessly and hugged her, feeling her trembling against him. It gave him an eerie feeling, as if he were hugging a ghost.

"I can't believe you're alive," he whispered. "I've been so sure for so long you were dead."

In November 1963, when "Sugar" and "Spice" O'Connor (none of the paying customers had ever been able to tell for sure which was which) had been the toast of Jack Ruby's Carousel Club and when Mollie was last seen in Dallas, she had been not quite 20 years-old. In his mind, her image had remained that way, frozen in time. But now, he realized, she would be just on the cusp of 44. Maturity had slightly hazed her innocent, almost hurtful prettiness, but it had also given her a gentler appearance than the girl who had danced and shed her clothes on the Carousel stage. Her hair was darker but still a true blonde, now with bright highlights of raindrops sparkling in it, and except for breasts that would have put a Greek goddess to shame, she was still slender, almost frail-looking. There were a few wrinkles around her eyes and mouth, but her facial features were as striking as ever.

She kissed him on the cheek. "For a long time, I felt the same way about you," she said. "God, Matty, can it have really been twenty-four years?

"I'm afraid so," he said, "but nobody'd know it to look at you. You look great, Mollie, really great."

Her smile conveyed a deep, infinite weariness. "I don't," she said, "but it's sweet of you to say so. You haven't changed that much, either. You were always the only real gentleman in the bunch." She laughed nervously, fumbled in her purse and extracted a package of cigarettes. "Want a smoke?" she asked.

"No," he said, "I quit a long time ago. You go ahead."

She produced a disposable lighter, touched the flame to the tip of her cigarette and inhaled deeply. "I have to congratulate you," she said. "You did a really good job of covering your trail when you left Chicago. I finally managed to convince your old boss, P. Q. Wallace, that I was trustworthy and it was a matter of life and death. Otherwise, I guess I'd never have found you. It took me nearly three years as it was, and several times I almost gave up."

"You talked to Wally?" he asked incredulously.

She lowered her eyes. "Well, I guess I might've done a little more than just talk to him," she said. "We had a kind of a relationship for three or four months. He kept me from cracking up. He's a nice man."

"Yeah," he said, "Wally was a lifesaver for me, too. But, hell, even he didn't know where I was."

"He had a rough idea from some of the things you said

before you left," she said. "I figured the rest out for myself.
It was clever of you, coming back this close to Dallas, I
mean. I figured you'd be in Maine or Oregon or someplace
like that."

"Well, now that you know all about me," he said, "suppose you tell me where you've been hanging out since 1963?"

"Oh, lots of places," she said, exhaling a plume of smoke.
"Mexico, the Caribbean, South America, Europe. Mostly
Mexico City, though. I just ran blindly for the first year after
it all happened, but then, sometime in '65, a most unlikely
person helped me get out of the country. He fixed me up with
a new identity, put me up in an apartment in Mexico City and
generally took care of me for almost twenty years—till 1984,
when the rotten bastards killed him. It was Dee Conlan,
Matty. I know that's hard for you to believe, but that's who it
was."

It was more than hard to believe, he thought; it was
impossible. "But, Mollie, he was in on it with them. Don't
you know that?"

She smiled sadly and shook her head. "No," she said,
"they just used Dee, that's all. He was like a child, Matt, and
they took total advantage of him. They knew he wasn't very
smart, and they used him and manipulated him and black-
mailed him until they got everything they wanted from him.
Then they murdered him. That's why I came back to the
states and started looking for you."

"I remember reading about it when Dee died," he said.
"The papers called it a heart attack."

"The papers were wrong," she said. "It only looked like a
heart attack. They gave him some kind of drug. I know they
did." There were tears in her voice.

"Just for the record, who do you mean when you say
'they,' Mollie?"

She put her head on his arm and dabbed at her eyes with a
tissue from her purse. "You know who I mean," she said
emptily. "Alex Sutton and Tommy Van Zandt have been the
ones behind this whole barrel of snakes from the start. Every
time they killed somebody, they just got richer and safer and

more powerful. And now Tommy has the balls to want to be governor of Texas. God, that sucks!"

"What makes you so sure about them, Mollie?"

"I know it, that's all," she said, in a voice thin with anger and longstanding fear. "I know it the same way you know it. The same way Jamie knew it. The same way Hollie knew it. Oh, Jesus, Matty, if we don't help each other now, it's going to be too late for both of us."

He squirmed in the seat, wishing he had a drink. He hadn't had one all day because he hadn't dared, and he was very uncomfortable. He put his arm around her, drew her up close to him, and felt her shaking all over.

"Look, Mollie, I'm sorry," he said, hating himself for saying it, "but I'm just not going to get mixed up in anything, especially anything that involves Alex and Tommy and all that stuff that happened in '63. I've spent half my life running away from that shit. Now I'm out of it, and I want to stay out of it."

"Oh, but Matty, you're *not* out of it," she whispered fiercely. "Neither one of us will ever be out of it as long as we live, and you know it as well as I do. Do you think what happened to your wife and daughter in Illinois was an accident? You can't seriously believe that."

A fleeting vision of Diana, his six-year-old daughter, flashed across his mind's eye. She was running down the driveway of the house in Naperville to greet him after work, her brown pigtails flying out behind her, her round little face wreathed in smiles. "Hi, Daddy! Hi, Daddy! Come look! I found a frog . . ."

He shuddered and shook his head. "I *do* believe it," he said in a breaking voice. "I've made myself believe it for four years, and I can't stop now."

"If you believed it," she asked, in a voice so low he could barely hear her, "why did you disappear without a trace the day after the funeral? Why did you never even come back to collect the insurance money? Why did you walk away from an $800-a-week job without telling a soul where you were going? Why, Matty?"

He couldn't answer her quiet, cutting questions. All he

could do was look wordlessly away and pray that she'd shut up.

"Just a tragic, unfortunate accident," she said, pressing the point unmercifully. "Just like what happened to Hollie and Jamie and Little Lynn. And Marilyn Moon and Angel Garcia and Mike Fisher and God knows how many others. And when the time comes, they'll probably say what happened to you and me was just an accident, too—unless you wake up, Matt."

"But there's no logical reason for it," he said desperately. "Christ, why should either of us be a threat to anybody anymore, if we ever were?"

"Because of what we know," she said, "and the evidence we have."

"I can't speak for you, Mollie, but if I ever had anything that might incriminate anybody, it's long gone. I was never sure what it was, even when I had it right in my hands, and I got rid of it a long time ago."

"I don't believe that," she said, "and they wouldn't either. They know you and Jamie and Mike were in Ruby's apartment that night before the cops had a chance to search it. Hollie told me herself that you found something, something that scared Jamie half to death."

"It's gone," he repeated. "I got rid of everything."

"Well, I didn't," she said. "I've still got mine. I've been collecting it in little bits and pieces since a couple of months before the Kennedy assassination, and I've gradually added to it over the past twenty-four years. Now I want you to have it, Matty," she said. "You're the only person alive that can do what needs to be done with it."

"Mollie, I don't want it, for God's sake!"

She opened her purse again and removed a small chrome-plated key. "This key fits a locker in the Greyhound bus station in Little Rock," she said. "There's a briefcase there with things in it that will boggle your mind—more than enough to fix Alex Sutton and Tommy Van Zandt for good. Combine it with whatever you found at Ruby's place that night, and it just might rewrite the history books on the assassination, too, if you could get it in the right hands."

"What makes you think I'll even try?"

She reached across and dropped the key into his shirt pocket. "I know you don't want to, Matt," she said, "but I'm begging you. Take the key and get the briefcase. If you don't do anything but mail the stuff to police intelligence in Dallas, at least do that much."

"Mollie," he moaned, "don't do this to me!"

She leaned heavily against him, put her arms around him and squeezed him hard. "I don't think I've got very long, Matty," she said dispassionately. "For the past week or two, I've had the feeling they were practically breathing down my neck. I'm sorry if I've blown your cover by doing this, but you're my only hope, old friend. You're *our* only hope. It's more than just punishing them for what they did to Jamie and Hollie and all the rest. It's more than just paying them back for screwing up our whole lives. It's also cleaning up something that's unspeakably ugly and vicious and wrong. Please help me do it, Matty."

He took the key out of his pocket and watched it glitter in the faint light. There was a number imprinted on it. "312," it looked like.

"How?" he asked resignedly.

"I can't go back to the bus station, or anywhere near it," she said. "They know what I look like, and they'd be waiting for me. If you don't want to go yourself, you could get someone else to do it. Getting the briefcase is half the battle. When you see what's in it, you'll know what to do. And if I'm able, I promise you I'll give a deposition or testify in court or do anything else I can to make the strongest possible case against them."

She was shaking even more violently now, so violently that she couldn't even manage to light a cigarette. He took the lighter and lit it for her, wishing he could keep her with him and comfort her, yet wishing he had never seen her again, all at the same time.

"I just don't know, Mollie," he said. "I'm going to have to think about it. In the meantime, what're you going to do? Where are you going to go?"

"I've got to try to get out of the U.S. pretty soon," she

said. "I have some friends in Mexico City who'll hide me if I can make it that far, but my life's not worth a box of Crackerjacks anywhere in this country."

He looked out the window, noting that the rain had slacked off to a slow sprinkle, and heard himself making an incredible proposal. "You could stay at my place for a few days," he said. "My house is out from town and there aren't any close neighbors, so nobody would have to see you."

"That'd be an awful risk for you," she said. "I've made enough trouble for you as it is."

He looked at her in the semidarkness, at the large, wet eyes, the rounded curve of her breasts inside the trenchcoat, the soft blonde hair against her cheeks, the gentle warmth of her mouth. It had been such a damned long time ago, he thought, and yet he still harbored a trace of the fierce and tender yearning he had felt for Mollie O'Connor every time he saw her in the old days. He had never told another human being, because Alex Sutton had always seemed such an inseparable part of her life that there had been no point in even thinking about it. But he had spent countless hours thinking about it, nevertheless.

"Not if you ditched the Lincoln somewhere and we went in my car," he said. "Heading north on Highway 81, there must be at least fifty dirt roads that wind off into the woods between here and the U.S. 65 junction. If we left the Lincoln out of sight of the highway on one of them, it might be days before anybody found it, much less reported it. And if we took the license plates, it could take a long time to link it to you."

"It's a better idea than any I've got," she said. "But do you really want to take that chance? Is it really worth it to you, Matty?" He saw quiet understanding in her eyes.

He nodded. "Some things never change," he said. "I used to envy a certain lieutenant of homicide more than you'll ever know." He paused and smiled. "And I still care about you, Mollie."

"Then I'd be a fool to say no," she said.

He glanced down at the locker key again, folded his fist

around it and shoved it into his jacket pocket. "Okay," he said. "You go first and take it slow. I'll circle around and follow you at a distance until we're a mile or so out of town, just to make sure nobody's tailing us. Then I'll pass you and lead you the rest of the way. I know a really good spot, but it's about fifteen miles up the road."

"Thanks, Matty," she said. "Thanks for everything." She leaned forward and kissed him softly, on the lips this time. Then she opened the door and jumped out, and half a minute later he heard the Lincoln's engine start quietly in the damp, empty night. The headlights flashed on, and the big car backed slowly out into the street, then pulled forward and stopped abreast of him as he started the Mustang. For an instant, he saw her face dimly through the window of the Lincoln, then she waved and pulled quickly past him. At the first corner, she turned right and headed for the highway two blocks distant.

As he watched the wide red band of the Lincoln's taillights fade gradually into the night, he reached out and touched the empty seat beside him, feeling her warmth still there and finding it strangely comforting. Then he drove slowly away in the opposite direction, cautiously scanning the surrounding streets and parking lots for any sign of other moving vehicles, but seeing none.

His intentional detour took him three or four blocks out of the way before he, too, swung back toward Highway 81. When he reached the highway and pulled up at the stop sign, the Lincoln was already out of sight over the slight rise to the north. At first, he was only mildly irritated when he noticed the big tractor-trailer rig creeping slowly out into the northbound lane just a block ahead of him. Then he saw that the truck was apparently fully loaded and having a difficult time picking up speed, and he felt a growing sense of unease. The Mustang's speedometer showed him piddling along at 25 miles per hour, which meant that, even if Mollie were driving only 45 or 50, she was getting further and further ahead of him with every passing minute.

By the time the trucker shifted gears and the speedometer

needle climbed past 30, they were almost to the outskirts of Star City. At that point, Matt pulled out and tried to pass on the narrow two-lane road, only to find himself face to face with a glaring set of oncoming headlights. He cursed under his breath, dove back behind the truck just in the nick of time to avoid a head-on, and became aware of a small lump of panic forming, then growing in his chest.

Chapter Four

October 25, 1987

The damned road seemed to be on a perpetual upgrade, causing the truck to continue having problems gathering a head of steam, and the rain-drenched pavement didn't help matters at all. Every time Matt would get close enough to attempt to pass, the truck's rear wheels would kick up a deluge of muddy water onto his windshield so that he couldn't see a thing. Each time it happened, he would drop back, and the horrible feeling that he was losing control of the situation would grow inside him.

Now they were a mile past the sign marking the corporate limits of Star City—and then two miles. The truck was still poking along at a little over 50, and Matt could have whipped around him easily, except for the wet pavement and the constant succession of hills and curves that obscured his vision. It wasn't going to get any better, either. It was starting to sprinkle again, and he knew from past experience that, at most, there were no more than half a dozen really safe places to pass between here and the 65 junction—even without the rain.

He stared in mounting frustration at the mud-spattered rear end of the 18-wheeler in front of him. The big green letters printed on the back of the truck said:

COUNTRY OAK FURNITURE MILLS
America's Finest Home Furnishings
Ruston, La.

It would be a cold day in hell, he thought savagely, when he ever bought any furniture from Country Oak Furniture Mills. He wouldn't have a goddamned stick of Country Oak Furniture Mills furniture in his goddamned house, not if it was the last goddamned furniture on earth.

He drummed his fingers on the steering wheel and eased out around the truck again. But through the spray of rainwater and mud, he could make out more headlights approaching, and he fell back again, swearing.

There was no need to get frantic yet, he told himself. Surely, by this time, Mollie would have realized that something was holding him up. Surely if she didn't catch sight of him pretty soon, she would just pull off onto the shoulder of the road and wait for a couple of minutes. If she did, everything would be fine. The only problem was, he was getting so much backsplash from the truck that he might not be able to see her when he went by.

Even at the risk of losing more time, he decided it would be best to ease off and let the truck outdistance him a little, at least until he was out of its wake. He lifted his foot from the accelerator while the speedometer needle descended to 40 and the green-lettered sign on the rear of the truck diminished to the size of a postage stamp.

Jesus, he thought, looking at the odometer, he was a good five miles out of town now. Where was she? Where could she be?

Suddenly, he saw the truck's brake lights flash on, and an instant later, through the black wetness beyond the truck, he could make out more lights. They were still perhaps 300 yards away and they seemed to be all over the road, but with the reflections the way they were, it was hard to tell.

He tapped the brake pedal, slowing the Mustang to a crawl, and the realization washed over him slowly. Only one thing caused traffic tie-ups out in the middle of nowhere on a night like this.

There was a wreck ahead, and it looked like a bad one.

Then he saw that part of the glow on the rapidly approaching horizon in front of him wasn't coming from car lights, after all. He could distinguish the white dots of multiple headlights, as vehicles coming from the opposite direction pulled off into the grass beside the highway, and he could clearly see the red dots of the truck's taillights and those of at least one other vehicle ahead of the truck.

But for the most part, it was the flames leaping furiously from the twisted wreckage of an overturned automobile that were lighting up the night sky. The car was lying almost exactly in the center of the highway, and the flames were rising 15 or 20 feet into the air.

The unthinkable thought exploded in his brain like a stick of dynamite.

"Oh, God," he whispered. "Please, God, not Mollie."

He jerked the Mustang to a stop behind the truck, threw open the door and ran as hard as he could go toward the burning car. A heavyset man wearing a wide-brimmed straw hat and carrying a large flashlight with a red plastic cone on the end of it came trotting toward him, motioning for him to stay back.

"You better not go no closer, mister,' the man said. "That sucker's liable to blow any second."

The panic had grown to the size of a football in Matt's throat and chest. He strained to see the burning car through the smoke and rain and darkness, but all that was visible from this angle were the wheels and undercarriage.

"Are you a cop?" he asked the heavyset man in a voice that sounded like someone else's.

"No, sir, I'm just a volunteer fireman. I think somebody's gone to call the state troopers."

He pushed roughly past the man and ran on, until he was no more than 30 feet from the blazing car and the heat was so intense that he couldn't force himself any closer. He backed up slowly toward the shoulder of the road, changing positions so that he could get an unobstructed view of the car's rear license plate. Then, in the reflected headlights of one of the other cars, he saw it plainly and read it aloud to himself.

"GKF-692."

For a split second, he thought seriously of throwing himself into the flames. He lurched toward the roaring fire, feeling the blistering force of it scorching his face. His clothes were so hot they were almost smoldering.

"Why?" he screamed. "Oh, God, why did you do this?"

He felt hands on him, several strong hands pulling at his jacket, arms restraining him, trying to drag him back away from the searing heat of the fire. He whirled blindly, swinging his fists in wild circles, but not hitting anything.

"Leave me alone," he gasped, grappling with the hands. "Leave me alone or I'll kill you!"

Somebody slapped him roughly across the face. "You just take it easy, feller," a voice growled. "I don't want to have to punch your lights out."

He let himself go limp. "Just leave me alone," he said. He knew that tears were running down his face, but he didn't care. It didn't matter anymore. Nothing mattered anymore.

"Listen, mister," the same voice said in a much gentler tone. "If you're looking for the lady that was in the car, she's over here. Looks like she was thrown clear when the car flipped, but she's in real bad shape."

Matt's head was reeling, but he wiped his eyes and focused them on the figure of the volunteer fireman. He was pointing his flashlight at a lump under a dark blanket in the roadside grass several yards away. There was a man squatting beside the blanket, and he seemed to be doing something to the lump.

Matt stumbled over to the blanket and looked down at Mollie. The front of her trenchcoat was mostly blood. The man had a tourniquet on her arm and was holding it there. The knuckles on his hands were white and so was his face.

"It's an artery," he said, glancing up at Matt. "I got it

closed finally, but she's so torn up inside I'm afraid she'll never make it.''

Matt knelt beside him and touched Mollie's face. There were two deep cuts across her forehead. One of them ran up into her hair and the other trailed down to her left ear. He took out his handkerchief and tried to wipe away some of the blood that covered her face. It didn't do much good. In a few seconds, the handkerchief was soaked, but the blood just kept coming. It seemed to be everywhere.

Her eyes flickered, and suddenly they were open, looking at him. He saw her lips form his name, but no sound came out. Then she tried again and this time he could hear her.

"Matty," she whispered, "Get away from here, baby. That's . . . the only thing you can do now."

"Hang on, Mollie," he pleaded. "Help's coming. It's on the way."

"I'm sorry," she said, "I don't think . . . I can wait."

"Can you remember what happened?" he asked. "Can you tell me?"

"I don't know," she said. "There was a car . . . came from somewhere. I lost control . . ."

Some of his tears ran down his cheeks and dripped onto her mangled face, and a series of huge, wracking sobs shook his body so hard that he almost fell over. He stroked her cheek and found it wet with his own tears. When his vision cleared enough to see her again, he didn't see her as she was, but as she had once been.

She was back on the stage at the Carousel, wearing her ponytail and cheerleader sweater with the big block-letter "S" on the front, right between her perfect, tantalizing breasts. Hollie was beside her, as identical as her reflection in a mirror. He heard the emcee's raucous voice:

"And now, ladcez and gentlemen, let's hear it for those sweet thangs from Sweetwater, Texas—the prettiest pair of little Irish shamrocks that ever grew in the Lone Star State. Let's give a big hand for Sugar and Spice O'Connor!"

Then they were dancing and singing, and they were surprisingly good. The two of them were old-fashioned burlesque at both its most titillating and most touching. In captivating sound and sensual motion, they recreated the timeless story of the birth of ambition and the death of innocence. They started out with "Tammy," as they almost always did, then followed it with "Patches" and "Teen Angel," and finished up with "Lullaby of Broadway." That was where both of them wanted to end up—on Broadway—and they were entirely serious about it. Serious enough to use part of their combined $500 a week salary to pay their tuition for drama and dance classes at SMU. When they were done, they had stripped down to sequined panties and bras. They had never once gone any further than that, and Matt Eastman had always been glad they didn't.

You were such a dream, he thought, and the way I loved you was my own special secret, but I'll never love anybody that way again. Not ever. Then the spotlights and the glitter and the music faded away and died. His imagination withered, and he was back amid the misery and gore and trauma of the present.

"Mollie," he whimpered, "Mollie, please don't die."

She tried to smile at him. "Poor Matty," she said, her voice barely audible. "I can't help it."

Down the highway, from the direction of Star City, he saw a pair of flashing blue lights approaching and heard the faraway wail of a siren. Just another accident, he thought. It would go into the books as just another unavoidable accident.

He remembered what she had said as they sat in the Mustang with the rain pouring down. Could it have only been an hour ago, maybe even less? "And when the time comes," she had said, "they'll probably say what happened to you and me was just an accident, too—unless you wake up, Matt."

He had awoken for a little while. For a few minutes back there in Star City, he had felt more awake and alive than he had in a long time. But now he just wanted to go back to sleep and blot it all out. If this was what being awake was all about, he didn't want any part of it. It hurt too goddamned much. Still, he couldn't help but wonder what sort of "accident" it would be when his turn came.

The patrol car bounced to a halt, its blue lights forming a peculiar contrast to the diminishing orange flames above the remains of the Lincoln. He looked back at Mollie. Her eyes were still open, and that look of fear and dread was still there, but he could tell she was dead.

It wasn't right, he thought. It wasn't fair. People shouldn't still look afraid when they were dead. People should be at peace and at rest when they were dead, but he was afraid Mollie wasn't.

"Goodbye, Sugar. Goodbye, Spice." His lips formed the words soundlessly, and he looked away from her haunted eyes.

Matt saw the trooper talking on his radio about an ambulance, and he almost started to yell that there was no need, but caught himself in time. Before the trooper finished talking and started toward the little group gathered around the lump under the blanket, Matt stood up and staggered away.

He made his way back to the Mustang, which was well shielded from the trooper's view by the bulk of the 18-wheeler from Country Oak Furniture Mills, and he had started the engine and turned completely around before anyone paid any attention to the fact that he was leaving.

"Hey, I thought that guy knew this lady," he heard a voice say.

"He acted like he did," someone else said, "but maybe he was just upset. Sure is a shame, ain't it?"

He pressed down hard on the accelerator, being careful not to spin the wheels or attract any unnecessary attention as the Mustang rapidly gathered speed. Then he was gone, hurtling through the night back toward Star City, studiously avoiding looking into the rearview mirror. He didn't risk a single glance until the needle on the speedometer was touching 70 and he was positive that there was only unbroken darkness ahead of him and behind him.

Inside his jacket pocket, his sweating fist closed like a vise around the little chrome-plated key, and he squeezed it until the metal cut deeply into his flesh.

He wished with all his heart that he could have promised

Mollie to do what she had wanted him to do with the key—but he was also glad beyond words that he hadn't. Making a promise that you couldn't keep to a dying person was one of the most despicable things he could imagine.

CHAPTER FIVE

October 26, 1987

It was well after midnight when he finally returned to the old Victorian house and parked the Mustang under the trees. For three or four hours he had driven aimlessly around the back roads of Southeastern Arkansas in a state of semishock, feeling only empty numbness where his insides should have been, while a mass of tangled images constantly twisted and turned in his brain.

He saw Lee Harvey Oswald with a lump on his head and a sneer on his lips as he was led in manacles into a Dallas police interrogation room. He saw an affable Jack Ruby smiling at a tableful of cops and reporters at the Carousel Club and expansively setting up a round of drinks on the house "because you guys deserve it." But then the images blurred and merged, and Ruby had the Colt in his hand and he was shooting Oswald. . . .

He saw Jamie Cade grinning at him over a stein of beer in the TV Bar on Elm Street. "Hey, you old cowchip," Jamie was saying, "let's go nose around and see what we can find." Then the grin dissolved into a grimace of pain and

Jamie's face turned black and he was lying dead on the floor of his apartment with a broken neck. . . .

He saw Hollie O'Connor's liquid eyes, flawless face and fabulous body in the merciless glare of the Carousel's spotlight as she slowly and tauntingly peeled off her cheerleader's sweater. Then he saw the same body, now crushed almost beyond recognition after a hit-and-run driver ran her down. . . .

He saw Colleen, the willowy blonde copywriter from Des Moines whom he had met and married in Chicago, holding their little girl, Diana, when she was about three and brushing her long brown hair. Then he saw the shattered, blackened remains of the house after the natural gas explosion in which they died. . . .

And again and again, interspersed with the jumble of other images, he saw Mollie trembling and chain-smoking and begging him for help. And then the flames from the Lincoln shooting up into the rain above the highway and life running out of Mollie's broken form under the blanket, her eyes staring and terrified as death closed over her. . . .

He vaguely recalled stopping for gas at an all-night service station in Monticello and seriously considering buying a pack of Winstons from the vending machine, despite not having smoked a cigarette in a dozen years. Then he lost track of time again, and the next thing he knew he was driving slowly past a closed and darkened Leon's Place and realized he was almost to Jefferson. He drove slowly on through the town, past the square and the courthouse, *The Jeffersonian* office, Riker's Drug Store, Western Auto, Sears. Then Safeway, Robertson's Exxon, Razorback Motors, Steadman Funeral Chapel, the First Baptist Church. He took a sharp right onto the blacktopped county road that led to the old Victorian farmhouse, and five minutes later he was home.

The air had turned chilly after the rain, but he sat absently in the car for awhile with the door open and the radio blaring. It was almost 1 a.m. on a Monday morning and most normal people were trying to sleep, but there was no one nearby to be disturbed by the noise, and he wouldn't have cared if there were. He sat there until the German shepherd at the house a quarter-mile down the road started barking at something.

Then he turned off the radio, slammed the car door and went into the house.

Hobo, who almost never barked and who should have been sleeping for hours, greeted him in the living room, wagging his tail and panting, then bounded into the kitchen ahead of him, seeming curiously excited. He put Hobo outside, where the dog communed with nature quickly and unceremoniously and was back scratching at the door in less than a minute. Inside again, Hobo looked at him with expectant brown eyes that said: "Have a heart, man. Can't you see I'm starving?"

"You're totally full of it," he told the dog tonelessly. "You know you've been fed already. Go to sleep." He relented after a minute though, opened a fresh can of dogfood and dumped half of it into Hobo's dish. The dog ate ravenously until the food was gone, licked the empty dish for a few seconds, glanced up to see if any more was forthcoming, belched, yawned and shuffled off to his favorite lurking place in the hallway.

Once he had Hobo taken care of, he went to the cabinet beside the sink, removed two glasses and set them side by side on the table. Then he crossed to the pantry, where he picked up a recently opened bottle of bourbon in his left hand and the bottle of amaretto containing the cyanide in his right. He brought both bottles back to the table and sat down. It felt cold and damp in the house, so he didn't bother to remove his jacket.

It was about time for a nightcap, he thought, carefully pouring three ounces of bourbon into the first glass—and it was also about time to check out of this mess. He could see no point at all in prolonging it. His career, his family, his friends and his hopes were all gone. His guts were gone, too, as surely as if they had been burned to ashes along with the Lincoln. The difference was, they had been gone long before the disaster outside Star City. In all likelihood, Sarah would soon be gone, too, and then there would really be nothing left.

Even if nobody came to kill him right away, he just didn't have the stomach for waiting and wondering and spending whatever life he might have left completely alone and with only a hollow cavity inside him.

He looked at the bottle of amaretto as he slowly drank the bourbon, and he wondered what it was going to feel like. It would probably hurt like hell for a few seconds, then it would be over. He knew he could make himself do it, but he might need quite a bit of bourbon before he got the courage to toss down a shot of the amaretto. He wondered if he should write a note. It seemed a little pointless, but most people who committed suicide did write notes, after all. It was like something you were supposed to do.

Since Sarah was the only person in town with whom he had more than a nodding acquaintance, and since he had made a will leaving her *The Jeffersonian*, the house and what little else he possessed, maybe he should write the note to her. On the other hand, why should he drag Sarah into something so sick and disgusting? One of those impersonal "To whom it may concern" notes would be much better, he decided.

It had been nearly a year ago, right about the time he had finally made up his mind to kill himself, that he had gone to the lawyer in Little Rock and had the will drawn up. After that, it had seemed of no particular consequence *when* he did the deed. After that, it had been a foregone conclusion in his mind, a *fait accompli*. As recently as yesterday, he had had absolutely no timetable for it, but the events of the past few hours had changed all that. He hoped Sarah didn't hate him too much for willing her the weekly hassle of *The Jeffersonian*. She didn't have to keep it forever if she didn't want to, she could always sell to somebody for a few thousand—maybe.

He reached into his pocket and pulled out the little silverish locker key, staring at it for a moment as though he had forgotten where it came from. The key disturbed him because he couldn't figure out what to do with it. It was like a last pending item of business on an agenda that otherwise had been swept clean—an untidy, unwanted, unfinished bit of business that refused to go away.

Because he had accepted the key from Mollie, however unwillingly, he knew that he couldn't simply throw it away.

The most intelligent thing he could do would probably be to put it in an envelope and mail it to the Little Rock police with a short note. They could open the locker and examine the contents of the briefcase and decide if it merited notifying Dallas authorities or the FBI or whoever. But this would mean hunting up an envelope, writing an explanation of some kind, driving to the post office and buying stamps, and he had neither the time nor the energy for all that.

To hell with the key, he thought angrily. He didn't want to think about the key anymore. He was too tired to think about the damned key. He shoved it deep into his pants pocket and poured himself another slug of bourbon.

He awoke suddenly and looked at the quartz clock on the kitchen wall. It was only a few minutes past 2 a.m., so he knew that he couldn't have been asleep very long, probably not more than 15 minutes or so. And that was odd in itself, since he usually slept for at least an hour or two when he nodded off while drinking late at night.

The bourbon glass stood empty a few inches from his right elbow. He was pretty sure that he had emptied it at least three or four times, and yet his head felt fairly clear. A short distance away was the other glass, still clean and untouched, and near it was the bottle of amaretto containing enough cyanide to wipe out half the town. Squarely in front of him was his ballpoint pen and a totally blank notepad, on which he had been preparing to write something—he had no idea even now what it might have been—when he lost consciousness.

He frowned, feeling a chill run up his backbone. Something had awakened him, but what?

Then he heard it, not really a sound at all, only the faintest suggestion of a sound, coming from somewhere in the front part of the house. He sat perfectly still and listened so hard he could feel himself straining. He heard nothing else right away, but as he listened, he recalled Hobo's unusual behavior when he had first walked in. Hobo was the type of so-called watchdog who would watch and wag his tail if a thief was stealing everything in the place. Unless the thief yelled at him, that is. If that happened, Hobo would slink away and hide. The old mutt loved people, all people, no matter who they were, as long as they didn't hit him or talk loud. That was why Hobo had been so happy and alert despite the lateness of the hour; he had had company.

Someone else was in the house, and whoever it was had most likely been hanging around the place for a good while.

Another infinitely soft hint of sound reached his ears. It was a little like a crepe-soled shoe stepping lightly on the thick carpeting in the living room.

A board creaked somewhere.

There was someone in the house, all right. Maybe a couple of someones.

He felt totally sober, which was fortunate, he supposed, although it might have been better to be drunk. He realized that he was shaking slightly, but he had no real sense of fear. Not yet, anyway. Maybe he would later, but he doubted it. He felt as though he were in a void of some kind, a semi-interested observer watching a play and waiting for the plot to unfold. In the back of his mind, he had expected to have at least a day or two of grace before they came for him, but they were here already, and he honestly didn't give a good goddamn.

They were going to such incredible pains to kill a guy who was in the process of trying to commit suicide. It was actually kind of funny when you stopped to think about it.

Maybe they had known where he was all along—maybe even for months—and had only been waiting for Mollie to make her move. Maybe they would be someone he knew, maybe a Dallas cop from the old days, maybe even Alex Sutton himself. No, he decided, not likely.

He fought down the impulse to turn and peer into the opaque darkness of the dining room and the pitch blackness of the living room beyond, knowing he couldn't have seen anything if he did. So he just kept sitting at the table with his back toward the dining room and shoved his cold hands into the slash pockets of his jacket. When he did, he was startled to rediscover the chilly bulk of the snub-nosed .22. He had forgotten it was there, and he almost wished it weren't. It gave him an option that he had no desire whatsoever to exercise.

"Don't move, Mr. Eastman," a pleasant voice said evenly from the dining room doorway. "Just sit as you are, but take your hands very slowly out of your pockets and put them on the table."

He did as he was told, reluctantly leaving the .22 behind. He knew they would search him, but they just might start shooting if they saw the gun in his hand.

"Very good," said the voice. "Now please remain perfectly still and keep your hands where I can see them at all times."

Someone moved in close behind his chair and he felt gloved hands expertly patting him down for weapons from his shoulders to his ankles. They quickly discovered the .22 and removed it, as he had known they would.

"A nasty little toy you're carrying, Mr. Eastman," the voice admonished gently. "Were you planning to shoot someone?"

He saw no reason to answer the question, so he didn't.

The man who was doing the talking stepped around the table into Matt's field of vision, turning slightly as he did and tossing the .22 to a second man, who was, at the moment, only an indistinct shape in the corner of Matt's right eye.

The first man, unmistakeably in charge, moved with graceful, catlike strides and held a silencer-equipped .357 Magnum pointed casually at the third button on Matt's jacket. He was slender, medium tall and dressed neatly yet nondescriptly in a narrow-brimmed brown hat, a tan trenchcoat, a brown suit and expensive cordovan oxfords. He had inquisitive eyes set in a narrow face, a thin, aristocratic nose, short, sandy hair going gray, and a triangular white scar on his left cheek. He looked to be about 40 years old, and he spoke in a well-modulated voice with a vague trace of an accent. All told, he looked and acted like no one else Matt had ever encountered in southeastern Arkansas.

"Take a good look around," the first man told his companion. "We don't want any surprises."

The second man nodded. He was dressed similarly to the first and identically armed with another .357 Magnum, but otherwise he and the other were almost total physical opposites. The second man was short and squatty, built along the lines of a miniature bull, with dark hair, heavy eyebrows and a round face. He moved heavily across the kitchen and disappeared into the hallway, still without saying a word.

When he was gone, the first man pulled out a chair at the far end of the table, rested one foot on the seat of it, and propped the hand with the gun on his knee while his eyes studied Matt. "A pleasure to meet you after so long, Mr. Eastman," he said. "You may not realize what a momentous occasion this is, but before the sun comes up this morning, we are going to write the final chapter in a very long story."

"How thrilling," Matt said cryptically. "I think I know how the story's going to end." He looked at the gun with the silencer. "Why don't you just go ahead and do it? I hate suspense."

The man shook his head. "Sorry," he said, almost apologetically, "but we prefer a somewhat less blatant last chapter. Something less inclined to arouse small-town suspicions. Auto accidents are always best, but whatever it is, I assure you we intend to make it all perfectly painless, so long as you don't do anything foolish, of course."

"Your thoughtfulness is overwhelming," Matt said.

The man smiled. "But first there's the small matter of a locker key, Mr. Eastman. We know you have it, so why don't you just give it to me now, or tell me where it is."

"Tough luck, my friend," Matt said, "but the key was in the Lincoln when it burned up."

"I don't believe you, Mr. Eastman. We know that Miss O'Connor was utterly desperate to place the key in your possession and would never have driven away without doing that. It would be much simpler and easier if you'd tell me where it is."

Matt shrugged. What the man said meant he must have thought Mollie was heading back to Little Rock when she left and didn't know that Matt was following her, not that it really mattered. It was a little late to start playing hero now. "It's in my pants pocket," he said resignedly.

The man with the gun smiled again. He seemed relieved. "Very good," he said. "Now if you'll just take it out of your pocket and slide it down the table to me, I'll be most grateful. Just be sure to move very slowly, Mr. Eastman."

Matt again did as he was told, then watched his uninvited guest pick up the little silverish key, check the number imprinted on it, and drop it into the pocket of his trenchcoat.

"Excellent," the man said. "Now, as soon as my slow-moving friend finishes searching the premises, we can get this unpleasant business over with."

"You, uh, mind if I have a drink first?" Matt asked, indicating the two bottles on the table in front of him.

"Not at all, Mr. Eastman," said the man. "In fact, I might even join you, if I may. It's been a long night."

"Absolutely," Matt said, feeling a sudden little thrill race through him. "I think that'd be the only civilized thing to do under the circumstances."

The man surveyed the two bottles with a critical eye. "I've never cultivated much of a taste for bourbon," he said, "but I'm very fond of amaretto. Do you mind?"

Matt bit his lip. He bit it very hard, hoping the man didn't notice. The thrill had become a huge, living thing, filling the empty space inside of him. It was all he could do to keep from laughing. It was all so fucking ludicrous.

"Not at all," he said. "Help yourself." He slid the clean glass and the bottle of amaretto down the table, using the same motion he had used a moment before with the locker key. "I think I'll have a slug of bourbon, myself," Matt said.

He slopped a generous portion of whiskey into his glass and watched the other man change the pistol to his left hand, pick up the amaretto bottle with his right hand and carefully pour himself about two ounces.

"You know, Mr. Eastman," the man said conversationally, "I was most disappointed when I learned we had failed to close your account four years ago in Illinois. But, as they say, things have a way of working out. Ironically, it was only because we missed you then that we were able to settle matters with Miss O'Connor tonight."

As the man lifted the glass of amaretto, Matt Eastman was unable to keep from grinning at the killer of his wife, his child, and the secret love of his young life.

He had thought he was no longer capable of hating or thirsting for revenge or even feeling simple anger, but in that instant he knew he had been wrong. Somewhere in the darkest, most suppressed reaches of his being, a spark of fury still burned. And somewhere justice of the most poetic type still lived.

"Your health," he said dryly and knocked back the bourbon.

"Cheers," the man said and took a large, appreciative sip of the amaretto.

CHAPTER SIX

October 26, 1987

When the telephone rang in the predawn darkness, Sarah Archer was already wide awake and staring into the black infinity of her bedroom ceiling. For close to an hour, she had been lying there in the moist stillness of the early morning, thinking and worrying about the decision she would have to make within the next 24 hours.

Whichever way it finally went, she doubted that she had ever faced a bigger or more critical decision in all her 27 years, not even when she had broken off her engagement to Kyle Morrison. Careerwise, there was no question that she would be better off taking the reporting job in Pine Bluff than staying where she was. That had been what motivated her to apply for the job in the first place. But there were other things to consider, too. While southeastern Arkansas offered a strictly limited future for a professional journalist, it did have certain endearing qualities. The life here was leisurely, the people friendly, the atmosphere peaceful, the surroundings as easy and comfortable as an old shoe. They were all she had ever known, and it would be hard to walk away from them into strange new surroundings and experiences.

If things had gone differently and she had married Kyle Morrison, she probably would never have thought about leaving—at least not until it was too late to do anything about it. Kyle was the extremely popular 30-year-old assistant principal at Jefferson High School, and everybody in town was pretty sure that when Old Man Purdy reached mandatory retirement age in three more years, Kyle would inherit his position as principal. To the townspeople, Kyle was a "fine young man," and at least 500 of them had told her so, either before or after she had broken the engagement. Because of his sterling reputation, not to mention the fact that his Uncle Arvin was a ranking member of the Board of Education, there was also speculation that Kyle would one day be superintendent of schools, one of the half-dozen most prestigious and best-paying jobs in town. But, as of the week before Thanksgiving 1986, whatever future heights might be achieved by Kyle Morrison were no longer any of Sarah Archer's concern.

It had been two and a half years since she had first sensed herself drifting away from Kyle emotionally, and almost a year since she had given him back the ring with the gorgeous half-carat diamond in it. Her mother had told her straight out that she was a fool for doing it. ("Just throwing happiness away with both hands! My God, girl, don't you ever want to amount to anything?")

Sarah had not even tried to explain what she had done in terms that people like her mother could understand. In a sense, she had done it for self-preservation. She was desperately afraid of becoming another smothered nonentity like the women she saw at Garden Club meetings and in the society section of *The Jeffersonian*. She had also come to hate Kyle's love affair with the status quo and his mindless stereotyping of everything and everybody, including himself. Yet the truth was, she still had no logical or reasonable explanation to offer for why she had ruthlessly destroyed a relationship that had become a treasured part of the hometown scene. Sometimes, though, she was almost certain it had had something to do with the man she worked for, David East.

Even after four years, she didn't know what to think of David East; all she knew was that she thought of him a lot. It was David East, more than anyone she had ever known, who had stimulated and encouraged her to look beyond the boundaries of her narrow, well-ordered world. And, ironically, it was David East whom she would miss the most if she decided to leave that world in order to satisfy the curiosity he had aroused in her. Although he was at least 20 years older than she was, she had never met anyone nearly as intriguing, and at times when she was around him, she found much more than merely her curiosity aroused. He had been more places and seen and done more things than all the other people she knew put together. He made Kyle— and every other eligible male in Jefferson, for that matter—seem plodding and boring by comparison. And yet, David East often seemed to see himself as the most boring, uninspiring one of all. He had a bitterly humorous way of putting himself down that both tickled and devastated her, and there was an underlying sadness about him that made her want to take him in her arms and mother him—or something like that. Anyway, it was going to be very hard to leave his employ, if that was the way the decision went.

The phone rang a second time, then a third, while Sarah sat up in bed and frowned at it. Who could be calling at—she squinted at the luminous dial of the clock on the nightstand—at 3:11 a.m. on a Monday morning? The strongest possibility was a wrong number. The second strongest was an obscene caller. The fad of telephoning women and talking dirty to them in the middle of the night had not yet caught on in Jefferson the way it had in the big cities, but it happened occasionally. It had happened to Sarah twice in recent months, both times a heavy breather who didn't say a word but just panted into the phone. She had thought fleetingly that it might be Kyle, but then she decided that was stupid. Within six weeks after their breakup, Kyle had started dating a sexy young teacher at Jefferson High. Now they were supposed to be married next June, and there was no indication that Kyle ever so much as thought of Sarah Archer anymore, much less did weird things like calling her up at 3:11 a.m. and panting at her.

A third possibility was Sarah's mother. Maybe there was some kind of emergency, or maybe her mother was simply calling to bitch her out again. She had spent the previous afternoon visiting her mother at El Dorado, as she did every Sunday, and had dutifully called when she got home to report her safe arrival back in Jefferson. But her mother had not taken the news well when Sarah told her she might be moving to Pine Bluff, not well at all. ("I hardly get to see you as it is. All you do is run in and run out again, and you'll probably never come down here if you move all the way to Pine Bluff.") Sarah told herself that her mother didn't mean to be the way she was, but she was still a selfish, grasping person, who felt an immense need to control her only daughter. And it had become much worse in the years since Sarah's father had died and her brother Jody had moved to Jackson, Mississippi, to work for an insurance company.

The phone rang again, sounding more insistent each time it did. She couldn't just ignore it; she wasn't built that way. Maybe one of these days when she got rich, she could get one of those answering machines.

"Hi there, this is Sarah Archer. I refuse to answer the phone in person right now, and there's not a thing in the world you can do about it. But if you want to leave your name and a message at the tone, I may call you back sometime, when I get damned good and ready. . . ."

On the other hand, maybe a big story had finally broken in Jefferson. Maybe a 747 had crashed into the county courthouse. Maybe City Hall was on fire and the mayor was trapped inside with his secretary, both of them naked, of course. Seriously, though, she had heard on her car radio that a woman had been killed in a fiery auto accident at Star City. If it could happen in Star City, for God's sake, it could happen in Jefferson.

She picked up the phone, shoved her long hair back to allow her ear access to the receiver and spoke huskily into the mouthpiece.

"Hello?"

"Is that you, Sarah?" a voice said. It sounded familiar, but it was so faint and slurred that she could barely make out the words.

"Yes, this is Sarah Archer," she said. "Who's calling?"

"Sarah, I. . . ," the voice began vaguely, then hesitated a moment. "Sarah, this is, uh, David East. I really hate to do this, but . . . well, I need to ask you a big favor. A very big favor. There's nobody else I can ask. If there was, I wouldn't bother you."

She pushed herself straight up against the headboard of the bed and strained to hear what he was saying. "David, I'm sorry, but I can hardly understand you," she said.

When he spoke again, his voice was a little louder, but there was still something vague and perplexing about it. "Sarah, could you . . . I mean, I know it's the middle of the night and I hate like hell to ask, but could you possibly come out to my place? Something's, uh, come up out here."

"Is anything wrong, boss?" she asked. He sounded about half-snockered, but there was something else, too—something she couldn't quite define.

"You, uh . . . Yeah, I guess you could say that, Sarah. See, I've got kind of a weird problem out here."

"What's the problem, David?"

"I, uh . . . can't tell you over the phone," he said. "But I . . . Shit, I hate to ask you, but I really need you to come out if you could. I need some help, Sarah."

She shivered and her heart jumped with sudden apprehension. "Are you sick, David? Are you hurt?"

"I'll be okay,' he said. "I'll tell you about it when you get here."

She was silent for a second or two, trying to think. Was he seriously in some kind of trouble, or maybe just a bit sloshed and pranking around? Even in her confused state, she didn't consider the latter a very strong possibility. David drank a lot, she knew, but he never seemed out of control. And he had never done anything like this before, never called her late at night, never asked her to come to his house, not even for coffee. In fact, when the subject came up occasionally, he invariably made excuses. The place was filthy, he would say, a total wreck, and he didn't want her to see it. Maybe he had finally gotten around to cleaning house and couldn't wait to show it to someone. Could that be it?

"It'll take me a few minutes," she said. "I mean I'm not dressed or anything." She felt her cheeks burning. "I . . . I'll hurry."

"Thanks," he said, "I really appreciate it. I hate to drag you out like this, but . . ." His voice drifted off, then added quickly, "Oh, by the way, there's one thing I ought to tell you."

"What's that?"

"Be very careful on the way," he urged. "Keep your eyes open for anything that looks . . . you know, unusual. When you get here, come to the back door, and make damned sure nobody's following you, okay?"

Now she was not only puzzled, but downright nervous as well, and she could feel herself trembling inside. "Okay," she said. It was the only thing she could think of to say.

She heard a click then, and she knew he had hung up

It was about 3:40 when she pulled the VW into the driveway and parked behind David's Mustang convertible. The front of the house was completely dark, but she could see some light through the rear windows. She had hurried as fast as she could, feeling jittery and agitated because of the way David had talked and because it all seemed so out of character for him. Her nerves were still on edge as she took the keys, got out of the car and made her way through the gloom past the front porch and along the side of the house. As instructed, she had kept a sharp eye out on the way over for anything out of the ordinary, but she had noticed absolutely nothing.

She opened the gate in the chain link fence surrounding the backyard and went up the walk to a set of steps that led to the back door. Trying the knob and finding it unlocked, she opened the door, stepped inside into the kitchen, and caught her breath sharply at the scene before her.

David East was sitting in a chair at the kitchen table with his eyes closed and his face very pale. He was gripping his left arm with his right hand and a bright red blood stain stretched from the collar of his shirt all the way down to the cuff on the left sleeve. She could see the rise and fall of his chest and knew he was breathing, but except for this movement, he was so completely still that she wasn't sure whether he was concious or not. That was bad enough by itself, but that was only the beginning.

The first dead man lay at the end of the table, his face contorted in unspeakable agony and tinged a hideous shade of reddish-black, his body grotesquely twisted and his features frozen in one final convulsion of pain. The second dead man lay sprawled half in the hallway and half in the kitchen, a gelatinous puddle of coagulated blood surrounding what was left of his head. Near his outstretched right hand was the biggest, ugliest pistol Sarah Archer had ever seen—except for the one just like it lying on the kitchen table in front of David East.

She felt her insides coil into knots and gag. She ran to the sink and retched violently into it, groping blindly for a paper towel off the holder to her left and wiping her mouth with it. She wanted to turn and run blindly out the same door through which she had just entered, but she forced herself to stand still while she fought the hysteria rising up inside her.

When she looked back at David East, she saw that his eyes were open and he was looking at her. "Thanks for coming, Sarah," he said quietly. "I wouldn't have got you into this for the world, except I didn't know anybody else to call."

She moved slowly toward him, trying to fight the faintness and nausea that kept flooding over her in great undulating waves.

"What happened, David?" she said stupidly. "Are you all right? Do you want me to call an ambulance?"

"No!" he said, in a surprising strong voice. "No ambulances, please. The bastard just nicked me and I think I got the bleeding stopped. I'm okay, and an ambulance wouldn't do either one of these guys a fucking bit of good. Excuse me. I'll try to watch my language."

He laid his head slowly on the table, and she went over to him and tried to pull his hand away from the wound just below his shoulder. "Come on," she said, feeling a little self-control returning. "Come on, let me help you. Which way's the bathroom?"

"Down the hall," he said, gesturing with a sickly grin. "Past old 'pretty boy' there."

He let her guide him slowly into the hallway, both of them carefully stepping over the corpse with half his head shot away and the pool of drying blood. When they got to the bathroom, she lowered the commode lid and sat him down on it. He made a face and so did she as she unbuttoned his shirt and peeled the bloody sleeve down his arm, then unwrapped the T-shirt he had wadded tightly around it and took a look at the wound.

From the looks of it, he was right. It had bled freely, but to her inexperienced eye, it didn't appear to be that serious. The bullet had sliced open the soft part of his underarm just behind the bicep and torn out a small chunk of flesh, but it had missed the bone, the artery and the main muscle mass. The wound looked to be clean, and the blood was barely oozing from it now.

"I think you're going to live," she said, tremulous but relieved.

"There's a bottle of alcohol in the medicine chest," he told her, "and some gauze and adhesive tape, too. If you'll just douse the damned thing good with alcohol and see if you can get some kind of proper bandage on it, I'll be fine."

She found some Advils in the medicine chest, gave him three of them to swallow with a glass of water, then took a couple herself. He cried out sharply and tears came to his eyes when she poured the alcohol directly into the wound. For a second she was afraid he might pass out, but he didn't, and after a few minutes, she had the bandage in place and was helping him down the hall toward his bedroom.

She was almost to their destination when she tripped over something dark and bulky in the hallway. Whatever it was made a grunting noise that sounded like "Oooof!" and scuttled out of the way.

"Good God, what was that?" she said, feeling a new surge of panic.

"Never mind," he said. "It's just Hobo, my old dog. He

likes to lie in the hall and blend in with the carpet and play camouflage tricks. He gets a real kick out of surprising people. That's what happened to the guy with his brains on the floor out there. Sonofabitch would've killed me for sure if he hadn't tripped over Hobo.''

None too steadily, she managed to guide him the rest of the way to the bedroom. "Okay," she told him, "you can lie down now.''

"I can't tell you how much I appreciate this, Sarah," he muttered, as she leaned him back onto the bed.

"It's all right, David," she said, lifting his legs and swinging them onto the mattress. "Why don't you try to rest a little now? We can talk later.''

"No," he said, "there's no time. There's too much to tell— and much too much to do. I've got to get started pretty soon or I'll never get it all done.''

She put her hand on his head. "Can you tell me what happened, David?''

He smiled painfully. "First of all, you ought to know something about me," he said. "My name's not really David East. It's Matthew Eastman and my friends call me Matt. If I have any friends left alive, that is.''

"You're carrying me a little fast," she said. "Maybe I'll just keep calling you 'boss.' It's less confusing that way. Who are those two . . . people in there?" She shuddered again as she thought about the bodies.

"I have no idea," he said. "All I know is they've been chasing me for the past eighteen years. Them or somebody like them. They specialize in murders that look like accidents. They killed my family in Illinois four years ago and an old friend of mine in Star City last night. Then they came here to do the same to me.''

"But why?" she said, her eyes wide. "God almighty, why?''

"It's a very long story," he said. "It'd take me days to tell you the whole thing.''

She looked at her wristwatch and saw that it was ten minutes past four. It seemed an eternity since she had answered the phone in her bedroom and this whole incredible sequence of events had begun, but it had actually been less than an hour. She hesitated even to think about what might lie ahead, but whatever it was, she knew she was part of it now, whether she liked it or not. If nothing else, though, she rationalized, at least it had gotten her mind off the job offer in Pine Bluff.

"You might as well give it a try, boss," she said, reaching down and taking his hand. "I'm a real good listener. If you feel up to it, I mean."

He seemed lost in thought for a moment. "You would've been every bit of three years old when it all started," he said, shaking his head in disbelief. "It was the fall of 1963 . . ."

CHAPTER SEVEN

November 22, 1963

It was 12:25 p.m. by the big white-faced Western Union clocks that frowned down on the fourth-floor newsroom of the *Dallas Times Herald*. The three-star edition had been put to bed for about ten minutes, and the presses were almost ready to start rolling downstairs. The mad scramble to update the main story and sidebars on the President's visit was over until 1:30 or so, when it would start up again for the four-star, and a quiet lull had fallen across the newsroom. Some of the cityside staff were drifting out to lunch now, and some were already gone. Others were still working special Kennedy coverage or enroute back to the office from scattered assignments across the city.

Around the U-shaped copy desk and the long, L-shaped city desk complex, a dozen editors, copyreaders and rewriters still held the fort, smoking and bullshitting and trying to relax. A dozen or so other people were clustered around the big windows overlooking Pacific Avenue in hopes of catching a glimpse of the motorcade as it passed along Elm Street a block away.

"There he goes," somebody said. "Hell, I barely saw him." Then it was over and the crowd at the windows broke up quickly and drifted away.

In the corner where the two angles of the city desk "L" came together, Matthew Eastman, a 24-year-old rewrite man only recently arrived in Dallas after a two year stint at the *Wichita Falls Record-News*, lit a Winston, hung his headset on his shoulder and stretched. It had been a long morning, but, all told, everything had gone as smoothly as anybody had a right to expect. They had even had some time to sit around and joke, in the peculiar black humor common to media types, about some whacko taking a shot at JFK. One smartass had actually written a mock obituary that made everybody laugh nervously and feel a little edgy.

Chances were, though, it would be an even longer afternoon. Another hour and Kennedy would be back aboard Air Force One bound for Washington, and the biggest news event of Matt Eastman's young career would be history. Later on, there seemed an excellent chance of the afternoon deteriorating into the kind of glacial, interminable boredom that so often followed a hot news day. And for Matt, even the fact that it was Friday held little solace, since he was working the 10:30 to 7:30 shift on Saturday, which not only wiped out the whole day but pretty well chilled any plans for the evening, too.

As the fill-in fifth wheel on the *Times Herald's* five-man rewrite staff—and its most junior member—Matt got the honor of working every holiday and lunch hour, as well as the least desirable weekend time slots. He also had the dubious distinction of being the regular "late man" during the week, which meant vegetating at the rewrite bank until 4 p.m. every afternoon, long after everyone else had gone home or to some bar. Since nothing short of World War III could possibly make print after the financial edition closed down at 2:15, the only thing a "late man" usually did was grow callouses on his backside and answer nut calls. Still, he knew he should not complain. Less than three months earlier, he had sought the job with almost romantic ardor. It had meant a $10 raise to $115 per week, and it had, praise be, gotten him out of Wichita Falls, which was the most important accomplishment of all.

The move to the *Times Herald* that September had also reunited Matt Eastman with Jamie Cade. True compatriot that he was, Jamie had spent his whole first year in Dallas touting his buddy Matt to the *Times Herald* brass, and eventually they had gotten around to giving Matt a call. He and Jamie had gone to college together at North Texas State, then worked together at San Angelo and Wichita Falls. Somewhere along the way, they had become best friends and it didn't bother Matt that Jamie was inevitably the star and he the plodding hanger-on. Right now, for example, Jamie was at Dallas police headquarters, right at the nerve center of everything, monitoring the police radio in case there was any trouble during Kennedy's visit, while Matt was stuck here in the background, twiddling his thumbs.

Where Jamie was flashy, Matt was conservative. Where Jamie was brash and impetuous, Matt was shy and reticent. Where Jamie had a natural talent for obtaining information from people and translating it into clever words on paper, every interview and every story was a struggle for Matt Eastman. He knew that Jamie's IQ was no higher than his, if as high; it was just that he couldn't seem to use his intellect as efficiently as Jamie somehow did. He and Jamie were not a matched set. They were, in fact, as different as day and night, but none of that really mattered. They were friends.

Matt felt a hunger pang and heard a low rumble in his stomach. It was still at least an hour before he could break away for a sandwich and a couple of beers at the greasy spoon on San Jacinto Street where he usually grabbed lunch. In the meantime, he considered trudging into the *Time Herald* coffee shop for another cup of their evil-tasting brew, but quickly changed his mind. He had had four cups of the stuff already, and that in itself might explain the growling in his gut.

He stubbed out the butt of the Winston and almost immediately reached for another one. It was exactly 12:30 p.m.

The telephone rang. Actually, it buzzed. That was what telephones did on the city desk; instead of ringing, they buzzed. He looked down at the flashing button and saw that it was the direct line to rewrite, which meant it was no-shit serious business and not just some random call from a subscriber, a crank or a psychopath.

He slipped the headset on, poked the flashing button with his finger, and spoke into the mouthpiece.

"Hot line. This is Eastman."

"Hang on tight, old cowchip," he heard Jamie Cade say grimly, with a slight quaver in his voice. "I think there's something super-bad about to break." Jamie paused to listen to something the police dispatcher was saying in the background.

"What's up, man?" Matt asked.

"Holy shit, this is it," Jamie yelled, his words shrill and urgent over the line. "Chief Curry's ordering all available units to the Triple Underpass. We got shots fired at the Kennedy motorcade. Sheriff Decker's down there. He says it looks like the President's been hit!"

"Hold on," Matt gasped. He whipped off the headset, jumped to his feet and screamed across the desk to the city editor, feeling the words tearing themselves out of his throat as though they had claws.

"Shots fired," he shouted. "Triple Underpass. Kennedy may have been hit!"

Not that he rejoiced over it, but as it turned out, that afternoon was probably the least boring of his entire newspaper career.

After the initial shock wore off, the *Times Herald* staff took hold and performed like professionals should. They didn't act like pros at first, though; they acted more like demented children. Some were crying, some were cursing, and some were wandering around in a daze, saying, "Oh God, oh God, how could this happen?" To get them functioning again, Felix McKnight, the executive editor, finally sat down at the rewrite desk, put on a headset and started typing the story that Jamie and George Carter, the paper's senior police reporter, were trying to dictate. McKnight's example served to calm the rest of them, and once they got themselves under control, they did okay.

Nobody wanted to admit it, but deep down inside, most of them sensed that Kennedy wasn't going to make it. The disjointed accounts filtering in from eyewitnesses in Dealey Plaza strongly indicated that he was dead already, and one reporter calling from Parkland Hospital quoted a trauma room intern as saying the President's wound was "incompatible with life." But it was still a shock when, just before 1 p.m., the bells started dinging wildly in the little glassed-in cubicle that housed the wire machines. Matt went running in, along with a bunch of others, and bent down to read the terse, totally predictable message as the teletype pounded it out.

FLASH!

DALLAS—TWO PRIESTS SAY KENNEDY DEAD.

About 45 minutes later, the city editor, who, as nearly as Matt Eastman could remember, had not addressed him directly from the day he was hired until the present moment, turned to Matt and said, "Hey, Eastman, get over to the police station as fast as you can. On top of everything else, we got a patrolman shot in Oak Cliff and the cops have a description of a suspect who may be good for both the cop killing and the hit on Kennedy. George and Jamie have more than they can say grace over, so just stay with them as long as it takes and do whatever you can to help. Got it?"

"Got it," he said, gratefully shucking the headset and running for the elevator. For once, he thought, instead of being lost out on the fringes of the action, he was going to be squarely in the middle of something—the biggest goddamn something that had ever happened in Dallas, Texas.

When he got to the police station in the old Muncipal Building at the corner of Harwood and Commerce Streets, it was just after 1:45 and the police press room on the third floor was in a state of aggravated bedlam.

"They got a suspect spotted in the Texas Theatre on Jefferson Avenue," Jamie yelled as he ran past him toward the homicide bureau through a corridor swarming with newspeople, FBI agents, Secret Service men and plainclothes Dallas detectives. "There's three or four squads on the scene right now, so we ought to know something pretty quick."

"What do you want me to do?" Matt asked uncomfortably. He had been in the police station a half-dozen times before, mostly just kibitzing and visiting with Jamie, but the proceedings whirling around him now were totally alien. He felt as though he were the only person in the corridor who had no business there.

Jamie ripped a ragged page off his notepad and handed it to Matt. "Here's the dead cop's name and badge number," he said. "Run over to the PIO office and get a file picture and a bio on him. Get everything you can, then take it on over to the city desk pronto."

"Okay. You want me to come back when I get through?"

"Sure, why not?" Jamie said. "We'll find something for you to do. Besides, I smell a whole bonanza of overtime in this caper, old cowchip. You might as well get your share of it."

"Fat chance," Matt said. "My regular shift isn't over till four o'clock."

"Don't worry about that," Jamie assured him. "Hell, we'll probably be here all night."

Matt looked down at the name scrawled on the scrap of paper. "J. D. Tippit," it said.

Suddenly, a big, burly detective in a white Stetson came charging out into the corridor. "They got the sonofabitch," he yelled. "He damn near shot another one of our guys, but his gun misfired and they got him. They ought to be on their way in with him in five or ten minutes."

Matt turned and ran down the corridor in the direction of the public information office. It would be close, he thought, but if he hurried, maybe he could get the stuff on Tippit to the city desk and get back in time to see the suspect when they brought him in.

They said his name was Lee Harvey Oswald. He was pretty beat-up, but still sneering and defiant, and looking like he would've shot the finger to everyone in sight if his hands hadn't been cuffed behind him. But from the very first, it was hard for Matt to believe that a skinny, sallow-faced punk like this had single-handedly done so much damage in such a short time.

He had assassinated the President of the United States, critically wounded the governor of Texas, killed one patrolman and done his damnedest to shoot a second officer—all within the space of an hour and a half. At least that was what the cops said, and the evidence against Oswald was already mounting. There was the Italian-made rifle found in a sixth-floor storeroom at the Texas School Book Depository, where Oswald worked and from which shots had definitely been fired at the motorcade; the rifle had Oswald's palm print on it. There were the cardboard boxes in the same room, which the assassin had apparently used as a gun rest; they had Oswald's fingerprints on them. There were photos found in Oswald's apartment, showing him holding the rifle and the .38 caliber pistol used to kill Tippit, and a crude map of the motorcade route had supposedly been discovered among Oswald's belongings.

Matt stood around while they booked the suspect and then watched them lead him into an interrogation room to talk to Captain Will Fritz, the head of the homicide bureau. Fritz was stout, bespectacled, balding and pushing 65. He looked more like somebody's grandfather than the Dallas Police Department's chief interrogator and obtainer of confessions in murder cases. "Cap," as most of the reporters and homicide cops called him, never raised his gravelly voice much above a whisper or used any threats or duress, but there was something almost uncanny about how he could persuade a guilty suspect to spill his guts. In his nearly 40 years with the department, hundreds of hardened killers had admitted their misdeeds to Fritz, and those who knew him had little doubt that he would achieve the same results with Lee Harvey Oswald.

Matt leaned against one of the dingy walls after they took Oswald away, fidgeting and feeling very unnecessary. Jamie was in the press room interviewing a detective about the rifle Oswald allegedly had used, and Carter was buttonholing an FBI agent named Hosty. At the *Times Herald*, they were still replating and grinding out extras, and somebody said that street vendors were getting up to $10 a copy for late editions with details on the assassination and Oswald's capture. Under the circumstances, Matt figured he ought to be doing something productive, but he had no idea what. Here he was, with the story of the decade—maybe the story of the century—sitting in his lap, and all he was doing was standing around shuffling his feet.

There must be a dozen stories in this room, he told himself. So find one, damn it. What was it Jamie always said? "If nothing's happening, hell, *make* something happen!" That's what he had to do now, he thought. But how?

Like a heaven-sent answer to his entreaty, Matt suddenly spotted Alex Sutton coming down the corridor. He felt his pulse quicken. Here, at least, was somebody he knew, and a fairly important somebody, at that. Alex was a lieutenant in homicide, a top aide to Will Fritz, widely respected in the department, and often mentioned as a possible successor when old Cap finally retired. Alex and Jamie were also close friends, and Matt had gotten to know him fairly well at a series of after-work beer-drinking sessions over the past couple of months.

Right now, the lieutenant seemed flustered, maybe even a little pissed about something. That was unusual in itself, since he was ordinarily one of the coolest, most unruffled characters Matt had ever met. But, pissed or not, Matt had no intention of letting Alex get away without talking to him, not when he might know something hot about the investigation.

"Hi, Alex," he said, stepping into the detective's path and extending his hand. "What's happening?"

Alex looked slightly startled, as if he didn't recognize him at first. Then he smiled tightly, although his eyes stayed cold and distant.

"Hello, Matt," he said, shaking hands. "What're you doing around here?"

"They sent me over to help George and Jamie," Matt said. "Had to send in the first team, you know." He laughed nervously, but his attempt at humor seemed to go right past the lieutenant.

"Where's the suspect?" Alex asked abruptly. "Have they booked him yet?"

"Yeah, he's in with Cap," Matt told him, a little disappointed that Alex seemed to know even less than he did.

Sutton appeared to relax a little. "That's good," he said. "This monkey thinks he's some kind of tough guy. So far, he's not talking at all, but Cap'll get a confession out of him before he's through. You watch."

Matt brightened and reached for his notepad. That was a pretty good quote. Maybe he could get something useable out of Alex after all, he thought.

"You think this guy pulled the whole thing by himself?" he asked.

Matt looked straight at him and their eyes met. Alex's eyes were still cold, but there was a weird kind of magnetism in them, too. It made Matt so uncomfortable that he wanted to look away, but it was hard to do when he tried. "I *know* he did," Alex said. "We've got all the evidence we need to put him in the electric chair right now. You know the guy's a Commie, don't you?

Matt shook his head. "Seriously?" he asked.

"Sure," Alex said. "Hell, he defected to Russia and the damned idiots in Washington let him back into the country."

"You think he's some kind of Russian agent?"

Alex snorted. "Not a chance," he said. "The Soviets are too smart to have a guy like this working for them. He's too unstable, too dangerous, too damned unpredictable. He's a sociopath with a chip on his shoulder for everybody, and no loyalty to anybody but himself."

For just a split second, Matt felt a troublesome twinge of curiosity, wondering how Sutton knew so much about Oswald, when, as nearly as Matt could tell, Alex had just come into the station and hadn't even seen the suspect yet. His next question was intended to dispel that twinge, but it didn't.

"Were you there when they arrested Oswald? At the Texas Theatre, I mean?"

"No, but I wish I had been," Alex said bitterly. "Strictly off the record, Matt, I think it's a dirty shame they brought this asshole in alive in the first place. He should've been blown away on the spot. The only safe place for people like him is a slab in the morgue.''

"But what if he's part of some kind of conspiracy?" Matt heard himself asking. "I mean, if Oswald's the only suspect and he's dead, how do we know if he was the only one shooting at Kennedy?"

Alex didn't answer, but turned quickly away, seeming distracted. "Hey, I've got to run, Matt," he said. "See you later. We'll have a beer."

"Sure," Matt said. "Yeah, sure."

He shook his head in disbelief as Alex walked off. Maybe the lieutenant was only reacting to the stress of the moment, Matt thought, but what he had just said seemed like a hellava strange thing to say—especially for a cop who was supposed to be investigating the first murder of a U.S. President in 62 years.

An investigator's job was to develop evidence, not obliterate it. Wasn't it?

CHAPTER EIGHT

November 24, 1963

There had never been a weekend like it in journalistic history. Matt was pretty sure of that. By noon Saturday, it looked as though every news organization on earth had sent people to Dallas. The city was swarming with reporters, photographers, cameramen and TV commentators. The police station was utterly overrun with them, and they all went through the same motions, asked the same questions, interviewed the same people, took the same notes, shot the same pictures, wrote the same stories. By Saturday night, he had accumulated 12 hours of overtime, and would almost have traded it for a day off, but it looked like that was too much to hope for.

He and Jamie had stayed at the police station until almost 10 o'clock, when the city editor told them to go ahead and take off but be back early Sunday. Captain Fritz was supposed to be about through questioning Oswald and wanted him transferred from the city lockup, where he had been kept since Friday afternoon, to more secure quarters at the county jail. It was pretty certain that the transfer would take place on

Sunday, when downtown traffic was at a minimum. But if anybody knew the exact time, it was a well-kept secret, so the only thing to do was camp out at the police station and wait.

After work, Matt had accepted Jamie's invitation to come along for a drink at Jack Ruby's Carousel Club, where, as usual, Jamie was meeting Hollie O'Connor when she got off. Hollie and Mollie finished their last show at 10:30, and after that they all sat around adjoining tables and talked for about an hour.

Jack Ruby stopped by for a minute, as he often did. Tonight, though, his broad face was grim and he was shaking his head. "It's such a shame," he said, "such a terrible shame. I just keep thinking about poor Jackie Kennedy and those poor little children. What a terrible, terrible shame."

Although they looked and sounded the same as always while they were on stage, both Hollie and Mollie seemed especially distressed about President Kennedy, and behind his thin smile, Alex acted just as uptight to Matt as he had the afternoon before, maybe even more so. Even Jamie was subdued and quieter than usual, and it seemed obvious, now that they had a few minutes to think about it, that all of them were still saddened and stunned by what had happened the day before—all of them except Tommy Van Zandt, that is.

When Tommy came in about 11 o'clock, he was talking exuberantly, grinning like a hyena, escorting a statuesque blonde in an expensive mink, and obviously having himself a blast. He was also a little tipsy, and every time he raised his glass, he offered the same loud toast.

"Here's to the good times; they're all ahead of us now."

Tommy Van Zandt could be one of the world's most charming people when he wanted to be, Matt knew, but he could also be one of the world's most perfect horse's asses. Everybody in the group knew about his Jekyll-and-Hyde personality, and most of the time they ignored it or took it in stride. They also knew what a political reactionary Tommy was, and how much he hated the majority of what John Kennedy and his New Frontier stood for, and usually they turned a deaf ear when he started ranting about "nigger lovers'' and ''welfare staters.'' Given the circumstances, though, Matt found Tommy's mood and tone not only callous but also completely out of place, and apparently so did the rest of the group.

After the third or fourth toast, the atmosphere started getting tense around the two tables. Matt saw Hollie and Mollie frown at Tommy several times, and at one point he heard Alex tell Tommy curtly to ''knock it off.'' But it was Jamie, of all people—who would usually put up with just about anything when he was with Hollie—who finally brought matters to a head.

''It may not make a shit to a rich, famous lawyer like you, Tommy,'' Jamie told him laconically, ''but some of us don't like what happened yesterday in Dallas a goddamned bit. So why don't you just shut the hell up before I christen you with this glass of beer.''

Tommy just laughed, but from then on, he quieted down a little, and a few minutes later, he got up and left, waving back with one hand and keeping a firm grip on the blonde with the other. Not long after that, Matt said good night, walked back to where he had parked his grubby Falcon, and went home to his cluttered East Dallas apartment, where he slept like a dead man until the alarm went off at 7 a.m.

As far as Matt was concerned, that Sunday morning didn't feel a damned thing like Sunday morning was supposed to feel. But then again, on a weekend like this one, there was no reason it should. He had agreed to come in early, so that Jamie would have an extra hour or so to sleep—or maybe roll around in bed with Hollie, he thought enviously. But when he got to the Municipal building a little before 8 o'clock, there were already close to 100 news people gathered there and more were arriving in a steady stream. Most were congregating in the basement, where, theoretically, Oswald would be put into an unmarked police car sometime that morning and whisked the six or seven blocks to the county jail.

It turned out to be one of those hurry-up-and-wait operations. The morning dragged by and nothing happened. At 8:30, a *Times Herald* photographer arrived and set up his camera and tripod in the basement, along with two or three dozen other still photographers. Around 9, Jamie showed up, carrying a thermos of coffee and looking as if he were still half-asleep. As soon as he had poured them both a cup of coffee, Jamie put in a call to Captain Fritz's office to see if he could find out anything about the move, but after talking to Fritz for a minute, he hung up and shrugged.

"All he says is he imagines it'll be sometime today," Jamie said, "but I'll bet you a beer it'll be before noon, old cowchip. Personally, I think Cap's tired of screwing with this guy, and he figures the evidence is strong enough to get a conviction whether the guy confesses or not."

"What do you think about all those eyewitnesses down in Dealey Plaza who were so sure the shots came from someplace else besides the Book Depository?" Matt asked. "From what I hear, even some of the cops in the motorcade thought they came from another direction. You think maybe Oswald had some help on this thing?"

"You mean do I think there's another assassin out there someplace?"

"Yeah, I guess that's what I mean."

Jamie shrugged. "I don't know," he said, "but I'll tell you one thing, old cowchip. If Oswald did it all by his lonesome, this boy's not only one hell of an accurate shot, he's also one hell of a fast shot. I just don't see how he did it with that damned old bolt-action rifle."

A little before 10, word started circulating in the corridors of the police station that the move was going to take place momentarily. By this time, Jamie and Matt had both been back and forth to the basement a half-dozen times, but now they went again and stood around with the milling, increasingly impatient crowd of newspeople.

One of the major problems in trying to cover the transfer was that there were no phones accessible to reporters in the basement itself or anywhere nearby. In fact, the closest ones were all the way up on the third floor in the Burglary and Theft Bureau, and there would undoubtedly be a stampede in that direction once Oswald was actually out of the building and on his way. Fortunately, Matt thought, the ulcerous urgency of the two-star and three-star deadlines wasn't facing them at midmorning on a Sunday; if it had been a weekday, it would have been an entirely different story.

"There's no sense in both of us standing around here with our thumbs up our butts, old cowchip," Jamie said at about 10:30. "Why don't you go up to the pressroom and call in a status report to the city desk. Oh, and on your way back down, bring me a Coke and a pack of Winstons." He dug in his pocket, withdrew a handful of change and tossed Matt three quarters.

"What do you want me to tell the city desk?"

Jamie grinned. "Hell, I don't care," he said. "Tell 'em we're pretty sure it'll be before noon. Tell 'em they'll be the first to know. Tell 'em to screw off."

Matt went upstairs, took a quick detour to the men's room, and was heading down the hall toward the pressroom when he was surprised to see Alex Sutton come out of Burglary and Theft and start in his direction. The lieutenant looked more uptight than ever. He also seemed to be in a terrible hurry.

"Hey, Alex," Matt called, "what do you hear from Fritz?"

Alex glanced at him without slowing down. "Nothing much," he said, not even breaking stride. "Sorry I can't stop to talk, but I've got to get downstairs on the double."

"Does that mean they're about ready to move Oswald?"

"Not necessarily," Alex said as he stepped into the elevator. "I'm just on my way to meet somebody, that's all." The elevator doors slid shut and Alex was gone, leaving Matt to wonder for one brief instant what a homicide detective was doing in the Burglary and Theft Bureau when there was so much going on up in Homicide.

Matt went on to the pressroom and telephoned the city desk as instructed. It was a pretty pointless gesture, except that it gave the bored wretch at the other end of the line a sense of doing something for a moment. Consequently, this particular wretch talked for much longer than necessary, while Matt sprawled drowsily on the couch in the pressroom, staring up at the life-size pinup picture on the wall, only half listening to what the guy was saying, and vaguely worrying that he should be getting back to the basement. Finally, spurred by a nagging feeling of guilt—plus the near-certainty that Jamie was out of cigarettes by now and poised on the brink of a nicotine fit—he told the guy he had to go, hung up the phone, and trotted for the stairs. He looked at his wristwatch as he went and was surprised to find that it was almost 11:15. He could only hope that Jamie wasn't too pissed off.

He stopped momentarily at the vending machines in the first-floor lobby for Jamie's Coke and cigarettes, then ran for the stairs and lumbered down the last flight toward the basement. He was only a few steps from the bottom when he heard something that sounded like a firecracker, followed by shouts and a wild commotion just below him.

Just then, the basement door burst open and a solid wall of media people came pouring up the stairs straight at him, every one of them fanatically intent on getting to those third-floor telephones. Matt could see nothing but confusion in the basement behind them in the few seconds before the crush of onrushing bodies pushed him back. He felt himself losing his footing and falling.

As he was flung backward and the canned drink in his hand was knocked loose and sent clattering down the stairs, the only clear thought in his mind was, "Thank God I didn't open Jamie's Coke!"

While feet pounded past him, he was aware of a struggle of some kind still going on in the basement. There was a huge knot of people flopping around and wrestling on the floor. Everybody in the place seemed to be screaming at once, but he could make out a few voices distinctly above the din.

"Get that sonofabitch," somebody hissed furiously. "Get the gun! Get the gun!"

"Jack, you bastard!" someone else howled.

Then Matt heard another voice, obviously a policeman, warning the scrambling members of the press corps. "Everybody stay where you are. Don't move or you're going down."

Suddenly Jamie materialized from somewhere. Ignoring the cop's warning, he reached down and pulled Matt to his feet. "Come on, let's get out of here," he said, "before some other fool starts shooting."

Jamie ran up the stairs with Matt struggling along behind him.

"What the hell happened?" Matt managed to ask.

"Oswald's been shot," Jamie shouted over his shoulder. "Looks like he's probably dead."

Matt felt sick and dizzy, and a confused procession of conflicting feelings raced through his mind—professional disgust with himself for not being there when it happened, personal regret at missing one of the great tragedies of history by no more than ten seconds, anger and revulsion over another vicious assassination so soon after the first, and fear that, if Oswald died, the world's only chance to learn the truth would die with him.

"But how?" Matt panted. "How could it happen with all those cops around? Who did it, for Christ's sake?"

They were at the third-floor landing now, and Jamie stopped and leaned against the wall, gasping for breath. When he turned to face Matt, his face was white and beaded with sweat.

"Our friend Jack Ruby shot him, Matt," he said. "Old Jack ran up and shot that asshole just as big as you please."

Matt couldn't believe what he was hearing. "You've got to be kidding," he said.

"Kidding, my ass," said Jamie. "Hey, did you get me some cigarettes? God, I need one bad."

Matt fumbled in the side pocket of his jacket, pulled out the pack of Winstons he had bought only moments before, and pitched it to Jamie. Jamie tore the pack open clumsily and lit one with shaking fingers.

"I saw the whole thing, old cowchip," he said. "I didn't even know Jack was down there, but all of sudden he came out of nowhere with a gun in his hand. He came right up within a foot or two of Oswald and said, 'You sonofabitch, you killed my President.' Oswald kind of drew back and tried to cover himself up, but he couldn't do much, because, shit, he was handcuffed. Then Jack shot him. He shot him right through the middle of his body while the whole goddamned world watched him do it."

As he would often reflect over the years that followed, the rest of that Sunday after it happened had more downright craziness crammed into it than any twelve-hour period that Matt ever experienced. The day of the assassination had been bad, but the atmosphere had been one of simple shock and straightforward grief, remorse and anguish. On the day that Ruby shot Oswald, however, something snapped under the force of the second shock wave in 48 hours, and the atmosphere turned utterly insane. As the whole country gathered in slack-jawed amazement around its TV sets to see the bizarre drama in the Dallas police station replayed again and again, most of the public seemed convinced that Dallas was one gigantic lunatic asylum. And as the day wore on, a lot of people in Dallas seemed determined to justify that conclusion.

By the middle of the afternoon, a wild, mindless kind of panic had descended over most of the girls who worked at the Carousel. Part of it stemmed from the increasingly obvious fact that, with Jack in jail and facing capital murder charges, his down-at-the-heels nightclub was now history, along with the jobs of everyone employed there. Jack was always broke or very close to it, and the Carousel constantly operated on the verge of bankruptcy. And even if he had any money now, everybody was pretty sure it would be absorbed by something other than striptease dancers' salaries. But the panic went far beyond mere job security or monetary considerations.

Bosomy Karen Carlin, for example, who danced under the name "Little Lynn" and who had been the Carousel's un-challenged star until "Sugar" and "Spice" O'Connor came along, was almost hysterical when she heard about Ruby. In some respects, she was almost like a daughter to Jack. In fact, the last thing Ruby had done before he went to the police station to shoot Oswald was stop at the Western Union office half a block away to wire some money to Karen to bail her out of trouble with her Fort Worth landlord. At about 4 o'clock that afternoon, she called the police pressroom and Matt answered the phone.

"This is Little Lynn," she said, and it was obvious that she was crying. "I've got to talk to Jamie Cade. It's very, very urgent. Is he there?"

When Jamie got on the line, Karen told him she had arranged to borrow enough money for bus fare and was leaving for Houston in less than an hour. "I won't be back," she said, "not ever, and if anybody should ask you, don't tell them where I went. Promise me, Jamie."

"Sure, I promise," he said, "but what's the rush, Karen? What's this all about?"

"Damn it, I'm scared," she said, her voice breaking apart. "I'm scared to death about some stuff that might come out about Jack and some other people. I can't tell you any more than that, Jamie, but I wanted to warn you about something."

He laughed. "Warn me? What do you mean?"

"Hollie and Mollie O'Connor are nice kids, and I'd hate to see anything happen to them. But Mollie's already got herself mixed up in something pretty deep, and if she's not careful, Hollie may get dragged into it, too. So for Christ's sake, tell Hollie to be careful, Jamie, and watch out for her. She's not directly involved in this, but Mollie is, and I don't know how much Mollie might've told her. Mollie knows how much danger she's in herself, but Hollie may not suspect a thing."

"You're not making a hellava lot of sense, Karen," Jamie told her. "What kind of danger?"

"I can't talk anymore," she said. "God knows, I've said way too much already. Just take care of Hollie. Get her away from Dallas if you can. It's probably too late for some of us, but not for her."

Jamie had been feeling pretty ragged even before Karen's call, but afterwards he turned as edgy as Matt had ever seen him. He had already been worried about Hollie, primarily because he didn't know where she was, or what she was doing, or how to get in touch with her. Less than an hour after the shooting, she had come into the press room and told Jamie that Mollie wanted to talk to her and insisted on going someplace where they would have complete privacy without disturbances.

Matt noticed Mollie waiting out in the corridor while Hollie and Jamie talked, and he was never able to forget the way she looked. Her eyes were puffy and red from crying, but they were also the stricken, desperate eyes of an animal caught in a trap. Her face was totally without makeup and sickly pale. Her lower lip was quivering uncontrollably, and she looked so tormented, so vulnerable that he wanted to go out and say something reassuring to her. But, as usual, he couldn't seem to find any appropriate words, so after a minute, he simply looked away.

"Mollie's really, really upset about what's happened with Jack," Hollie had told Jamie. "She made me promise not to tell a soul where we're going, not even you. And whatever you do, if you see Alex, don't say a word about this to him. I'm not sure why, but Mollie doesn't want him to know anything at all about it. I'll call you as soon as I can, but I just don't know when it'll be. From the way things look, it might not be until tomorrow sometime. I'm sorry, honey, but please try to understand, okay?"

Jamie, however, was in a less than understanding mood by the time he hung up from talking to Little Lynn. He banged the keys on his old Royal upright unmercifully and chain-smoked like a blast furnace while he put the final touches on his story about the shooting and dictated it to the rewrite desk. When he finished, it was shortly after 6 p.m., and Matt had already been through with his two sidebar stories for 20 minutes or so.

"I've had all the nutty broads and screwball phone calls I can abide for one day, old cowchip," he said then, relaxing a little, "and I'm in the mood for some serious beer-drinking. An epidemic of mass insanity seems to have taken over this whole fucking town today, so what do you say we go out and play with the rest of the crazies?"

"Suits me," said Matt, who had just chalked up his 22nd hour of overtime for the weekend. "I've got just about enough energy left to make it to the TV Bar."

There was lunacy in the very air over Dallas that night. And maybe—just maybe—that was what caused Matt and Jamie to end up doing the impulsive, illogical, inexplicable things they did later that evening.

Since the TV Bar was one of the few watering holes within walking distance of City Hall that was open on a Sunday evening, they found the place swarming with customers—cops, newspeople and lawyers, mainly—and most of the booths and tables already occupied. But Jamie quickly spotted Mike Fisher, a reporter for the *L.A. Times* with whom he had struck up an acquaintance the day before. Fisher was sitting at a table with Howard Thompson, a well-known young criminal lawyer who did occasional legal work for Ruby, and two other attorneys, Melvin Ring and G. C. Griggs.

"Hi, guys," Jamie said. "You got a couple extra seats at this table for members of the hard-working press?"

They sat down and Jamie introduced Matt to everybody while they waited for the waitress to come back with another round of the 18-ounce steins of beer that the TV Bar was famous for. The beer had just arrived when Matt noticed a small, middle-aged man making his way slowly toward the table. The lawyer named Ring also saw the man at about the same time.

Ring waved his hand and yelled, "Hey, Jake, come on over here and have a beer."

The man came over and smiled wanly. "Thanks, Mel," he said, pulling a chair over from another table and sitting down. "I've been feeling really bad all day," he said. "I'm so fidgety I can't sit still."

"Gentlemen," Ring said, addressing the three newsmen at the table, "I'd like you to meet Mr. Jacob Snyder, Jack Ruby's roommate. These fellows are reporters, Jake. They might like to ask you a question or two."

That was a classic understatement, of course. For the next half-hour, Jamie and Mike bombarded Snyder with questions about Ruby's home life, his personal habits, what it was like to live under the same roof with him, and so on. Even Matt thought of two or three questions to ask. But after awhile it grew fairly obvious that Snyder knew little more about Ruby than Matt and Jamie did, and the conversation gradually drifted away from Jack's roommate to other Ruby-related topics.

Later on, Matt couldn't clearly recall who first suggested that they all drive Snyder home and pay a visit to the apartment he shared with Ruby. Regardless of who made it, however, by the time the suggestion came up, they had been sitting there for close to two hours and Matt was feeling mildly sloshed. He and Jamie had downed five or six rounds of beer, and Mike Fisher had presumably consumed even more than that, since he had been there longer. At any rate, they all thought going to Ruby's place was a great idea.

They piled into two different cars, with Snyder and the three lawyers riding in Ring's Lincoln, and Matt, Jamie and Mike following in Mike's rented Chevy. It took less than 15 minutes, or just about long enough to finish another round of beers enroute, to get to the apartment, which was in an older neighborhood just off Jefferson Boulevard in the Oak Cliff area on the west side of the Trinity River. Matt had never realized how close Jack lived to the Texas Theatre, where Oswald had been arrested, until they passed by the brightly lit marquee just a few blocks before reaching their destination.

The apartment was so messy and disheveled that even Jamie commented on its condition. "Jesus, what a dump," he said. "I thought my place was bad, but it looks like the Adolphus penthouse compared to this."

They moved some clothes and other clutter off the living room furniture, and everybody sat down and opened some fresh beers. Mike Fisher flopped into a chair and put his feet on the coffee table, obviously somewhat the worse for wear. Before long, Fisher was dozing, the lawyers were talking in low, sympathetic tones with the shaken Snyder, and Matt and Jamie were left to their own devices.

They wandered into the kitchen, where they were more or less out of earshot of the living room. "Hey, old cowchip," Jamie said with a conspiratorial grin, "want to nose around a little?"

Matt shrugged. "Why not?" he said. "It beats sitting around talking about poor old Jack."

So they ambled down the hall, glanced briefly into the bathroom, and then turned toward the closed door of a bedroom. Jamie pushed the door open slowly, switched on the overhead light and looked around. The pictures on the wall were of strippers and comics and Ruby himself, so it was obvious that it was Jack's bedroom. The floor, the bed and the furnishings were all piled and littered with clothes, shoes, hats, boxes, books, newspapers, various other personal items and just plain trash.

"Old Jack sure could've used a housekeeper," Jamie said disgustedly. He reached for the light switch and started to pull the door closed again, but for some reason, Matt grabbed his arm.

"Wait a minute," Matt said. "Maybe we ought to take a closer look. I mean, if there's anything here that would give us a clue to why Jack did what he did today, it's got to be in this room."

Jamie frowned, then nodded. "I guess you're right," he said. "Come on."

They paused to listen for a moment to the unbroken drone of voices from the other end of the apartment. Then they slipped into Ruby's bedroom and pulled the door closed behind them.

And it was there in that dingy, unkempt room during the next ten minutes or so that Jamie Cade sealed his fate and Matt Eastman found a lifetime's worth of fear and trouble.

CHAPTER NINE

October 26, 1987

With considerable effort, Matt used his good arm to raise himself into a sitting position against the headboard, pulled back the curtains on the window behind the bed and looked outside. It was full daylight on a bright, crisp Monday morning, and he had spent far too long trying to recount and explain things that probably no longer made any sense or any difference. He felt very sore and tentative, but it was well past time to get started taking care of the matters confronting him—matters that were no less unpleasant or confusing than those of his past, but matters that demanded his immediate, urgent attention in the present.

He stood up very slowly, holding onto the headboard for support as he looked at his wristwatch, and was alarmed to see that it was almost 7 a.m. "See, damn it, I told you," he said, irritated with himself. "Here I've been talking nonstop for over two hours, and I've still hardly gotten started with this stupid story."

He felt a little light-headed, and almost lost his balance as he started across the room, but he was determined to shake the feeling off. As much as he longed to lie back down on the bed and sleep, maybe for the rest of the day, he knew that was entirely out of the question. He would sleep when his two unwanted guests had been disposed of and the most distressing indications of their presence in his house erased, and not a minute before.

Sarah had been sitting cross-legged on the foot of the bed and watching him with rapt, wide-eyed interest, but now his movement broke the spell and she drifted reluctantly back to the present. From his very first words, she had listened in awed silence as he reconstructed the events of that long ago November, and he could tell that she was nowhere near ready for him to stop. Her instinctive reporter's curiosity was far from satisfied.

"But aren't you even going to tell me what you and Jamie found at Jack Ruby's place?" she asked disappointedly.

"It's hard to explain," he said, moving unsteadily to the closet and taking out a shirt that was reasonably clean, but old enough and sufficiently frayed around the collar to be worn for the dirty task at hand. "There was some stuff scribbled on a piece of notepaper in what looked like Ruby's handwriting. We thought we knew what some of it meant, but we weren't sure. There were a couple of photocopies of checks that were payable to Ruby and endorsed by D. Wingo Conlan, and there was a photograph that had been torn in half, wadded up and thrown in a wastebasket. That was by far the most interesting thing because one of the people in the picture was Oswald and another one was Tommy Van Zandt. There was somebody else in the picture, too, but we couldn't tell who it was because of the way the picture was torn."

"Then this meant Tommy Van Zandt and Oswald knew each other," she said, "and maybe Van Zandt had something to do with the assassination, right?"

He shrugged. "Seems like a reasonable assumption," he said. "And now Tommy's worth God knows how many millions and he'll probably be the next governor of Texas."

"That's incredible," she said. "Do you think it was him who sent those two men after you?"

"I don't know," he said, "but, again, it seems like a reasonable assumption."

"But what was Ruby doing with the picture in the first place, and how did he get it?" she asked. "Do you think the picture had something to do with him shooting Oswald?"

He turned his hands palms upward in the classic "who knows?" gesture and was immediately sorry for doing it, because it made his wounded arm hurt. "Now you're getting into the hard part," he said, wincing. "I can't come any closer to answering that question now that I could twenty-four years ago."

"So what did you and Jamie do with this stuff?"

"Nothing really, except worry a lot about what it might mean and about what might happen to us if the FBI ever found out we took it. After Jamie was killed, the only thing I wanted to do was get rid of it, so I buried it on my parents' old farm out east of Dallas. As far as I know, it's still there."

"What happened to Jamie?" she asked. "How did he die?"

"Somebody broke his neck with a judo or karate chop," he said without emotion. "The cops never charged anybody in the killing, so it's still on the books as an unsolved murder."

"But I thought when a big-city reporter got murdered it was pretty important news," she said. "Surely there was an investigation."

His lips twisted themselves into a bitter imitation of a smile. "Oh, certainly there was," he said, "but it's kind of hard to have a meaningful investigation when the guy who did the killing is the same guy doing the investigating, if you get what I mean?"

Her mouth fell open and she looked stunned. "You mean it was that detective? That Alex Sutton?"

He stood there for a minute, holding the hanger with the frayed shirt and staring into space. Then he took the shirt off the hanger, shoved his arms into the sleeves, crossed the room to the dresser, opened a drawer and took out a pair of clean socks. It was almost as if he had forgotten she were there, until he said, "I don't know. It's just a feeling I've had for a long time. There's never been anything tangible to support the feeling, but . . ."

He stopped and smiled at her. It was a real smile this time, not an imitation. "Jesus Christ, Sarah," he said, "you'll have me standing here babbling all day if I'm not careful. Why don't you get on out of here now and go home for awhile? I really appreciate your help, but I've got a nasty job to do and I think you'll be happier somewhere else while I'm doing it."

The reminder of the two dead bodies just down the hall seemed to startle and unsettle her. She bit her lip. "No," she said, "I don't want to run out on you. I want to help you. You're in no shape to try to do it by yourself."

"I don't feel real chipper," he said, buttoning the old shirt and sitting down on the edge of the bed to put on his socks, "but I can manage the messiest part. It's no job for somebody with a weak stomach, and I've already made you throw up once."

She seemed embarrassed. "I'm sorry about that," she said. "I've always been bad about upchucking at the slightest pretext, and when I saw all that blood and those two bodies . . . God!"

"Well, you won't have to look at them again, except on your way out the back door. I'll take care of all that, but if you're really sure you don't mind, there's a couple of other things you could do."

"No problem," she said. "What are they?"

"Judging from these," he said, reaching into his pants pocket and pulling out a set of keys on a Hertz key ring, "those two characters left a car somewhere around here within walking distance." He tossed the keys across the bed to her. "I found them on the guy in the hall doorway," he explained. "The car'll probably be an '87 model of some kind and it'll have some of those little yellow Hertz stickers on it. If you can find it, bring it back here and pull it up in back of the house where it'll kind of be out of sight, okay?"

"Sure, boss," she said. "I think I can handle that. Are you positive you don't need me here?"

He shook his head firmly. Then he took her by the arm and

guided her carefully down the hall and around the carnage on the carpet. Hobo roused himself as they passed his favorite lurking spot, stretched, got to his feet and bounded along after them. The dog stopped briefly to sniff at the trouser cuff of the dead man in the doorway, then snorted and pattered on into the kitchen.

When Matt looked at her, Sarah's face was pale and she was shaking a little again. "Shut your eyes, Sarah," he said. She did and he put his arm around her, gave her a small hug and propelled her toward the back door. When he touched her, he could feel her soft warmth, but beneath her enticing physical surface, he could also sense the deeper strength and vitality that always attracted him to her. Within that instant, he wanted to cling to her, to take a death grip on both her outer softness and her inner strength as if they were the last slender threads between himself and oblivion. He wanted to hold her and kiss her and try to forget the heavy, hopeless weariness inside him, but he knew he had to turn her loose—at least for now.

"Okay, get going," he told her, "Give me a good twenty minutes, maybe a little more, and I promise the surroundings will be a lot less upsetting when you get back." He gave her arm a final squeeze. "Be careful, Sarah," he whispered.

She nodded and ran down the steps without looking back.

As soon as he knew she was gone and had put Hobo out into the yard, he decided to tackle the worst job first, before he lost his new-found nerve and changed his mind. He went to the pantry and took out a recently opened box of the heavy-duty, oversized plastic trash bags that he normally used to transport his household garbage to the dumpster down on the county road a mile from the house. Twice a week, a sanitation company under contract to the county dispatched a packer-body truck to empty the dumpster, but that was the closest thing there was to garbage service outside the town of Jefferson itself. All rural residents in the vicinity were required to either bury or burn their trash or haul it to the dumpster. And Matt had long ago learned that the light-weight, economy grade of garbage bags from the supermarket had a nasty habit of coming apart enroute and befouling the trunk or back seat of the Mustang. So, for the past two years or more, he had paid an additional dollar or so per box for a type of extra-large, three-mil-thick bag stocked by Jefferson Hardware. Now he was very glad he had indulged in that small extravagance.

Even with the extra-large bags, he found it took two of them to enclose a single human corpse. He started with the one beside the kitchen table, removed the contents of his pockets, piled them on one of the chairs to examine later, picked up the narrow-brimmed brown hat that had come off the man's head during his dying contortions, and stuffed the hat into one of the bags. Then he pulled one bag over the man's feet and legs and up to his chest, slipped another bag down over his ghastly, discolored face, his shoulders and torso, and finally secured the ends of the two bags together with wide strips of silver-gray duct tape.

Matt was immeasurably relieved when he could no longer see the agonized expression or the puffy, burnt cherry-hued skin of the dead man's face and neck. The horror of the corpse's appearance was intensified by the realization that it could just as easily have been Matt himself lying there dead of cyanide poisoning. If the man had asked for bourbon some five hours earlier instead of the amaretto, Matt was almost certain that it would have been he who swallowed the liqueur with the cyanide. At this moment, he still couldn't be 100 percent sure, but that was the way he had planned it in his mind. That was the deal he had made with himself. Whatever his visitor chose to drink, he would drink the opposite. So fate had decreed that the other man die and that he live, at least for now.

It brought a chilling new meaning to the old expression, "Name your poison," he thought. It also caused him to pause from what he was doing long enough to go to the pantry, where he had taken pains to replace the bottle of amaretto not long before Sarah had arrived, and push the bottle to the very back of the top shelf where it was well out of sight. One of these days, he thought, he might be able to bring himself to dig a deep hole somewhere behind the house, pour the amaretto into it, cover it up again, and forget he had ever had it. But for the moment, he still felt too dependent on it to do that.

After a minute, he returned to the primary chore at hand and bent down to remove the remaining contents of the second man's pockets, being careful to keep them separate from the first man's belongings. Then he repeated the process with the plastic bags. Because the first man was moderately tall and had already been stiff with rigor mortis, getting two bags to cover him had been a close fit. But bagging up the body of the second man was considerably easier, because, although he weighed more than the first, the second man was much shorter.

When Matt was through with the wrapping job, he dragged both the bodies into the unfurnished spare bedroom and shoved them into the bottom of the closet. He closed the closet door firmly then and leaned against it, breathing heavily. He was already tired from the exertion, and the bullet wound in his arm was hurting and throbbing, but he knew his task had barely begun.

He got a pail and a sponge from the broom closet in the hall, filled the bucket with cold water, and added a splash of liquid cleaner. Then, holding his breath and gritting his teeth, he sponged up the dried and clotted blood from the linoleum by the doorway into the hall. It was stuck like glue, but with repeated wipings, the linoleum finally came perfectly clean. Fortunately, not much blood had gotten on the hall carpet, and what stains were left after his sponging would be next to invisible on the dingy, dark-brown shag, anyway. Twice, he took buckets of bloody water and dumped them down the commode, and, finally, when he finished with the third bucket, he was convinced that he had done a thorough job.

Once the floor was done, he quickly examined the contents of both men's pockets. The wallet belonging to the first man, the one killed by the cyanide, contained several credit cards and a Virginia driver's license in the name of Theodore Arnold Shroeder, photographs of an attractive blonde woman and a boy who looked to be about 12 years old, various other papers and $223 in cash. The other items from the first man's pockets included a chromium cigarette lighter, an opened package containing three small cigars, a pair of fingernail clippers, a plain white handkerchief, about $3 in change, and the locker key he had taken from Matt.

There were similar cards and identification papers in the second man's wallet, except that this one's driver's license was from Texas and his name was listed as Victor Michael Zandoli. He also had been carrying something over $300 in cash, two opened packages of Lifesavers, one cherry and one peppermint, and a double-bladed pocket knife with a pearl handle.

Except for the cash and the locker key, which he transferred to his own pocket, Matt placed the items in two separate small plastic bags, of the type usually used to store frozen foods. He took them into the bedroom and put them into the bottom right-hand drawer of his dresser, not really wanting to keep them, but thinking that when he dumped the bodies across the state line in Louisiana that night, the fact that they bore no identification might serve to buy him a little extra time before the next two bastards showed up.

He went back to the kitchen then, let Hobo in from the back porch, where the old dog was sitting and methodically scratching the paint off the screen door, and he even wiped the accumulated crumbs and sticky spots from the table and countertop. He was in the process of brewing a pot of strong coffee in the percolator when he heard a car pull into the driveway. When he looked out the windows over the kitchen sink, he saw Sarah climbing out of a teal blue Thunderbird with a satisfied little smile on her face.

They started out a little after 8:30 that night on a macabre journey that neither of them wanted to take. Although her misgivings over what they were doing were perfectly plain, to Sarah's credit she never once suggested that they call the sheriff and tell him the truth about what had happened. Nobody would believe the truth, and she understood that as well as Matt did. So Matt drove the rented Thunderbird with the two bodies in the trunk, and Sarah followed along behind him in the Mustang convertible as they headed south on Highway 81. The papers in the glove compartment of the

T-bird showed that it had been rented four days earlier at the Little Rock airport, but it was now on its way to the vicinity of Monroe, Louisiana.

Sarah had spared him the onerous chore of going to the office that day. She had, in fact, been very adamant in her insistence that he stay home and take a nap, while she took care of matters pertaining to *The Jeffersonian*. He had had no idea how exhausted he really was until about ten minutes after she left, and then, despite having just consumed three large cups of coffee, he barely made it to the bedroom before he conked out. It was midafternoon before he woke up, and although his arm still hurt a little and the tension inside him quickly returned, he felt better than he had at any point since he had left to meet Mollie in Star City. He couldn't believe that less than 20 hours had passed since then. It seemed as though it had been at least a week.

The road to Monroe was long, narrow and tedious, especially after they crossed the state line and Highway 81 became Louisiana Route 139. Matt had always hated Louisiana highways. Even the interstates were bad in Louisiana, and Route 139 was little more than a paved cow trail, on which any attempt to pass a truck was a life and death adventure. He made no effort to pass anything, however, not even when the 18-wheeler that was perpetually ahead of him geared down to 35 or 40 miles an hour on the curves and grades. He was still tormented by the nightmare of the evening before, and he had no intention of losing the Mustang's headlights in his rearview mirror—or the reassuring knowledge that Sarah was right behind him—even for a second. And he was grateful that, unlike the last time, the road was at least dry and visibility was excellent.

By the time they made it to the town of Bastrop and picked up U.S. 165, the worst part of the trip was behind them. It was only another 20 miles into Monroe, and the road was pretty decent from this point on. The traffic even thinned out somewhat and there were stretches where Matt was actually able to set the speedometer needle on 55 for a few minutes.

It was a little after 10 when they reached Monroe, and five or six minutes later, they came in sight of Interstate 20 and the concentration of brightly lighted gas stations, fast-food restaurants and motels along it. Their destination was a large shopping mall on the south side of the interstate and about five miles east of downtown Monroe, which Matt remembered from previous trips in this direction, so he swung onto the I-20 service road, and then eased into the eastbound lane of the interstate. The stores in the mall would all be closed by now, so there was a good chance that no one would notice their arrival in the parking lot. During the daylight hours, when regular business was in progress, the T-bird would most likely go unnoticed among all the other cars for quite some time—at least until the grisly cargo in its trunk began to smell. And as cool as it was, that might not happen for four or five days, possibly even longer. At least it would give them a little time to try to figure out their next move.

The parking area was huge and well-lighted, but there were only a handful of cars scattered around it, and no signs of human activity at this hour of the night. Matt parked the T-Bird in what he hoped was an unobtrusive spot, not too close to any of the mall entrances, but not out on the remote edges of the parking lot, either. He removed the envelope containing the rental papers from the glove compartment and shoved it into his jacket pocket. Then he wiped off the keys with his handkerchief, placed them in the ashtray on the dash and shoved it back into the closed position. Finally, he took a hand towel that he had brought along for the purpose and wiped off every possible surface inside the car in hopes that he would leave no fingerprint. He made sure that all the doors were locked, then repeated the motions with the towel on the exterior, paying particular attention to the doors and windows.

Finally, he walked over to the Mustang, where Sarah was waiting with the headlights off and the engine idling softly. He opened the door and tossed the towel into the back seat.

"Okay," he said. "I guess I'm done. Want me to drive back?"

"No," she said, "I'm fine, and I love this spirited little pony of yours. I'll drive and you can rest. Get in."

He slid into the bucket seat and leaned back, stretching his legs out and trying to ease some of the tiredness and tension that started at the back of his skull and ran all the way down to his heels. He looked at her and saw her smiling at him, and that made him feel better. Then she reached over and massaged the taut spot directly between his shoulder blades for a moment, and that made him feel better yet.

"Thanks," he said, "I needed that."

"Are you okay?" she asked, rubbing his neck.

"Yeah," he said. "I think I'm going to make it. I'll feel a thousand percent better, though, once we're out of sight of that damned T-bird."

"Just settle back and relax and consider it done," she assured him. She dropped the gear selector into drive, gave the old convertible some gas, and the tires squawked on the asphalt as the powerful 289 engine responded and sent them streaking across the parking lot. He closed his eyes for a few seconds, and when he opened them again, they were sailing along the interstate at a steady 65 miles per hour.

They stopped at one of those combination grocery store-service station-delicatessens, and while he filled the Mustang up with gas, Sarah went inside and bought a six-pack of beer, a couple of packaged sandwiches, several varieties of chips and a large cup of coffee. Neither of them had eaten all day, and although neither had felt particularly hungry up until then, they quickly discovered that the presence of food made them utterly ravenous. They wolfed down the sandwiches and chips in short order, while Sarah drank the coffee and Matt disposed of two cans of beer and started on a third.

Matt laid his head against the back of the seat, sipping his beer and feeling more contented and at ease than he could remember feeling in a long time. He looked out the window at the uninspiring north Lousiana countryside streaking past in the darkness outside the Mustang, and he thought for a few minutes that he could go to sleep. But after a while, he realized that he was too keyed up to sleep. Besides, he thought, the very least he could do was stay awake and keep Sarah company on the long drive back to Jefferson.

"Are you awake, boss?" she asked, as though she had read his thoughts.

"Yeah, wide awake," he said. "Why? What's on your mind?"

"Oh, nothing, really," she said. "I just thought you might tell me some more about, you know, the things that happened after the assassination—if you're not too tired, I mean."

"If that's your idea of a good time," he chided, "you must really be bored."

"Come on, boss," she said. "It may be old stuff to you, but it's all brand-new to me."

He thought for a moment. "Well, okay," he said, taking a sip of his beer, "but don't blame me if it doesn't make a damned bit of sense."

CHAPTER TEN

Although the pain and grief gradually eased somewhat with the passage of time, and even the notoriety finally diminished a little, the aftereffects of "Assassination Weekend" lingered on, especially for Matt and Jamie. The weeks drifted by in the "city of hate" (as Ruby's flamboyant chief defense lawyer, Melvin Belli, branded Dallas) and the daily routine at the *Times Herald* settled into the same predictable, repetitious pattern as before. Outwardly, it was again business as usual for most people, but deep inside, Matt knew his life would never be the same. Too many things had irrevocably changed.

For one, Mollie O'Connor had left town suddenly and under very peculiar circumstances, and nobody—not even her sister, Hollie—knew where she was. About 36 hours after the Oswald shooting, Hollie had returned from her hush-hush session with Mollie and contacted Jamie. She had stayed overnight with Mollie at a motel in Weatherford, west of Fort Worth, but Mollie had refused to come back to Dallas, even long enough to collect her personal belongings. Instead, she had arranged for Hollie to send her things, plus her half of their joint savings, to their parents' home in Sweetwater, where she said she would pick them up in a day or two. From there, she told Hollie, she intended to head west, possibly to California, and promised to stay in touch. She had tried to persuade Hollie to go with her, but Hollie had told her it was out of the question, that she would never consider leaving Jamie.

Hollie herself was a totally changed person after Mollie went away, however, and the change was definitely not for the better. She was no longer the bubbly, carefree girl she had been before that fateful weekend. It was as though, within the space of three or four days, she had aged 15 or 20 years. She was often depressed and withdrawn, and she worried incessantly about Mollie. She wouldn't repeat or discuss anything that Mollie had told her on their last day together, but from that day on, she quietly but steadfastly refused to be part of any social gathering that might include Alex Sutton or Tommy Van Zandt. And her mood wasn't helped by the fact that the only communication she received from Mollie between late November 1963 and mid-March 1964 was a single scribbled postcard, postmarked Phoenix and bearing no return address.

Hollie worked briefly as a dancer at a strip joint on Harry Hines Boulevard, but both the manager and the customers could tell that her heart wasn't in it. Jamie hated the place anyway and was genuinely relieved when she was fired after three or four weeks. Not long after that, she got a job as a waitress at a North Dallas restaurant, and everyone who knew her could tell that her dreams of a show business career had somehow vanished along with Mollie. Jamie asked her to move in with him, but she said she wanted to hold onto the apartment she had shared with Mollie, in case Mollie decided to come back. In desperation, Jamie finally even asked her to marry him, but she said she just wasn't ready to get married yet and asked him to wait awhile.

"It's not that I don't love him, Matt," she confided one night as they sat across from each other in a booth at the TV Bar while Jamie was making a phone call. "It's just that I'm so . . . oh, I don't know . . . confused right now, I guess. I don't think I'd make a very good wife, anyway.''

The rest of the nation seemed outraged all over again in the spring of 1964, when a Texas jury sentenced Jack Ruby to die in the electric chair for killing Oswald. But most of the leaders and ordinary citizens in Dallas not only seemed to think the verdict was just and appropriate, but also seemed in a terrific hurry to put the whole affair behind them. They wanted to get Melvin Belli out of town, try to forget the outburst of invective he had leveled at Dallas during the trial, and move on toward the bountiful destiny they envisioned for their city.

Even in Dallas, Ruby's trial and subsequent appeal were major news, of course, but insofar as the amount of space they consumed in the local press, they ranked well behind such objects of civic pride as the completion of the 52-story First National Bank Building and the opening of the new North Park Mall, one of the nation's ritziest shopping centers. One industrious copy editor at the *Times Herald* actually measured the space devoted by the paper to the entire Kennedy case since the day of the assassination and compared it to the amount given the completion and grand opening of North Park. The shopping center won, hands down, he reported.

For Matt and Jamie, the Ruby trial seemed to go on forever, and every day that it lasted brought them new anguish, misgivings and feelings of guilt. On at least a dozen occasions after their visit to Ruby's apartment, they sat down and tried to assess the importance of what they had found and decide what to do with it, but somehow they never seemed to get any closer to resolving that question.

On the surface, the evidence didn't look like much, but the torn photograph was undoubtedly the most important single item. When the ragged edges of its two wrinkled halves were placed together, it showed Oswald and Tommy Van Zandt seated at a table in what appeared to be a courtyard of some sort. There were drinks on the table and lush tropical plants in the background, and Oswald and Van Zandt seemed engrossed in conversation. Apparently, neither was aware that the picture was being shot, and the grainy quality of the photo suggested it had been shot from a considerable distance and then enlarged.

The most troublesome and puzzling thing about the photograph was the person sitting between Oswald and Van Zandt. Because of the rough manner in which the picture had been ripped in half and then wadded up, it was impossible to tell who the person in the middle was. It looked like a man, but it could conceivably have been a woman wearing pants and a shirt. There was no way to know because too much of the emulsion had been destroyed when the picture was torn and crushed.

From the beginning, Matt argued that because Ruby almost certainly had seen the picture and could identify this third person, it could be important evidence in his trial. A good guess was that it had been Ruby himself who tore the picture, and his reasons for doing so might help to explain why he shot Oswald.

Jamie took an entirely different view, however. "Hell, old cowchip," he said, "the outcome of the Ruby trial is a foregone conclusion. Several million people saw Jack commit murder, and the only possible defense is insanity, so what's the testimony of an insane man going to prove about this picture? The real significance of the picture is what it might mean about the Kennedy assassination itself. I say we should sit on the picture and see what we can find out about Tommy Van Zandt."

And so they sat on it. They sat on it until it was too late to do anything but keep sitting on it.

In the end, they did the same with the crumpled sheet of notepaper they had found beside an overflowing wastebasket in Ruby's bedroom, although there was no way they could convince themselves that Jamie's argument about the photograph also applied to the sheet of paper. The sheet was covered with the kind of jumbled notations a person might make while he was talking on the phone to someone. At the top of the page, in what they both recognized as Ruby's handwriting, was a first name and initial:

"Alex S."

All five letters had been traced over several times with a ballpoint pen, so that their impression was deeply embedded in the paper. A bit further down the page, in a lighter hand, Ruby had written:

"Transferring Osw.—City Hall basement—sometime after 11"

And still further down:

"Meet A. at Main St. ramp—no problem getting in"

The bottom third of the page was decorated with crude drawings and artwork. There was a doodled Star of David, its six points outlined over and over again in blue ink. Just to the right and slightly below the star was another drawing, this one of a pistol with smoke curling out of the barrel. And finally, there were three distinct, heavily inked letters, letters that had been written over and over again with hard, angry, jabbing strokes that had almost torn through the paper. The letters spelled a profane and universally known abbreviation:

"S.O.B."

Minutes before Oswald was shot, Matt remembered Alex Sutton passing him on the third floor of the police station. He had been hurrying to the basement to "meet somebody," he had said. Could that somebody have been Ruby? Was it possible that a Dallas homicide detective had actually, knowingly served as an accomplice in the murder of the man accused of assassinating the President? The idea was unthinkable, absurd, insane—and yet it was precisely what the words on the notepaper suggested.

"What're you going to do, Matt?" Jamie demanded. "Call up the D.A.'s office and tell Henry Wade you've got this scrap of paper with a bunch of doodles on it that make you think a cop helped set up Oswald for the kill? Christ, man, do you realize how stupid that sounds? You'd probably either be hauled off to the psycho ward at Parkland or laughed out of town—or, hell, maybe both."

The other evidence was even more nebulous. It consisted of photocopies of two checks, both payable to Ruby and both endorsed by D. Wingo Conlan, president of and principal stockholder in Conlan Universal Aerospace Corporation, one of the largest manufacturing firms in Texas. One check, dated

November 6, 1963, was written for $8,000; the other, dated November 21, 1963, was for $5,000. Obviously, the total of $13,000 would be a piddling amount to pay for a murder, and there were plenty of less sinister reasons why the checks might have been written, since both Jamie and Matt knew that Conlan was an acquaintance of Ruby's and had been a frequent patron of the Carousel. But there could also have been other Conlan checks that Ruby didn't bother to photocopy. And the fact that the copies of the Conlan checks had been found only inches from the torn picture of Oswald, Tommy Van Zandt and an unknown third party made them still more intriguing, especially since Van Zandt was one of Conlan's most intimate associates. Could Conlan be the third man in the torn photograph?

Matt went around and around with Jamie about it, but they always emerged from each discussion as far as ever from any mutual agreement on what to do. Jamie wanted to keep the evidence to themselves and conduct their own investigation into what it might mean, and he had no qualms about using his friendship with Alex and Tommy to find out as much as he could about their activities and associations—particularly with Ruby, Conlan and Oswald.

But the whole idea gave Matt an aggravated case of the sweats. And within a month after the Ruby trial ended in March, matters were destined to become even sweatier.

It was a few minutes before 4 p.m. on a warm afternoon in late April, exactly five months to the day since the assassination (although neither of them consciously realized it at the time), when Jamie called the rewrite desk and asked Matt to meet him for a beer after work. It was something they normally did at least twice a week, so Matt thought nothing about it. But a half-hour later, when he walked into the Lavender Room, a lounge at the corner of Main and Columbia in East Dallas, not far from where each of them lived, he knew instantly from the expression on Jamie's face that something was wrong.

"You don't look too happy, man," Matt said, slipping into

the other side of the booth where Jamie was sitting alone, a half-finished glass of beer in front of him. "Something on your mind?"

Jamie nodded. "Remember Mike Fisher, the guy from L.A. who went to Ruby's place with us that night?" he asked.

"Sure," Matt said flippantly, "is a pig's ass pork?" Hell, he remembered everything about that night. He remembered it in great detail, no matter how hard he tried to forget, and he could still picture Mike Fisher dozing on the couch in Ruby's trashed-out living room. "What about him?"

"He got scragged yesterday," Jamie said matter-of-factly. "He was sitting at his desk in the pressroom at the L.A. police station when some off-duty cop's gun went off and killed him—stone, cold dead. They say it was purely an accident. You know, just one of those tragic, unavoidable things that happen." He paused long enough to drain the glass in front of him. "I just hope to shit they're right," he said.

Fortunately, the waitress showed up about then with two fresh beers. Matt seized his and drank thirstily, trying to ease the sudden dryness in his throat. "Hey, it's a damned coincidence," he said. "It's got to be."

"That's what I keep telling myself, old cowchip," Jamie said quietly. "I just haven't made myself believe it yet."

"Aw, come on, Jamie," Matt said. "You don't think . . ."

"I don't know what I think," Jamie interrupted shortly. He drank a third of his new glass of beer in one gulp, then asked in a softer tone, "Did you hear about Tommy Van Zandt?"

Matt shook his head, feeling stupid. "No," he said. "Should I have?"

"Well, I don't know," Jamie said. "It's pretty big news. Our friend Tommy was just named a vice-president at Conlan Universal Aerospace. There was a little story about it in the business section yesterday. And I also picked up an interesting tidbit of information down at the cop shop today concerning another dear friend of ours."

"I'm listening," Matt said.

"It seems Alex Sutton's also gone to work for Conlan,"

Jamie told him. "It's only a moonlighting job in plant security, and he's not leaving the P.D., at least not right away. But the rumor mill says he's knocking down some really major dinero from Conlan, something in the neighborhood of two and a half thou a month. Does that start any wheels turning in your head, old cowchip?"

Yes, Matt thought, he could feel those wheels turning in his head right this minute. He could also feel the sweat forming in his armpits and the persistent dryness growing in his throat, a dryness that no amount of beer could wash away.

On another evening exactly five months later, Matt again drank beer with Jamie Cade. This time, it was a Saturday in September, and this time, they met at the Surf Bar at Fitzhugh Avenue and Bryan Street, only two blocks from where Jamie lived. And this time, as it turned out, was the last time.

They didn't talk about the Kennedy case at all that night. They talked about the "good old days" instead, about their broke, hungry college days in Denton and the roach-infested apartments where they had lived, about their concurrent stints at the *San Angelo Standard-Times* and wild weekend trips down to the Mexican border, about dust storms, prostitutes and all-night drunks at Wichita Falls.

They stayed there until after 10 o'clock, when Matt looked at his watch and asked Jamie if he wasn't going to be late meeting Hollie. Jamie and Hollie always got together on Saturday night after she finished work; it was a ritual with them, but tonight the ritual was broken.

"We had kind of a fuss," Jamie said. "I don't even know for sure what it was about, but we decided to take the night off. Sometimes I don't know about Hollie, Matt. Sometimes it seems like we're kind of drifting apart."

Matt was surprised, but he tried to reassure Jamie. "You'll work it out," he said. "Hell, you've got to work it out. You two characters were made for each other."

Shortly after 11 and very much the worse for wear, Matt left Jamie sitting there in the booth at the Surf, staring groggily into his glass of beer. Later, Matt vaguely recalled staggering down Bryan Street to where he had left his Falcon parked and then precariously weaving his way home through the quiet streets of East Dallas. With his last ounce of energy, he climbed the stairs to his one-bedroom apartment on Gaston Avenue, collapsed across the bed still fully clothed and lost consciousness, not realizing that he would never see Jamie Cade alive again.

He woke up about 9 the next morning with a terrible hangover, and spent the next two hours swallowing Alka-Seltzer and strong coffee, trying to rid himself of the cobwebs in his head and the black butterflies in his stomach, while he leafed absently through the Sunday newspapers. By early afternoon, he felt better and tried calling Angel Garcia, the diminutive, dark-eyed Mexican girl who had worked at the Carousel, but got no answer at her place. Then, as he did almost every Sunday, he put in a dutiful long distance call to his parents at the little Kaufman County farm where he had grown up, talked to his mother for ten minutes or so, and said hello to his dad.

This chore completed, he shaved, showered, put on a sport shirt and a pair of jeans and drove out to White Rock Lake. He stopped twice on the way, once at Roscoe White's Drive-In for a six-pack of beer and a barbecue sandwich, and once at a bait shop on Garland Road for a carton of red wigglers. Then he found a likely looking spot on the lakeshore, where there weren't too many kids running around, and spent the rest of the day drinking beer, listening to KLIF on the car radio, and pretending to fish. He stayed at the lake until dusk without ever getting a serious nibble. On the way home, he picked up another six-pack, and finally settled down in front of the TV set until bedtime.

At 5:50 the next morning, the strident ringing of the telephone beside the bed awakened him. He swore under his breath and groped blindly for the receiver, knowing he wasn't due at the rewrite desk until 7:30 and wondering what sadistic bastard could be calling so early. He grunted into the mouthpiece and heard the irritated voice of an assistant city editor at the other end.

"Hey, Eastman," it said, "have you seen anything of Jamie Cade?"

Matt tried to think and rub the sleep out of his eyes at the same time. "No," he said, yawning uncontrollably, "not since Saturday night. Why?"

"He's supposed to be working early police," the assistant city editor said, "but he hasn't shown up and we can't seem to locate him. It's left us in a helluva bind. I thought you might know where he is."

Working early police on Monday was one of the few jobs at the *Times Herald* that was worse than being a junior rewrite man. It meant getting to the police station at 4:30 a.m., digging through mountains of weekend reports and trying to come up with at least a half-dozen stories for the one-star edition. Jamie caught the trick every other week, and he hated it.

"Did you try his apartment?" Matt asked.

"Yeah, about five times. There's no answer."

Matt threw back the covers and sat up on the edge of the bed. He knew Jamie and Hollie had had a fight. Chances are, they had made up and Jamie had spent the night at Hollie's place, he thought. Even so, it was very unlike Jamie not to report for work on time. He was very conscientious about that kind of thing.

"I can try his girlfriend," Matt said. "She might know where he is."

"I'd appreciate it," the assistant city editor said. "If you find him, tell him to get his ass down here on the double, okay?"

Matt hung up and started to dial Hollie's number. Then he stopped. He had called there enough times to know the number by heart, and he considered Hollie a good friend, but it was still extremely embarrassing to have to call there at this hour of the morning. He would probably stammer and get all tongue-tied if Hollie answered the phone. And, God, he thought, what if Jamie wasn't there? Then he would really have opened up a can of worms.

He swallowed hard and finally forced himself to dial, feeling his palm sweating against the receiver. He heard the phone ring once, then twice, then a third time. He held his breath during the fourth, fifth and sixth rings, then exhaled loudly on the seventh. Maybe Hollie was in the shower, he thought, and Jamie had already left. The phone rang at least a dozen more times before he hung up, after which he spent the next three or four minutes pulling on some clothes, thinking that would give Hollie time to finish whatever she might be doing. As soon as he was dressed, he called back, and this time, he let the phone ring 30 times or more, but there was still no answer.

It was damned odd that Jamie and Hollie were both gone, he thought. Where could they be? He wondered for an instant if they had run off to get married. He smiled at the thought, but it hardly seemed likely. He would have been very disappointed if that had happened and Jamie hadn't asked him to be a witness.

Then he thought about Mike Fisher and the smile froze on his face. He grabbed his jacket out of the closet and ran for the door.

It took no more than ten minutes for Matt to get to his car and drive to Jamie's apartment, located in a new two-story, 16-unit building that looked almost identical to 50 other apartment complexes in East Dallas. He took the stairs two at a time to the second floor and knocked on Jamie's door. There was no response, but he could hear a sound of some kind coming from inside. It was a rhythmic, scraping sound that he couldn't identify.

He knocked again, louder this time. Still nothing.

"Hey, Jamie," he yelled, with his mouth close to the door. "Are you in there?"

From behind the locked door, there was no reply. There was only that odd, repetitive sound continuing softly at regular intervals every few seconds. It sounded like:

Scra-a-ape, click-click, silence. Scra-a-ape, click-click, silence. Scra-a-ape, click-click, silence. . . .

A cold, hard lump of apprehension was now lodged just below Matt's Adam's apple. It grew larger as he ran to the window on the stair landing and looked down at the parking lot at the rear of the building. Jamie's car, a sporty red

Karmin Ghia, was plainly visible in its usual space near the west end of the building.

If Jamie's car is here, Matt heard a voice shouting inside his head, where the hell is Jamie? If he's not at Hollie's and he's not at work, then he has to be here. But if he's here, why doesn't he come to the goddamned door? Why . . . ?

He felt suddenly weak in the knees as he ran back down the stairs to the manager's apartment on the first floor. He punched the bell five or six times and then started beating his fists against the door as hard as he could. After a minute, he heard muffled noises from inside, but he didn't stop pounding on the door until someone came and furiously jerked it open.

The manager appeared in the doorway, trying to pull a robe around himself, breathing hard and swearing. He was a middle-aged man with a bubble gut, a hairy chest and an unpleasant disposition, and he obviously didn't appreciate being so rudely disturbed so early in the morning.

"What the hell's going on out here?" he demanded. "What the hell do you want?"

"This is an emergency," Matt said, showing the man his Department of Public Safety press card. "I think there's some kind of trouble in Apartment 207. I need you to let me in there."

"Why the fuck should I?" the man demanded. "You ain't no cop."

Matt felt himself losing control. He reached out, grabbed the front of the man's robe and yanked him forward until his face was only a couple of inches from his own.

"I think my friend's in there," Matt said between his teeth, "but I can't get him to come to the door. I'm afraid something's happened to him, and I know goddamned well something's going to happen to you if you don't get your passkey and let me into that room."

"Okay, okay," the man said, pulling away from Matt's grasp, "you don't have to get mean about it."

The manager took a ring of keys off a hook beside the door, and Matt followed him up the stairs and waited while he searched for the right one. Finally he got the door unlocked, flung it open with a disgusted motion and stepped back to let Matt go inside.

Everything looked normal enough at first glance. Jamie had never been the world's greatest housekeeper, but the apartment was no more untidy than usual, and there was nothing particularly messed-up or out of place, as far as Matt could see. There was a half-full bottle of Pearl beer on the coffee table, along with a large ceramic ashtray piled high with cigarette butts, part of a package of Winstons, and a well-thumbed copy of *Playboy*. Some dirty clothes and newspapers were scattered around on the furniture, but nothing was broken or torn apart. The scraping noise Matt had heard was coming from a record that was still spinning on the turntable of Jamie's portable phonograph. The needle was stuck in the eject groove and the record just kept going around and around, dragging the needle with it and making the same sound over and over, as it had apparently been doing for hours.

There were no signs of burglary, robbery, forced entry or a struggle. Overall, it looked like a typical bachelor apartment a lot like Matt's own, in fact —except for one thing.

Jamie was lying on the living room floor with his eyes open. He was wearing only skivvy shorts and a T-shirt, and his face was somewhat discolored. You could tell by the position of his head in relation to his body that his neck was broken. Even to a total novice like Matt, it was obvious that he was dead and most likely had been for some time. (Eight or nine hours, the medical examiner would later rule, which meant it had happened sometime between 10 and 11:30 the night before.)

"Oh, my God!" Matt heard the manager gasp. He turned and saw the man standing behind him, staring dumbstruck at the body, his eyes as white and round as two cue balls in his gray, unshaven face. "Oh, my God, my God!" he said again and stumbled out into the hall.

Matt picked up the phone on the end table beside the couch. He called the police emergency number first, told the dispatcher in a surprisingly calm voice that he wanted to report an apparent homicide, and gave her his name and the address. After that, he called the *Times Herald* city desk, asked for the city editor, and told him Jamie Cade was dead.

Then he sat down on the couch, waited for the cops to get there, and wept as he had never wept before in his entire adult life.

CHAPTER ELEVEN

After giving a brief statement to the police and driving back to his own apartment, Matt felt too physically ill to do anything but go to bed. He barely had the strength to call the city desk and tell the disembodied voice that answered that he wouldn't be in until he felt better. Then, at a little after 9:30 in the morning, he crawled under the covers and stayed there until noon the next day. During that period, he budged from the bed only three or four times, and then only long enough to go to the bathroom or swallow some aspirin. He didn't eat a bite of food during this period and promptly vomited back up the only beer he tried to drink. There was no way to tell how long he might have stayed there if Hollie hadn't called on Tuesday afternoon to tell him the funeral was scheduled for 2 p.m. the next day in Jamie's hometown of Seymour, Texas, about 40 miles southwest of Wichita Falls.

"I know he'd want you to be there, Matty," Hollie said, "and I was hoping maybe I could ride out with you, if you feel like going. I just got back from Sweetwater yesterday. I was driving back when I heard about Jamie on the radio, and

I don't think I'm up to making another trip alone right now." Her voice was husky from crying, but she seemed to have herself pretty well under control at the moment.

He hesitated for a second. "Well, sure," he said, not really wanting to commit himself, but not knowing what else to say. "What time do you want to leave?"

"Oh, about 9:30 in the morning, I guess. That ought to give us enough time."

"Okay," he said, "I'll pick you up."

They made the long dismal drive across the rolling North Texas prairies under dreary, overcast skies and in silence for the most part, reaching the funeral chapel with only a few minutes to spare. There were 100 or so mourners in the chapel when the services began, but they were mainly relatives, hometown friends of the family, and people that Jamie had gone to high school with. Except for Hollie and himself, Matt didn't see anyone else from Dallas, and Ross Purvis, an older reporter from the *Record-News* in Wichita Falls, was the only other person he even recognized.

Hollie wore a plain black dress, a little black pillbox hat and a string of pearls that he knew Jamie had given her. With her long blonde hair wound tightly into a bun and only a trace of lipstick and a hint of eye makeup accentuating her pale face, she looked more like a member of one of the local church choirs than a girl from the Carousel Club. She wept quietly during the chapel service, which consisted of two hymns, two prayers and a brief eulogy read by a Methodist minister, who repeatedly referred to Jamie as "James" and therefore seemed to be talking about somebody else.

"While we must rightfully grieve over the loss of one so young and full of promise, and over the sudden and violent manner in which he was taken from our midst, we must also realize that the Lord moves in mysterious ways," the minister said. "We do not always understand these ways, but we must accept them, just as we must accept the fact that James has now moved beyond our realm of understanding and gone on to a better place . . ."

Once, in the middle of the minister's talk, Matt tried to

imagine what Jamie's reaction would be if he were sitting there listening.

"Sounds like a crock to me, old cowchip," he could almost hear Jamie saying.

As a light mist of rain fell on the windblown little cemetery at the edge of town, Matt and Hollie stood off by themselves a few yards away from the others around the gravesite. Matt put his arm around Hollie's shoulders and felt them shaking as the tears ran silently down her cheeks. He watched the pallbearers unload the silver-gray casket from the hearse, carry it under the little green canopy where the family was seated, and slide it onto the platform above the grave. He heard the minister somberly intone the words of the burial ritual.

"Yea, though I walk through the valley of the shadow of death, I will fear no evil . . ."

For a moment, Matt expected his own tears to start flowing again, but his eyes remained dry. His tears were all gone now. His sorrow was spent, and all the other emotions that would eventually follow had yet to form. For now, he was left with only numb emptiness inside. He feared no evil, at least not yet, because reality had not yet set in for him. He felt almost nothing, and nothing seemed quite real. Even the strangers clustered around the grave were like cardboard figures, the minister's voice like a monotonous recording.

They drove back toward Dallas in a steady rain that grew harder as they moved further east. By the time they were a dozen miles out on Highway 114, Hollie had stopped crying. She repaired her mascara, freshened her lipstick, tossed the little pillbox hat into the back seat, and brushed out her hair. When she pulled it back into the familiar ponytail, she looked almost like herself again, except for the dullness in her eyes. Then she lit a couple of cigarettes and handed one across to Matt.

"Are you all right, Matty?" she asked.

"I don't know," he said, taking a drag from the cigarette and tasting her lipstick on the filter. "It's hard to tell. I'm just kind of drained, I guess."

"Jamie told me about the stuff you found at Jack's place,"

she said. "He wouldn't admit it, but he was scared of it, Matty. I mean really scared. He worried about it a lot. Sometimes he even talked in his sleep about it. Do you think that stuff had anything to do with . . . what happened to him?"

"I don't see how it could," Matt said. "Nobody but you and me and Jamie knew anything about it."

"Maybe so," she said, "but a lot of people knew you went to Jack's apartment that night. Maybe whoever killed Jamie didn't have to *know* what you found. Maybe just suspecting was enough to set them off. And maybe you ought to think about looking for a job in some other town, Matty. That's what I'm going to do. I can't take it in Dallas anymore, not after this."

Hearing her talk about leaving only made the emptiness inside him grow more cavernous. "I'm sorry you feel that way, Hollie," he told her, "but I don't blame you a bit. Where do you figure on going?"

"I'm not sure," she said, "but I'll tell you something if you promise you won't repeat it." Her tone was suddenly low and conspiratorial, and he thought absently how much she still seemed like a high school girl sometimes.

"I promise," he said.

"Well, I talked to Mollie yesterday for the first time since she left," Hollie said excitedly. "She's been in Los Angeles for three months, and she'd read about Jamie in the L.A. papers. She said she was so worried about me she just had to call. She wants me to come out there, and I think I'm going to do it, Matty. I've missed her something terrible, and I really want to be with her again—especially now."

Matt nodded. "Sure," he said, "I understand."

"You could to to L.A., too, Matty," she said. "You could find a job out there; I know you could. Maybe the three of us could, you know, help each other out, at least until we got settled."

"Well, thanks, Hollie," he said, "but I don't know. I never thought much about moving that far away from Texas. How soon do you think you might go?"

She shrugged. "Mollie's supposed to call me back in a day

or two," she said. "I'd like to leave in a couple of weeks, if everything works out. She's already got a place out there. It's not much, she says, but it's big enough for the two of us." She smiled and her eyes regained a little of their old brightness, as she reached across the seat and nudged him playfully in the ribs. "Shoot, I bet she'd even let you sleep on the couch if you want to come along," she said. "Mollie always did kind of like you. I could tell."

He smiled back at her, but his heart wasn't in it. "I'll think about it," he said, "and I really do appreciate the thought, Hollie."

"I hope you'll think really hard about it before you say no, Matty," she urged, her tone totally serious again. "Being in L.A. instead of Dallas just might be the difference between being alive and being dead."

Maybe, he thought glumly, but it certainly hadn't done Mike Fisher very much good.

Hollie O'Connor never made it to Los Angeles, of course.

Just nine days later, her shattered remains were carried by ambulance to Parkland Hospital and deposited on a cold metal slab in the morgue. Virtually every bone in her body was broken, the medical examiner said. No one got a good description of the car that struck her that midnight as she walked from the restaurant where she worked to the parking lot across the street. But one witness told police the car appeared suddenly out of a side street with its headlights off, accelerated at full throttle and was traveling at nearly 50 miles per hour when it ran her down. The driver made no attempt to stop, and, in fact, never so much as slowed down after the impact, which hurled Hollie over the top of the car and into a parked vehicle.

Matt Eastman never saw her alive again after he let her out in front of her apartment house that Wednesday night following Jamie's funeral. She called him four days later, on Sunday, to say she was still waiting to hear from Mollie and ask if he'd reached any decision about leaving or staying. He told her he was still mulling it over, although he had known all along that he had no genuine intention of going. He felt incapable of getting enthused about anything, but the last thing he wanted to do under the circumstances was dampen whatever enthusiasm Hollie could manage to muster. That was why he didn't tell her the truth.

She called again on Friday afternoon, only a few hours before she died, and caught him just as he was getting off and about to leave the rewrite desk to begin another bleak evening in one bar or another. He knew how ridiculous it was, but he had still spent most of his nights since the funeral carrying out a lonely quest for any information that might produce a lead in Jamie's murder—and usually drinking himself into a stupor in the process. He had worked through the list of bars that he and Jamie had frequented, then started on others with which he was not familiar but which were conveniently located in the area around Jamie's apartment. Sometimes he asked the bartenders and patrons if they had known Jamie Cade, if they had ever seen him drinking with anyone else, if they had ever heard him arguing or having words with anybody. Other times, he merely sat and listened to other people talk, hoping against hope that some overheard fragment of conversation might provide some sort of clue to what had happened.

He remembered later that Hollie sounded happy, almost giggly, on the phone that day.

"Mollie called this morning," she said excitedly, "and it's all set. She's got a job lined up for me and everything. In another week or so, I'll be on my way to Hollywood. Oh, Matty, meet me for lunch tomorrow and let's talk, okay?"

"Sure, Hollie," he said, trying his best to sound cheerful.

"Would you tell me the honest-to-God truth about something, Matty?" she asked, and there was a sudden note of concern in her tone.

"I'll do my best," he said.

"Do you think Jamie would mind if I went away and didn't come back?" she asked. "Does that seem like it's being, you know, unfaithful to him, or anything like that? I wouldn't want him to think it meant I didn't care anymore."

"He wouldn't think that, Hollie," he assured her. "Jamie

believed people ought to do what they have to do. I know he'd understand."

"I sure hope so," she said sadly. "I'll always love him, Matty. I just hope he knows that, wherever he is."

If you believed in the hereafter, you could also believe that less than eight hours later, Hollie was reunited with Jamie and able to tell him of her love herself. The accident happened almost exactly at midnight, but Matt didn't find out about it until about 2:30 a.m. He had come home around 11 that night and had been carrying a pretty good load following a sustained period of "research" with no solid food except for a couple of bowls of popcorn. He had peeled off his clothes, collapsed on his unmade bed and passed out the instant his head hit the pillow. He woke up suddenly some three and a half hours later when the doorbell began to ring with urgent, demanding redundancy. There was a throbbing ache in his head, a disgusting taste in his mouth, and a dreadful sense of apprehension in his heart. It must have been a premonition of some kind.

He pulled on a pair of pants, went to the door and looked through the peephole. The young, neatly dressed Mexican-American man standing in the corridor outside looked vaguely familiar. Matt didn't know his name, but he recognized him as a junior-grade homicide detective.

He took off the chain lock and opened the door. "Police," the officer said. He held his badge out as identification, but Matt waved it away.

"I don't remember your name," Matt told the cop, "but I recognize you from the police station. What's going on?"

The young detective's face was grim and unsmiling. "I'm Detective Antonio Canales, Mr. Eastman," he said quietly. "Do you mind if I step inside for a minute? I need to talk to you."

Matt shrugged, stepped back into the room and allowed the cop to come into the apartment. "Okay, what can I do for you?" he asked, shutting the door after his visitor.

"I'm afraid I've got some pretty bad news, Mr. Eastman," Canales said. "Do you know a Miss Hollie O'Connor?"

"Oh, Jesus Christ," he said, feeling a choking sensation rising in his throat. "What's happened? What's wrong?"

"I'm sorry to have to tell you," Canales said gently, "but she was killed late last night by a hit and run driver."

Matt's legs went limp and he sank back against the wall, wondering how much death one person could stand in such a short time. He could still see Hollie's face as she had looked in the car on the way back from Seymour. He could still hear her excited voice as it had sounded on the phone just a few hours ago. He wanted to cry, or scream, or curse, or something. But all he could do was lean there, staring at the detective and shaking his head.

"I know it's tough, Mr. Eastman," Canales said uneasily, "but we'd appreciate it if you'd come down and give us a positive ID on the body. We haven't been able to locate any relatives locally, and we were told you probably knew her better than anyone else in Dallas. We also know the deceased has an identical twin sister somewhere, and we need to establish formal identification for the record."

As a reporter, Matt had seen quite a few dead bodies, but he had never been to the morgue. He had also never been asked to do anything like this before, and he wasn't certain he could handle it. He thought he might fall completely to pieces when he looked at her, but he didn't. He thought he might go berserk and scream or run away, but he didn't do that, either.

On the contrary, once he had made the identification, he just kept on staring at what was left of Hollie O'Connor. He kept on staring until Detective Canales finally pulled him away and signaled the morgue attendant to push the drawer back into the cabinet. He kept on staring despite the fact that he knew he would see Hollie's torn corpse in his nightmares for years to come.

And the worst part wasn't the blood, the splintered bone and the mangled flesh. It was the look of ultimate, surprised horror in the glazed, unseeing eyes that stared back at him from Hollie's face.

During the weeks that followed, Matt withdrew into a far corner of himself, where he existed alone in a bubble of desolation and dispair. His world became a void in which time seemed to stand still and the day-to-day rush of events had no relationship to him. For the most part, he went down to the beige brick building on Pacific Avenue each morning and eventually ended up at home again each evening just as he had always done. He drifted through the motions of working the rewrite desk, gathering surface information and composing meaningless stories about people and events in which he had no remote interest whatsoever.

At night, he often continued to go out by himself to the bars that he and Jamie had frequented, but somewhere along the way, he stopped pretending that he was looking for information and confessed to himself that his only purpose was to dull the pain inside him and postpone the inevitability of going home as long as he could. On the nights when he went straight to the apartment and tried to avoid drinking more than two or three beers, he inevitably lay wide awake into the small hours of morning, sometimes never managing to fall asleep at all. Even when he did manage to lose consciousness, his sleep was fitful and marred by an endless succession of bad dreams.

Surprisingly, one of the few bright spots during this awful time turned out to be Tony Canales, the same homicide cop who had brought him the devastating news of Hollie's death. Over the next few months, he would help to restore some sanity to Matt's life and become his closest friend in the process—as well as the only person in Dallas in whom Matt dared to confide, even partially.

Their friendship began in a highly unlikely fashion on a chilly evening in December 1964. It was a Monday, the night before Matt's usual day off, and he had stayed at the Surf until the 1 a.m. curfew descended. He had no rational explanation for why he was drawn back to the Surf so often, unless it was because it was the last place he had seen Jamie alive, but scarcely a week went by that he didn't kill at least one or two evenings there.

As usual, he had parked the Falcon in the decaying residential neighborhood a half-block down Bryan Street. Also as usual, he was drunk enough to be slightly unsteady as he made his way toward the car. But he was not so drunk that it didn't give him a start when a dark figure materialized abruptly from behind a tree, stopped directly in his path and addressed him by name.

"Hello, Matthew Eastman. Let's you and I talk for a minute, okay?"

Matt paused warily, balling up his fists and backing up a step or two. "Maybe okay and maybe not okay," he said tensely, squinting into the darkness. "Who the hell are you, anyway?"

"Ease up, man," the figure said. "It's Tony Canales from homicide. You remember me, don't you? I thought maybe I could buy you a cup of coffee, that's all. What do you say?"

Matt relaxed a little, but still felt far from calm. "I don't know," he said. "Is this cup of coffee in the nature of official business or what?"

"Well, not exactly," Canales said. "I'd say it's more like unofficial business. Come on."

They got into the detective's unmarked white Ford with the telltale buggywhip antenna and "Exempt" license plates, and then drove slowly down Bryan Street without saying anything else to each other. Canales whistled softly under his breath while in the background the police radio squawked and chattered a garbled, staccato message about a signal 31 at East Side and Fitzhugh. Canales paid no attention, and after a couple of minutes, he pulled the Ford into a parking place under the red and white canopy at the Rose of the Rancho, an all-night eatery a block east of the telephone building, where they got out and went inside. There were only a few customers in the place and none of them so much as looked up as the detective led the way to a booth by the front windows and sat down.

"Buenos noches," he said, grinning at the little gum-popping Chicana waitress when she came over. "Hey, you want something to eat?" he asked Matt.

"Just some coffee," Matt said, sinking back against the red leatherette seat cushions and feeling the beer taking its toll.

"I'll have a bowl of chili with beans, some tamales and a cup of coffee," Canales told the waitress.

"Si, mi Capitan," the girl said. She winked at him and her lips formed a kiss in the air as she twisted back toward the counter. Canales was obviously a late-night regular at the Rose, Matt decided, and just as obviously, the waitress found his suave good looks very appealing.

"It'd never do for me to bring my wife in here," the officer remarked when the girl was out of earshot.

"I wouldn't recommend it," Matt said. "But on the other hand, what do I know? Hell, I don't even know what this is all about."

Canales' face turned suddenly serious, and he sat silently as the waitress brought their coffees and repeated the winking routine. When Canales spoke again, his voice was almost a whisper. "It's about life and death, amigo," he said, "and about which one of those you want for yourself."

"I don't know what you're talking about," Matt said coldly.

"Let me give you some friendly advice, Matthew," Canales said. "You'll stay a lot healthier a lot longer if you stay away from seedy bars and quit asking people you don't know about what happened to Jamie Cade."

"I don't know why you should care," Matt said, feeling the locked-up bitterness beginning to simmer inside him. "I mean, what business is it of yours, for Christ sake?"

"I'm not sure how to answer that," Canales said. "Maybe it's because I can understand how much it hurts to have two friends killed. I think I know what you're trying to do, but in the long run, you're only making trouble for yourself." He seemed to hesitate for a moment, but when Matt didn't say anything, he plunged on. "Did you ever have any reason to think Jamie Cade might be a homosexual?" he asked bluntly.

Matt almost dropped his coffee cup, then he slammed the cup into the saucer so hard it nearly shattered. "Are you fucking nuts?" he snarled. "What kind of goddamned question is that? I mean, he was my best friend, man, so if I thought he was queer, what the hell does that make me?"

"Look, I'm not trying to insult anybody," Canales said,

"but I'm asking you a deadly serious question, and I'm looking for a serious answer. What evidence we have right now suggests that Cade picked up some guy in a bar, invited him up to his apartment for some hanky-panky and the guy killed him. We've turned up a couple of witnesses who say Cade made homosexual overtures to them under similar circumstances during the past few months. And now Cade's family even seems convinced it's some kind of queer deal. They're afraid to see the grand jury indict anybody because of the embarrassment it might cause them."

Matt couldn't believe his own ears. "That's the stupidest goddamned thing I ever heard," he said. "You mean to say Jamie's own family'd let the sonofabitch who killed him get off scot-free just because of some bullshit like that?"

"I didn't say that," Canales told him. "All I'm saying is if some known deviate comes to trial for Cade's murder, the testimony could get really nasty. It's the kind of thing that'd be tough for any bereaved family to go through."

"Have you got a suspect?"

"There's a guy we've been talking to," Canales said, "but everything we've got against him is purely circumstantial. We've been able to place him in the neighborhood the night Cade was killed, and he's a bully-boy type who knows karate. He's got three previous arrests for assaulting and robbing homosexuals. No convictions, though. The grand jury let him off every time because his victims either couldn't or wouldn't identify him."

The waitress came and refilled their cups, flirting with Canales with her eyes and giving him a fabulous view of her cleavage as she leaned over the table. Matt poured sugar into his coffee and stirred it. He felt as sober as if he hadn't had a drink all week.

"This just doesn't make any sense," he said. "I knew Jamie for more than five years, and there was never any indication of anything like that. I mean, hell, he had a steady girlfriend. He spent every spare minute he had with her. Does that sound like homosexual behavior?"

"Some guys can conceal things like that," Canales said. "Sometimes it's just an urge that hits them every so often.

Some guys are, you know, AC-DC. They can go either way. I'm not saying Cade was any of those things. I'm just telling you what some of the thinking is on the subject. For instance, some people say Cade's girlfriend found out about him and had already dumped him when he got killed.''

In spite of how utterly absurd it all sounded, Matt caught himself remembering the fight that Hollie and Jamie had had a short time before his death. She told Matt later she had gone home to Sweetwater for a couple of days and had, in fact, still been there the night he was killed. Jamie himself had mentioned the possibility of breaking up with Hollie. And yet, her very last words to Matt had been an expression of her undying love for Jamie.

"That's not true," Matt said. "They had an argument of some kind, that's all. Did you ever know of any couple that didn't have an argument once in a while?"

Canales offered no reply, except for another far-out question. "Do you think Hollie O'Connor might have killed herself?" he asked abruptly. "In your opinion, could she have been depressed enough to do that?"

"Oh, hell no," Matt said. "Absolutely not. No way. She was making plans to get out of Dallas and put her life back together. She'd been in touch with her sister in California, and she was excited about the idea of going out there."

"That's interesting," said Canales. "If it's true, it certainly shoots down another theory I keep hearing about this case."

"What theory?"

"A theory offered by the same people who think Cade's murder was homosexually related. They also seem convinced that Miss O'Connor threw herself in front of that car on purpose. They're pretty sure she committed suicide."

Matt folded his arms on the table and laid his head on them in a gesture of total dismay. The only thing he could think of was how exhuberant Hollie had sounded the last time he had talked to her on the phone. She had been so eager to get to L.A., so utterly convinced that she and Mollie could pick up right where the "Sugar and Spice Sisters" had left off when the Carousel closed down. There was no way on God's earth she would have committed suicide that day, and it didn't take a psychiatrist to figure that out. Killing herself had been the furthest thing from her mind.

"Then why was the car driving with its lights out?" he demanded. "Why did the driver just keep going and never even slow down? Do they think Hollie hired the bastard to run over her? Is that the idea?"

Canales finished his chili and tamales and pushed the dishes away. "So you think the theory might have a few holes in it," he said dryly.

"I can't believe this shit," Matt exploded. "I can't believe a word of it."

"This is strictly off the record, Matthew," Canales said, "but to tell you the God's honest truth, I can't quite buy it, either. That's one reason I wanted to talk to you and hear what you had to say. I also want to give you a word of warning, my man. You're the only person in this town who knew both subjects well enough to challenge these theories in court. I'd be careful if I were you."

Matt gave the detective a puzzled look. "What're you telling me all this for?" he asked.

"Mostly for your own protection," Canales said, "and because you'd be a valuable witness if any of this ever comes to trial. But I've got to admit there's something else, too. I'm not one for rocking the boat or questioning anybody's judgment, but, just between you and me, none of this theory stuff jibes with anything I've been able to find out, and that bothers me. It bothers me a lot."

The realization hit Matt with the force and suddenness of a flash of lightning, and within the space of one split second, all the pieces of a giant jigsaw puzzle seemed to fall together in perfect order in his mind. When they did, he could see the whole, ugly picture as clearly as if it had been painted on the table in front of him.

"I'll bet you twenty bucks I can tell you who's in charge of this investigation," Matt said softly. "And then I'll bet you another twenty I know where every damned one of these so-called theories originated."

There was no verbal response from the detective. His black

eyes remained unblinking and expressionless as they stared back at Matt, but they seemed to be inviting him to go ahead and say what was on his mind.

"Lieutenant Alexander Sutton," Matt said. "That's who it is, on both counts, isn't it?"

There was still no expression in Canales' eyes, but Matt noticed the faintest trace of a smile playing at the corners of the officer's mouth.

"I'm glad I'm not a betting man," Canales said. "If I was, I'd have just lost forty dollars."

CHAPTER TWELVE

One Friday afternoon about three weeks into the new year, the city editor called Matt aside and told him he was being taken off the rewrite desk and reassigned. At first, Matt was afraid he was being punished for his poor initiative, lack of concentration and low level of productivity over the past four months. It would have come as no surprise if he had been banished to the Siberia of the copy desk—unquestionably the worst fate that could possibly befall a *Times Herald* staff writer—there to languish among the other misfits, has-beens and never-weres for the duration of his career at the paper. But as it turned out, the city editor actually had a promotion in mind instead.

"We're putting you on Jamie Cade's old beat at the police station, effective immediately," the city editor said. "You'll report there at 7 o'clock tomorrow morning, have Sunday off, and then be back for the early shift Monday. And, by the way, there'll be a $10-a-week raise beginning with your next paycheck. Good luck."

Somehow, it seemed to Matt that the city editor's final two

words were strangely prophetic. As he walked out the back door of the building and turned down Patterson Street toward the parking lot that afternoon, he was feeling better than he had felt in a long time. He had almost forgotten how pleasant the sensation of well-being and satisfaction could be, and it was all he could do to keep from feeling guilty about enjoying it.

It was a bright, sunny afternoon with temperatures in the low 60s, one of those exhilarating January days that make up for all the erratic and unpredictable excesses committed by Texas weather. He felt so good that he stopped at a self-service carwash on the way home and gave the Falcon its first bath since the previous summer. Then, when he reached the apartment, he actually spent well over an hour straightening the place up, washing the piles of dishes in the kitchen, taking out the trash, bagging up his dirty laundry, vacuuming the carpet, and even changing the sheets on the bed.

When he finished and was still feeling good, he picked up the telephone on an impulse and dialed Angel Garcia's number. Once, a few months earlier, he had known the number by heart, but now he found he had forgotten it and had to look it up before he could place the call.

He was gratified to catch Angel at home at a little after 6 p.m. on a Friday, and even more gratified at how pleased she sounded to hear from him.

She recognized his voice instantly and let out a shrill, delighted little yell. "Hey, muchacho, que paso?" she cried. "Oh, Matty, I've been missing you something awful, and I was worried to pieces about you, honey. I thought you'd forgot all about your poor little ol' Angel. Now why you want to go and worry me like that, huh?"

"I'm sorry I haven't called," he said. "I've missed you, too, but I've been feeling really bad lately, and everything's been so screwed up I haven't been able to think straight."

"I know, Matty," she said sympathetically. "I heard all about Jamie and Hollie. That was a terrible thing. I couldn't hardly believe it."

"Listen," he said, sidestepping the subject, "I've finally

got a Saturday night off tomorrow. I know it's late to ask, but I was hoping maybe you and I could do something together.''

Her laughter was soft and musical, and he could close his eyes and picture the way she looked right now. After all this time, just the sound of her was enough to make him almost unbearably horny. "You got anything special in mind?" she asked suggestively.

"I'll think of something," he assured her, blushing. "What do you say?"

"Well, sure, honey," she said. "There's no way I could pass up a deal like that."

Angel's spacious two-bedroom garden apartment had always struck Matt as pretty plush quarters, even for an exotic dancer with a full-time job. But as he pulled up in front of her building at 6:30 the next evening, he found himself even more puzzled by her ability to afford it, since, as far as he knew, she had been without regular employment for the better part of a year.

After the Carousel closed down, Angel had found now-and-then work in several even less respectable nightclubs and topless bars. She was about a half-inch shy of five feet tall, with a round, babyish face framed by long, silky black hair, round, wet, doe-like eyes, skin the shade of a chocolate milkshake, and a body that was almost unreal. All in all, she was one of the most alluring women Matt had ever seen, and yet, careerwise, she had two strikes against her, in Texas anyway: (1) She was an illegal alien, who could be deported at the slightest pretext, and (2) she was a dark little chili pepper in a town where guys who shelled out big bucks to watch burlesque vastly preferred pale-skinned, blonde-haired, blue-eyed "Miss U.S.A." types. That was why Hollie and Mollie O'Connor had been headliners, and Angel Garcia had never been anything more than a warm-up act.

And yet, if Angel had any worries about making financial ends meet, they were hardly apparent. Her apartment was located just a block off Abrams Road on the north edge of Lakewood, one of the city's more exclusive residential areas. It was furnished rather garishly, but quite expensively, with ornate white and gold furniture, thick pink carpeting and luxurious floor-to-ceiling drapes. The kitchen where Angel kissed him and handed him a margarita in a salt-rimmed champagne glass contained every kind of major and minor gadget imaginable. And the bathroom where he went to wash his hands was all gold and marble fixtures, velvet walls, full-length mirrors and Hollywood-style lighting. Matt was pretty sure that his entire monthly after-tax income wouldn't have paid the rent and utility bills on the place.

Knowing that Angel never tired of Mexican food, he took her to dinner at the Acapulco Café, one of the few places in Dallas where you could get decent cabrito, and afterward to a movie at the Palace Theatre downtown. Later, as he drove back toward East Dallas in the Falcon, he held his breath and tried to sound casual as he asked if she felt like stopping by his place for a drink. In all honesty, he could see no real reason why she would want to, but he had spent four or five hours scrubbing and polishing the place and had even augmented his usually meager supply of liquid refreshment with a fifth of tequila and a bottle of Kahlua, just in case.

He needn't have worried about Angel's response.

"Sure, baby," she whispered teasingly, "but only if you promise not to run me off after one drink." Simultaneously, he felt her hand slide up his thigh to his crotch and the tip of her tongue running around inside his ear "It's been so long, I thought maybe you'd ask me to stay the night," she said.

He stopped for a red light and turned giddily to kiss her warm mouth, cupping the soft roundness of her breast in his hand as he did.

"I'm not just asking," he told her hoarsely. "I'm begging."

For the first hour after Matt got the apartment door unlocked and slammed it shut behind them, they did nothing but make love. They did it with total abandon and without conversation or preliminaries, shedding their clothes as they struggled across the living room, then throwing themselves on the bed and losing themselves completely in each other. As the night wore on, Matt lost count of how many times they made love. They did it until the delerious, pent-up frenzy inside him finally spent itself; then they did it with calm, unhurried appreciation, savoring the intimacy between them like the kind of rare vintage champagne that you seldom taste in a lifetime.

And finally, sometime before dawn, they propped themselves up on the pillows and lay there clinging to each other, relaxed and drowsy, but still unwilling to give themselves up to sleep just yet.

"You are some kind of guy, you know that?" she said with her cheek against his chest.

"I am?" he said. "How so?"

"Well, you're a muchisimo lover, honey," she said, kissing him lightly. "But when you invite a lady over for a drink, don't you think you really ought to give her one?"

"Oh, hell, Angel, I'm sorry," he said, feeling stupid. "I forgot all about it. Wait right here and I'll bring you something. What do you want?"

He tried to get out of bed, but she grabbed him from behind, pulled him down onto the pillows and giggled. "No, man," she said, "you rest up and get your strength back, and I'll get us some drinks, okay?"

Matt started to protest, but she was already up and gone.

He couldn't resist a grin as she hopped across the room, as nude as a little tan noodle with her pert, perfect breasts bouncing like golden melons against her ribs, and stooped to retrieve his discarded shirt off the floor. She slipped it on demurely, covering herself from her shoulders to her upper thighs, but her breasts still struggled and strained against the incumbering fabric and tried their best to spill out as she buttoned the shirt.

She turned and smiled back at him then. "I got to be properly dressed," she said tauntingly, "in case the neighbors are window-peeking when I turn on the lights. Where do you keep the booze?"

"There's Carta Blanca in the icebox," he said, "and some tequila and Kahlua in the cabinet under the sink. You know where the glasses are."

"I'll be right back," she said. "Why don't you get my cigarettes out of my purse—it's somewhere around here—and light us a couple?"

Matt felt around on the carpet until he found his undershorts, then pulled them on and continued his search, finally locating the small clutch handbag on a chair in the living room. He took it back to the bed, where he opened it in the faint light from the streetlamp outside, and immediately saw a box of Marlboros and a gold Ronson lighter inside.

Feeling slightly theatrical, he stuck two cigarettes in his mouth and lit them at the same time, just as he had seen somebody do it in the movies once, then removed one of them and took a deep drag off the other. The effect was quickly spoiled, however, because as he reached over to place the extra cigarette in the ashtray on the nightstand, the purse slid off the bed and fell to the carpet, scattering part of its contents across the floor.

"Shit," he said under his breath.

He got down quickly on all fours, grabbing the articles off the floor and stuffing them into the purse, hoping to have everything replaced before Angel got back and discovered how clumsy he was. As he picked up Angel's white leather billfold, he spotted the green and white corner of a treasury note protruding from it. Unthinkingly and without paying the slightest attention to the denomination of the bill (but assuming it was probably no larger than a 10 or 20), he unsnapped the leather catch and opened the wallet to shove the currency back inside.

When he did, he was amazed to see that it was a brand-new $100 bill, still crisp and unwrinkled, except for the protruding corner. And a second later, he was even more amazed to discover that, underneath the first bill, there were eight more just like it.

He was still standing there with the billfold in his hands when he heard Angel coming back. He turned and saw her in the doorway, holding two glasses of Kahlua and frowning at him. "What're you doing, honey?" she asked.

"I dropped your purse," he said, deciding there was no point lying about it. "Your billfold fell out and I saw all that money. Jesus Christ, Angel, you shouldn't be carrying so damned much cash around with you. That's just asking for trouble, don't you know that?"

She just smiled, shrugged her small shoulders and handed

him his drink. "Don't worry about it, baby," she said non-chalantly. "I'll be sending it to Mexico tomorrow, anyway."

Matt sat on the edge of the bed and took a sip of his Kahlua. It was sweet and smooth and pleasant on his tongue, and it grew even more so when she came and sat beside him and began to stroke the back of his neck. But he couldn't keep from wondering and worrying about the bills and where they had come from. Hell, he thought, he didn't take home $900 every two months, after taxes, so how could a semi-unemployed alien like Angel Garcia get her hands on that kind of money? And how could she be so blasé about it?

Somehow, though, he managed to keep from asking the questions that gnawed at his mind. And when they finished the Kahlua, they both fell asleep with the first faint light of Sunday morning filtering in through the blinds and Angel's dark little head resting in the hollow of his arm.

She stayed with him all the rest of that day, cooked breakfast for them about noon, insisted on serving him his in bed, and later made love with him twice. In the afternoon, they sang in the shower together, drank tequila sunrises, and listened to the Beatles on his stereo while they watched the sun go down. It was, all in all, one of the best days he had ever spent, and he was gratified that Angel seemed as sorry as he was to see it end. At about 9 o'clock that night, she told him she had to leave, and although his loins briefly urged him to argue, he figured it was probably for the best, since he had to report to the police station at 4:30 the next morning to begin his first full week on his new job.

So he drove her back to her apartment, gave her a five minute goodnight kiss (which made him hope she might invite him to come up for awhile, although she didn't), told her he would call her in a day or two, and went home, feeling tired but happy.

And through it all, not another word was ever said about the contents of Angel's purse.

Starting the following Tuesday, Matt tried every day for a week to reach Angel by phone but got no answer at her apartment. He even drove by the place two or three times, but there was no sign of Angel's white Buick convertible in the parking lot, and he could only assume that she had gone out of town for some reason. If she had, he wondered why she hadn't bothered to call him. They had seemed so incredibly close on Saturday and Sunday—so "made for each other," as corny as it sounded—that he couldn't imagine her taking off somewhere without letting him know. And yet, he could only conclude that she had, and the harder he tried to rationalize about it, the more jealous, angry and deserted he felt.

On Thursday of that week, while he was in the homicide bureau following up on the murder of a convenience store clerk during an armed robbery, he ran into Alexander Sutton for the first time since his reassignment. He had, in fact, seen Sutton only twice since Jamie's death, and after what Detective Antonio Canales had told him about the lieutenant's role in the Cade murder investigation, Matt had been wondering what he was going to say to Alex the next time they met.

One part of Matt yearned to tell Sutton off in no uncertain terms about the stupid, off-base implications and innuendo he was spreading about Jamie, and maybe even taking a swing at the sonofabitch. But another part of him told him to act as uninformed as usual, keep his resentment to himself, and try to find out what he could about where the investigation was heading—if, indeed, it was heading anywhere.

Matt was still trying to control his conflicting feelings when Alex came over, smiled with unexpected warmth and stuck out his hand.

"Hi, Matt," he said congenially. "I heard you were taking over Jamie Cade's old beat. Welcome aboard."

Matt's reply was guarded, but he took pains not to sound unfriendly. "Thanks, Alex," he said. "I just hope I can do half as good a job over here as Jamie did."

"I'm sure you'll do fine," Alex said. "If there's anything I can do to help out, be sure and let me know."

"Matter of fact, there is something I need to talk to you about," Matt said. "We haven't had anything on the Cade investigation in a month or so, and the city editor wants me to put together some kind of update on how things are going.

You know, any new leads or theories you might have, stuff like that. I understand you're the man in charge, right?"

"I guess you could say that, Matt, but to tell you the truth, there's just not very much to report. The investigation's pretty well at a standstill right now."

Matt tried to make his grin convincing. "Well, you know how city editors are—or maybe you don't," he said. "Sometimes they can be a real pain in the ass when they get fixated on something. His position is that Jamie was a *Times Herald* reporter, after all, and so we've got to run a follow-up on the thing periodically. Even if there's not enough for a story, I at least need to write up a memo of some kind to keep this guy off my back."

Alex smiled patiently. "Okay, sure," he said. "I'll be glad to go over what little we have. You want to come down to my office?"

The lieutenant led him down a corridor and around a corner, then motioned him into a cramped glassed-in cubbyhole that was barely large enough to hold the desk, two chairs and four-drawer file cabinet crammed into it. He pointed to a straight-backed chair wedged between the front of the desk and the wall. Then he removed a manila folder from the top drawer of the file cabinet and sat down behind the desk with it.

"Here it is, such as it is," he said, opening the folder. "So where do we start?"

For a long, puzzled moment, Matt studied Alex, noticing how strangely small he looked behind the bulky desk. Because his presence usually seemed so commanding, Matt had always thought of Alex as being relatively tall, but now he realized that the lieutenant was actually quite short. The realization gave him a weird feeling, as if Alex were no longer the same person he had been before.

"With suspects, I guess," Matt said. "Are there any?"

Alex made a wry face. "None we can make a case against," he said. "We talked to one character who might be good for it, but there's nothing concrete to charge him with. We know he was in the area the night of the killing, we know he has a black belt in karate, and we know he's been charged before with assault and robbery. We're also pretty sure he'd crossed paths with Cade at least once or twice. But that's not nearly enough for the grand jury to indict this monkey."

Again, Matt studied Alex silently for a moment. For some reason he was remembering the only other time he had ever heard Alex call someone "this monkey." It was the day of the assassination and his reference had been to Lee Harvey Oswald. It also struck Matt as odd that he could never recall hearing Alex refer to Jamie impersonally as "Cade" before.

"I want to ask you something straight out, Alex," he said, "and I'd appreciate a straight answer."

"Well, sure, Matt," Alex said, acting a little taken aback. "You know I'll be as straight with you as I can."

"I guess maybe you've heard some talk, just like we have down at the paper, that Jamie's murder might be some kind of queer deal," Matt said. "What do you think about that?"

Alex kept his eyes lowered to the open folder in front of him for several seconds before he answered. "Look, Matt," he said finally, "nobody's saying for sure that Jamie Cade was a homosexual, at least not at this point, and there's certainly no reason you'd want to print something like that in the paper."

"That's not the point, Alex," Matt said. "I'm asking you what you think."

"Listen, you know the guy was a friend of mine, too," Alex said, "but we've talked to several male witnesses who say he propositioned them."

Deep within, Matt could feel the two conflicting parts of himself fighting for dominance. He could also tell that one side was winning and the other was losing. "Who are these witnesses, Alex?" he asked.

"I'm sorry, Matt, but I can't tell you that. It's immaterial, anyway, because we don't have a case."

"It's not immaterial, Alex," Matt said coldly, still trying to hold back the fury inside him, "because you and I both know it's a goddamned lie. What about Hollie O'Connor?"

"What do you mean?"

"I mean somebody killed her, Alex. Somebody murdered her just like they murdered Jamie."

"The facts don't support that kind of conclusion," Alex said. "On the contrary, the facts suggest she committed suicide. She was a very troubled person, Matt. You understand that as well as I do." By now, Alex was clearly losing patience with Matt's allegations, but Matt no longer cared.

"To hell with that, Alex," he said. "The only thing I know for sure is that Hollie was murdered, and I think you know it, too. I hear you've got a witness who saw a car with no lights deliberately run her down. And even if you don't, I still know it wasn't suicide because I talked to Hollie myself a few hours before it happened."

"I didn't realize that," Alex said. "What did she tell you?"

"That she was going someplace to meet Mollie," Matt said bluntly. "You *do* remember Mollie, don't you? Did you ever wonder what happened to her when she disappeared so suddenly, or did you just figure she committed suicide, too?"

Alex's face was very white, except for two spots of livid color high on his cheeks, but his voice remained surprisingly calm when he spoke again. "Where did she say she was going to meet Mollie?" he asked.

Matt smiled. "I don't recall, Alex," he said, "and I don't think I'd tell you if I did."

If looks could have killed, Matt knew he would have been dead where he sat. "You're totally out of line, Matt," Alex told him icily, "and you're screwing around with things that could get you into deep, deep trouble, my friend."

"Maybe so," Matt said, "but I think you're just trying to cover up shit with more shit, Alex, and one of these days I'm going to find out why."

In years to come, he would wish a million times he had kept the angry half of himself under tighter rein that day and never said these things. But after that moment, it was everlastingly too late.

Outwardly, Matt and Detective Antonio Canales were even more different than Matt and Jamie had been, and yet their two brief initial meetings had ignited a spark of friendship between them, one that burned steadily brighter in the days immediately following Matt's big flare-up with Alex Sutton. So, although Matt had effectively destroyed one bridge into the homicide bureau, he quickly discovered another, much more reliable one in the person of Tony Canales.

On the surface, they had practically nothing in common. Matt was a white ex-farmboy from middle-class surroundings in the sticks of Kaufman County while Tony had spent his childhood as a poverty-stricken, inner-city Hispanic kid fighting to survive in the barrio called "Little Mexico" just north of downtown Dallas. Although he was less than three years older than Matt, Tony had already accumulated a wife, two kids, and a mortgaged tract house in the suburbs, while Matt had never had a single serious thought in those directions. Tony was a devout Catholic who went to mass every Sunday, and Matt was a Protestant backslider who hadn't been inside a church since his high school baccalaureate. Tony didn't even like beer very much and probably didn't average even a six-pack of the stuff in a month. But during this period, he began to stop off occasionally with Matt for a quick one (it was exactly that, too; it was quick and it was one, never two or three) on his way home to hearth and family.

After a few weeks, Tony went so far as to invite Matt to his house for Sunday dinner, and Matt promised to accept the invitation as soon as he could set up another date with Angel Garcia and bring her along. That never happened as it turned out, but his friendship with Tony Canales was destined to prove a godsend, not only at the outset but many years later.

After more than two weeks of dogged persistence, Matt finally got an answer when he dialed Angel's phone number. But when he did, he didn't do a much better job of controlling the angry side of himself than he had with Alex Sutton. It was just past noon on a day in mid-February, and an almost overwhelming thrill raced through him the instant she picked up the phone and he heard her voice. But the thrill quickly faded and soon soured into a desperate, combative frame of mind after only a few minutes. To say the least, her reaction to his call was far removed from what he was hoping for. He could tell something was wrong; he just couldn't figure out what.

"Hey, buenos tardes, honey," she greeted him vaguely. "What you been up to lately, baby? I been out of town for awhile, you know."

"Well, I kind of figured you must've been somewhere," he said in a voice heavy with chagrin, "since I've been trying to call you every day since the week before last. Why didn't you tell me you were leaving?"

"I . . . I didn't know, honey," she said. "It was something that came up kind of sudden, you know."

"Well, where'd you go?" he asked bluntly, despite knowing it was none of his business.

"I went down to Mexico," she said. "I had to go see my little old Mamacita, and I got to go back again pretty soon, too. My mama, she's real sick, you know."

He thought of the nine new $100 bills he had seen in her purse. Maybe the money had been to pay her mother's doctor bills, he thought, but that still didn't explain where it came from in the first place.

"I'm sorry to hear that," he said, feeling a momentary twinge of guilt for being jealous. "Hey, I missed you so much I almost went crazy while you were gone, and I'm dying to see you, Angel. Is it okay if I come by this afternoon after I get off work?"

"Oh, no, honey," she said quickly. "I can't see you today. I'm, you know, real busy. I got all kinds of things to do." Her voice sounded nervous and evasive.

"But, damn it, Angel, I want to see you. Don't you understand?"

"I'm sorry, baby. I just can't work it out right now. Let me call you sometime, okay? I'll call you and we'll get together."

"Yeah? When?"

"Oh, pretty soon. When things settle down a little bit, okay?"

"Come on, Angel, I'm only asking for a few minutes. At least meet me someplace for a drink, okay? Please."

"No," she said firmly. "No, I can't. Not today."

"Tomorrow then."

"No, honey, not tomorrow. Not the next day, either.

There's no way, so just back off, all right? I don't know when I can see you again. That's all I can say.''

He felt totally crushed and rejected. "I thought you and I had something really special going," he said lamely. "I guess I was wrong."

"Oh, Matt, honey, you know I like you a lot, but you don't understand. I got some real heavy obligations right now, and there's just no way I can get out of them."

"You're tied up with somebody else, aren't you?" he said, wondering why it had taken him so long to figure that out. "That's where the money and the apartment and all the rest of the stuff comes from, isn't it?"

"I'm sorry, honey," she said. "I got to go now."

She hung up before he could say another word, and when he called back, there was no answer. He tried the number a dozen times that afternoon and evening, usually letting the phone ring 20 or 30 times before he broke the connection, but it was utterly fruitless. The next morning, he went through the same procedure with the same lack of success, and when he got off he drove by Angel's apartment in Lakewood. Her Buick was there this time, parked right where it should have been, but there was only silence when he rang her bell over and over again.

Although he doubted it would do any good, he left a terse, six-word note under the windshield wiper on the driver's side of the Buick. All it said was:

"Angel,
Call me, damn it.
—Matt"

He never heard from her again, but when he got home about 9 p.m. on the night of Wednesday, March 10, 1965, Matt found Tony Canales waiting in an unmarked squad car in front of his apartment house.

"Better brace yourself, amigo," Tony said flatly. "It's more bad news."

Somehow Matt knew what it was without having to be told.

"It's Angel Garcia, isn't it?" he said.

Tony nodded. "Border patrol found her body yesterday morning," he said. "It was washed up on the bank of the Rio Grande south of Laredo. She'd been dead about a week, and this one was no accident, Matt. Looks like real Al Capone stuff. She had a dozen bullets in her."

CHAPTER THIRTEEN

The edition of *The Jeffersonian* that arrived in 1,423 mailboxes around the county that Friday was probably the worst and weakest edition of the paper in all of Sarah Archer's six years as its editor. It was, to be perfectly frank, a thrown together mess, wherein two press releases from state agencies appeared practically verbatim on the front page, and the main story was the local police department's threadbare annual warning to parents on the perils of Halloween trick-or-treating. The article was accompanied by a rather cute photo of four preschool kids dressed up in their witch and goblin outfits, but that was the high point of the entire eight pages.

Still, considering all the distractions of the past four days, Sarah thought, it was a minor miracle that the paper had gotten out at all. It was too late now to do anything but forget about it, and she firmly resolved not to waste her time worrying. The important thing was that it was finally Friday and the humdrum daily routine at the newspaper office was mercifully over until Monday morning. Besides, in all likelihood, the current edition of *The Jeffersonian* wouldn't retain the rank of "worst ever" for very long. The way things were going, next week's paper would most likely be even worse.

If she had accomplished nothing else that week, however, she had at least settled the question of whether she would stay in Jefferson or move away. On Tuesday morning, still in a semidaze from the trauma of the previous 24 hours, she had called the managing editor of the *Pine Bluff Commercial* and told him she had decided not to accept his job offer. Despite the momentary feeling that she had just burned one of the few remaining bridges between herself and the outside world, she knew there was no way she could walk away now. Like a moth being drawn inexorably into a burning candle, she was too mesmerized by the engima in which she was now enmeshed—let alone, with the man she still found it difficult to call Matthew Eastman.

Although she had no idea as yet what could be done with it, she knew she had stumbled onto a much bigger story right here under her nose in Jefferson than anything that might have awaited her in Pine Bluff. But she also knew she would be lying to herself if she pretended this was the only reason she had elected to stay. Ever since the telephone had rung beside her bed in the early hours of last Monday morning, she had seemed unable to get Matthew Eastman out of her mind for more than a minute or two at a stretch.

Even when she was at the office and he was recuperating at home from the gunshot wound in his arm (she told everybody in town that he was in bed with the flu), she was unable to concentrate on her work for thinking of him. Each evening, she had fixed his dinner and stayed with him until he fell asleep, and twice she had spent the whole night at his house, sleeping very properly on the rollaway bed in his spare bedroom, but having some less than proper dreams about him. A few of the dreams actually made her blush when she replayed them mentally later on, but even so, she replayed them again and again.

"Good lord, I can't seem to disengage from this," she admonished herself constantly during those four days. "And what's worse, I can't even make myself *want* to disengage, so what am I going to do?"

On Thursday, he had insisted on coming back to work, and she thought that might relieve her mind, since she would no longer have to worry about what might be happening at his house while she was at the office. But it hadn't really helped. Instead of wondering if someone were shooting at him, she merely found herself sitting in a sort of stupor and staring at him as he tried to get out the monthly ad billings and complete other necessary chores.

Now it was Friday and the situation was really no different from what it had been three days ago as far as Sarah could see. She was still full of confused, conflicting feelings, still uncertain what her next move should be, and still trying to comprehend everything he had told her since Monday morning—not that he had told her all of it yet. On the contrary, she was sure beyond the slightest doubt that he hadn't, but she was equally certain that he eventually would, if she gave him enough time.

Unlike most Fridays, Matt had worked at the office almost all day. He had pulled together various odds and ends of stories for next week's paper, written an editorial about the traffic problems on Highway 81, and arranged for Julie Bliss's boyfriend, an amateur photographer, to shoot pictures of both tonight's Jefferson-Sheridan football game and tomorrow night's Halloween goings-on.

Before leaving for home shortly after 3 that afternoon, he had stopped by her desk, leaned down close to her and asked in a loud stage whisper, "Think you could stand spending another evening with me, or are you totally burned out on that kind of stuff?"

When she looked up at him, there was no way she could keep from smiling. "I was afraid you'd never ask," she said with perfect candor.

"Well, I've been feeling like getting out and stretching my legs," he said. "I thought we might take a walk before it gets dark. And if you'll take some money out of petty cash and pick up some steaks on your way out, I'll show you what a great backyard chef I am later on. Doesn't that sound exciting?"

"It sounds great," she said. "I'll be there."

"Don't bullshit me now," he told her sternly. "If there's

something else you need to do, or even something else you'd rather do, I understand. Really.''

She smiled again. "Hey, I said I'll be there," she said. "Don't start trying to back out on me, okay?"

"Okay," he said, "but you'd probably better bring along some walking clothes. I mean, that dress looks really nice on you, but I don't think it'd be too practical for tramping around through creek beds, high grass and barbed wire fences.''

Much as she doubted the wisdom of spending so much time at his place, and much as she wondered where their association was leading her, she could hardly wait to see him. By the time he had been gone an hour, in fact, she was so eager that she told Julie Bliss to lock up at 5 and left the office more than 45 minutes early, something she would never have thought of doing ordinarily. She also stopped by her rooming house long enough to change into jeans, a sweatshirt and sneakers, and while she was there, she rather self-consciously tossed a few essentials into an overnight case. Now that he was almost well, she knew there was no legitimate or innocent reason for her to stay over, but on the other hand, she thought, there just might be a couple of not-so-innocent ones.

On her way out, she paused to spray a little extra cologne on the back of her neck and behind her ears. Then, as she was hurrying down the stairs with the overnight case in her hand and already feeling very self-conscious, she came face to face with Mrs. Mitchell, her austere, narrow-minded little landlady.

"Sakes alive, young lady," Mrs. Mitchell said with disapproval heavy in her voice, "I just don't know why you bother to rent this room. You've hardly been here a night this week."

"I'm, ah, going out of town to visit some friends, Mrs. Mitchell," Sarah said, her heart pounding at the certainty that Mrs. Mitchell could see through her lie like a sheet of cellophane. "See you later."

"Well, you'd best be careful, young lady," the old woman admonished sourly. "Otherwise, you're just liable to end up dead someplace."

And now here she was, at a little after 4:30 in the afternoon, again driving up in front of his house, her palms sweating on the steering wheel of the Volkswagen, just as they always seemed to do when she knew she was going to see him, and an eerie, unexplainable anticipation coiled like a spring under her ribs.

She parked behind Matt's convertible, picked up the paper sack with the T-bones, mushrooms and salad fixings from the supermarket, and went through the gate into the backyard. She paused at the backdoor, shifted the bag of groceries to her left arm, and knocked as loud as her fragile, thin-skinned knuckles were capable of knocking. By this time, she was getting used to the idea of coming here, but for the first few moments she still always felt strange and awkward, and under no circumstances would she have dared walk in unannounced, even if the door were standing wide open.

"Hey, it's unlocked," she heard him yell from inside. "Come on in."

Matt was leaning against the sink with a bottle of beer setting on the counter beside him. He was wearing jeans, a plaid flannel shirt and tennis shoes, and he was grinning at her. Propped against the counter a few feet away was an ancient shotgun with double blue-steel barrels and a dark, well-worn stock. The sight of it gave her sort of a queasy feeling, but she tried not to show it.

"Gee, Sarah," he said, taking the bag of groceries from her and looking her up and down appreciatively, "you could pass for a real country girl in that outfit."

She grinned back at him. "Listen here, city feller," she said lightly, "if I'm not a real one, then there ain't no such thing."

"Well, come on then," he said, "and I'll give you a chance to prove it."

He handed her an extra beer to carry, laid the shotgun on his shoulder and whistled for Hobo. The dog got to his feet slowly, stretched for a minute, then ambled over to the back door and waited expectantly.

"Let's go find us a rabbit, boy," Matt said, and Hobo whined in anticipation.

They must have walked five miles that afternoon, across the rolling fields behind the house, where the needlegrass was knee-high, through stands of pines and hardwoods, where the ground was red and moist and there was no grass at all, and down a meandering, almost dry creek bed, where their feet sank ankle-deep in the soft sand.

At one point, Hobo flushed a cottontail rabbit out of its hiding place. The dog froze as the rabbit burst out of a clump of tall grass and into the open. Matt raised the shotgun and sighted intently along the barrel, while Sarah put her fingers in her ears and held her breath in anticipation of the explosion. But after a second or two, he lowered the gun again and watched the rabbit vanish into the shadows of a thicket 100 feet away.

"I don't guess I feel like cleaning a rabbit today," he said sheepishly, uncocking the shotgun. "In fact, I don't guess I feel like shooting anything today, either. I think it may be quite a while before I feel like shooting anything again."

He walked to the edge of the copse of woods where the rabbit had disappeared, eased himself down on the fallen trunk of a dead pine tree and put the gun down beside his leg. After a minute, she came and sat next to him on the tree trunk. Hobo was sniffing his way across the meadow in wide, sweeping circles, his nose close to the ground and all his attention focused on the mingled scents around him. A deep, all-encompassing silence seemed to hang over the countryside. Except for the faint chirp of a bird somewhere, there was no sound at all.

"My dad used to take me hunting sometimes when I was a little kid," she said. "He liked hunting birds mostly." She laughed very softly. "I used to be his retriever."

"Yeah," he said, without looking at her, "my old man liked to hunt birds, too. My old man liked to hunt anything. Once when I was about six, he took me squirrel hunting early one morning and left me sitting on the bank of a creek while he tried to maneuver around to get a shot at some squirrels in a big hickory tree. It seemed to me like he was gone for hours, but I guess it really couldn't have been more than fifteen or twenty minutes. Anyway, I got scared there all by myself and worried that he wasn't coming back, so I took off for the house. Man, he was mad when he caught up with me. I mean, I guess he was more scared than mad, because he thought something had happened to me, but I thought for sure he was going to bust my tail.''

"What did he do?'' she asked.

"Nothing really. My mother got on his case pretty good for leaving me alone that way in the first place, and she told him she didn't blame me for coming home. He cussed a little and slammed the door, and that was about it. But you know, it's funny. I don't think he ever took me squirrel hunting again after that. He took me hunting for other stuff, but not squirrels.''

"I'm glad you didn't shoot the rabbit,'' she said, in a voice so soft that he could barely hear the words.

When she spoke, he turned toward her, and they looked straight into each other's eyes for what seemed like a full minute, with their faces only a foot or so apart. Then he reached out and took her face between both his hands and kissed her.

He kissed her softly at first, then with ravenous passion, as though he had been wanting to kiss her forever. He kissed her as if his very life depended on kissing her, as if he never wanted to stop, as if he could go on and on kissing her for the rest of eternity.

And she kissed him back as though she didn't care if he did.

Strange, unintelligible little sounds came from them as they both gave themselves totally to the kiss and lost themselves in the great, churning vortex of it. Their mouths were like two wild, living things, each insatiably intent on devouring the other, and their bodies seemed intent on fusing themselves into one writhing entity.

When the kiss finally ended, they had slid off the log and were tangled together on the ground. He held her tightly against him and stroked her hair. Hobo came sauntering up about that time, wagging his tail and panting, his stubby muzzle dripping with water from the creek. He stared at them for a moment, as though trying to figure out why they were lying there like that. Then he flopped down beside them and started rolling in the grass.

Matt propped himself up on one elbow and looked at her. "You can't imagine how many times I've wanted to do that over the past four years," he said.

She laughed nervously and rubbed her face against his shirt. Her lips were numb from the kiss, but the rest of her felt as if it were on fire. "What took you so long?" she asked.

He laughed, too, just as nervously. "No guts, I guess," he told her. "Most of the time, you were engaged to somebody else. Then I was afraid you wouldn't like it, and where would I have been if that had happened? I mean, after all, I'm no Robert Redford."

"Oh, I don't know," she said. "You're no Tom Cruise, but I'm not so sure about Robert Redford."

He kissed her again, but kept it under some measure of control this time. "It's getting dark," he said then. "I guess we ought to be heading back to the house."

"Yes," she said, "I guess so."

They trudged the half-mile or so across the fields through the gathering dusk, moving slowly and holding hands. Neither of them broke the silence until they eventually reached the chain link fence around the backyard, where Matt whistled for Hobo and let the dog through the gate. They followed Hobo into the yard, then stopped beside the ramshackle old toolshed. Both of them were breathing hard, but not so much from the walk itself as from the emotions they had unleashed. She had thought the hike back might cool them off, but she had been wrong.

He jerked open the door of the shed, shoved the shotgun back into one corner of it, and pulled the door shut again. "I'd better get that thing out of the way," he muttered. "As giddy as I'm feeling, I might shoot my foot off."

He turned blindly toward her then, and they both reached out for each other. Their open mouths collided, and suddenly it started all over again, only this time she knew there was only one way for it to end. For several months, she had very calmly and rationally considered the likelihood of this happening sometime, and she had wondered again and again if she really wanted it to. Now she could no longer think at all, but at least she didn't have to wonder anymore. She knew beyond any doubt what she wanted.

The whole world seemed to be whirling insanely before Sarah's eyes, and she found it impossible to focus on anything, as the warm, intimate weight of Matthew Eastman pressed her back against the shed and a pulsating infern of desire blazed up inside her. She was trembling so violently that she could feel both of them shaking, and she wondered for a fleeting instant why she had never felt anything even remotely like this with Kyle Morrison.

Matt's hands were under her sweatshirt. She felt them on her bare back, under her bra straps, on her breasts. They were good hands, gentle hands, but very demanding hands, too. She loved his hands. She couldn't give enough of herself to them. She wanted them all over her at once.

"God, I want to make love to you, Sarah," she heard him say. "I want it more than I ever wanted anything in my whole life. I never knew anybody could want anything so much."

Her mouth flew hungrily back to his and her hands tugged at his shirt. "Oh, Matthew," she gasped as she pulled him toward the back door of the house, "can't you tell I feel the same way?"

It was odd, she thought vaguely, but that was the first time she had ever called him by his real name. So that was another hurdle of sorts out of the way.

She knew she would never call him "boss" again.

Matt awoke with a small start sometime after midnight, feeling the soft, unfamiliar warmth of Sarah's nakedness in his arms, and unsure for a second where he was and who he was with. Then he turned slightly and looked at her, marveling at how beautiful she was in the faint moonlight from the window and mentally savoring the returning recollection of the last several hours. She was asleep, with her face against his shoulder, one arm across his belly, her mouth slightly open and her dark hair spread around her on the pillow. She looked like something he might have dreamed on an exceptionally good night, and he had to feel her to make sure she wasn't some trick of his imagination. It was still that hard to believe she was actually here.

In the four years since he first came to Jefferson, his encounters with the opposite sex had been so rare that he might as well have been a priest—except for a couple of brief interludes. There had been Cheryl, a sweet but shopworn waitress at Leon's, who had allowed him to pick her up and obliged him with her favors on three or four occasions before running off with some truckdriver, as barmaids were prone to do. And there had been the widowed, matronly secretary at the county tax collector's office, whom he had made the mistake of dating out of sheer loneliness a few months after he arrived in town. She had fed him fried chicken and pot roast, talked constantly about marriage, and proceeded to mother and smother him for six or seven weeks until he couldn't stand it any longer and broke it off. There were, after all, some things worse than loneliness, and a few even worse than enforced celibacy, when you got right down to it—and Mabel Simpson (he had called her Mabel, but always thought of her as Mrs. Simpson, even when they were in bed together) had been one of them. She still worked at the county courthouse, and the idea of running into her always made him uneasy when he had to go there.

But there had never, ever been anyone in his life like Sarah. He was already thoroughly convinced of that. Certainly not Cheryl or Mabel Simpson. Not Colleen, the only woman he had ever married. Not even Angel Garcia, as sexy as she had been. And none of the others even came close. He got a strong impression that Sarah hadn't made love very many times, but there was no need to practice something when you were already perfect at it. Just the memory of her spontaneous, unrestrained sensuality aroused him all over again. She not only made him feel younger, more virile and more energetic than any old duffer of 47 had a right to feel; she also made him half-believe that his luck might have finally changed for the better.

And yet, along with the positive vibrations and the unmatched thrill of actually having her there in his bed, a sense of guilt and foreboding continued to gnaw at him. He should never have gotten her involved in his secretive, screwed-up past. No matter what kind of excuses he might make for dragging her into the endless, sucking whirlpool in which he existed, they could never begin to justify his doing it.

The specter of what lay ahead was impossible to forget for more than a few seconds, even amid the delirious ecstasy of making love to Sarah.

He had made it a point to read one or both of the Little Rock papers every day that week, and so far nothing had shown up in either *The Democrat* or *The Gazette* about the two bodies they had left in the shopping center parking lot on the outskirts of Monroe. But with the warmer weather of the past day or two, the smell had to be getting terribly obvious by now. Soon, the bodies were bound to be discovered. In fact, they could very well have been discovered already. Then it would be only a matter of time until some other sonofabitch with a gun came looking for him.

There would always be another sonofabitch with a gun. There would always be a next time. He was as certain of that as he was of the sun coming up in another six hours or so. And if anything happened to Sarah because of it, he would spend eternity hating himself.

There would always be a next time, unless . . .

Unless he took the goddamned initiative for once in his miserable life, he thought.

He remembered the little silverish locker key, still safely tucked away in his pants pocket. He thought of Mollie O'Connor's briefcase waiting in the bus station in Little Rock, and in spite of himself he wondered what kind of evidence was really in it. He thought of the other evidence, the stuff from Jack Ruby's place that he had put in a plastic case and buried a few paces from the old cistern in the pasture behind his parents' house. He wondered if it was still there after all this time, and if there was any way to get his hands on it again.

Matt wondered if any of his friends and allies were still alive and well in Dallas. Could Tony Canales conceivably still be around somewhere? Was it just barely possible that he was still wearing a Dallas Police Department badge? If he was, would he still remember a promise made more than 18 years ago? And what about Sam Garrett? Was Sam still an editor at the *Times Herald*? Was he still as bullheadedly convinced that the truth had never been told about the Kennedy assassination as he once professed to be?

God knows, he had tried running. He had tried hiding and covering up, pretending and forgetting, living a lie and even lying to himself—but none of it had done any good. Maybe it was time to try a different approach. Maybe that was the only way not to be caught sitting here, vulnerable and hopeless, when the next sonofabitch with a gun showed up. Maybe it was the only honest chance he had to keep Sarah from being a victim of the "accident" meant for him.

She stirred beside him, murmuring something that he couldn't understand, and he could tell she was waking up well before she opened her eyes. She stretched, stifled a yawn, then smiled and reached up to touch his face.

"Hi," she said. Then the smile abruptly faded. It was almost as if she were reading his mind. "You're worrying again, aren't you?" she asked.

"Yeah, I guess so," he said, seeing no point in further pretense. "I'm trying to figure out what to do. I want to just lie here with you from now on and forget everything else, but I don't think that's going to work."

"No," she said, "I don't think so either."

"I'm sorry I got you into this, Sarah," he said. "It was weak and stupid of me, and I'm truly sorry."

"Hush," she said, pressing her fingers to his lips. "It was no such thing. I'm glad you asked me to help you. Between the two of us, we'll figure out what to do. I know we will."

He wished he could make himself believe that, but the truth was, the shit was only going to get deeper from here on, and there was still so much she didn't know. For one thing, he hadn't even mentioned the locker key yet.

He heard his stomach complaining about the fact that he hadn't eaten in more than 12 hours, and it seemed like a good time to change the subject. "We, uh, sort of forgot about dinner," he said sheepishly. "Are you hungry?"

She giggled and gave him a wet kiss. "Now that I think about it, I'm absolutely starving," she said.

So he got an old robe out of his closet for Sarah to wear, put on the same disheveled clothes he had been so anxious to discard early in the evening, and they got up. They ate the T-bones for breakfast at about 1:30 on Saturday morning, along with potatoes baked in the microwave and a tossed salad that Sarah made while he was getting the fire going in the charcoal grill behind the house. After they ate, he stretched out on the living room couch with his feet on the coffee table to finish his second beer, and Sarah came and put her head in his lap. It was a moment of quiet but complete contentment, a moment they both knew couldn't last very long but tried to hold onto nevertheless.

"Want to talk?" she asked finally, when the beer can was empty.

"Not really," he said, "but there's still some stuff I ought to tell you before we go any further."

She pulled his mouth down to hers and kissed him. "I don't see how we can go much further than we already have," she said softly. "I'm afraid I'm in love with you, Matt."

"I've known for a long time that I was in love with you, Sarah," he said, "but I kept telling myself I wasn't going to do anything about it. Now I can't say that anymore."

"I think fate plays a role in things like that," she said. "What happened last night was meant to be, and besides, it was just too right to be wrong."

"I know that," he said. "But I hope you still feel the same way after you hear what I've got to say."

CHAPTER FOURTEEN

When he got out of the Army that spring, after spending 21 months in Vietnam, Matt toyed with the idea of not going back to Dallas at all. He knew there was an investigative reporting job waiting for him at the *Times Herald*—a job that paid well above the average newsroom salary in Texas—because Sam Garrett, the new city editor, had taken the trouble to write him about it. But for a month or two, he thought it would be nice to go somewhere else and start over fresh, even on a smaller paper where the work was harder, the pay lower and the hours longer. It would be a relief not even to think about the Kennedy assassination again, much less keep digging up stories about it. And it just might be a damned site safer somewhere else, too.

Except for his friendship with Sam, who had come to the *Times Herald* as an assistant city editor a year before Matt had left, he didn't really feel any strong ties to the paper anymore. He still had plenty of acquaintances there, but outside of Sam, his only true friend in Dallas was Tony Canales. A lot of things had changed since he had joined the

Army in disgust in mid-1966, both in Dallas and within himself.

For one thing, his father had died of a heart attack the previous year at the age of 63, and his mother had had to give up the family farm (the only real home Matt had ever known) and move into a small house in the town of Kaufman, where his two younger sisters lived. The images of the farm as it had been when he was six or seven years old were frozen forever in his memory, and as he flew home for the funeral, he had reviewed them all with feelings of infinite sadness.

On the military jet high above the Pacific, he could close his eyes and see the old-fashioned, high-gabled white house, the hulking red barn behind it, the rusting John Deere tractor pulling the plow through the sandy earth, the four big oak trees in the front yard, the White Leghorn hens stretching in the chicken yard. He could smell bacon frying on a cold morning and pies and cornbread dressing baking at Thanksgiving. He could hear Mack, his scrawny old bird dog, barking at the schoolbus, and his mother calling him to supper.

On his last visit to the farm before leaving for basic training, he had buried the plastic box containing the items from Ruby's apartment a couple of hundred yards behind the house. And while he had no desire to retrieve those things, the knowledge that he would never be able to go home again and find the farm of his childhood made him somehow even sadder than knowing his father was dead.

In truth, Matt and his dad had never gotten along very well, and although they had never feuded openly, Matt had known since high school that he was a disappointment to the old man. David Crockett Eastman had never quite understood how his son could turn his back on the fine farm he had built with his own two hands and go to the city to write stories. In the neat, narrow furrow of David Crockett Eastman's world, grown men didn't write stories for a living. Matt's father respected doctors and schoolteachers, tolerated preachers and lawyers, and realized the necessity of druggists and shop-keepers, but he had little use for most other people who wore suits and ties to work. To him, there was no higher calling than working the land.

After his dad died, Matt could tell by the tone of his mother's letters that she was pretty miserable, and he tried to write at least every couple of weeks and make his own letters as positive and cheerful as possible. He also sent her some money whenever he could scrape together an extra 50 or so. She had been left with very little besides the farm itself, and with the steady migration to the city, farmland in Kaufman County was a drug on the market. By the late '60s, as many old farmsteads were standing vacant as were still occupied in the county. Much as he wanted to help his mother, though, Matt couldn't stand the thought of going back to Dallas just to mark time nearby during her declining years. His sisters would simply have to fill that role if anyone in the family were going to.

The likeliest alternative to Dallas was Chicago, where Matt's recently discharged friend, Sergeant Percivale Quincy Wallace (with a name like that, how could you blame the guy for calling himself "Wally"?), had landed the managing editor's job with a mass circulation tabloid called the *National Tattler*. Wally had extended an open-ended offer to Matt to join the *Tattler* as an articles editor at almost twice what he could make back at the *Times Herald*, and Matt was sorely tempted to take him up on it.

When he got back to the States, he went so far as to fly directly to Chicago to look the situation over. Wally picked him up at O'Hare, and they spent the next two days drinking and reminiscing while Wally extolled the easy lifestyle and hefty monetary rewards of tabloid journalism. He was on the verge of accepting the *Tattler* job and called Sam Garrett in Dallas to tell him so, but something Sam said on the phone caused him to change his mind.

"I can't match the Chicago salary, Matt, but I really need you down here," Sam said. "I think we're onto one of the biggest stories this town ever saw. It's genuine Pulitzer Prize caliber stuff, and you're just the guy who can write it. I promise you'll have total freedom to work on it for however long it takes, and nobody'll be bothering you with crap assignments.''

"Okay, you've at least got my curiosity aroused, Sam," Matt said. "What is it?"

"Are you familiar with a super-rich industrialist named D. Wingo Conlan?" Sam asked.

A small but unmistakable chill scampered up Matt's spine. "I'm afraid so," he said. "I even have an ex-friend of sorts who's some kind of big wheel with Conlan's company."

"Well, that could turn out to be a major advantage on this story," Sam said, "because it looks like our man Conlan's into some very, very deep shit."

"What's new about that?" Matt asked. "He's been up to his neck in one kind of shit or another for as long as I can remember."

What came immediately to Matt's mind, of course, was Conlan's unexplained involvement with Jack Ruby and his possible connection to Lee Harvey Oswald. But beyond that, Dee Conlan was also among the most notorious prodigal sons in Dallas history. He was a wastrel-playboy extraordinaire, and long before he had inherited controlling interest in Conlan Universal Aerospace Corporation on his father's death in 1961, Dee had been making news of one kind or another. Paternity suits and barroom brawls seemed to be among his specialties.

"If our preliminary information's correct," Sam said, "all you have to do is name it and he's into it. For starters, we're talking large-scale drug smuggling—and I *do* mean large. I mean deals worth two or three million bucks apiece. We're talking big-time, hardcore pornography, too. It looks like Conlan's running a massive distribution system for the stuff. We also could be talking white slavery—and maybe even murder."

Sam's accusations surprised Matt, whereas rigged bids, bribes and kickbacks on government contracts would not have. And as much as Matt wished he weren't interested in what Sam was telling him, he knew he was.

"But, hell's bells, Sam," he said, "Dee Conlan's already got more legitimate money than you and I could count. Why should he want to get into all that high risk stuff when he's raking in billions in defense contracts?''

Matt's thoughts raced back to certain articles he had read during his boring, interminable tenure as a press officer attached to Army headquarters in Saigon. Stateside newspapers were usually two or three weeks old by the time he saw them, but he had perused them religiously even so, and now and then he had run across something really intriguing—something that had brought Dee Conlan's slack, insipid face into sharp mental focus, even from 10,000 miles away.

One of the most thought-provoking articles had been a *Washington Post* interview with Theodore White, author of the series of the best-selling "Making of the President" books. Right after the assassination of South Vietnamese President Nguyn Diem, White said, President Kennedy had made a firm decision to end the U.S. military presence in Vietnam altogether. In fact, White contended that Kennedy had scheduled a meeting with General Maxwell Taylor and Ambassador Henry Cabot Lodge for November 24, 1963, at which he planned to order the total withdrawal of American troops. The only problem was, Kennedy never made it to that meeting. He was killed two days before in Dallas.

Not long after that, as the war escalated under Lyndon Johnson, Conlan Universal Aerospace became one of the largest beneficiaries of the U.S. military build-up. Matt had read several news stories about major contracts awarded to CUA, and one article in particular noting that between January 1, 1964, and January 1, 1969, CUA had landed more than $2.4 billion worth of Defense Department business overall. The point was, if Kennedy had ended the war, the vast bulk of those contracts most likely would never have been awarded at all. Every time Matt thought about it, he also thought about Dee Conlan, and he wondered if Dee could possibly have been (a) smart enough or well-connected enough to figure the situation out in advance, and (b) vicious enough to plot a presidential assassination to keep it from happening.

"I don't know," he heard Sam Garrett saying. "Maybe Conlan's crazy. Maybe he's just greedy. Or, hell, maybe he's both. That's what we want to find out, Matt. Over the next few months, we want to learn everything there is to know about D. Wingo Conlan.''

Matt heard a warning voice in his head saying something about curiosity killing a whole lot more than just cats. But a few minutes later, he reluctantly asked Wally for a rain check on the job offer in Chicago. Early the next morning, he was on a plane back to Dallas.

As Sam Garrett had predicted, the *Times Herald's* investigation of Dee Conlan dragged on through most of the summer. Even then it was hard to see any end in sight, but by late June, Matt was convinced that they were really onto something.

Most of the paper's initial information on Conlan's alleged racketeering had originated from a single source, an attractive, 27-year-old former administrative assistant at CUA named Lisa Feagan. She had worked for about seven months as Conlan's personal secretary and taken three or four trips with him to Mexico and South America. During this time, she claimed to have seen large quantities of what she believed to be cocaine or heroin loaded into a secret compartment aboard the company plane, stored in a false-bottomed credenza in a CUA office, and in the physical possession of Conlan and other CUA officials. She also said that Conlan had openly snorted cocaine in her presence many times and had frequently offered it to her and others present. When Matt asked her straight out, however, if she had seen either Tommy Van Zandt or Alex Sutton with suspected drugs, her answer was an unequivocal "No."

Lisa Feagan had been fired from her $12,500-a-year job, she said, after rejecting a series of proposals from Conlan that had nothing to do with designing, manufacturing or marketing jet aircraft, missiles and other military hardware. She accused Conlan of offering her, on various occasions: $15,000 to pick up a five-month-old infant in Ciudad Acuna, Mexico, bring it across the international border as her own child, and deliver it to an address in Del Rio, Texas; $5,000 per day (with a ten day minimum guarantee) to star in a feature-length porno movie being filmed somewhere in West Texas; and $1,000 per minute to perform oral sex on him.

The woman obviously fell into the category of "disgruntled former employee," a species of which any reporter has to be wary. But the more Matt checked into Dee Conlan's background, the more convinced he became that she was not only telling the truth but probably only scratching the surface.

The clip files in the *Times Herald* morgue told part of the story. There was a separate file filled with brittle, yellowed articles about Conlan's father, Carter W. Conlan, who had built CUA into one of the country's top armament manufacturers during World War II and Korea, while managing to retain almost 70 percent of the company's common stock. The elder Conlan had been a confidant of governors, senators and congressmen, as well as a well-respected businessman, community leader and established member of the so-called Dallas oligarchy. But Dee's own file told a markedly different story—the story of a wealthy, privileged son who had apparently been a black sheep and degenerate from the beginning. Early articles in the file included one on a paternity suit in which the jury found for the plaintiff and ordered Dee, then only 22, to pay her $10,000 in a lump sum, plus $200 per month until the child turned 18. Another told of aggravated assault charges being filed against Dee after a fistfight at a debutante ball, another about his arrest for DWI and possession of marijuana after an accident on North Central Expressway. There were also numerous superficial mentions of him in name-dropping nightclub columns and social notes.

At age 32, however, Dee became the nation's youngest chief executive officer of a major aerospace company when he took over at CUA in 1961. After that, the stories in the files were mostly on such subjects as important contracts, company growth, Dee's elevation to chairman of the board of CUA, and various other business ventures he undertook in energy and real estate, many of them apparent financial flops. There was a notable and total absence, though, of articles about any type of civic involvement, community service or charitable endeavors. If Dee had ever participated in anything of that nature, it was a well-kept secret.

But it was Tony Canales who supplied the information that really brought the Conlan investigation to a head. Tony had been promoted to the number two spot in the police department's Intelligence Division while Matt was overseas, and as it turned out, he had his own thick file on Dee Conlan. When Matt persuaded Lisa Feagan to give Tony a sworn statement about what she had seen and heard at CUA, Tony generously agreed to share with him all the bits and pieces of information that intelligence had collected over a period of more than three years.

"We know he's running drugs, Matt, lots of drugs," Tony said. "But both the FBI and the DEA are in on this, and we don't want to make a move until we're sure we've got a provable case. And when we do move, we want to destroy as much of the drug network that Conlan's built as we can. Getting him out of the picture isn't going to help much if somebody else just steps in and takes his place in a few days or a few weeks."

"I know a lawyer named Tom Van Zandt," Matt said. "He's a VP of some kind at CUA. Is there any indication he's involved in this?"

"No," Tony told him. "We've checked Van Zandt, and he's as clean as a pin as far as we can tell. It looks like he's the one who's actually running CUA on a day-to-day basis and turning it into one of the most profitable big companies in the country in the process, I might add—while Conlan's out dealing drugs and racketeering."

"Where does Alex Sutton fit in?" Matt asked.

Tony shrugged. "Hard to say," he said. "Frankly, his involvement with CUA while still an official member of this department was one of the main reasons we got into this thing in the first place. There's an obvious question of ethics and conflict of interest here, and I think the chief's pretty close to asking for Sutton's resignation. But Sutton's played it very cool so far, and there's really nothing to hang him with yet."

Matt smiled tiredly. "Alex used to have quite an eye for the ladies," he said. "You think he might be in on this porno movie deal?"

Tony didn't return the smile, and his tone was grim when he replied. "I don't think so," he said. "I think that's strictly Conlan's baby. But as long as we're on the subject, Matt, there's something I guess I ought to tell you. It's not very pleasant and it's not something I enjoy talking about, but I think you've got a right to know."

"It sounds bad," Matt said. "What is it?"

"We got hold of a print of one of the films we think Conlan produced," Tony told him. "I'll let you watch it if you want to, but I don't think it'll turn you on. Angel Garcia's in it."

Matt just stared at him without speaking for a minute. It all seemed as though it had happened ages ago, but now he finally understood the whole thing—the flashy apartment, the white convertible, the $100 bills, the unexplained absences, the odd behavior, the whole bit. At least he thought he did, until Tony went on.

"That's not all, Matt," he said. "We're pretty sure Angel was also a courier for the drugs. Conlan apparently likes to use good-looking women for that job. That's probably why he tried to recruit Lisa Feagan for the same sort of assignment."

"So who killed Angel?" Matt asked. "Any ideas?"

Tony shook his head. "Could've been Conlan. Could've been some rival drug dealer. Could've even been the Mexican police. Holy Mary, the kind of dangerous games she was playing, Matt, it could've been almost anybody."

Yes, Matt thought, it even could have been the same person who killed John Kennedy. But he didn't mention that thought to Tony. After all, they were talking about drugs and porn, and the Kennedy thing was another investigation entirely.

Or was it?

At times, Matt grew so weary of the Conlan thing that he simply had to do a story on something else. When he did, the stories always seemed to relate back to the assassination. After all his years of research, nobody was better versed on the subject or more adept at cranking out copyrighted articles for the *Times Herald* on the many twists and turns of the case. The "Dealey Plaza Irregulars," as the corps of local conspiracy buffs called themselves, had long since adopted him as their favorite journalist. They also provided him with an endless chain of theories and ideas.

For example, he interviewed a car salesman who claimed to be the third victim of the shots fired in Dealey Plaza on November 22, 1963. The man had been standing almost directly across Elm Street from the presidential limousine and had been struck in the cheek by either a bullet fragment or a piece of concrete when one bullet slammed into the curb beside him.

The salesman had insisted—first to Dallas police at the very moment Oswald was being questioned in an adjoining room, and later to any reporters who would listen—that the shot that injured him had come from directly across Elm Street, not from the School Book Depository 300 feet away. Now the other reporters were all gone, but Matt would still lend an ear.

A sheriff's deputy, who refused to let Matt use his name in print, told of receiving information from several reliable witnesses that at least one or two shots had been fired from behind the wooden stockade fence at the top of the now-legendary grassy knoll. One witness reported seeing a man hurry away from that spot immediately after the shooting, but once Oswald was in custody, everybody lost interest in this other suspect, the deputy said.

Matt also talked to a Dallas police officer who was standing on top of the Triple Underpass when the shooting started. The officer was certain he had heard four shots, not the three shots eventually established as the official number by the Warren Commission. The officer also insisted that he clearly saw a shower of sparks fly where one bullet struck a manhole cover on Elm Street.

Perhaps the most significant story grew out of what the Irregulars called the Sewer Theory. Some of them took him behind the wooden fence atop the grassy knoll and showed him an inconspicuous sewer grate there. Directly beneath the grate was what amounted to a small concrete room measuring about four feet square, and leading away from it was a sewer pipe that was large enough for a small man to slither through. The pipe led directly to a drain opening in the north curb of Elm Street at almost precisely the spot where the infamous third shot—the one that had exploded Kennedy's head—had hit the President. Not only had none of the officers present that day apparently known of the sewer opening, but for some peculiar reason, neither it nor the pipe leading to the drain in the Elm Street curb even appeared on official maps of the city's sewer system.

At Matt's request, a motorcycle patrolman who had been just to the left rear of Kennedy's limousine and caught a faceful of blood and brain tissue when the fatal shot struck the President, accompanied him to Dealey Plaza to look at the sewer opening, the pipe and the drain. The look of genuine surprise that crossed the patrolman's face sent a surge of excitement through Matt.

"Did you know this was here on assassination day?" Matt asked.

"I never knew it was here until right now," the patrolman said. "As far as I know, nobody else knew about it, either. I thought the shots came from this direction and I ran up the hill to look. I was within a few feet of this thing and never saw it, so I know for sure nobody checked it out that day."

Matt also showed the opening to Deputy Buddy Walthers, one of Sheriff Bill Decker's top aides, who had also been in Dealey Plaza when JFK was shot. Walthers, too, seemed surprised that the opening was there, and Matt couldn't resist posing a totally outrageous question, one he probably wouldn't have dared ask of 95 percent of the policemen he knew.

"Just for the sake of argument," he said, "let's suppose some Dallas cop wanted to shoot Kennedy that day and knew about this sewer opening. If he stashed the rifle here in advance, used it to shoot the President, left it in the hole when he was through, and then came back for it later, can you see any reason he couldn't have gotten away with it in all the confusion?"

"That's a helluva broad supposition," Walthers said, "and I'm certainly not saying I think it happened. But off the record, no, I can't. I think there's a good chance he could have done it without anybody knowing."

And finally, there was the story that cut the deepest into Matt's own emotions—the recounting of the more than 20 unexplained deaths of persons in some way associated with either Ruby or Oswald or both. The list began with Mike Fisher, Jamie Cade, Hollie O'Connor and Angel Garcia, but over the past five years it had steadily continued to grow.

Howard Thompson, one of the lawyers present at Ruby's apartment along with Mike, Jamie and Matt, and the attorney originally tabbed by Ruby to lead his defense, dropped dead of an apparent heart attack at the ripe old age of 46. He had no previous history of heart disease.

Karen "Little Lynn" Carlin, whose fear of something had been amply demonstrated by her frantic phone call to Jamie and her even more frantic flight from Dallas a few hours after Ruby shot Oswald, obviously hadn't run far enough or fast enough to avoid her place on the list. She was found dead in a Houston hotel room with a bullet through her head.

Marilyn Moon, another Ruby stripper, who also left Dallas in the wake of the assassination, discovered that there was no safe harbor for her, either, not even as far away as Omaha, Nebraska. An unknown killer found her alone in her home there one evening and shot her seven times.

There were many others, some of them obscure figures who had only marginal connections with the case. One was Thomas Killam, whose wife once worked for Ruby and whose best friend roomed in the same house where Oswald lived. He was found dead on a sidewalk in Pensacola, Florida, after "accidentally" falling through a plate glass window and cutting his throat. Another was Harold Russell, the only apparent eyewitness to the shooting of Officer J. D. Tippit as he tried to arrest Oswald. Ironically, Russell himself was beaten to death during a struggle with a police officer who was trying to arrest him in the small town of Sulphur, Oklahoma. Yet another was William Wahley, the taxi driver who picked up Oswald and took him to his apartment minutes after Kennedy was shot. Wahley later became the first Dallas cabbie to die in a traffic accident in 40 years. And still another was Oswald's landlady, Earlene Roberts, who had also been acquainted with Ruby through her sister. Mrs. Roberts had testified that shortly after the assassination a police car pulled up in front of her rooming house, honked its horn twice, then drove away as Oswald remained hidden in his room. Her death, too, was attributed to heart failure.

Before that fall was over, Matt would have every reason to believe the list was still far from complete.

It was a balmy Wednesday afternoon in late September, and Matt was feeling particularly frustrated over the snail's pace with which the *Times Herald* lawyers were reviewing his four-part series on Conlan's drug connections. The series had been ready to roll for two weeks or more, but the lawyers continued to hedge and nit-pick, as lawyers were paid to do. Both Sam and Matt kept assuring them that, even as idiotic as Conlan seemed to be, he would never dare to file a libel suit. If Conlan should ever venture into a courtroom to contest what the stories said, he would be laying himself wide open for criminal charges. But still the lawyers kept equivocating.

At a little after 3 p.m., the phone rang on Matt's desk and he picked it up without thinking, half-expecting it to be Sam, offering to console him by buying him an after-work beer. But when he realized who it actually was, he felt himself break out in a cold sweat.

"Howdy, Matt," the voice said amiably. "How's everything going, old buddy? This is Tommy Van Zandt."

He seemed to lose his voice temporarily, and it took him a few seconds to locate it. "Well, hello, Tommy," he finally managed to say. "It's been a long time."

"It has, indeed, old buddy. Matter of fact, it's been way too long. I want to get together with you, Matt. I've got a business proposition for you—a proposition I think you might find mighty attractive. I'm not at liberty to talk about it over the phone, but if you'll drive out to our North Dallas offices, I'll be glad to lay the whole thing out for you."

Matt's brain was whirling, but the gears didn't seem to be meshing. "That sounds fair enough," he said. "When do you want me to come?"

"Sooner the better, Matt. I'm prepared to do it right away, this very evening, if that's agreeable with you."

"Just tell me what time."

"Why don't you come about 6:30. I'll be expecting you."

At 6:25 sharp, Matt pulled into the landscaped and virtually deserted parking area surrounding the highly restricted CUA executive complex in an isolated area of far North Dallas a mile or so beyond the new I-635 loop. He stopped at the guard's station, gave the uniformed security officer inside his name, and told him he had an appointment with Mr. Van Zandt.

The guard showed him where to park, although there were no other cars on the lot except for a white Ford with the CUA logo on its sides and a dark blue Mercedes sedan. Then he led Matt to a pair of large glass doors, where he pressed a buzzer, waited a moment, and let him inside.

"Take the elevator to the second floor, turn left down the hall, and it'll be the first office on your right," he said pleasantly.

There was no one in the outer reception room when Matt got there, so after a moment's hesitation, he walked across to a massive door of sculptured oak and pushed on it. It opened with amazing ease for its size, and he was suddenly standing in the inner office and face to face with Tommy Van Zandt for the first time in nearly six years. Tommy had gotten a little jowly and put on a few extra pounds around the middle, but otherwise he looked the same as always—handsome, sharply dressed and ultra-confident.

He stood up, grinned behind his cigar and extended his hand. "Good to see you, Matt," he said. "Glad you could come. Sit down."

From the first, the grin bothered Matt a little. It was a Cheshire Cat grin and there was something very unsettling about it. After they shook hands, he lowered himself silently into a heavy leather chair in front of Tommy's huge mahogany desk and assumed a waiting posture.

"You're looking well," Tommy said. "Army life must've agreed with you."

"I've been back awhile," Matt said.

"Yeah, I know," Tommy said, grinning again, "and you've been one helluva busy little feller, I understand."

"I don't know what you mean," Matt said. He could hear the defensiveness in his own voice.

"Sure you do, Matt," Tommy said. "Hey, there's no use in two old buddies bullshitting each other, now is there? Mr. Conlan's very impressed at how thorough you've been in turning up information about him. Fact is, he's so impressed he wants to offer you a job."

Matt made a snorting sound. "Yeah, I'll just bet he does," he said sarcastically, as his mind shouted questions at him. How the hell could Tommy possibly have found out about the series? Somebody at the *Times Herald* must have snitched, but who? Matt knew it couldn't have been Sam, but it had to have been somebody

"I'm completely serious, Matt," Tommy said. "We have an opening at CUA for a public relations director, and Mr. Conlan and I both feel very strongly that you're the perfect man for the job. It pays thirty thousand a year, which has to be at least three times what you're making now, and it doesn't even involve that much writing. You see, at CUA we're just as interested in what doesn't get in the paper as in what does, if you know what I mean."

"I think I know exactly what you mean, Tommy," Matt said, "but I'm not for sale. Not even for thirty thousand."

"That's only the starting salary, of course, Matt. There could be a lot more money down the road, once we know we can depend on you. There could be some pretty attractive perks, too—like expense-paid trips abroad, stock options, your own company car and life insurance." He grinned again. "CUA has a wonderful insurance program."

"Thanks for the offer," Matt said, standing up and feeling extremely unsteady, "but no thanks."

"Why don't you think it over for a few days before you decide?" Tommy said blandly. "I'd really hate to see you make the wrong decision. You know, turning down an opportunity like this could be the worst mistake you ever made, old buddy."

Matt tried his best to slam the heavy oak door on his way out, but the damned thing wouldn't slam.

As he strode across the empty parking area, the security guard came out of his little house and watched him. The guard wore a disconcerting grin on his face that looked exactly like Tommy's.

"Good night, Mr. Eastman," he called cheerfully. "Do be careful driving home."

Several times on the way back across town, he had the distinct and eerie feeling that he was being followed. The same dark blue Mercedes stayed in his rearview mirror all the way down Midway Road, and he saw it again after he turned onto Forest Lane. It looked like the one he had seen on the CUA parking lot, but he couldn't be sure, and after he got to Abrams Road he didn't notice it anymore. By then, though, it was really too dark to tell, so he drove around for a while and stopped for a couple of beers at Willie's Lounge on Beacon Street before he went home.

When he walked into his apartment, it was after 8:30 and the phone was ringing.

At first, he was actually afraid to answer it, but when it kept ringing, he finally went over and jerked up the receiver.

"Hello," he said.

"This is Tony Canales, Matthew. Are you all right?"

"I don't know," he said truthfully. "Is something wrong?"

"Yes, I'm sorry, but it's Lisa Feagan," Tony said. "She was killed about half an hour ago."

"Goddamn it, Tony," Matt snapped irrationally, "everytime you call me at home it's to tell me somebody else is dead. I don't think I can take it anymore." He felt like crying—not for Lisa Feagan, but for himself.

"It does seem that way," Tony admitted. "I wish I didn't have to, but I thought you ought to know."

"What happened?" Matt asked.

"It was another hit-and-run, almost identical to the Hollie O'Connor case a few years ago, and that's what worries me, Matt," Tony said. "She was crossing a street when this car with no headlights came along like a bat out of hell and smeared her all over the concrete. I'm not saying it's got anything to do with this Conlan thing you're working on. I just think you ought to be damned careful, that's all."

Matt thought he could feel himself coming totally apart. He went out that same night and bought a .22 pistol at a pawnshop. He carried it to work the next morning in his inside coat pocket. It wasn't much reassuance, but it was better than nothing.

Two days later, on Friday, Sam Garrett told him the Conlan series had been put on hold indefinitely. "With our only quotable source dead, the lawyers and the top brass think it's just too risky right now," Sam said.

A week to the day after that, at 11:15 on another Friday night, Matt was almost run down in his apartment house parking lot by a big sedan with no lights. It missed him by inches and then only because he managed to roll under a parked vehicle. It was hard to be sure, but the car looked like a dark blue Mercedes.

On Saturday, he called Wally about a job in Chicago, and on Sunday, he packed what little he planned to take with him.

On Monday, he called in sick and spent the day ransacking his own apartment to make it look as if the place had been searched. After dark that evening, he drove his car to Samuell-Grand Park, cut his hand with a razor blade and squeezed out some blood on the driver's seat. Then he walked to Samuell Boulevard and called a cab to take him to a motel near Love Field.

Early the next morning, David East caught a plane to Chicago and Matt Eastman disappeared from the face of the earth.

CHAPTER FIFTEEN

It was a painful subject, but sooner or later, Matt knew he was going to have to talk to Sarah about it. All week, he had kept inventing reasons to wait a little longer and a little longer and a little longer until he was thoroughly ashamed of himself for his lack of courage. By late Saturday morning, though, he had run completely out of excuses. It was now or never, he thought.

"There's, uh, still one other thing I haven't told you about," he said hesitantly, hating to spoil the mood of the morning.

For understandable reasons, they had slept late, and it was already almost 11 o'clock. They were sitting at the kitchen table, where they had just finished their second breakfast in the past eight hours, this one a mushroom omelette Sarah had fixed, and Matt was sipping his third cup of coffee. Outside, the skies were cold, gray and overcast with a threat of rain, and he doubted that they would see the sun all day. Dreary weather usually had a way of dragging him down mentally and emotionally, especially on weekends, but today he was virtually oblivious to climatic conditions. Except for this one nagging concern, he felt closer to contentment and peace than he had in years and would just as soon have gone back to bed and spent the rest of the day making love to Sarah. He had no desire to disrupt the tranquility that had settled over them, but he figured he had postponed the inevitable about as long as he could.

If it hadn't been for the troublesome matter of the little chrome locker key, he might have felt downright sunny inside, rain clouds or no rain clouds.

She smiled at him and took another sip of her coffee. Her eyes were clear and blue, and they smiled at him, too, over the rim of the cup. She had on one of his turtleneck sweaters and the same jeans she had worn the afternoon before, and her hair was pulled back in a ponytail. He had never seen her look prettier.

"Well, come on, out with it," she said teasingly. "I want to know every last one of your secrets."

He set his cup down, dug the key out of his pants pocket and laid it on the table. He wished one last time that he could have made himself throw the damned thing away and forget it, or that he had mailed it to the cops, or done something with it other than what he was doing now—but he hadn't. The only thing he had done was carry it around in his pocket for close to six days and worry about it. In another few seconds it was going to be too late to do any of those other things he might have done, but he had the ominous sensation that the worrying might just be beginning.

"This was given to me last Sunday night," he said, pushing the key over beside her coffee cup. "That woman who was killed in Star City handed it to me a few minutes before she died. She begged me to take it and I begged her not to give it to me, but she did. Now I'm stuck with it, and believe me, I'd about as soon have a case of AIDS."

Sarah blinked. "I think I'd a whole lot rather you had the key," she said self-consciously. She picked it up, turned it over and squinted to read the number imprinted on it. "What kind of Pandora's box does this fit?" she asked.

"She said it fits a locker at the bus station in Little Rock.

There's supposedly a briefcase in the locker, and it's supposedly full of some kind of evidence. She wanted me to get it and turn it over to the police or the FBI or somebody.''

Sarah's face was suddenly very serious. ''Who was this woman, Matt?'' she asked.

He looked puzzled, then shook his head. ''Sorry for the mystery,'' he said. ''I guess I just assumed you knew it was Mollie O'Connor.''

''My God,'' she said in disbelief. ''You mean the stripper? The one who disappeared in 1963?''

''The very same,'' he said, ''and everytime I think about it, it spooks the hell out of me. For over twenty years, I was sure she was dead. Then suddenly I find out she's alive, after all. So I meet her and spend maybe an hour with her, and then . . . then she really *is* dead. Jesus Christ, it still makes me sick every time I think about it.''

''But, Matt,'' she said, ''I read about the accident in *The Gazette*, and that wasn't the name in the story. It didn't say anything about Mollie O'Connor. How can you be sure it was even her? I mean, it's been so long . . .''

''Look, if it had been me, the story wouldn't have said anything about Matthew Eastman, either,'' he said shortly. ''It was her, all right. There's not the slightest doubt about that.'' He shuddered as he remembered how Mollie had looked there beside the highway with the blood all over her.

Mostly for Sarah's benefit, but partially because he felt a need to sort the whole thing out in his own mind, too, Matt spent the next half hour going back over the events that had culminated in Mollie O'Connor's death. Two or three times, his own words brought tears to his eyes, but he kept plunging on with the story, being careful to include every detail he could remember, and he found that just talking about it to someone was mildly therapeutic. When he was through, it was past noon and a light rain was falling outside, not unlike the rain that had been falling the night Mollie died. His eyes were red and his throat was dry and hoarse, but he also felt a deep sense of relief.

Sarah reached out and touched his face. She ran her hand through his hair and leaned forward to kiss him. ''You cared about her, didn't you?'' she asked. ''I mean, she was a whole lot more to you than just some casual face out of the past, wasn't she?''

He nodded. ''I guess so,'' he said. ''I never really knew how I felt about her. I never had much of a chance to find out. I had kind of a crush on her in the old days, but it wasn't just her I cared about. I cared about a lot of the people who got killed, and when those two bastards killed her, it was like they were killing the rest of them all over again. A week ago, I think I really wanted them to kill me, too, just to get it over with.''

''How do you feel about it now?'' she asked.

''I don't know,'' he said, ''but I don't feel the same, that's for sure.'' He looked at her and pulled her close to him, close enough to feel how good she felt through the turtleneck sweater. He kissed her while his hands moved hungrily over her and his senses feasted on her closeness.

''I much prefer you alive,'' she whispered.

''Now I feel like I've finally got a reason to stay that way,'' he told her. ''But you know, Sarah, that scares me a little bit, too. Before, it was like I didn't have anything left to lose, but now I know I do. It makes me want to grab you up and put you in the car and carry you off someplace five thousand miles from here, someplace where maybe we'll be safe for awhile, someplace where they can't come take you away from me like they've taken everything else I ever cared about.''

''Oh, Matthew,'' she said, hugging him, ''I know how you feel, but running away again won't help. Sooner or later, the fear and regret would only catch up with us, even if those other people didn't.''

''It might buy us some time, though,'' he said, ''and I can't see anything else to do.''

''Listen to me,'' she urged. ''There are only two ways to end this thing once and for all. You can die, like you nearly did last weekend, or you can go after these people, whoever they are. Thanks to your friend Mollie, you may finally have the tools you need to do the job after all these years.''

The last part of what she said didn't even register with him. All he really heard was the first part.

"I probably ought to die," he said bitterly, "and if I could get you off the hook by dying, I wouldn't even mind. But now I'm afraid they'd try to kill you, too. I've wished a hundred times I'd never gotten you into this mess, Sarah, but if I had it to do over, I'm pretty sure I'd go right back and do the same thing all over again. I guess I'm too damned weak to do anything else. Face it, Sarah, you're about the only strength I've got left."

Her eyes suddenly flashed sparks in his direction, and she hit the table with her fist, rattling the cups in their saucers. Then she spat out the first expletive he had ever heard cross her lips.

"That's just plain bullshit," she said, her voice rising. "You're not weak, so you might as well quit saying and thinking you are. A lot of awful things have happened to you, Matthew, things that would make anybody want to run or hide or give up. But a weak person could never have done what you did when those two men came to kill you the other night. You didn't need my strength to do that; you did it on your own. And if you were going to give up, I think you'd have done it right then. So just knock it off, okay?"

He made a wry face at her. "Sure, just call me Superman," he said.

"Maybe I will," she shot back at him. "And I'll tell you something else, too. If you were so weak and cowardly and dependent, you would have thrown this key away and never shown it to me or told me how you got it."

She picked up the key and closed her fingers tightly around it. "Because now that you have," she added pointedly, "you know perfectly well what we're going to have to do with it."

"I do?" he said. "What?"

"We're going to Little Rock and open that locker, of course," she said resolutely. "Then we're going to see exactly what's in that briefcase and take it from there." She stood up and shoved the key into the back pocket of her tantalizingly tight jeans.

"Come on," she said, reaching down for his hand. "We can be there inside of two hours if we hurry."

Despite Sarah's eagerness, Matt was full of precautions that afternoon, especially since it was a Saturday and he knew the streets in downdown Little Rock would be much more sparsely populated than they would have been on a weekday. This was good in one respect, because there would be less traffic to slow them down on their escape from the area. But it was bad in another way, because they would have no chance to lose themselves in a crowd if somebody started chasing them—or, worse yet, shooting at them.

He insisted on bringing along one of the .357 Magnums left behind by the two hitmen, but he agreed to stow it under the driver's seat of the convertible and actually carry just the old .22 under his jacket. The difference between the two pistols was approximately the same as the difference between a BB-gun and a cannon, but the .22 was a lot lighter and less bulky, and the six hollow-point slugs in it were totally capable of stopping somebody at close range.

Matt's edgy, unsettled frame of mind wasn't helped at all when they stopped at a 7-Eleven on their way out of Jefferson and he bought a morning edition of the *Arkansas Gazette*. His fears about the imminent discovery of the two bodies they had dumped in Monroe had been well-founded, as it turned out. The story was right there, just below the fold on page one, and it was much more prominently displayed than he had expected. The two-column headline read:

CAR CONTAINING TWO BODIES
WAS RENTED IN LITTLE ROCK

Underneath it, a smaller subhead added:

Louisiana police, FBI agents seek to identify
slaying victims found at Monroe shopping mall

He read the first three or four paragraphs aloud to Sarah as she drove north through the drizzle on Highway 81:

"Monroe, La.—The automobile in which the decomposing bodies of two unidentified men were discovered Friday was rented more than two weeks ago in Little Rock, and the victims actually may have been killed in Arkansas, then driven to Louisiana, investigators say.

"Because of the apparent interstate character of the slayings and the possibility that the two men were kidnapped and transported across a state line, Louisiana authorities have asked the FBI to enter the case. No identifying papers were found either in the car or on the bodies, leading investigators to believe they were removed by the men's killers in an effort to delay identification.

"One man apparently died of a bullet wound in the head, a preliminary coroner's report said, but the cause of the second man's death had not been determined late Friday. There were no visible marks on the second body, according to police. Autopsies were ordered on both victims.

"The bodies were discovered shortly after 3 p.m. Friday in the trunk of a 1987 Thunderbird which witnesses said had been parked for several days in the parking lot of a Monroe shopping center. Police were called to the scene after passersby noticed an unpleasant odor coming from the car.

" 'We're asking anyone who might have seen the car when it arrived at the shopping center to come forward and help us with this case,' said Capt. Wilfred Mouray of the Monroe police. 'From all indications, the people responsible for these murders are cold-blooded professional killers.' "

Matt finished reading the rest of the article to himself, although there was very little additional information in it. Then he folded up the newspaper and tossed it into the back seat.

"Well, they certainly make you sound like a dangerous character," Sarah said, smiling uneasily. "How long do you think it'll take the cops to find out who they are?"

"Probably not long if they've really got the FBI involved," he said. "One of them signed the rental papers on the car, of course, but my guess is that neither of them was using his right name. The problem is, whoever they were working for can probably guess who they are from the descriptions of the men and the car. So can anybody who might have been working with them."

"What does that mean?"

"It means if I had to do it, I should've told you about the damned locker key three or four days ago instead of screwing around until they found the bodies," he said. "This way, we may have given them enough time to put somebody else on stakeout at the bus station."

"Stop worrying," she said. "All you have to do is stay out of sight and let me get the briefcase out of the locker. They won't recognize me, and I can be in there and gone before anybody knows what's going on."

"How do you know they won't recognize you?" Matt asked.

"There's no way they could," she said. "They've never seen me before."

He stared at her glumly. "How do you know that?" he said again.

It was just after 2 p.m. when they turned off U.S. 65 onto Interstate 30 west of the city. Ten minutes later, following an impromptu plan that Matt had thrown together since leaving Jefferson, they backed the Mustang into one of the outer spaces on the parking lot behind the downtown Sheraton Inn, which overlooked the interstate, and went into the lobby to call a taxi.

Making the short jaunt to the bus station and back in a cab would serve several purposes, he reasoned. For one, it would give them a degree of anonymity and keep anyone at the bus station from knowing what kind of car they were driving. For another, it would allow both of them to go inside, instead of one of them having to sit in the car with the motor running. He had decided to let Sarah open the locker, as she suggested, but he wanted to keep her in sight every second while she was doing it. Finally, it would leave the Mustang only a few hundred feet from the I-30 freeway, where Matt knew it could out-accelerate and outrun practically any recent standard car that might be pursuing it.

The cab was a Pontiac that had seen better days. The driver was an amiable young black man who was playing his radio loud enough to peel paint and who shouted the same identical three-word response above the blast of the music to virtually every question or comment.

"We need to go to the bus station," Matt yelled.

"No problem, man," the driver yelled back, as the cab chugged into the street and turned left, leaving a thin, blue haze of oil smoke in its wake.

"We're just going to run inside for a minute and come right back out," Matt said, leaning over the back of the front seat to make himself heard. "Can you double-park in front and wait for us?"

"No problem, man."

Matt tossed a five-dollar bill on the seat beside the driver. "I don't want you to move from in front while we're inside, not even for a cop," he said. "Understand?"

"No problem, man."

Matt dropped another five on top of the first one. "I also want you to keep your eyes open, and if we come out of that bus station running, be ready to floorboard this thing and get the hell out of there as soon as we hit the seats, okay?"

The cabdriver grinned. "No problem, man," he said, pocketing the two bills.

The bus station was about as deserted as the rest of downtown Little Rock at midafternoon on a Saturday. As the driver had promised, it was "no problem" parking squarely in front, because no other cars were around the entrance, but the absence of people moving around inside also disturbed Matt. The lobby was practically empty, and there were no more than two or three dozen people in the waiting room. It made everyone in the place stand out like a sore thumb.

Sarah winked at him as they got out on different sides of the cab and walked into the building separately, trying not to make it obvious that they had arrived together. Since neither of them was familiar with the premises, they strolled around unhurriedly and about 30 feet apart until Sarah spotted the lockers. Their eyes met for an instant, and he saw her nod quickly toward them as she moved in that direction.

A moment later, Matt followed at a distance, trying his best to appear casual and disinterested, but pretty sure he wasn't doing a very good job of it. He briefly assumed a leaning position against the wall, then walked across to a poster and pretended to read it, then fumbled in his pockets as if he had lost something, then strode over to a water fountain and got a drink.

Through all these meaningless motions, he could feel the hard, cold bulk of the .22 under his jacket. He could also feel himself trembling inside, sometimes so violently that he wondered why other people couldn't see him shaking, but no one apparently did.

Sarah was walking along the bank of the lockers now, peering at the numbers and looking for the one marked 312. She seemed to be having a hard time locating it. Was it possible, he wondered, that the lockers weren't numbered consecutively? The idea seemed ridiculous, but he could think of no other reason why it could be taking her so long. His eyes made another long, sweeping pass around the bus station, and he felt thick, sticky panic rising in his throat.

Don't be a fool, he told himself through clenched teeth. There was no reason to get so frantic, no reason to feel the sweat pouring down his ribs under his clothes, no reason to want to take back the locker key and hurl it across the room and say to hell with the briefcase forever, no reason to succumb to the overwhelming urge to grab Sarah and run before it was too late.

Then he saw the sonofabitch standing there watching her, and he knew there *was* a reason, after all.

The man was a good deal closer to Sarah than he was to Matt, and he had been partially obscured from Matt's view by an offset in the wall. But Matt realized that Sarah had seen the man, too. That was the reason she was hesitating.

Matt eased forward, keeping his head down and his face in the opposite direction until he was sure he could get an unobstructed view of the man. Then he turned and looked directly at him for a split second. When he did, something snapped into place inside his head.

The man wore a trenchcoat over a dark gray suit, a white shirt with a burgundy tie, and a black Tyrolean hat. He had a small moustache, and he didn't look like anybody you'd expect to see in a bus station—not in Little Rock, Arkansas, or anyplace else, and not on Saturday afternoon or any other time. In dress, bearing and mannerisms, he looked a lot like the two men Matt had seen in his kitchen early last Monday morning.

He carried himself like a cop, Matt thought fleetingly, but the man was certainly no cop, at least not a legitimate one. He was the third piece in a matched set, and Matt had left two other pieces of that set lying broken and stinking and dead in Monroe, Louisiana.

Now, Matt thought, unless a fourth piece to the set was lurking around somewhere nearby, there was an outside chance that he and Sarah just might get out of this place alive. But they were going to have to deal with the sonofabitch in the trenchcoat before that could be accomplished.

He put his hand in his jacket pocket and closed it tightly around the butt of the .22 pistol. Then he sauntered forward, as though he were taking a shortcut across the locker area on his way to somewhere else, until he was within six or seven feet of where she was standing. She turned toward him and he saw naked fear and something close to desperation in her eyes.

"Go ahead and open it," he mouthed silently as he passed.

Praying that she had understood, he moved quickly past her, so that he was between her and the man in the trenchcoat.

He heard the metallic sound as she inserted the key into the keyhole, followed by the click as she turned the knob and opened the locker door. In the corner of his eye, just as he brushed past the man in the trenchcoat, he saw her slide a dark brown briefcase out of the locker. Then the man moved between them and he could no longer see Sarah.

Matt ducked out of sight around a corner, flattened himself against the wall, held his breath and listened.

"Hold on a minute, Miss," he heard the man say. "I want to talk to you."

"What about?" Sarah asked.

Matt crept forward on his tiptoes and peered back around the corner. The man was blocking Sarah's path, reaching inside his trenchcoat with one hand and grabbing for the briefcase with the other.

"You're going to give me the briefcase and stand where you are," the man said with quiet authority. "Then you and I are going to walk out of here together very calmly, and you're going to act as if nothing at all is wrong."

"But it doesn't belong to you," Sarah protested.

"I don't think it belongs to you, either," the man said. "I have a gun under my coat, but if you do as you're told, nothing will happen to you. Otherwise, I promise you I'll kill you right here."

To Matt, the next ten seconds seemed to last for ten minutes. Every frantic thing that took place during those seconds was played out in slow-motion and Matt didn't even seem to be part of what was happening.

He pulled the .22 out of his jacket, tensed his legs underneath him and catapulted himself toward the man in the trenchcoat with the pistol high in the air. Then he hit the man across the back of the head with the barrel of it as hard as he could swing his arm. The man grunted and stiffened, and the black Tyrolean hat tumbled to the floor. He tried to turn with his hand still tangled inside his trenchcoat, but Matt raised the gun and hit him again. He saw blood gush from the man's head and run down the side of his face. Several drops of it splattered against the front of the lockers. He could feel the stickiness of it on the hand that held the .22.

The man was already falling when Matt hit him the third time.

He saw Sarah's shocked face. She was clutching the briefcase and shrinking back in horror.

"Run, goddamn it," he hissed between his teeth. "Get to the cab."

The man was flat on the floor now, threshing his arms in convulsive, insensible motions. Then Matt heard a confused jumble of sounds coming from the direction of the waiting room, as he stooped and ran his free hand inside the man's trenchcoat.

He found the weapon there and awkwardly wrestled it out, not at all surprised to see that it was another .357 Magnum. The bastards were a matched set, all right.

He looked up to see a fat black woman lumbering toward him.

"Great gawd a'mighty," she bawled, pointing at Matt. "He done killed that man!"

"Get back," he yelled, jumping to his feet and waving both the Magnum and the .22 in wild circles above his head.

He thought of firing once or twice into the air, but he must have looked enough like a maniac as it was, because the black woman was suddenly lumbering in the opposite direction. In fact, everybody he encountered on his way back to the front entrance of the bus station seemed more than anxious to get out of his way. When they saw the guns in his hands, they cleared a wide path for him all the way to the door.

Sarah was already getting into the taxi, and he pushed her on through the door, then threw himself in behind her.

"Drive!" he told the driver and jammed the barrel of the Magnum hard against the back of his neck. "Drive or you're dead!"

"N-no fuckin' problem, man," the driver cried, and the tires screamed as the taxi peeled away from the curb.

Matt glanced behind them and saw a small knot of people spilling out of the bus station. A few of them ran out into the street, shouting and pointing after the smoke-belching taxi.

He was dimly aware of Sarah crying in the seat beside him and hugging the briefcase against her. His heart was pounding like a bass drum in his ears, and he was afraid he was going to pass out, but he knew he couldn't.

Not yet. Not yet.

They wheeled up to the main entrance of the Sheraton, where the cab had picked them up, and Matt ordered the driver to stop there. Except for a young couple talking intently to each other perhaps 60 feet away, there was nobody around as Matt opened the door of the taxi and got out on rubbery legs. He listened for sirens for a moment, but heard nothing, then swayed drunkenly as he reached back inside the cab, took Sarah by the hand and pulled her toward him. She stumbled out onto the sidewalk and stood there, glassy-eyed and blinking back tears, but still keeping a tight grip on the briefcase.

Holding the Magnum in his left hand, he pulled a small wad of currency out of his pocket with his right and tossed a $20 bill through the window at the cabdriver.

Matt pointed the big pistol at the driver's jawbone. "I want you to get your ass out of here and forget you ever saw us," he said. "In return, I'm going to forget I ever saw you. But if you tell anybody about us—and I mean anybody at all—I'm going to remember you damned fast. You got it?"

"No problem, man," the driver gasped, his eyes glued to the gun.

"Then move."

The old Pontiac roared forward and shot into the street, leaving them in a pall of blue smoke. Matt watched until it was out of sight, then caught Sarah by the arm and steered her hurriedly toward the parking lot.

Two minutes later, the Mustang convertible was streaking west down the I-30 freeway, its speedometer needle hovering at 85. They had gone only three or four miles when they passed a state trooper heading in the opposite direction, his blue lights flashing. Matt's heart almost stopped for a moment, but the trooper never so much as broke stride, and in a matter of seconds he was out of sight.

After that, Matt cut the speed back to a more respectable and far more unobtrusive 68 miles per hour. But he kept his eyes fixed on the rearview mirror and drove past the U.S. 65 turnoff without slowing down, opting to stay on the interstate all the way to Malvern and take U.S. 270, a narrow, more out-of-the-way route, back to Pine Bluff.

They were more than 30 miles out of Little Rock and approaching the Malvern exit before he felt sufficiently under control again to talk.

"Are you all right, Sarah?" he asked.

"No," she said bluntly, "but I guess I'll live. I'm not sure anybody can say as much for that man back in the bus station, though."

"I'm sorry it happened," he said, "and I'm doubly sorry you had to end up in the middle of it."

"You hit him pretty hard, Matt. Do you think he might be dead?"

"I don't know," he said, "and at this point, I don't really care, either. You know how us cold-blooded professional killers are."

"I feel so stupid about the whole thing," she said. "All the way over there, I kept thinking you were worrying about nothing. Now I know better. It . . . it upset me a lot when you hit that man, but I understand why you had to do it. I think I understand a lot of things now that I didn't understand before. Do you think we got away clean?"

"If you mean do I think somebody's hot on our heels, the answer's no," he told her. "Beyond that, it's hard to tell. I don't think anybody can connect this car with what happened at the bus station, not even the cabbie, so we ought to be okay for awhile. I just hope you don't hate me for what I did back there."

"I don't hate you; I love you," she said simply. "And as scared as I am, I can hardly wait to see what's inside this thing. Whatever it is, I feel like I've got a real stake in it now."

Matt felt relieved when they were able to get off I-30 and turn onto U.S. 270 toward Malvern. He stopped at a service station just off the interstate, went to the men's room and washed the dried blood off his right hand. On the way out, he bought some Cokes and candy bars, hoping they would help to get rid of the weak, empty feeling inside him until they could get some real food somewhere.

It took a good while to get through the town, because of the narrow streets and bumper-to-bumper traffic. It was strange, he thought, how different downtown Malvern was from downtown Little Rock on a Saturday afternoon.

Within 15 minutes, though, they had negotiated the detour down U.S. 67 and were back on 270 heading south toward Prattsville and Sheridan. Then the dense pine forests closed in around the narrow two-lane road and they drifted along behind a farmer's pickup truck at 45 miles per hour for a long way.

Matt didn't care. It was as though he didn't know where they were going and had absolutely no desire to get there. He didn't share Sarah's curiosity about the briefcase, either. On the contrary, he dreaded having to open it up and look inside. The one thing he did wish he had was some beer—about a case of beer, to be precise—but this was dry territory and he wouldn't be able to buy so much as a single can until they got to Pine Bluff.

He looked across at Sarah and saw her staring straight ahead through the windshield and holding the briefcase fondly, almost possessively, in her lap. As he drove, he silently asked himself the same question he had asked so often before.

"Why didn't I throw that damned key away while I had the chance?"

And, as usual, there was no answer.

CHAPTER SIXTEEN

Partly as a precaution and partly because they both felt exhausted by the time they got to Pine Bluff, they decided to spend the night there and finish the trip back to Jefferson the next morning. Sarah worried about leaving Hobo alone in the house all night, but Matt assured her it had happened plenty of times before, and the consequences would be no more serious than a puddle and a pile beside the back door and an accusing look in the old dog's eyes.

Despite her concern about Hobo, Matt could tell that Sarah was glad they weren't going all the way home until later. It meant she could get a look at the contents of the briefcase that much sooner, and there was no doubt that had been uppermost in her thoughts ever since their escape from Little Rock.

It was barely 4 p.m. when they checked into a Holiday Inn on U.S. 65 at the southern edge of Pine Bluff, but from the fatigue in Matt's bones and the tension in his muscles, it felt more like midnight. The first thing he did was take off his jacket, open a beer from the 12-pack he had just bought at a package store a block away, and flop across the bed, while Sarah went into the bathroom to wash her face, brush her hair and redo her worn makeup. After a few minutes, he felt himself beginning to relax a little as he gulped the beer and the knots inside him slowly loosened. He even grew slightly drowsy and might have drifted off for a short nap if Sarah hadn't come out of the bathroom about that time and snuggled up beside him on the bed.

"I feel a lot better now," she said. "How about you?"

"I'm kind of zonked out, but I'll be okay," he said. "The last couple of hours just took all the starch out of me."

It felt really good when she put her hand lightly on his forehead and even better when she leaned down and kissed him. "You just keep surprising me," she said, "but it's a little bit scary, too. It's hard for me to reconcile what you did this afternoon with the David East I knew—or thought I knew—all that time."

He smiled tiredly. "Even a cornered rat's been known to fight for its life," he said. "Then again, maybe you just bring out the bad-ass in me."

"Do you want to rest for awhile before we open the briefcase?" she asked expectantly.

He knew what she wanted him to say, so he obliged her. Besides, he had to admit he was also curious, especially after all they had gone through to get their hands on the damned thing.

"Nah, bring it on over here," he said. "We might as well see what I've been shooting people and beating them over the head for. Otherwise, the cops—or someone even worse—may be pounding on the door before we get a chance."

She got the briefcase off the table where she had put it when they first came in and laid it flat on the bedspread between them. It was made of lustrous dark brown cowhide with shiny metal hardware and had obviously cost a lot of money. But knowing Mollie O'Connor, that wasn't surprising. Mollie always did have expensive tastes.

"You do the honors," Sarah said. "You've earned the right."

He shoved back the bright brass catches on either side of

the handle and the latches snapped open with two sharp metallic clicks. His eyes met Sarah's for an instant as he started to raise the lid.

"Do you think we're opening up a real can of worms here, Matthew?" she asked nervously.

"Probably more like a real barrel of snakes," he said and flipped the briefcase open.

By this time, he was prepared for almost anything, from a shrunken head to the components for a submachine gun, but the visible contents of the briefcase looked pretty bland at first glance. They consisted of several bulky, unlabeled manila envelopes, the exterior of which gave no clue as to what might be inside. Matt picked up the one on top, unfastened the metal clasp, thrust his hand inside and pulled out a thick stack of glossy eight-by-ten photographs.

At that point, things started to get a lot more interesting.

None of the pictures would have won any photography contests for style or composition. They were all slightly fuzzy, a little out of focus, and had obviously been shot from a considerable distance and then blown up. But with all their flaws, the photos would have been worth a fortune on the international media market.

Lee Harvey Oswald was readily identifiable in each of the first dozen pictures in the stack. In most of them, he was joined by D. Wingo Conlan, the late Dallas industrial czar, and Tommy Van Zandt, the man who now aspired to be governor of Texas.

There were several different sets of pictures, but they all looked as if they had been taken somewhere in Mexico. The first group showed Oswald, Conlan and Van Zandt standing together in a desolate, arid outdoor setting. Except for an automobile of uncertain make and vintage, part of which was visible in several of the shots, the only objects in the background were rocks, sand and cacti. Three of the photos distinctly showed Oswald in various attitudes, holding a long-barreled rifle that closely resembled the 6.5-milimeter Manlicher Carcano which he had allegedly fired at the Kennedy motorcade. In a fourth photo, Oswald appeared to be handing the gun to Conlan, who was grinning like an idiot.

From the very first glimpse, the background in the second set of pictures looked hauntingly familiar to Matt. In these photos, Oswald, Conlan and Van Zandt were again visible, this time seated around a table in what looked like a courtyard of some kind, talking animatedly and drinking. It was apparent that the pictures had been shot in sequence over a considerable length of time. The entire sequence showed a waiter replenishing the three men's drinks, then Van Zandt apparently leaving and two, attractive, dark-haired women joining Oswald and Conlan, then one of the women embracing Oswald and the other sitting in Conlan's lap.

"I'll be a sonofabitch," Matt said, staring hard at the pictures of the women. "See that girl in Conlan's lap? I'm almost positive it's Angel Garcia."

"What about the girl with Oswald?" Sarah asked, looking over his shoulder. "Do you know her, too?"

"No," he said, "but I'd bet five thousand bucks she didn't live very long after this picture was made."

The last photo in the sequence showed Conlan and Angel Garcia standing, as if they were about to leave. Conlan had one hand on Angel's shapely behind, and he was shaking hands with Oswald with the other.

At the very bottom of the stack was a series of four other photos, and when Matt saw them, he felt a little current of electricity run through him, making the hair stand up on the back of his neck. These final pictures in the collection had apparently been shot just seconds apart, and they were almost identical, but not quite. They showed the same table in the same courtyard, but this time the group at the table had changed somewhat.

This time, Conlan wasn't present and someone else was seated between Oswald and Van Zandt. In one picture, this third party was handing Oswald what appeared to be a large wad of currency.

Matt knew instantly that he had seen one of these same pictures many times before, although the last time had been many years ago. It was still almost as familiar to Matt as his own reflection in a mirror, and yet three of the pictures were so nearly alike that he couldn't be sure which of them it was.

Except for the picture with the money, it could have been any of them—not that it really mattered.

The point was, the first time he had seen the picture was on the night of November 24, 1963, when he and Jamie had found it lying on the floor of Jack Ruby's bedroom. It had been crumpled and ripped in half so that the person in its center couldn't be identified. As far as Matt knew, the two halves of that other picture were still buried in a plastic box on the old Eastman farm in Kaufman County, Texas, as it had been for more than two decades. But he still remembered what it looked like with perfect clarity, and beyond the slightest doubt, it had been a print of one of the same photos lying in front of him now.

The recognition came as a jolt, especially when he remembered all the times he had stared at the picture and tried to figure out who that mysterious third party could be. Now, in one earthshaking split second, he finally knew. And along with the shock of knowing, he could only wonder how many lives might have been spared over the last 24 years if he had known from the beginning—assuming he had the guts to do something about it.

If he had, Jamie Cade might still be alive. So might Angel Garcia. And Hollie and Mollie O'Connor. And so many others that it made him ill to think about it.

"Alex, you miserable bastard," he whispered.

The third person in the picture was Lieutenant Alexander Sutton of the Dallas Police Department—the same homicide detective who had told Matt so vehemently in an unguarded moment on assassination day that Oswald should never have been taken alive.

Yes, under the circumstances, Matt could understand how a live Oswald could have been a monumental embarrassment to Alex Sutton.

And suddenly, Matt knew so much that his mind could scarcely contain it all, much less process the raw knowledge into orderly, rational conclusions. The realization whirled like a tornado in his brain, flinging a wild confusion of thoughts, almost-forgotten memories and other mental debris into every corner of his consciousness. It made him so dizzy momentarily that he had to lie back on the bed and close his eyes.

"What is it, Matthew?" Sarah asked in mild alarm. "Are you all right?"

"My head feels like it's going to explode," he said. He would have to wait until later to explain the situation, he thought. He simply wasn't up to it right now.

She got some aspirins from her purse and handed them to him, along with another beer to wash them down, and after a few minutes he felt well enough to replace the photographs and open the second manila envelope in the briefcase.

This one was stuffed with dozens of letters, notes, memos and other papers, some on official Conlan Universal Aerospace Corporation letterheads and some on personalized stationery with the initials D.W.C. It took Matt a minute to determine that the initials belonged to Dee Conlan. Many were personal messages from Dee to Mollie O'Connor, whom he always seemed to address as "M." Others apparently pertained to corporate matters at CUA.

It would have taken at least a full day to read everything in the envelope, but Matt paused long enough to take a close look at a few of the communications that caught his eye. One of them, written in shaky longhand on Dee's monogrammed stationery and dated March 23, 1983, began:

"Dear M—

I would have been to see you sooner, but I was scared to leave. They've gotten control of so much of the company now they might lock me out of my own office while I'm gone. I gave Tommy all them stock shares to keep him quiet, but that wasn't enough, he just keeps taking more. I don't see how he does it, but he knows how to pull all that legal stuff and I think my other lawyers are in on it with him and Alex, too. They are robbing me blind, baby, but I just can't figure how to stop it. Sometimes I think I ought to just get out of this whole thing and let them have it, then I could come down there and be with you all the time . . ."

Another, typed on a CUA Executive Offices letterhead (but obviously not by a secretary, judging from the number of typos), was dated 8/11/72 and was unsigned. It read:

"Dee:
   Unless the 10;000 shares we talked about are signed over to me by Friday, don't expect me to cover for you when the FBI comes around and starts asking questions about certain things. I can get them off your back, at least for awhile, but if you think I'm going to stick my neck out to protect you for nothing, you'd better think again. I'd better hear something from you soon, or it looks like you're going to end up in deep trouble."

The third envelope held the strangest collection of all. There were two yellowed billfold-size pictures of the same little boy—the kind of pictures school photographers used to take every year by the millions —one of which showed him at six or seven years of age, the other at about ten. Printed on the white border underneath each of the photos was "School Days, Van Wert, Ohio." One was dated 1941, the other 1944. It took Matt a few seconds to comprehend that the little boy was apparently Alex Sutton.

There were also two photographic copies of pictures from a high school yearbook. In both pictures, a beardless, crewcut Alex Sutton smiled out at them, once from above a football jersey with the number "55" on it, and once from beneath a graduate's mortarboard. At least it certainly *looked* like Alex Sutton, and the information printed beneath the senior class picture seemed to confirm that assumption. It said: "Franklin Alexander Sutton ('Good Old Alex')—honor roll 3 years, football 2 years, track 2 years, junior class treasurer, senior class parliamentarian, Quill & Scroll, Spanish Club."

Along with the pictures, the envelope also contained a typed, notarized three-page statement. It was dated July 10, 1984, and signed by one Mary Cockrell of Van Wert, Ohio, who apparently had once been engaged to marry the same "Good Old Alex." But from the gist of the statement, which Sarah read aloud, the relationship had come to an abrupt and puzzling end right after Sutton returned from military service in 1957.

"I had the feeling something was wrong even before he got home," Mary Cockrell's statement recalled. "Alex and I always wrote each other at least twice a week, but for the last month or so he was in Germany, I only got one short letter and one postcard from him. Then, when he came back to town, I didn't even hear from him for a day or two, but he finally called and asked if he could see me. 'You must be kidding,' I told him. 'I've been waiting for months to see you.'

"He acted so peculiar that night I was afraid he was sick or something. We went out and got a hamburger and then drove around for awhile, but it was almost like he didn't know me. Sometimes it seemed like he didn't even know where he was. He looked just the same as always, but there was something different about the way he talked and acted. I mean, Alex and I had been dating since we were juniors in high school, but all of a sudden, he was like a stranger to me. I was sure he would want to make love after being away for so long, but he acted like he didn't even want to kiss me. When he took me home, he told me he was planning to leave Van Wert for good. He said he wanted to go to Texas and try to get a job as a policeman.

"I said that was fine with me, that I'd always thought I'd like Texas, and that seemed to make him real uncomfortable. He said he was going to be leaving in just a few days and thought it would be best if I stayed in Van Wert for awhile. He said he'd write when he got settled. I got the feeling that he just wanted to get away from me, and I told him so. He made some excuse about Army life changing his way of thinking and said he wasn't so sure he wanted to get married, after all.

"I started to give him his ring back right then, but I decided to wait and hope that he'd be more like himself the next time—only there wasn't any next time. Two days later, I called the rooming house where he was staying, and they told me he'd moved out. I never saw him again after that or even heard from him. He left without saying a word, and I couldn't understand it. It just broke my heart at first.

"When I kind of got over it, though, I started thinking about how different he had been. I got out some of his old letters and compared the handwriting in them with the writing in the last letter and postcard he sent me. The writing looked a lot different, and even the way he said things was different. I also talked to three or four other people who had known Alex before and seen him after he got home. They all said they thought he acted real weird.

"I'm convinced that the person who came back from the army wasn't Alex Sutton at all, but just somebody who looked like him. I know it sounds crazy, and I can't explain it, but I swear it's true. I knew Alex so well for so many years, and I know he'd never have just run off like that with no explanation. I know girls who get jilted are bitter sometimes, but it's not just bitterness that makes me say that, either. I also know engagements get broken all the time, but the real Alex Sutton wouldn't ever have done it this way. He was too honest and decent for that.

"This may sound silly, but I'm convinced the man who came back to Van Wert in May 1957 was some kind of imposter. I don't know why or how this could be, but since I knew Alex better than anyone else in town, I also believe this imposter was afraid I would guess the truth, and that was why he left so suddenly. I only hope that someday I find out what really happened."

Attached to the statement were photocopies of two of the letters Mary Cockrell had received from Alex Sutton. One had been written in the summer of 1956 and the other in the spring of 1957 just a few weeks before he was to return home. The contrast she had noted in the handwriting was readily apparent, even to Matt's untrained eye.

"How strange," Sarah said, studying the two letters. "Mary Cockrell sounds a little nutty, but it really *does* look like two different people wrote these letters."

Matt didn't say anything. He had no idea what *to* say. All he knew was that he was dog-tired, both physically and mentally, and that he was growing uneasier and more disturbed by the minute.

Nevertheless, he resolutely took the fourth and final manila envelope out of the briefcase, opened it and turned it upside down over the bed. The contents consisted of three tape cassettes which tumbled out onto the bedspread. They were labeled "Mollie O'Connor Taped Depositions I, II and III," and each was capable of holding up to 60 minutes of conversation.

He was instantly relieved that they hadn't brought a tape recorder. At this point, he thought, listening to three hours of talk might be more than his mind and body could stand.

Sarah, on the other hand, was clearly as disappointed as he was relieved. "God, how frustrating," she said. "This whole thing is dynamite, but the tapes could be the best part yet. It makes me want to go out and buy a tape recorder right now." She looked eagerly at him. "What do you think?"

"First of all, I think I'm worn to a frazzle," he said, opening another beer and sprawling in a chair. "Second of all, I'm not sure I can stand to listen to Mollie O'Connor's verbal memoirs tonight. I think it's going to be very painful and upsetting, even tomorrow. Third of all, I think I'm too goddamned old for this cloak-and-dagger shit."

"But Matt," she protested, "we've got hold of something really strong here, something you could take to the authorities and get their attention for sure. And just think what a great story it'll make. This is Pulitzer Prize stuff. Don't you realize that?"

"The only thing I realize," he said sourly, "is that I'm too beat to think about it right now."

She shuffled the three cassettes in her hands for a moment, then dropped them resignedly back in the briefcase. "Okay then, we'll wait until morning," she sighed, "but at least tell me what you think this all means."

"I don't know," he said, "and I'm too tired to even guess."

Sarah went slowly around the room, switching off all the lights, except the one in the bathroom, leaving the room almost as dark as the sky outside. Then she came over and sat on the arm of his chair. "I'm sorry," she said, with her mouth close to his ear. "I know you're tired, and you've got every right to be. Do you want me to order some food from room service so we don't have to go out?"

"Why don't you just order something for you?" he said. "I think maybe I'm too tired to eat, too."

She leaned down and kissed him. The contact started softly and casually, but it quickly escalated into an encore of the kiss outside the toolshed the afternoon before. When it ended, her jeans and sweater were somewhere on the carpet and they were back on the bed. This time it was just the two of them—without the briefcase.

"On second thought," she whispered breathlessly, "we could just go straight to bed and have an early breakfast instead."

He pulled her hungrily, needfully to him, feeling her legs tightening around him and her fingers struggling with the buttons of his shirt. It was awesome, he thought, how quickly and completely she could arouse him, even when he was scared, nervous and weary to the very core of his being.

"That's the one thing in the world I'm not too tired to do," he said, smiling in the darkness.

By half past ten the next morning, they were in *The Jeffersonian* office with the front door securely locked and the first of Mollie O'Connor's three cassettes unwinding on Sarah's tape recorder.

At first, Matt was almost transfixed by the sound of Mollie's voice. He had expected it to be an eerie, uncanny experience—one he had approached with equal amounts of dread and curiosity—and it fulfilled those expectations completely. The surprising part was that, before they were over, the next three hours would also become one of the most enlightening, intriguing, and even strangely satisfying, interludes of his entire life.

"My name is Mollie O'Connor," the slow, precise voice on the first cassette began. "I'm forty-three years old and of sound mind. Today is June 1, 1987, and I'm recording this in Room 216 of the Gulfstream Motor Hotel in Biloxi, Mississippi, where I'm registered under the name Marguerita Ocala. The information I'm about to give is in regard to the assassination of President John F. Kennedy on November 22, 1963, and several unsolved murders related to the assassination.

"In the summer of 1963, my twin sister Hollie and I were working as exotic dancers at Jack Ruby's Carousel Club in Dallas when I met Lieutenant Alex Sutton, a homicide detective in the Dallas Police Department. He was ten years older than I was and had a reputation as one of the toughest cops in town, but Jack said I should be nice to him because he was a very influential person who could help me and the Carousel. Jack was always trying to play cupid and match up the girls who worked for him with his favorite customers, but I didn't mind. I liked mature, rugged men, and I thought Alex was very handsome and charming. I was young, impulsive and not very smart, and I fell in love with him almost instantly—at least I thought I did.

"Within two or three months, I knew I had made a bad mistake. I didn't really know how bad it was at the time, but it turned out to be the biggest mistake of my life. Underneath his charm, I discovered Alex was cruel, cold-blooded, insensitive, self-centered, domineering and jealous. On top of that, there was something even worse about him that was hard to pin down. He gave me the feeling he could kill somebody and enjoy doing it, and I was scared to death of him. He was always very suave and proper when we were around other people, but when we were alone, he got a kick out of hurting me. He knew lots of ways to hurt people, both physically and psychologically, so that it didn't show and nobody else could tell. By early fall, all I wanted to do was get away from him, but he had me so intimidated I was afraid to try to break up with him, so I just went on. I didn't know what else to do.

"In October 1963, Alex told me he had to go to Mexico on business, and he insisted that I go with him. We went in a private plane owned by Dee Conlan, president of Conlan Universal Aerospace in Dallas. Several other people I knew also went, including Conlan, a lawyer named Tom Van Zandt, and Angel Garcia, another girl who worked for Jack Ruby.

We flew to Monterrey and stayed in one of the big hotels there for three days.

"While we were there, Alex told me to take some pictures of Dee Conlan, Tom Van Zandt and another man I didn't recognize. First, at Alex's instruction, I photographed them out in the countryside while they were looking at a rifle and taking some practice shots with it. Later, I also photographed them while they were having a meeting of some kind out in the hotel courtyard. Alex showed me how to focus the camera on the table where they were sitting and said I was to shoot the pictures from the balcony outside our room and not let anybody see what I was doing. He also told me to be sure and not get him in any of the pictures with the others.

"I don't know what made me disobey him. I guess it was just because of the way he'd hurt me and all the degrading, humiliating things he'd done to me. And maybe it was partly to prove to myself that I didn't always have to do everything he said. I was terrified at what he might do if he found out, but I hated him so much I did it anyway. After I took the pictures of the others, I used a separate roll of film and took several shots of Alex with the man I didn't know. Then I hid that roll of film until I got back home and had it developed.

"I discovered later that I could have saved myself all that worry and trouble. It wasn't that Alex trusted me—at least not in the way I define trust—but he was so sure I wouldn't do anything to cross him that he let me take all the film to be processed. When the prints were made, I ordered an extra set for myself, which is how I obtained the photos accompanying these tapes. At the time, I didn't have the slightest idea who the stranger in the pictures was or why I bothered to be so secretive, but something told me they might come in handy sometime. I didn't realize until the day President Kennedy was shot that the other man in Mexico was Lee Harvey Oswald.

"I spent the night of November 21, 1963, at Alex's house in North Dallas. Since he was working the day shift, he got up early the next morning and left me in bed. He thought I was asleep, but I heard him leaving the house and ran to the bathroom, where I could look out the window and see the driveway and the garage. I watched him bring a rifle out the back door of the house and put it in the trunk of his unmarked police car. It looked a lot like the rifle I had seen Alex and Oswald and the others looking at in Mexico, but I'm no firearms expert, so I can't be sure. Anyway, I remember wondering what Alex was doing with a rifle. He always carried a pistol, as all Dallas police were required to do, off-duty or on, but I'd never known him to have a rifle in his car.

"About five hours later, the President was killed, and the moment I first saw Oswald on TV, I panicked. From then on, I was sure Alex was involved in the assassination, but I didn't know how or why. By this time, I also sensed something strange and really sinister about the man who called himself Alex Sutton, and I wasn't sure that was actually his name at all. Sometimes, strange people would come to his apartment in the middle of the night. Once in a while, he would make me sit in the car while he met somebody in some out-of-the-way place after dark. When this happened, Alex and the other person would take small objects out of their pockets and exchange them back and forth.

"Another scary thing that Alex did was hypnotize people. At least I guess that's what it was. He had the most penetrating eyes I ever saw. Sometimes they could bore holes right through you. Other times, they were like magnets. I mean they could catch and hold another person's eyes so tightly the person couldn't look away. Alex did it to me dozens of times, and he did it to other people, too. He once bragged to me that he could make my boss, Jack Ruby, buy drinks for every customer in the Carousel on a Saturday night, even though everybody knew how tight Jack was with money. And Alex did it, too. I never understood how he did it, but it had to be with some kind of hypnosis or post-hypnotic suggestion.

"He called Jack over to the table where a bunch of us were sitting and said, 'Hey, Jack, what do you hear from Chicago?'

"Jack just looked kind of blank for a minute. Then he waved a couple of the waitresses over and told them, 'Give everybody a drink on the house—whatever they want. It's on me.'

"Alex just looked at me and winked. I couldn't believe it, and I still can't explain it. The only thing I could figure out was it must have had something to do with the word 'Chicago.'

"Two or three times, I also heard Alex talking in his sleep in a foreign language. I didn't have any idea what language it was, only that it was something I'd never heard before. It wasn't any kind of Latin language like Spanish or French, and I didn't think it was German, either. There was a Russian guy in my dance class at SMU, and one day I asked him to say something in Russian. When he did, I was pretty sure that was the language Alex had been using in his sleep.

"I'd had the pictures I took secretly in Mexico processed right after we got back. Hollie's boyfriend, Jamie Cade, worked for the *Dallas Times Herald*, and he took them down to the paper and got someone in the photo lab to make eight-by-ten prints of them for me free. The day after Kennedy was killed, I took one of the pictures to Jack and told him I was afraid Alex was mixed up in the assassination somehow. Lots of people said Ruby was sleazy, immoral and crooked, but to me he was always a decent sort of guy. He was good to the girls who worked for him, and he was about the only person in Dallas except for Hollie that I felt like I could trust. But when I showed him the picture, Jack got madder than I'd ever seen him—not at Alex for buddying around with Lee Harvey Oswald, but at me. He called the picture a damned fake and grabbed it out of my hand and tore it in half. I tried to tell him I knew it wasn't a fake, because I'd taken it myself, but he wouldn't listen.

"After that, the panic just got worse and worse, and when I heard the next day that Jack had shot Oswald, I almost went crazy. In my mind, I just knew Alex had made Jack do it somehow, by hypnotizing him or brainwashing him or something. I was deathly afraid Jack might have told Alex something about the picture, too. I didn't have any doubt that Alex would kill me if he ever found out about that.

"That same afternoon I decided to leave Dallas for good. I asked Hollie to go someplace with me and spend the night. I told her I had to get out of town and begged her not to ever let Alex know where I was, but I didn't tell her about all the other stuff because I was afraid I'd only get her in trouble. I don't know whether it was because of me or because of something Jamie Cade did, but Hollie got in trouble anyway. Less than a year later, she and Jamie were both killed, and I knew Alex was responsible. I knew it in my heart, but there was no way to prove it, of course.

"For several months, I blamed myself and wished I could have died in Hollie's place. But then I got to thinking that God must have left me alive for some special reason. I finally came to the conclusion that my purpose in life must be to get even with Alex Sutton, to punish him somehow for what he did to us, and for what he did to so many other people. So that's what I decided to do, no matter how long it took . . ."

CHAPTER SEVENTEEN

November 3, 1987

He and Jamie were sitting in the TV Bar on Elm Street, just like in the good old days, and Jamie was grinning at him over the rim of one of those giant beer steins.

"It's about time to go to Dallas, old cowchip," Jamie was saying.

"But Jamie," Matt heard his own voice protesting. "We're *in* Dallas."

"No, we're not in Dallas, old cowchip," Jamie said. "We're in a fucking mess of trouble, that's where we are. Why don't we go over to Jack Ruby's and see what kind of corpses we can find in the closets? Ha-ha-ha!"

Suddenly, Jamie's grin became a grimace of pain. His eyes bugged out, and his face turned black. Then his flesh rotted and fell away, and Matt was staring at a bleached white skull across the table. Suddenly, Hollie and Mollie were sitting on either side of the skeletal Jamie. Their eyes were glazed and sightless, their hair bloody and matted, their faces gray masses of dead, torn flesh. But they were wearing their cheerleader sweaters and singing:

> "The eyes of Texas are upon youuu . . .
> All the livelong dayyy . . ."

Matt woke up screaming on a sweat-soaked sheet in the predawn darkness of a Tuesday morning, clawing at the apparitions in the air around him.

And even after Sarah took him in her arms and drew him close to her, as a mother might hold a frightened child, his body continued to shake—not so much from the vivid horror of the nightmare, but from the real life trauma that he knew lay ahead.

About noon that day, Matt accepted the inevitable scenario into which the locker key, the briefcase and the cassette recordings had inexorably drawn him over the past week or so. In all probability, he had actually accepted it a day or two earlier, but the bad dream had helped crystalize the acceptance in his mind. Thus, it was at this particular juncture, as he and Sarah were lunching on ham sandwiches in his small private office at *The Jeffersonian*, that he finally admitted the inescapable truth to himself.

He had to go to Dallas, try to get in touch with Tony Canales and maybe Sam Garrett, and see if there was any way to undo a twisting, tangled web of intrigue and deceit that spanned nearly a quarter of a century. It had reached the point where he had no other choice, and if he ended up facing criminal charges himself, then he would just have to deal with it when the time came.

So far, he and Sarah seemed to be in the clear on the incident in Little Rock. Sunday's edition of *The Gazette* had carried a short, superficial story about it on an inside page. It said that a man identified as Nicholas Trego, an import-export broker from Dallas, had been hospitalized with a fractured skull and severe concussion after being pistol-whipped in an altercation with another man and a woman at the bus station on Saturday. One witness was quoted briefly to the effect that the fight seemed to be over a briefcase the woman was carrying. The story said police had questioned a cab-driver who had driven the two suspects from the bus station to the Sheraton Inn. The driver denied seeing any getaway car and the suspects were described only as a white woman between 25 and 30 with long dark hair and a brown-haired white man of medium height and build in his mid-40s, both wearing jeans and jackets.

An even shorter story in Monday's edition said the injured man had regained consciousness and his condition had been upgraded from critical to serious. He told police he had no idea who the suspects were or why they attacked him, which came as no surprise to Matt. He knew the last thing this character wanted was to see Matt and Sarah—and maybe the briefcase, too—safely tucked away in police custody.

"I think it's time I took a little trip west and got this nasty business laid to rest once and for all," he said, washing a last bite of sandwich down with a swig of Dr. Pepper. "Do you think you can manage things around here without me for a few days?"

"No," she said bluntly, "absolutely not. You and I are in this together, Matthew. In fact, you wouldn't be in it nearly so deep if it weren't for me, and if you think you're going to Dallas without me, lover, you'd better just think again."

He wasn't surprised. He had expected her to react this way, and his plan called for appealing to her sense of responsibility. "But, Sarah," he said, "somebody's got to put out the paper. We can't both just walk off and leave it. I was counting on you to keep it functioning while I'm gone."

She smiled slyly. "I'm way ahead of you, Matthew," she said. "I knew this was coming, and I started getting ready for it first thing yesterday morning."

"What do you mean?"

"I mean I've got all the stories written for this week's paper, and I've got Blanche Abercrombie, who used to work for the paper at Warren, lined up to finish the paste-ups and take them to the printer's. Julie Bliss's mother is going to watch the front desk until Julie gets out of school in the afternoons. There's no reason why we can't both take the rest of the week off."

"But this could take more than a week," he said lamely, knowing she had outflanked him.

"If it does, we'll just have to cross that bridge when we come to it," she said.

"Look, Sarah, I don't want to see you dragged any deeper into this shit."

She arched her eyebrows, and her eyes were wide behind her glasses, her usually soft mouth set in a firm line. "Don't be bullheaded, Matthew," she said bullheadedly. "I'm going with you, and that's final. One of these days, I'm going to help you write this story, and I want to be there to see the rest of it happen. Besides, I've never even been to Dallas, and I want to check it out." The firm line dissolved into an impish smile. "After all, I might want to look for a job there sometime."

"You'd better be kidding," he threatened, "or you bloody well will stay here."

She was still smiling when she came over and kissed him. "The simple truth is, I don't want to let you out of my sight for a minute," she said. "I love you, damn it, and I don't want anything to happen to you—not unless it happens to me, too. I can't stand to think about you going into this thing all alone. Even you can use an ally, for God's sake."

At that point, he officially capitulated. He was out of excuses anyway, and on the rare occasions when Sarah was moved to profanity, however mild it might be, he knew there was no point arguing with her. Her mind was made up.

"All right," he said, "but if I can make contact with Tony Canales and set up something for tomorrow, be ready to leave this afternoon."

Her smile widened into a grin. "I'm ready right this minute," she said. "I've been packed since yesterday."

By 5 p.m., they had turned *The Jeffersonian* over to Blanche Abercrombie, who agreed to put the paper out and mind the store for the rest of the week for $90, loaded a couple of suitcases, two sleeping bags and an ice chest into the convertible, left a sad-eyed Hobo in a kennel in town, and were driving north on Highway 81 toward Star City. For expense money, Matt took along the slightly more than $550 in cash he had removed from the bodies of the two hitmen. It seemed ironically fitting that those two should posthumously finance a trip to Dallas for a showdown with whomever hired them.

With no unforeseen delays, a three-and-a-half-hour drive would put them in Texarkana for the night, where they would be over halfway to Dallas. On Wednesday morning, they would put the convertible in storage and rent a car for the drive to Greenville, Texas, about 45 miles east of Dallas, where a stunned Tony Canales had agreed to meet them. After that, Matt's plans were less clearly defined, but at some point on the trip, he did intend to go back to his family's old farm in Kaufman County and try to locate the plastic box he had buried there.

Talking to Tony earlier that afternoon had been a little spooky, kind of exciting—and almost, but not quite, fun in spots. When he had first placed the call to Dallas police headquarters, Matt was concerned that Tony might not even work there anymore. If he didn't, Matt had no idea who to confide in, much less get to listen to his bizarre story, but he quickly discovered he had nothing to worry about on that score. Tony Canales was not only still very much a part of the DPD; he had also risen through the ranks to become one of its top-level administrators.

"I'm trying to reach Antonio Canales," Matt told the switchboard operator. "He used to be in the homicide bureau, but I'm not sure where he is now."

"One moment please," she said, not volunteering any information.

There was a long pause, followed by a series of metallic clicks. He thought he was about to be disconnected, but then he heard another female voice on the line.

"Deputy Chief Canales's office. May I help you?"

Holy Christ, Matt thought, Tony was a deputy chief? The kid from Little Mexico had really come up in the world since the last time they had seen each other. "Yes," he said, "is, uh, Chief Canales in?"

"Could I tell him who's calling?"

"Just say it's got something to do with the Jamie Cade-Hollie O'Connor murder case back in 1964. Tell him it's a hundred percent on the level and very, very urgent."

For about 30 seconds, there was only dead silence. Then he heard Tony's unmistakable voice—the flawless English flavored with the faintest trace of comino and chili pepper. His tone was guarded and slightly bemused.

"This is Canales. What can I do for you?"

Matt felt a little breathless. "Hello, Tony, this is Matt Eastman," he began, "and I'm hoping you might be able to save my life."

The next few minutes made Matt appreciate what Mollie must have gone through the day she had called him so suddenly out of the blue. In the beginning, Tony obviously thought the call was some kind of sick joke, but after three or four minutes, Matt managed to convince him that he was really who he claimed to be. Even after that, it took Tony a while to get over the shock of talking to someone he had given up for dead 18 years ago, but when Matt asked him to meet them the next day at the Holiday Inn in Greenville, his old friend didn't disappoint him. As an incentive, Matt told him he would share a briefcase full of evidence that might help clear a half-dozen murders in Dallas and otherwise make the drive worthwhile. There were other items, Matt added, that the FBI, and possibly even the CIA, might be extremely interested in, but he declined to be more specific than that on the phone. Finally, he elicited Tony's solemn promise to come alone and not tell anybody else where he was going.

"Okay, I'll be there, Matthew," he said. "I figure I owe you that much for old times' sake, amigo. You be careful on the way."

"You do the same," Matt said warily. "By the way, does good old Alex Sutton still work there?"

"Fortunately, no," Tony said. "He was invited to leave about eight years ago."

"That's good to know," Matt said. "I've got some really interesting material to show you about good old Alex. Do you think your phone's safe? I mean, it couldn't be tapped, could it?"

"Por dios!" Tony said. "I hope not."

"So do I," Matt told him, "but if we both make it to

Greenville in one piece tomorrow, I guess we can assume it's not.''

It was practically dark by the time they passed through Malvern and turned onto Interstate 30. From here on, there would be no more of the stops, starts and infernal slowdowns that had characterized the first part of the trip, so Matt set the Mustang's speedometer on 65 and settled into the endless stream of headlights and taillights plowing through the night toward the state line. Meanwhile, Sarah laid her head in his lap and went sound asleep.

. The scenery on this stretch of road was uninspiring enough even in the daytime, and at night there was absolutely nothing of interest to see, so Matt switched on the radio, found a station with decent C&W music, fixed his eyes on the monotonous highway, and lost himself in thought.

It had been nearly two and half days since they had played the tapes from the briefcase, but the tortured sound of Mollie's voice still echoed hauntingly in his ear. Sometimes he thought he would be able to hear it crying out to him from beyond infinity for as long as he lived.

She told how she had wandered all over the western half of the country during the first 15 or 16 months after her flight from Dallas. She had worked at waitress or sales clerk jobs or whatever else she could find, always afraid to stay in one place more than a few weeks, especially after Hollie's death. In March 1965, she had ventured as close to home as El Paso, where she picked up a newspaper one morning and, quite by accident, happened to see a story about Angel Garcia's murder.

"I remembered Angel from the trip to Mexico with Alex and Dee Conlan and Tom Van Zandt," she said. "I knew she'd been Dee's regular girlfriend for a good while, but I also knew that Dee could never be faithful to any one woman. He just wasn't built that way, and when Angel wasn't looking, he'd made more than one pass at me over the time I'd known him.

"On an impulse, I decided to call Dee. I was desperate by this time and didn't know what to do next. I thought if Dee was still interested in me, he might help me get out of the country, or at least someplace where I could feel safe for a while. In one way, the idea of calling him scared me silly, because I knew Alex worked for him and they were pretty close, but I also knew they weren't really friends. The truth was, Alex considered Dee an absolute fool, just somebody to take advantage of, and he'd told me so a hundred times. 'I'm playing this rich moron like a Stradivarius,' Alex used to say, 'and he's too damned simple-minded to know what's going on.'

"Dee really wasn't very bright. Alex was right about that. I'm sure now that he was mildly retarded. That's how Alex and Tom Van Zandt were able to use him and manipulate him and eventually steal his company right out from under him. Dee was literally like a twelve-year-old boy. He had no self-control and was totally ruled by his senses. He had the money to buy whatever he wanted, at least he did for a long time, and he lived a life of total excess. If he liked something, he just couldn't get enough of it—whether it was sex or drugs or liquor or food or whatever.

"To Dee, if one woman was good, ten women were better. He used to pay Jack Ruby just to introduce him to girls. That was how he got hooked up with Angel Garcia in the first place. He thought nothing of picking up three or four show-girls or cocktail waitresses and paying them a thousand apiece to go to bed with him, all at the same time. He thought if normal sex was good, then the kinky, weirdo kind had to be even better. It was the same with drugs and booze. If he was high on cocaine, he always thought there ought to be a way to get higher. He almost killed himself a dozen times by over-dosing, until he finally got it through his head that he had to set some kind of limits.

"On the other hand, Dee could be as sweet and gentle and loving as any man I ever knew, if you handled him right, and fortunately I discovered how to handle him pretty fast. To make a long story short, he was, to say the least, very receptive when I called him. He wired me a thousand and told me to fly to Mexico City. Three days later, he met me there, and that was the beginning of a relationship that lasted over eighteen years. I was Dee's mistress, although I never kidded myself that I was the only one, and I did just about whatever he wanted to do sexually. In return, he gave me a comfortable life and protected me. I told him straight out that if he ever let Alex know where I was, Alex would kill me, and Dee never breathed a word. That was probably the only thing in his whole life that Dee was careful about, but he kept the secret right up until Alex and Tom Van Zandt killed him.''

With Dee Conlan's often unwitting help, Mollie had collected the letters and other papers in the briefcase over a period of many years. They told, in graphic detail, the day-by-day, week-by-week story of how Tommy Van Zandt and Alex Sutton gradually took control of Conlan Universal Aerospace through legal subterfuge, threats and blackmail.

''What really broke my heart,'' Mollie said, ''was that they were using the pictures I took in Mexico to blackmail Dee into signing over huge blocks of CUA stock to them. Dee hadn't known Lee Harvey Oswald from Adam when they met him in Monterrey, and he stayed so stoned and drunk most of the time that he didn't even remember what he was doing. He was just having a good time and that was all he cared about.''

Under Mollie's guidance, Conlan had managed over the years to get his hands on several documents that were highly incriminating to Sutton and Van Zandt. Mollie had realized the futility of trying to explain the significance of the documents to Conlan, but she had kept them and added them to her collection. A few of them struck very close to home with Matt. There was, for instance, a handwritten note which said:

''Alex—

   I've made the overture to Eastman about the P.R. job, and, as expected, he turned it down flat. It looks like we'll have to go to another plan of action on this.

   I hope you're taking care of the Lisa Feagan matter, as promised. She's much too dangerous to be walking around loose. If the feds should start digging into her allegations about C's tomfoolery, there's no telling what else they're liable to come up with.

                                                     T.V.Z.

The note was dated 9/24/69, and although Matt could no longer be sure of the exact date of Lisa Feagan's fatal "accident," he was certain it had taken place within a day or two of the time this note was written. That was one of many things he wanted Tony Canales to check out.

It had also been Conlan who reminded Mollie of something she had heard previously, but forgotten—that Alex Sutton claimed to be from Van Wert, Ohio. Mollie had originally gone there out of curiosity, simply to dig up any information she could about Alex's early life, and she had stumbled onto Alex's ex-fiancée Mary Cockrell in the process.

Although Mollie's collection provided near-proof that Sutton and Van Zandt were blackmailers, racketeers, conspirators in the Kennedy assassination—and, in all likelihood, mass murderers, too—Matt doubted that her evidence would support her final charge against them. Mollie was certain they had murdered Conlan in late 1984 by administering some type of sophisticated drug whose effects mimicked the symptoms of a heart attack. Knowing everything else they had done, the charge was probably true, Matt thought, but with the kind of life Dee Conlan had led, he would have been a prime candidate for a heart attack, even though he was only 53 when he died. It would take an exhumation and an autopsy, at least, to prove the cause of death was something else, but maybe Tony could arrange that, too.

God knows, Alex and Tommy had every kind of rationale for getting rid of Conlan by that time. They had already syphoned off most of his corporate wealth, and, as Mollie's evidence indicated, gained virtually full control of CUA, so he was of no further use to them. Because of his profligate lifestyle, Conlan also could have been the kiss of death for Tommy's political aspirations. And, finally, retarded though he may have been, Dee had still been the only living witness—outside of Mollie herself—to the meeting with Oswald in Mexico. If he had ever been hauled into court for anything, the whole sordid story could have come pouring out. That had to be why Tommy went to such lengths to keep the series on Dee from being published in the *Times Herald* back in '69.

As Mollie had put it: "Dee wasn't very bright, but he was smart enough to know that Alex and Tom Van Zandt engineered the Kennedy assassination and implicated him in it. He knew what they were doing to him, but he just couldn't stop them and I couldn't either.

"It's my personal belief that Alex used Oswald the same way he used Dee, the same way he used Jack Ruby, and the same way he used me. I've never understood what his exact purpose was, but I think he picked out Oswald as a tailor-made fall guy in the Kennedy assassination, somebody who was so obvious he couldn't possibly be overlooked. I don't think he trusted Oswald to do the job alone, though.

"To make certain there were no slip-ups, I think Alex decided there had to be two assassins in Dealey Plaza on November 22, 1963. And I believe with all my heart and soul that Alex Sutton was that other assassin . . ."

Halfway across the State of Arkansas, Matt kept replaying the tapes in his mind. Occasionally, Sarah stirred and mumbled something to him, but by the time they got to Hope, she was still dozing, and eventually he forced himself to turn his thoughts to other things.

He was finally going home again, back to a place that no longer seemed like home at all. In all the years since he had run away to hide, he had been back only three times on furtive, flying trips to visit his mother in a nursing home in Kaufman, and the last one of those had been in late 1979. He wasn't sure if anyone had told her he was dead or missing, and her mind had been failing so badly by then that she may have thought his visits were only a dream. She seemed to enjoy them in a vague kind of way, but she cried each time he told her he had to leave, and although he suspected she did the same thing whenever anyone told her that, her tears almost tore him apart.

He had called at least once a month to check on her, always identifying himself merely as a family friend, and he also sent her a cashier's check for $50 or $100 now and then. In June 1980, the woman who answered the phone at the nursing home told him she had died about a week earlier. The news affected him much worse than he had thought it would.

The door between them had been almost shut for a long time, but now it was closed completely and he felt stabbing twinges of guilt for not having been a better, more attentive son. Missing the funeral wasn't that important, though, he told himself. Even if he had known in time, he wouldn't have dared to go, and even if he had gone, it would have been too late to do anything meaningful.

To soothe his conscience a little, he sent his sister a cashier's check for $2,000 and an anonymous note asking her to use it to help pay for the funeral and a headstone. The check had a phony name on it—and even phonier name than David East—but he figured his sister probably knew who sent it anyway.

Now, 18 years after he had last thought of himself as part of it, he was heading back to a place that had become fearful and alien to him. He knew that Dallas would be vastly different from the city it had been in the 60s, or even the one he had seen on his last overnight trip there in '79. The outward changes were of no concern to him, but because of all the unpleasant memories that his impending return stirred up in his mind, going back was like plunging into some kind of deep psychological abyss.

For some reason, though, he didn't feel so negative about seeing the old family farm again. In fact, he felt enthusiastic, almost excited at the prospect. He hoped nobody was living there, not just because he had some digging to do in the pasture behind the house, but because he thought he would really enjoy poking around the place again after all this time, maybe even rediscovering some of his favorite boyhood places and showing them to Sarah. If everything went well, he thought they might even end up staying there for a day or two. That was the main reason he had brought along the sleeping bags.

Beyond that, the farm also figured into a plan that had been slowly taking shape in his mind ever since he had made the decision to go back. The more he thought about the plan, the more he liked it, but he still wasn't sure if it would work or not.

A green and white sign flashed past the car that said

"Texarkana, next 7 exits" just as Sarah finally roused herself and sat up, rubbing her eyes and yawning.

"Well, welcome back," he said. "I wondered if I was going to have to carry you in when we got to the motel."

She laughed groggily. "I didn't mean to desert you like that," she said. "I thought I was just shutting my eyes for a few minutes, but then I absolutely died. Where are we?"

"About a mile from Texarkana," he said, "and getting closer to trouble all the time."

CHAPTER EIGHTEEN

November 4, 1987

Although he was 46 years old, had put two children through college, and was due to be a grandfather early next year, Deputy Police Chief Antonio Canales still bore certain telltale traces of the dapper young detective who had prowled the nighttime streets of East Dallas in the 1960s. There were streaks of gray at his temples and an extra inch or so around his waistline, but the younger women still gave him the eye sometimes. Maybe he was a half-step slower and a few pounds heavier, and maybe he did have to wear glasses to read things up close, but other than that, he liked to tell himself nothing had changed. Most of the time, he could make himself believe it, but not today. Today he was feeling every one of those mounting years, gray hairs, added inches and excess pounds.

He had been at work since before 9 o'clock that morning, taken only a 15 minute break for a sandwich at lunchtime, and still had to leave a pile of unfinished business on his desk to make the hour-long drive to Greenville. Now it was pushing 8 o'clock in the evening and Tony Canales was tired, hungry and slightly muddleheaded from everything he had seen and heard over the last four hours. And he still faced a long haul back to his house in Lake Highlands and his wife, Christina, the only woman he had ever loved.

If it had been anybody but Matt Eastman, he probably would never have agreed to the meeting in Greenville at all. If anybody else had called him up with some wild story about a briefcase full of evidence implicating a former veteran police officer and the leading candidate for the Texas governorship in everything from extortion to serial murders to conspiracy to assassinate the President of the United States, he would have been hard to sell. "Hey, man," he might have responded, "if it's such hot stuff, why don't you just bring it on down to my office? I don't make out-of-town house calls anymore."

But it had been Matt Eastman, his long-lost friend—the same Matt Eastman whose bloodstained car he had examined one night in 1969 in Samuell-Grand Park, and whom he hadn't seen or heard from since. A year or two later, Tony had come to the reluctant conclusion that Matt was really dead, although officially he had remained listed only as a missing person.

Tony had looked forward to their reunion with an odd mixture of nervousness and anticipation. He knew from what Matt had told him on the phone that much of the evidence pertained to Alex Sutton, and the subject of Alex Sutton always made Tony Canales a trifle edgy. Between his stint in the homicide bureau, where he had first learned to distrust Sutton, and his appointment as deputy chief two years ago, Tony had headed up both the criminal intelligence and internal affairs divisions of the DPD. In this process, he had developed a consuming, almost insatiable interest in the incredible career of Lieutenant (later Captain) Alexander Sutton. Ironically, this interest had been born out of Tony's conversations with Matt Eastman some 20 years in the past, and now, it seemed, matters had come full circle.

That was another reason—perhaps the primary reason—why he had been willing to come all this way to sit for four hours in a motel room with a man he had assumed dead until yesterday and an attractive young woman he had never seen before, while they barraged him with a tidal wave of information. As expected, much of the information did, indeed, relate to Alex Sutton, and it ranged from intriguing to downright devastating. Some of it tied in very neatly with what Tony had already learned during his own lengthy investigations into Sutton's activities, but it went far beyond that, too.

Tony's investigations had led, at least in part, to Sutton's forced resignation from the force eight years ago. Tony had always hoped it would lead to something much more serious, but conflict of interest was the only thing he had been able to make stick. What he really wanted, at the very least, was to see criminal charges brought against Sutton for obstruction of justice, intimidation of witnesses and official malfeasance. He wanted that because Sutton was a scumbag, a *cabron*, a liar and a conniver, who had enriched himself at the public's expense. He was a discredit to the whole law enforcement profession, and now it looked as if he were a whole lot more. If what he had just been shown was true, Sutton was not only a protector of hired killers, porno dealers and drug smugglers; he was quite likely a murderer, to boot. Tired as he was, Tony was glad he had made the trip.

"This is strong stuff, Matthew. No doubt about it," Tony said, taking out his handkerchief and wiping first his glasses, then his face with it. "I'd give a hundred-dollar bill to see Alex Sutton's reaction to what you've got here."

"My fondest hope is that you get to see the bastard's reaction for free, Tony," Matt said. "but the question now is, where do we go from here? How do you think we ought to proceed on this thing? How fast can you move?"

"Well, we've got a pretty complex situation here," Tony said. "There's a lot of possibilities, but a lot of loose ends, too. It's not going to be as simple as just going out and arresting Tom Van Zandt and Alex Sutton. I wish it was, but it's not—especially not with Van Zandt. He's one of the wealthiest, most powerful people in Texas, and he's got lots of friends in high political places, both in Austin and Washington. The last thing we want to do is go off half-cocked."

"I can buy that," Matt said, "but how soon can you get something started?"

"One of the first things I want to do is brief some of our other top people in the department and show them what you've got," Tony said. "Then we'll start the legal machinery moving. We'll have to get the DA's office involved, and I think we ought to bring in the FBI just as quick as we can. Anything that relates back to the Kennedy assassination is federal stuff, and they'll be the ones to handle the case. I've got a very solid relationship with the special agent in charge of their Dallas office."

"Have you told anybody else about this, Mr. Canales?" the girl named Sarah asked. "Does anybody else know who you were meeting or where you were going? I mean anybody at all?"

Tony flashed her his best Latin lover smile. Sarah Archer looked young enough to be Matt Eastman's daughter, but that was far from the situation. Matt was registered at the motel as David East, and this was obviously "Mrs. East."

"No, ma'am, not a soul," he said. "All I told my secretary was I had some business to attend to. Even my wife doesn't know where I am—and that's unusual, I assure you."

This Sarah was quite a dish, too, he thought as she smiled back at him—not quite as sexy as Angel Garcia, maybe, but certainly enough to wear out any two guys Matt Eastman's age. Hey, cut that out, he admonished himself; you're too tired for ideas like that. Besides, Christina would kill him if she knew what he was thinking.

"That's good, Tony," Matt said, "because I've got an idea. I know we're keeping you late, but I'd like to tell you about it—if you've got time."

"Sure," he said, looking at his watch. It was 8:15, and the way things were going, it was going to be 9:30 or 10 by the time he got home.

"Why don't you have a beer, Mr. Canales?" Sarah offered. "You can consider yourself off-duty by now, can't you?"

She was halfway to the ice chest in the corner of the room before he could protest, so he smiled again and shrugged.

"Well, maybe just one," he said. "I got a long drive ahead, and I sure wouldn't want to get busted for DWI."

He loosened his tie and took a sip from the cold can of Lite she handed him. He had never been much of a drinker, but in the length of time it took the beer to travel from his lips to his stomach, he felt a little better. "Okay, what's this idea of yours, Matthew?" he asked.

"First off, there's something you need to know," Matt said. "At least three people have already been killed over this damned briefcase in the past week and a half. One of them was Mollie O'Connor, the girl on the tapes. The others were a couple of hired guns who killed Mollie and then came after me. If all that hadn't happened, I wouldn't be here in the first place."

Tony took a large gulp of his beer. "What happened to these guys who came after you?" he asked.

"One of them did me the favor of poisoning himself, and I shot the other one in the head in self-defense. Before that happened, one of them was kind enough to tell me that they were the same ones who blew my wife and child to bits in Illinois four years ago. They'd been real broken up when they learned I was out of town at the time. Maybe you can imagine how sad I was to see them die."

"Mother of God, Matthew, I'm sorry," Tony said, shaking his head. "It sounds like you've been living in the middle of a regular little war."

"You could say that," Matt said. "I also fractured some other guy's skull in Little Rock last weekend when he tried to keep Sarah and me from getting the briefcase. He's using the name Nicholas Trego, and he's supposedly an import-export broker from Dallas. Personally, I think he's something else entirely, but he's still in the hospital over there, so you can check it out."

Tony took a small notebook out of his inside coat pocket and wrote the name down. "I'll do it first thing tomorrow," he said. "We can get Little Rock PD to hold the guy for investigation if we have to. Do you think this Trego was in with the first two?"

"I don't know," Matt said. "All I know is they dressed

similarly and were all packing heavy heat." He went over and pulled a long-barreled .357 Magnum out of a suitcase. "Like this," he said.

Tony whistled softly between his teeth. "With that kind of cannon," he said, "I guarantee they weren't out hunting quail."

"This is why we had to be so bloody careful about setting up this meeting," Matt said. "It's also why I'd rather you didn't risk taking any of this stuff back to Dallas with you tonight. Somebody wants this briefcase awful damned bad, so maybe you ought to send a couple of squads for it when the time comes. Meanwhile, I'm hoping you'll give me a couple of days to see if we can use it to bait a trap."

"I don't think I follow you," Tony said, "but I know I don't like the sound of this. What kind of trap?"

"Outside of the three of us, nobody knows we're here or what we have in this briefcase—not a living soul—right?"

"Absolutely right. I told you."

"I don't want you to come totally unglued when you hear this, Tony," Matt said, "but what if I were to send Tommy Van Zandt copies of a few of the choicest tidbits in this collection? What if I told him the whole thing was for sale for, say, five hundred thousand dollars and invited him to meet me at some out-of-the-way place to finalize the transaction? What kind of response do you think that might get from our boy Tommy?"

Tony finished off his beer and set the empty can down on the table with a loud bang. "I don't know, but I think you'd have to be crazy as a jaybird to try it," he said. "Come on, Matt, you know I can't have any part in something like that. Let's do this the right way, okay?"

"But listen, Tony, I've thought the whole thing out, and it's worth a shot," Matt insisted. "Otherwise, we're probably looking at months of legal maneuvering and a good chance Alex and Tommy could slip away somehow. If they find out what's happening before you and the DA and the FBI can make a move, they may be out of the country and gone. And I'm not interested in just spoiling Tommy's election campaign or costing him and Alex a few million bucks. I want to see those two bastards really hung out to dry. You understand?"

Tony sighed. "Sure, I understand that," he said. "What I don't understand is how you figure something like this is going to accomplish that. I think you'd be playing with dynamite, and you just might get yourself blown away."

"Look," Matt said, "I'd as soon cut my own throat as try something like this with Alex Sutton, because he's mean as a snake and twice as shifty. At this point, I don't know what else he may be, but I'm convinced he's a killer—as ruthless, calculating and cold-blooded a killer as they come. But I think Tommy Van Zandt's a whole different ballgame, and that's what I'm counting on."

"How do you mean?"

"First of all, Tommy's got an ego about the size of Texas Stadium," Matt said. "He wants power and recognition as bad as anybody I ever knew, and even without criminal charges, if this stuff gets out in the press, he's dead politically for all time to come. Secondly, Tommy's a businessman. With him, everything has a price. He tried to buy my cooperation once before a long time ago by offering me a high-paying, do-nothing job at CUA in return for not running a series of exposé stories on Dee Conlan. I think he's still got the same mentality, but this time I can make him incriminate the hell out of himself."

Tony still wasn't accepting Matt's line of reasoning completely, but he had to admit it was an interesting concept—interesting, but very, very risky. It was the kind of thing a deputy chief of police could never, ever sanction—not officially, anyway. "Do you think I could have one more beer, Sarah," he asked, bending his empty can between his fingers.

"Since nobody else knows we're here or what we have, it's a totally controlled scenario," Matt said. "If we get any response at all, it's got to be coming from Tommy, because he's the only one who knows. And if he does respond, it's a clear indication of guilt. Doesn't that make sense?"

"Maybe, but what if he doesn't respond?"

"Then the plan fails. It's that simple. If he doesn't take the bait, then we've got no choice but to go the longer, more complicated route and hope we can nail him and Alex in time. If he does take it, though, and you're there as a witness, it looks to me like we've got him by the you-know-what.''

"If he did respond, how do you think he'd do it?''

"I figure he'll either come in person with a sackful of money, or he'll send a bunch of guys with guns,'' Matt said, "or maybe both.''

"Even if I agreed to this—which I definitely haven't, by the way—we'd need at least a dozen guys from the tactical squad to cover an operation like this.''

"No, Tony,'' Matt said fiercely. "No way. You start bringing a lot of other cops into this, and you'll blow the whole deal. The only way this can work is if nobody knows about it but the three of us and Tommy, or somebody Tommy tells. Half the DPD would find out if you tried to get a tactical squad involved, and I'm not so sure Alex Sutton doesn't still have some friendly eyes and ears inside the department.''

Tony nodded grimly while he did some serious work on his second beer. He didn't feel nearly so tired anymore, but he did feel slightly tipsy. He would never be a beer drinker if he lived to be 100, he thought. Before he left Greenville, he'd probably have to stop for some coffee and something to eat to counteract the effects of the alcohol.

"You're right,'' he said. "That wouldn't surprise me at all. Since he became chief of security at CUA, Alex has hired dozens of cops away to work for him, and there's quite a few others still in the department who have part-time jobs out there.''

"Listen, I know you don't like the idea,'' Matt told him, "but if you'll go along with it, the whole thing can be done in two or three days. If it doesn't work, the only thing we can do is turn the evidence over to you and get out of the way. Sarah and I'll just have to go hide someplace and wait to see if the justice system can do anything with Sutton and Van Zandt.''

Tony shook his head. "Short of arresting you or confiscating the evidence, there's not much I can do to keep you from doing this, Matthew,'' he said, "but I just can't approve what you're suggesting. It's way too dangerous, and I could never take that kind of responsibility. Is that clear?''

"Sure," Matt said, "I wouldn't want you to."

"But as soon as you get the when and where established, you call me and I'll be there. I guess we can decide then if we need extra manpower, but I want to hear from you by Friday afternoon at the latest. Say no later than 2 o'clock, and I want your word on that.''

"You've got it," Matt said, "but I want your word on something, too. I want you to promise me you won't bring any other cops into this until then, okay?''

Tony sighed. "Okay," he said reluctantly, "I promise."

"Good. If everything works out right, I'm going to set up the rendezvous with Tommy at my parents' old farm near Kaufman. If we do it there, we can minimize the risk by keeping watch on the place from a distance while we wait for Tommy to make his move, just in case he decides to get violent. Would you do me one last favor on your way home tonight?''

Tony laughed. "I guess so," he said, finishing his second beer. "What's one more at this point?''

Matt went to a suitcase lying open on the dresser and removed two nine-by-twelve envelopes, one thin and the other fat and bulging. He handed them both to Tony.

"This is for Tommy Van Zandt," he said, indicating the thin envelope. "It's copies of two photos and two particularly incriminating memos. If you'll drop it in a mailbox after you get to Dallas, it'll get to him that much sooner." Tony took the envelope, noting that it was already stamped, addressed to Van Zandt at the CUA Executive Offices, and marked "Extremely Personal.''

"And this," Matt added, handing him the fat envelope, "is the ID on the two guys who came to my house to kill me. Their bodies were discovered last weekend in Monroe, Louisiana, if that's any help to you. Both names are probably aliases, but if you can find out who they really were, it might come in handy.''

"You didn't tell me anything about those two, either,''

Tony said. "If anybody asks, this stuff came through the mail with no return address. But, yeah, I'll run it through the computer and see what happens."

Matt stood up and stuck out his hand.

"I can't tell you how uneasy I am about this whole thing, amigo," Tony replied, shaking Matt's hand firmly. "I'll be waiting to hear from you. Be careful."

"You, too," Matt said.

Tony paused on his way out the door. He winked at the girl named Sarah. "Goodnight, Mrs. East," he said.

On his way to the car, the tiredness started coming back. His stomach was churning, partly from hunger and partly from a gut-wrenching feeling of dread that he couldn't shake.

Tony looked at his watch when he got to the car and saw that it was past 9 o'clock. He decided not to stop for anything to eat, after all, because he didn't have time. In spite of the lateness of the hour, and the fact that he knew Christina was going to be very unhappy, he knew he was going to have to go by the police station before he went home.

It wouldn't take the DPD photo lab more than five or ten minutes to make copies of the photos and memos in the envelope Matt had given him. Then, first thing tomorrow, he could put the copies in the hands of Special Agent Peter Benedict of the FBI. It wouldn't be as good as giving Benedict access to the whole briefcase, but it would at least give him a preview, a starting point. The evidence linking Van Zandt and Sutton to the Kennedy assassination was the strongest of the lot, and the sooner the federal machinery started to roll on that score, the better.

"You're breaking a promise," a small, insinuating voice inside his head told him. "You're violating a confidence."

No, I'm not, he told himself firmly. He had promised not to get any other Dallas cops involved in this; he hadn't said a word about the FBI. Besides, Matt wasn't leaving him any choice.

So maybe it *was* a little bit underhanded, maybe even slightly dishonest, but this thing Matt had hit him with was much too big, much too important to sit on, even for two or three days while Matt played this little game he wanted to play. Tony Canales wanted Alex Sutton's hide every bit as much as Matt Eastman did, even if he didn't have as much of a personal stake in the matter, and he was convinced that Pete Benedict could help him get it.

Matt would thank him later for what he was doing. In the meantime, he told himself resolutely, what Matt didn't know wouldn't hurt him.

CHAPTER NINETEEN

Actually, except for the overgrown yard and the leaning, straggling condition of the barbed wire fence out front, the old Eastman Place didn't look much different from the road than it had when Matt had last seen it. Until you got closer, you didn't notice the tattered screens, missing shingles, broken windows, peeling paint that had almost vanished in many places, and general wholesale rot that was quietly going on everywhere. It was only when you picked your way across the sagging front porch and peered past the warped and buckling front door into the dim, time-ravaged interior, that you knew the house wasn't long for this world.

Only the central part of the structure was still fairly well intact, enough so that at some recent point in time someone had used the living room to store hay. But there were no windows at all left in the rear, and part of the siding was falling off the back wall. The back portion of the roof had apparently been leaking for a long time, and the floor of what had been his parents' bedroom had fallen through in spots, and the rest of it was to the point of being hazardous to walk on. The musty smell of rotting wood also prevailed in the kitchen, where a patch of blue sky was visible through one corner of the ceiling.

Matt wasn't especially surprised by the condition of the place, just slightly chagrined.

"Hell, we can't stay in here," he said disgustedly, following their first cursory inspection of the remains. "We'll have to get a tent or sleep outside or go a motel in Kaufman. The house is just too far gone."

"Oh, I'm not so sure about that," Sarah said, continuing to prowl around the premises after he sat down in a relatively safe corner of the front porch and popped open a beer.

The drive from Greenville had taken longer than Matt expected. They had followed narrow, two-lane Highway 34 from Greenville down through Terrell and Kaufman, then veered back east on U.S. 175 to Kemp, and finally gone north on the farm-to-market road until they located the old oil-topped byway that led eventually to the house. Now it was pushing noon, and a tense weariness was hanging heavy in Matt's chest.

He had awakened that morning feeling shaky and uncertain about the trap he had so glibly proposed laying for Tommy Van Zandt during the meeting with Tony Canales the night before. In the cold, clear light of day, it seemed a lot less likely that anything positive could come of it than it had when he was touting it to Tony, and now it was Matt who was feeling trapped by the plan. Surely, Tommy was either too shrewd to fall for something so outlandish or too ruthless to let Matt get away with it—or maybe both. Still, if Tony had done as he said he would, the envelope was already on its way to Tommy, and sometime within the next 24 hours or so, Matt would have to summon up the courage to try to make telephone contact with him.

"I think we can manage this just fine," Sarah said, cutting through his negative thoughts, "if you don't mind driving back to town and picking up a few things."

"Are you serious?" he asked, pretty sure she was saying it just for his benefit. "I mean, we really don't have to stay here."

"Don't be silly," she said. "The living room looks dry and cozy. All we need is a broom to clean it up a little and some plastic to put over the broken windows, and we'll be fine. There's plenty of wood lying around for the fireplace and plenty of water in the well out back, and we've got our sleeping bags. I even found a few old pieces of furniture that may be usable. I think it'll be kind of fun."

Sarah was like some sort of miraculous tonic for him, he thought. He could actually feel her enthusiasm lifting his own sagging spirits.

"Okay," he said, "you asked for it."

They drove back to Kaufman and found a supermarket right on the highway where they could get everything they needed. Sarah's shopping list included a broom, two rolls of heavy-duty plastic film, some duct tape, a plastic pail and nylon cord for drawing water, another plastic pail for cleaning, a package of sponges, dishwashing liquid, soap, matches, candles, large plastic garbage bags, several rolls of paper towels, two small pans, plastic plates and cups, plastic knives and forks, a roll of aluminum foil, charcoal, charcoal lighter and a small portable barbecue grill. They also bought instant coffee, sandwich fixings, canned beans, chili, cheese, sirloin steak, baking potatoes, onions, tomatoes, orange juice, breakfast rolls, eggs and fresh fruit.

"Jesus Christ," Matt said as he loaded five large paper sacks filled with supplies into the back of the station wagon, "you must be planning to stay here permanently."

"I wouldn't mind," Sarah said cheerfully.

The following 18 hours or so proved to be a surprisingly pleasant interlude, even with the thought of what soon had to be done gnawing at the backs of their minds. It was hard work, but with his help, Sarah made the wreck of the house so almost-livable that he started to wonder if it might not be possible to salvage the old place yet. They swept out the living room thoroughly, starting with the cobwebs and dust on the walls and ceilings and working their way down to the hay and accumulated dirt on the floor. Sarah scrubbed the grime off a wobbly table in the kitchen, and Matt used a piece of flooring from the ruined back bedroom as a splint for its broken leg, binding it in place with duct tape. They found a wooden crate and a backless chair to complete their makeshift dinette, and then arranged their sleeping bags in an inside corner near the fireplace.

As the afternoon wore on, it became obvious that the night would be nippy, with a temperature likely to drop into the low 40s by morning, so they also set about weatherproofing their quarters as well as possible. They covered the broken windows with plastic film and secured it with duct tape, then taped garbage bags over the doorless doorway into the back of the house to cut off the chill wind that knifed through the gaping holes in the rear wall. Finally, once he managed to wedge and prop the front door shut and they got a fire going in the fireplace, it wasn't at all uncomfortable.

In a way, Matt was pretty sure he was using this tidying-up routine as a good excuse to postpone one of the main chores that had brought him back to the old farm in the first place. But as the sun was sinking low in the west and Sarah was deeply occupied with the finer points of setting up light housekeeping, he ventured back into the pasture behind the house to try to locate the plastic box he had buried there more than 21 years before. He had forgotten to bring anything along to dig with, but luckily he found a rusty spade with a broken handle at one corner of the tumbledown barn. Since he remembered burying the box only a few inches deep, he figured he could manage to dig it up with that—provided he could still find it after all this time.

The weeds were high in the pasture, so high that he even had trouble at first locating the old cistern he had used as a marker. Finally, though, he quite literally stumbled upon it—so literally, in fact, that he came close to falling into it. That would have been a hell of a way for things to end, he thought, almost amused at the idea. The brick sides of the cistern had been broken off almost to ground level, and a portion of the inside wall had collapsed, allowing dirt to wash in and partially fill the hole. It was no more than seven or eight feet deep now, with broken bricks and other debris at the bottom of it, and it was dry except for a puddle containing about a dishpanful of muddy water.

He stood with his back to the cistern, looking for the oak tree he had used as a visual reference point at the time of the burial. On that day in 1966, he had been in a hurry, doubtful that he would ever want to find the box again anyway, but determined to keep the directions simple in case he should. He had taken ten paces from the cistern directly toward the tree, which had been about 25 yards away and all by itself at the time. The problem now was that the pasture had become so overgrown with sprouts and small saplings that he couldn't even see the trunk of the oak from where he stood. So unless he wanted to take the time and trouble to chop down an entire young forest, he would have to guess at it.

He dug a half-dozen holes over the next hour without success. He dug until the sun had slipped out of sight behind the trees to the west, and rubbed a painful blister on his right hand in the process. He was about ready to give up until morning when he drove the point of the spade into the soft turf one more time and heard it strike something hollow. The spade made a tearing, crunching sound as it ripped through the thick mat of grass and roots, and as soon as he had turned up three or four shovels of the moist brown earth, he caught sight of the box. It had been dark blue, if he remembered accurately, and maybe it still was underneath, but what he could see of it was pretty much the same color as the dirt.

It took some doing to free the box from its resting place, and in the process, he discovered that it was pretty thoroughly rotted. By the time he had it in his hands, it had cracked in numerous places, and the lid came off completely when he tried to open it. Inside, though, everything was remarkably intact, even the several layers of plastic wrapping he had fastened around the papers with cellophane tape. The plastic itself had turned yellowish-brown and the papers smelled musty and felt crumbly around the edges, but, amazingly, he could still easily read the terse notes that a mesmerized Jack Ruby had written to himself so long ago:

"Alex S. . . ."

"Transferring Osw . . ."

"Meet A. at Main St. ramp . . ."

"S.O.B."

He replaced the papers gently inside the ruined box and carried it slowly back toward the house, thinking how nearly insignificant it all seemed now, in light of the legacy Mollie had left him. Still, it had been significant enough to cost an indeterminable number of lives, and soon it would go where it should have gone 24 autumns ago. In a sense, he thought, digging up the box was almost like opening the grave of a long-buried corpse. It gave him an eerie feeling and caused him to quicken his pace slightly. As he did, the lines of a Robert Frost poem ran briefly through his mind.

> "The woods are silent, dark and deep,
> But I have promises to keep,
> And miles to go before I sleep. . . ."

For a moment, he imagined himself as a boy again, hurrying home to supper in the failing light of an early evening, knowing he had stayed out later than he should have. And now, as then, he felt himself mildly spooked by the whispered suggestion of noises and hints of unseen movement in the quiet, darkening meadows and thickets behind him.

He knew it was silly, just as he had known it was silly long ago. But once, in spite of himself, he glanced over his shoulder into the gathering dusk, half-expecting to see Jamie Cade's grinning ghost floating along beside him.

Then he was back in the house again, back to the comforting sounds of the fire crackling in the fireplace and Sarah humming along with the music from her portable radio; back to the enticing aromas of steak sizzling on the grill at the edge of the hearth, potatoes baking in the coals, and a plate of freshly sliced onions and tomatoes waiting atop the ice chest; back to the cozy sight of the gimpy old table, now spread with a "tablecloth" of paper towels and neatly set for dinner, complete with glowing candles and a bouquet of late-blooming wildflowers in a fruit jar "vase." It was hard to believe it was the same place they had first seen that morning.

She grinned at the look of amazement on his face. "Welcome home, Paw," she said, quietly but triumphantly.

He set the box down and looked at her. "It sure is good to

be back, Maw,'' he murmured, holding her urgently against him, desperate for a transfusion of the strength and resolve that only she could give.

He opened his eyes the next morning to yet another peculiar sensation of *deja vu*. The first thing he saw was the orange glow of the sunrise in the dusty windows of the east wall, and it reminded him of looking out those same windows at the first light of thousands of other new days. But as full consciousness slowly returned to him, he realized that none of those other days had ever felt anything like this one. He was waking up on the floor of the house where he had been born—something he might never do again—and sharing a sleeping bag with someone who had still been in diapers the last time he had spent a night here. It was at once an end and a beginning, and as strange as it felt, he also found it oddly satisfying. Not only had he finally confronted the two conflicting halves of himself, but he had forged them together somehow as they had made love on the decaying floor.

Somewhere in the distance, he heard the faint, shrill crowing of a rooster on the chilly morning air. It was amazing, he thought, how far some sounds carried when there was no other noise to compete with them. Unless the crowing came from a game chicken running wild in the woods, the sound would have to be originating more than a mile away, because he knew there was no occupied dwelling closer than that. On the way back from Kaufman yesterday, he had checked the distance between the last inhabited farmhouse down the oil-topped dirt road to the south and the abandoned Eastman Place. It has been just over 1.2 miles by the odometer on the rented Escort station wagon, and there was nothing for three or four miles in the other direction.

In fact, the oil-topped road now ended at a ravine less than half a mile north of the Eastman Place. Matt remembered the ravine once being spanned by a rickety bridge and the road eventually intersecting the farm-to-market road that meandered on into the village of Prairieville. But the bridge had apparently washed out years ago, and because of the sparse traffic (mostly pickup trucks hauling feed to the cattle in the pastures along the road), it had never been replaced. Instead, the taxpayers' only expense had been for a black and white wooden barrier across the roadbed to keep anybody from driving off into the ravine.

Lying here, it was hard to imagine that the heart of Dallas was only a shade over 40 miles beyond the western horizon. If anything, this part of Kaufman County was even quieter and emptier than the countryside around Jefferson, Arkansas. And yet, just ten or so minutes south was the U.S. 175 freeway, and once you hit that, you could be inside the Dallas city limits in less than half an hour, even if you kept your speed under 65, which almost nobody did.

At any rate, he knew exactly how the rooster felt. As he looked down at Sarah and touched the new familiarity of her inside their zipped-together sleeping bags, he could damned near have crowed himself. He nuzzled her neck, heard her laugh low in her throat and felt her kissing his shoulder, even though he could tell she was still semi-asleep.

He tightened his arm protectively around her while he felt on the floor with the other hand until it came in contact with the long-barreled pistol he had left there the night before. Actually, up to now, he had felt as safe and secure in the ramshackle old house as he had felt anywhere in a long time. It was just that the precaution of keeping a gun close by seemed only logical under the circumstances. Hell, even a timber wolf or a bobcat just might pay a midnight call to a house that had been deserted for as long as this one had.

By this time tomorrow, though, such four-legged prowlers would likely be the least of their worries. By then, if everything went according to plan, intrusions by varmints of the two-legged variety would be a much stronger possibility.

There was a breathlessness under his ribs that made it hard to fill his lungs with air, and he could feel his heart pounding as he dialed the main number he had received from information for Conlan Universal Aerospace Corporation. It was a minute or two after 11 a.m., and he had waited as long as he could force himself to wait. The envelope had had more than enough time to reach its destination by now, and although common sense told him that any one of a hundred things could have delayed it, he knew he had to get this over with before his nerve deserted him completely.

He was in a phone booth beside a two-pump service station at Kemp. Sarah was standing next to him and reassuringly squeezing his free hand, but his palms were still wet with sweat and a cold ball of tension was coiled in the pit of his stomach. Above his own galloping pulse, he heard the thin rasp of the telephone ringing far away. Good God, what if Tommy hadn't even seen the envelope? What if he were out of town? What if he were halfway around the world on some kind of business trip. What if . . .

The phone rang once. Then twice. Then three times . . .

"Good morning. CUA." The switchboard operator's voice was harried.

"Ah, Tom Van Zandt, please."

"Thank you. One moment."

Strains of recorded music came wafting gently over the line to him. It was "The Impossible Dream." How utterly appropriate, he thought. How totally quixotic.

"Tom Van Zandt's office."

He struggled to fill his lungs with oxygen. "This is Matt Eastman," he said, in a voice that sounded weak and choky in his ears. "I need to speak to Mr. Van Zandt please."

"I'm sorry, sir, Mr. Van Zandt's in a meeting right now. Can I take a number?"

He swore silently while he tried to decide what to do next. He had never expected to be put straight through to Tommy. That was too much to hope for; things like that just didn't happen. But now what was he supposed to do?

"Are you there, sir?" the secretary's voice inquired, somewhat irritably.

"You listen to me, lady," he said between tightly clenched teeth. "I want you to give Mr. Van Zandt a message for me. I want you to give it to him right now, no matter where he is or what he's doing. Otherwise, you're both going to be very, very sorry."

"But I can't interrupt his meeting, sir."

"Oh, yes, you can," Matt assured her. "You tell him to

call Matt Eastman. He'll recognize my name. Tell him to call me at—" he tried to focus his smarting eyes on the number printed on the dial of the pay phone "—at 214-887-7944. You got that?"

"I have it," she said coldly and read the number back to him for verification.

"Tell Tommy he's got ten minutes to call me," he said, gaining a measure of control over his voice. "Otherwise, my next two calls will be to the FBI and the Associated Press. Understand?"

"I understand, sir," she said, with a bit more deference in her tone, "but I'm not sure I can get through to Mr. Van Zandt in time for him to do that. He left word he's not to be disturbed."

Matt bit his lip. "All right," he said. "Fifteen minutes then. Fifteen minutes from right now, but not one damned second longer. Fifteen minutes, or Tommy Van Zandt's hopes of being governor will be all over. Fifteen minutes, or he'll be in federal custody by this time tomorrow, and I mean that, lady. Believe me, I mean it."

He slammed the phone back onto the hook, wiped his sweating palms on his pants legs and turned to Sarah. He laughed shakily, feeling somewhat light-headed. "I always wanted to say something like that to one of those haughty, smart-ass secretaries," he said, "but now that I did it, I'm too godawful nervous to even enjoy it."

"Just take it easy," Sarah said. "You did just fine. It'll be okay."

He walked over and leaned heavily against the front fender of the Escort station wagon. Despite her reassurance, he wished fervently for a pack of cigarettes, and he would have given $50 for a shot of bourbon.

The next 15 minutes were going to last forever, he thought, glancing at his watch. It was 11:06.

If Tommy didn't respond in the allotted time, regardless of the reason, he had made up his mind not to wait any longer. If no call came by 11:21, he and Sarah would get in the Escort wagon and take the briefcase straight to Tony Canales at Dallas police headquarters. They would turn it and everything it contained over to Tony, and by midafternoon they would be back on I-30 heading for Arkansas.

He paced the length of the car and back, then looked at his watch again. It was 11:08.

In all honesty, he had come very close to changing his mind about calling Tommy anyway. The interlude he had just spent with Sarah at the old farm had convinced him beyond any doubt that there were other things in life besides fear and hopelessness and thoughts of revenge. Even if they had to leave Jefferson, there were plenty of places left to go, places where they could forget everything that had gone before and just concentrate on being with each other and being happy. Chances are, it would be much better in the long run if Tommy *didn't* call back. What was the use in complicating things, anyway, now that he knew what he wanted?

He paced some more. It was 11:10.

The only thing he wanted anymore was for it to be over. And now that he had made the move and crossed the bridge in his own mind, he told himself, he could end it whenever he wanted to. He didn't need Tommy Van Zandt's cooperation. He didn't really even need Tony Canales, not in the final analysis. All he needed was Sarah. As long as he had her, he could live with any situation that fate could throw at him.

He tried to smile at her, and she smiled back, but her eyes were worried—probably because of the way he looked. She was probably afraid he was going to have a heart attack and keel over dead on the spot. He was a little bit afraid of that, too. He took a deep breath and looked at his watch.

11:11. Ten minutes to go. Ten more eternal minutes, and then he could leave. He could walk away and forget the call, forget he had ever even thought about it, and go on to something better. Maybe he would sell *The Jeffersonian* and they would move to another part of the country—New England, maybe. He had always liked New England, especially Vermont and New Hampshire. If he sold everything, they could move up there and buy one of those old inns or something and get snowed in for the winter. Then they could spend all their time making love. He might last about a week if he took lots of vitamins. Oh, but what a week it would be, though.

11:13. The hands on his watch must be stuck. Surely, it was later than that. Maybe he ought to go into the service station and ask the man what time it really was. It was probably at least 11:30 by now, and they were standing around out here for nothing. The man inside the station had looked quizzically at them several times already. They must have looked pretty suspicious—or maybe just slightly crazy. What the hell was wrong with this silly watch? He shook it and looked at it again. The second hand seemed to be moving quite normally.

It said 11:15.

Tommy wasn't going to call. That much was obvious by now, so what could he hope to prove by standing around there like an idiot for another six minutes? The whole idea had been preposterous from the very start, and Tony had known it all along, Matt told himself, but had just decided to play along to keep him from getting upset. Tommy was much too clever to be conned this way. Otherwise, he never could have gotten one-tenth as far as he had. Any fool should be able to see that.

11:16. Five lousy minutes to go, if they dared to wait that long. At CUA, they probably had some sophisticated way of instantly determining the precise location of the phone number he had given the secretary. They probably had high-speed, missile-equipped helicopters standing by and were already on the way to blast the telephone booth and the entire town of Kemp into radioactive dust. At 225 miles per hour, the helicopters could cover the distance from CUA's North Dallas headquarters to the spot where he was standing in less than 15 minutes. Sure, he thought, that was why the secretary had insisted on more time. Tommy had undoubtedly already briefed her on what to say when Matt called.

11:18.

Matt scanned the cloudless sky above the rolling landscape to the west. He listened intently. What was that? Was it the sound of rotors in the distance? Jesus, maybe he was going insane, but it *was* possible. What if they were coming after them? Maybe they should seriously consider heading for cover before it was too late.

11:19.

"I think we ought to get the hell out of here," Matt said, pacing the length of the car for the hundredth time. "He'd have called by now if he was going to."

"Just relax," Sarah said soothingly. "Let's give them the full fifteen minutes first. Just a couple more minutes to go."

11:20.

The phone rang suddenly in the booth—as loud and strident as a cheap alarm clock in a tin washtub—and Matt jumped as if he had been shot.

He grabbed it after the second ring. "Hello," he said.

"Is that you, Matt, old fella?" asked the smooth, unmistakeable voice of Tommy Van Zandt.

"Yeah, it's me, Tommy," Matt said. He couldn't explain it, but now that the die was cast, he could feel himself calming down inside. His heart was still pounding, but now it was more from anticipation than from hysteria. "Did you get the package I sent you?"

"Indeed I did," Tommy said, sounding as unflappable as ever, "and I understand you're interested in talking about a little business proposition pertaining to that package. Am I right?"

"Exactly right," Matt said. "What I sent you is just a small sample of what I have for sale. I've got a really fantastic collection of goods, and I'm looking to get rid of the whole lot. There are several other interested buyers, but I wanted to give you first crack at it—just for old times' sake, you might say."

"That's real white of you, old buddy," Tommy said. "What kind of price are you asking?"

"Well, once upon a time, about eighteen years ago, you offered me a $30,000-a-year salary. Remember that?"

"I do for a fact," Tommy said. "I remember it very well. I also remember I didn't see much of you after that."

"I've decided to accept your offer retroactively," Matt said. "Eighteen times $30,000 comes to $540,000, so that's the price tag, Tommy. You deliver that amount to me in twenties and fifties within twenty-four hours, and you've bought yourself my entire stock of merchandise. It's all yours, and I promise you'll never hear from me again. I think that's a real cut-rate price, considering what you've cost me in grief over the years.''

"I want to tell you one thing, Matt," Tommy said. "What happened to Jamie and Angel Garcia and the O'Connor girls was none of my doing, and neither was what happened in Illinois. That's not my style, old boy, and I hope you believe that.''

"If I didn't, I'd be looking for you with a gun, not offering you any cash buyout deals," Matt said. "I always figured you for a practical guy, Tommy, and this is a pure business transaction as far as I'm concerned. Once it's done, I'm willing to call it even, and I mean it, but the deadline's not subject to negotiation. It either happens within the next twenty-four hours, or it doesn't happen at all, and I mean that, too. Otherwise, look for yourself all over the front pages of Sunday's newspapers.''

"No need for that," Tommy said blandly. "You just tell me where to come, and I'll be there with the dinero by this time tomorrow at the latest. What I'm telling you is you've got yourself a deal.''

Matt smiled. After all the sweat, it had been so easy, he thought, so incredibly easy.

Then, as quickly as it had come, the smile faded.

It had been *too* easy, much too damned easy.

The trap was set—but for whom?

CHAPTER TWENTY

Even Tony Canales agreed—although reluctantly and with unconcealed misgivings—that the plan seemed sound enough on the surface. It called for setting up a phony camp just behind the house, complete with a small tent, a bedroll covering two crude dummies made of garbage bags stuffed with grass and leaves, and even a smoldering campfire. They would leave the rented Escort station wagon parked nearby and hide Tony's unmarked police car behind an old shed a quarter-mile south on the oil-topped road. The shed, located about midway between the farmhouse and the wooden barricade at the ravine where the road ended, was barely standing. But it was sufficient to conceal the car, and any visitors they might have weren't likely to be traveling that far down the dead-end thoroughfare anyway.

By midafternoon, when this was all done and the stage was set, everybody would retreat to an observation post in a dense patch of woods on a slight rise about 300 yards away, where they could keep the house and the bogus campsite under surveillance without being seen. Then, if Tommy showed up alone as specified, Matt would go down, also alone, and make the exchange. If other people with less peaceful intentions appeared instead, the observers would be well-removed from immediate peril while they determined how to counter the intrusion.

Meanwhile, they would stash their equipment in the hidden position and establish a legitimate camping place there for the night. Then they would simply have to wait and see what happened, taking turns keeping watch through the night if necessary. There was no way to tell how long the wait might be, but if no one had showed up by 11:30 a.m. the next day, Saturday, Matt agreed to call the whole affair off and let Tony take over from there.

Immediately after giving Tommy Van Zandt directions to the farm, Matt had called Tony and told him the rendezvous was set for the farm sometime within the next 24 hours. Less than an hour later and well before 1 p.m., Tony was at the farm himself. He had been worried about Tommy somehow beating him to the scene, but Matt had been confident it would take even Tommy Van Zandt a little time to react to his demands, regardless of what type of reaction Tommy chose to make.

Tony arrived prepared for the worst. He was wearing camouflage coveralls, armed with two riot guns in addition to his .38 service revolver, and equipped with various outdoor gear, a camera with a telephoto lens, binoculars and a powerful electronic recording device to be hidden at the dummy campsite to pick up whatever incriminating sounds might be forthcoming. Despite Matt's repeated earlier objections, Tony was also accompanied by another officer, Sergeant Bruce Cannaday of the DPD tactical squad.

Tony hadn't said a word on the phone about bringing anybody with him, and when Matt saw the two of them drive up in the white Dodge Diplomat, his first impulse was to feel angry and betrayed. He shook hands with Cannaday, who was also wearing camouflage clothing and a .45 automatic on a cartridge belt around his waist, and allowed Tony to introduce Sarah to the sergeant, but his attitude made it clear that he wasn't happy about the extra company.

"Look, Matthew," Tony said, calling Matt off to one side to explain, "I didn't tell Bruce what the mission was or where we were going until we were over halfway here, so there's no chance the information could've leaked to anybody else. Bruce is an ex-Marine, who saw lots of front-line action in Vietnam. He's an excellent marksman and knows everything there is to know about hand-to-hand combat and wilderness survival. He's been with the department seven years, won twenty commendations, and I trust him implicitly. If all hell breaks loose out here, you couldn't ask to have a better man on your side."

"Whether I like it or not, it's a little late to do anything about it now," Matt said resignedly, "but frankly I can't see why you think it's necessary. Even if there's trouble, we ought to be safe enough over in the woods without the extra firepower."

"I hope you're right," Tommy said. "I hope Van Zandt drives right up here and hands you the money in small bills, then takes the briefcase and drives off again, but somehow I just don't expect that to happen."

"What exactly *do* you expect?" Matt asked. He remembered his fantasy of less than two hours earlier in which he had envisioned helicopters with nuclear devices attacking Kemp, so he knew how easy it was to let your imagination run away with you.

"I don't have the slightest idea," Tony said. "I just believe in being prepared, that's all. For instance, what if he *did* hand you $540,000? Have you ever thought about what you'd do?"

"Well, sure," Matt said. "I'd give him the briefcase and let you radio your guys to pick him up while he had the evidence in his hot little hands. You said you already have search warrants covering his office, home and car, right?"

"That's right, but what if he decided to dump the stuff someplace or destroyed it before we could get to him?"

"No sweat," Matt said. "Sarah and I could always testify about the contents of the briefcase. We also made copies of most of the stuff and left them in Arkansas."

"You're getting very shrewd in your old age, Matthew."

"Not really," Matt said, "but after you've had so many disasters, you start looking over your shoulder and keeping one eye on your ass at all times. Besides, it was Sarah's idea."

"Not that I think you're going to have to worry about it," Tony said, "but have you thought how it'd feel to hold that much money at one time? You might get a hankering just to keep it, instead of surrendering it as evidence."

Matt considered the idea for a minute. It seemed funny, but it had never once crossed his mind until now. It wasn't that he was all that scrupulously honest, he thought; it was just that keeping the money was so totally beside the point.

He grinned. "I might slip a couple of fifties out while you're not looking," he said, "but I don't seriously think so. I set such a high price just to make it sound convincing to Tommy, but the money itself doesn't mean a thing to me. All I want it to do is buy me a ticket to see Tommy and Alex with their balls in a vise."

"Maybe it's too late now," Tony said, "but I'm convinced we could do it without this crazy stunt, Matthew. I did some checking into Dee Conlan's death, and I found out that he was alone with Sutton and Van Zandt when he died. I could get an exhumation order pretty quickly with the evidence you've got, and I can get the feds moving on the JFK thing at a moment's notice. Why don't you let me try it before we risk any more mayhem? We can leave Bruce on stakeout here and take the evidence straight downtown right now."

For a moment, Matt felt tempted by Tony's logic, but then he shook his head. "Look, we've already agreed on this," he said. "We can do all that before noon tomorrow if nothing happens in the meantime. A deal's a deal, right?"

Tony shrugged heavily. "I guess so," he said, "but I don't mind telling you I'm worried. We've got a very dangerous situation on our hands, Matthew, and it may be a lot more dangerous than you realize."

Matt felt a puzzled frown on his face. God knows, they'd *had* a dangerous situation on their hands with Alex and Tommy for 24 years—so dangerous that people kept dying like flies because of it—but Tony seemed to be talking about something else entirely. He acted as if there were an additional cause for concern that Matt didn't know about.

"I don't follow you," Matt said. "If anybody ought to know how dangerous these people are, it's me, for Christ's sake."

"I appreciate that, Matthew," Tony said, "but I think you still may be underestimating who and what we're dealing with here. Maybe it's just Van Zandt's ego and political pipe dreams, like you said, or maybe it's something a lot bigger and a whole lot meaner. That's why I brought Bruce along and the riot guns and all the rest. And it's why I'm still saying a couple of Hail Marys and just hoping we haven't bitten off more than we can chew."

Matt stared uncomprehendingly at the deputy chief of police. He shook his head.

"I get the distinct feeling there's something you haven't told me," he said.

Before Tony answered, he took his .38 service revolver out of the shoulder holster under his coveralls and carefully checked the cylinder to make sure it was fully loaded. Then he shoved it back into the holster again and looked at Matt.

"Those two guys who came to your house in Arkansas," he said quietly. "Did you ever stop to wonder who they *really* were?"

"Once or twice," Matt said. "I figured they were ex-cops or maybe CUA security people or just free-lance pistoleros. Anyway, that's why I gave you their IDs. What about it?"

"I took their papers over to the FBI first thing yesterday morning and asked them to check out the IDs through their computer," Tony said. "The names they were using—Theodore Shroeder and Victor Zandoli, I think it was—were both aliases. All their papers were fakes."

"That's not so surprising," Matt said. "Hired killers do travel under assumed names sometimes, they tell me."

"The weird thing was, though," Tony said, ignoring Matt's sarcasm, "there was nothing at all in the FBI computer on either one of those names. At first, it looked like we'd drawn a blank, but when they interfaced into the CIA computer and cross-checked their international espionage files, they turned up something. It's something that really bothers me, Matthew. Something you ought to know before we go any further with this deal.''

Matt could tell by Tony's tone that there was no joke involved. "Okay, I'm listening," he said.

Tony licked his lips uneasily, and his expression was both grim and confused as his eyes met Matt's.

"I'm still having a hard time believing this myself," he said, "but unless the CIA computer screwed up somehow, I guess it's got to be true. According to the computer, those aliases have cropped up a number of times before and in several different countries.

"So what the hell does that mean?" Matt asked, genuinely puzzled.

"I don't know," Tony said, "but the only guys who ever used them before were known contract agents for the KGB.''

Sarah opened her eyes and listened to the night sounds in the underbrush around her. She shifted slightly in the sleeping bag to ease a cramp in her shoulder, then lay perfectly still again, looking up at a scattering of stars in a sky that was only a half shade lighter than the coal-black limbs of the trees overhead. In retrospect, sleeping on the floor of the old house seemed almost like a luxury now. The boards had been hard, but the ground was somehow even harder, and it was also colder. The damp chill from it seeped up through the plastic moisture barrier, the multiple layers of down-filled sleeping bag and her clothes, boring its way directly into her muscles and bones. And tonight, for the sake of propriety, she didn't have Matt's arms around her to keep her feeling secure, or his body heat next to her to keep her warm. He was lying close by, near enough for her to reach out and touch, but it wasn't the same as having him zipped up in the same sleeping bag with her. That was one of the coziest, most comforting sensations she had ever experienced, but the memory of it only made her feel worse at the moment.

Right now, all she wanted was for this interminable night to be over. She wanted whatever was going to happen with Tom Van Zandt to be put safely behind them. She wanted to be alone with Matt again, the way they had been before Tony Canales and Sergeant Cannady had come, before they had put everything on a war footing and gone into hiding. She wanted to drive into Dallas and see the sights, go to a nice restaurant and maybe even a nightclub or two. She wanted to drink one of those frozen margaritas, take the elevator to the top of Reunion Tower, ride through the West End in a horse-drawn carriage, and see the Kennedy Memorial and the School Book Depository. Those were the things she always heard people talking about after they made a trip to Dallas, and she wanted to experience them all.

After that, though, it wouldn't matter what they did or where they went, as long as they were together. For all she cared, they could come back to this old overgrown farm and stay here indefinitely. If they did, though, she would at least have to insist on some way to take a bath or a shower and wash her hair. It was now sometime in the wee hours of Saturday morning, and she had almost forgotten what hot water felt like. The last time she had been freshly showered and shampooed had been Wednesday afternoon at the motel in Greenville. During the nearly 60 hours since, the best she had been able to do was wash her hands and face, sponge the rest of her off with cold water and paper towels, and spray some deodorant in strategic locations. Consequently, her hair was a stiff, oily mess, her clothes smelled of stale sweat and woodsmoke, and she was beginning to feel really gross all over.

She had to admit one thing, though. She had finally gotten out of the pine thickets of southeastern Arkansas and discovered some excitement. Who would ever have dreamed that little Sarah Ann Archer, the 1978 sweetheart of the Warren High School Future Farmers of America Chapter, would find herself up to her ears in murder, assassination and international intrigue? It was still next to impossible for her to comprehend it herself. And her prim landlady, Mrs. Mitchell, would surely wet her lavender-scented britches if she were to catch a glimpse of Sarah Ann Archer right now.

"My stars, I couldn't believe my eyes. There she was, out in the middle of the woods with three armed men in a sleeping bag, and dirty as a pig. And she seemed so proper and well-brought-up at first, too. I tell you, you just never know. It's them drugs they take nowadays. Poor thing, she's probably hooked on that LSD . . .''

And what about Kyle Morrison? What would Little Lord Kyle (who always seemed to wear his pajamas while they made love and sometimes launched into lengthy discussions of the merits of accelerated classes or the advisability of an extended school term immediately after his orgasm) think about the circumstances in which she presently found herself? And, forget Kyle, what would her mother think, for godsake? Even worse, what would her mother *say*?

"I always knew you'd come to a bad end, child. I always knew you'd do it just to spite me. I worked and I slaved to give you a good home and bring you up right and get you through school, so you could make something out of yourself, so you could have it better than I did—and this is the thanks I get! Oh, Lord, where did I fail? Where did I go wrong?''

In the nearly total darkness ten feet away, Sarah heard a soft, sudden noise that made her start, until she realized it was only Sergeant Cannaday changing his position slightly. The men had decided to divide the period from 7 p.m. Friday until 7 a.m. Saturday into three four-hour shifts. Tony had insisted that Matt take the first shift, which ended at 11; Tony had taken the 11-to-3 shift, and now Cannady was standing watch for the final four hours. Sarah had offered to take a turn, but they had all insisted—either out of chivalry or inbred male mistrust of her guarding abilities—that she try to get a full night's sleep instead.

Fat chance, she thought. What dozing she had done had occurred in short, fitful stretches at best, and each catnap had been separated from the next by a period of worried wakefulness. After Matt had turned in a little after 11, they had furtively held hands for a while, but when he had drifted off into a sound sleep, she had turned over and tried her best to do the same, mostly without success. For the past hour, she had been acutely and uncomfortably conscious of everything around her, and by now she was fairly sure that she was awake to stay.

She sat up and hugged the top of the sleeping bag around her, instantly wishing she had remained horizontal for a while longer. A few seconds in a sitting position told her that her bladder was uncomfortably full, which meant an urgent relief expedition was only a few minutes away at most. Sometimes it was such a pain being a woman. All a man had to do when the time came was step behind a tree, unzip his fly, and *let* fly. A woman, on the other hand, had to peel off half her clothes, expose her bare bottom to the cold, be careful not to sit on any foreign objects when she squatted, and usually end up splattering herself in a most unsanitary, unladylike fashion before it was all over. She didn't know which was more distasteful, the idea of blundering around through the bushes in total darkness to get this untidy business done, or waiting until daylight broke and having to conceal her errand from curious masculine eyes. But she knew it was destined to be one or the other—and pretty soon, too—as she peered through the darkness toward the spot where she heard Cannady moving around.

"What time is it, Sergeant?" she inquired in a loud stage whisper.

She heard him push back the sleeve of his camouflage shirt and got a mental picture of him checking the luminous dial of his digital watch.

"4:47 a.m., ma'am," he replied. "A little over an hour yet till first light."

"Is anything going on?" she asked.

"Not a thing," he said. "It's as quiet as a tomb down there."

She would just as soon he had used some other descriptive metaphor, she thought, struggling to get some of the sleeping bag up around her shoulders to ward off the cold. If only they could build a fire here, things would be a hundred times better. Not only would it give her something to do and a means of warming her icy hands and feet, but she could also use the pretext of looking for firewood to take care of the other matter. But given the circumstances, a fire was obviously out of the question, so it was pointless even to think about it.

And it was just as pointless, she decided, to sit here in torment and postpone the inevitable.

"I've got to go commune with nature, Sergeant," she said bluntly, "so if you hear something crashing around in the brush, I'd appreciate it if you didn't shoot it."

"Yes, ma'am," he said stiffly.

"If you hear someone screaming for help, however, you have my permission to come get me. Okay?"

"Yes, ma'am," he said again.

She thought he was laughing, but she couldn't tell for sure.

Sarah picked her way past the indistinct forms of Matt and Tony Canales and into the dense growth that began only a few feet from where they were sleeping. It was so dark that she found it necessary to hold her arms up in front of her face to keep from being slapped and clawed by unseen brambles and tree limbs. After about 30 seconds of this, she emerged into a small clearing, where a patch of starlit sky was visible overhead and shaggy tufts of winter grass grew under her feet.

She paused to listen for a moment but heard nothing at all. Even the night sounds seemed to have been startled into silence by her presence, and a heavy hush hung in the air. This was definitely far enough, she decided, scarcely caring if the sergeant heard her wetting the grass. Although she couldn't have ventured more than 15 yards from the campsite, she felt indescribably isolated and alone and was already concerned about finding her way back. She pulled down her jeans and panties and squatted unceremoniously, holding onto a scrubby tree sprout to keep her balance.

The deed was done in a matter of seconds, and she shivered, sighed with relief and reassembled her clothing.

"Big deal," she whispered to herself. "Now all I have to do is retrace my steps and I'm home free."

The problem was, though, while she was hopping around in the clearing, she had managed to lose her sense of direction. And since there was no sign of a path through the brush and not a sound or speck of light or even a smell to follow back to where she had come from, there was nothing to do but plunge back into the thicket and hope she was going the right way.

She wasn't, of course. Lord knows, you never get that lucky on the first try.

Mentally, she tried to calculate the time she was spending groping her way through the undergrowth, and it soon became apparent that it was taking far too long. If she had been headed toward the campsite, she would already have stumbled across it, she thought. She would also have been able to see the slightly lighter backdrop of the sky beyond the edge of the woods, but there was nothing but more dark, dense forest in front of her.

She stopped dead and listened with all her might, praying for some sound that might guide her, thinking she would have given anything to hear a human cough. There was nothing but an eerie, unbroken silence in all directions. A short time earlier, Tony's snoring had disturbed her sleep. So why in heaven's name wasn't he snoring now?

There was absolutely no cause for hysteria, she told herself firmly. She would simply turn around in her tracks and start back the other way. Then, once she got back to the little clearing, she could reorient herself and get her bearings.

Only she couldn't find the little clearing. She walked at least twice as far as she had come since leaving it, but found no sign of it at all.

She felt reassured, although also somewhat embarrassed, when she recalled her last remark to Sergeant Cannaday—the one about coming to find her if she should scream for help. She was approaching that point, all right, but it would only be as a last resort. She would try one more time on her own, she thought, striking out in yet another direction.

Her efforts were totally pointless by this time, of course. She had no remote idea where she was, she admitted disgustedly, and she might as well face it. At this very moment, she could be as little as ten yards from the campsite, or, God forbid, as much as 100 yards away, perhaps even more. She had done that much aimless thrashing around. She bit her lip and felt like crying, not so much from fright as from sheer frustration.

The time had plainly arrived to swallow her pride and accept defeat. She could almost hear Matt chiding her and Tony and Cannaday chuckling. She cringed at the idea, but that was the price you paid when you couldn't even go pee by yourself. It was all so silly and demeaning, but anything was preferable to this.

"Sergeant," she called softly, "can you hear me?"

She waited expectantly, but there was no reply.

"Sergeant!" she repeated, considerably louder than before. "I can't find you. How about making some noise or something?"

This time she waited for a prolonged period, thinking that Cannaday or one of the others might be coming after her, rather than risk a lengthy exchange of shouts that could threaten the secrecy of their hiding place. She waited for what must have been five minutes or more, in fact. She waited until she began to experience the illusion of the sky growing lighter above the trees.

Then she realized it was no illusion.

Dawn was about to break over the eastern horizon, wherever that was. But where in God's name was she? And where were the others?

"Use your head, Sarah," she told herself fiercely. Surely the light could only help matters. If the sun rose in the east, then the sky would be brighter to the east. Since she knew their campsite was west of the house, which was, in turn, west of the oil-topped road, it stood to reason if she went toward the sunrise, she would eventually encounter the road, even if she missed the campsite. Then, simply by following the road, she could eventually find her way back.

How stupid, she thought, sitting down on the ground to catch her breath and allow the pale eastern sky to shed a little more light on the subject before she moved on again. How utterly stupid!

With the coming day gradually diluting the gloom, she discovered it was lucky she had waited as long as she did. Just a dozen yards from where she had stopped, the ground suddenly fell away into a steep creek bank laced with exposed tree roots and vines. She could see now that it was at least ten or twelve feet to the dry, sandy bottom of the creek bed, but if she had come upon it in the dark, she might have fallen right into it.

As it was, however, the creek now gave her yet another point of reference. She certainly hadn't crossed the creek, so that meant she should turn and head in the opposite direction. And since trees and bushes ordinarily grew thickest along a creek, moving away from it should take her toward an open area where she could at least tell where she was going—if not where she had come from.

She was gratified to find, after fighting her way through the undergrowth for only a few steps, that her reasoning had been correct. She emerged from the thicket into a wide, rolling meadow, interrupted only here and there by patches of scrub cedars and immature young oaks and blackjacks. Ahead of her, she spotted a straggling barbed wire fence, and beyond it, the oil-topped road. And as she trotted toward it with an immense burst of relief, she caught sight of the roof of the old farmhouse, barely visible off to her left.

All at once, as she was nearly to the fence and already turning toward the house, she realized exactly where she was in relation to the campsite. If she swung an additional 90 degrees to her left, her path would take her directly back to the point in the fringe of woods where this whole absurd episode had started. She could only guess how long she had been gone—probably not even a half-hour yet—and she hoped Sergeant Cannaday hadn't unnecessarily alarmed the others. And if he had, she hoped Matt wasn't too wor . . .

What was that?

She whirled and saw two cars rumbling toward her up the road, the rhythmic roar of their engines and the crunching hum of their tires shattering the pastoral stillness of the countryside, their headlights cutting through the thin early morning mist along the roadway.

"Oh, shit!"

She felt, rather than heard, the startled expletive hurtle

from her lips. She couldn't hear her words for the sound of her heart jumping into her throat.

In a single frantic motion, she threw herself to the ground and rolled behind a small cluster of cedars. As she cowered there, holding her breath and wondering if she had been seen, she heard the cars braking to a stop, their wheels kicking up little puffs of dust at the roadside.

She heard car doors opening and then quickly closing again. There was a low rumble of baritone voices, accompanied by faint metallic rattles and jinglings and finally the sound of multiple hurried footsteps padding along the road.

When the footsteps moved off to the north, Sarah inched forward around the cedars on her hands and knees, her face close to the ground, the prickly evergreen boughs scratching her cheeks, and took a look.

Their company had arrived—not a millionaire politician in a chauffeur-driven limousine delivering a suitcase packed with money, but a small army of methodical mercenaries. And of all the times they could have picked, they had arrived when the sky was the color of a tea rose in the east and she was separated from Matt and the others by several hundred yards of mostly open grassland. Even if she tried to slither along on her belly like a snake, she had grave doubts that she could reach the safety of the woods without attracting their attention. And, inexperienced as she was at such things, she had enough sense to know if they spotted her in the open meadow, she wouldn't have a chance.

Had Cannaday seen or heard the cars? Had Matt and Tony already been awake because of her unexplained absence? Did they know what was happening? What could she possibly do to warn or help them? Even with the snubnosed .22 revolver that Matt had insisted she keep in her jacket pocket ever since the nightmare at the Little Rock bus depot, she felt childlike, powerless and terribly alone. She would just as soon confront these commando-style invaders with a water pistol.

She counted eight of them—eight men dressed in what appeared to be dark-green Army fatigues; eight guerrillas with blackened faces, running at a crouch in the ditches on either side of the road; eight members of an assault team, moving rapidly and stealthily toward the old farmhouse that was their target; eight booted storm troopers, all with sidearms hanging from their belts, with at least some of them carrying large, lethal-looking weapons at the ready.

They were weapons like nothing Sarah had ever seen before outside the movies, weapons like the ones in "Platoon" and "Apocalypse Now."

She gasped as recognition slowly dawned along with the pink-tinged dawning of a new day—a day that might be the last one any of them would ever see.

To think she had actually been praying for daylight just a few minutes ago. Now she would have given anything to be lost again in the cold, dark woods, where there was nothing more sinister than an invisible creek bank, an unseen tree limb or a lurking varmint to threaten her.

She raised her head and stole another look at the column of anonymous marauders moving away from her along the mist-shrouded road.

Dear God, she thought, all eight of them had submachine guns!

CHAPTER TWENTY-ONE

November 7, 1987

Matt jerked awake in the rosy light of the early dawn. He felt Tony shaking him and heard Tony's low, anxious voice repeating his name.

"Matthew. Hey, Matthew. Come on, wake up."

Matt fought with the thick web of sleep that enveloped him. He shook his head. "What's going on?" he mumbled.

"We've got major problems, my friend," Tony said. "Bruce just saw some headlights down on the road. Looks like at least two vehicles have stopped down there." He hesitated for a second. "And Sarah's gone," he added heavily.

Matt struggled to get his legs free of the encumbering sleeping bag as he glanced frantically around. Tony was right. Sarah's empty sleeping bag was still there on the ground close beside him, but she was nowhere to be seen. When he reached over to feel the lining of the sleeping bag, he found it cold to the touch, with no remaining body heat left. That meant she'd been gone for quite a while, longer than just a minute or two, anyway. He felt confused and suddenly afraid.

"But where the hell is she?" he asked, rubbing his eyes.

"I don't know," he heard Cannaday's voice saying. "She said she had to take care of a personal matter and went off into the bushes. But that was over half an hour ago, and I haven't seen her since."

"Christ, I've got to find her," Matt said. He pulled the .357 Magnum out of his sleeping bag and started toward the dense curtain of trees and brush a few feet away, but Tony grabbed his arm.

"Easy, man," Tony said in an urgent whisper. "It was dark when she left, and she probably just lost her bearings. Anyway, you can't go crashing off looking for her right now. Our biggest problem is down there." He gestured in the direction of the road. "I'm sure Sarah'll be okay, if those guys don't see her before she finds her way back."

Cannaday was lying on his elbows, staring through his binoculars. "I see some guys on foot now. They're moving toward the house in the ditches beside the road. Looks like seven—make that eight—of them altogether, Chief. They're wearing military-type gear and operating almost like an infantry platoon. I guarantee you they didn't come to talk or trade."

Tony knelt beside the sergeant and squinted through his own binoculars. "I hate to say I told you so, Matthew," he said grimly, "but we never should've put ourselves in this position. We've got some super-serious trouble on our hands now."

Matt squatted beside him, trying desperately to comprehend the situation that was suddenly boiling up around them, but too worried about Sarah to pull his thoughts together long enough to concentrate on anything else. Where in God's name could she be? How could Cannaday have just let her wander off into the dark by herself? What if the men coming up the road had already spotted her?

"What do you think they're going to do?" he asked.

"Nothing we're going to enjoy very much," Tony said, studying the scene below them through the binoculars again. "They look like a bunch of damned commandos or something, man." He paused, then added excitedly, "Mother of god, Brucc, do you see that?"

"I sure as hell do," Cannaday said.

"See what, for Christ sake?" Matt demanded.

"Automatic weapons," Cannaday said. "They've got automatic weapons. AK-47s, as nearly as I can tell. We're looking at enough firepower right now to blow away everything within a mile of here." He lowered his binoculars and looked at Tony. "What's our next move, Chief?"

"Well, we can't afford to just sit here and watch, that's for sure," Tony said. "We need to move now and try to get some support in here pronto."

"That means somebody has to get to the radio in the car," Cannaday said. "Want me to try for it?"

"I'd rather you'd cover my tail and let me do it," Tony said. "Matt should be okay here as long as he stays out of sight. How far do you figure it is to the car?"

"Quarter of a mile," Matt said. "Maybe a little more."

"If we follow the edge of these woods, how close can we get before we have to get out in the open?" Cannaday asked.

"I don't know," Matt said. "Two or three hundred yards probably."

Tony grinned nervously. "Well, that's no hill for a climber," he said. "I could run the hundred in a shade over ten seconds when I was in high school." He checked his service revolver and looked at Cannaday. "Are you all set, Bruce?"

"Whenever you are, sir."

"But what about Sarah?" Matt said. "We can't just forget about her."

"I don't intend to, Matthew," Tony assured him. "But, believe me, this is the best way. Sarah's a smart girl, and under the circumstances, she's bound to have enough sense to stay out of sight. We can have a couple of choppers on the scene within twenty minutes after we call in, and I'll have them alert the Kaufman County Sheriff's Office so they can block off this road. If we can get enough manpower in here in a hurry, we'll have these guys where we want them, and *then* we can find Sarah, okay?"

"Okay," Matt said. "I don't guess I have a whole lot of choice in the matter, do I?"

Tony smiled unhappily and shook his head. "No, old friend," he said, "you don't have any choice. Just keep low and keep quiet, and even if somebody should come up this way, I'd think twice before I did any shooting if I were you. That Magnum's a helluva gun, but even it doesn't match up very well with an AK-47."

As if the mention of the weapon were some sort of cue, a short, staccato burst of gunfire suddenly shattered the cool silence of the morning. It was followed by another short burst, then another.

Even with his naked eyes, Matt could see a faint pall of dust and blue smoke rising from the area around the old farmhouse. Tony studied the scene through his binoculars for a few seconds, then handed the glasses over to Matt.

"Just in case you've got any remaining doubts about these bastards' intention, take a look down there, Matthew," he said.

Matt took the binoculars, scanned the trees and meadows until he found the eight gunmen, then watched them approach the house and the dummy campsite behind it in a wide semicircle. There was no firing at the moment, but they all held their weapons at the ready, prepared to spray everything in their path with bullets.

Methodically, two of the crouching figures approached to within 20 or 30 feet of the small tent and opened fire simultaneously. In seconds, the tent was collapsed and ripped to shreds. Nothing inside it could possibly have been alive, but they kept on firing until the tent and its contents were reduced to a smoking pile of tattered rags. Then, in the ringing silence that followed, one of them walked over and kicked at what was left of the dummies. Matt could see him turn and say something to the other one.

"They know they've been had now," Matt said, "and I think they're slightly pissed off."

They lost no time in demonstrating that fact.

A moment later, the whole group of them turned back in unison toward the house and the rented Escort station wagon a few yards away. Three or four of them opened fire on the house while two others concentrated on the car. Matt could see the splinters flying from the tortured walls of his boyhood home, the remaining windows disappearing in a snowstorm of shattered glass, and whole boards hurtling crazily away from the structure, torn from their ancient moorings by the force of the barrage.

He saw the tires of the station wagon go suddenly flat and the car settle slowly onto its hubs. The windows clouded, then vanished, and one of the doors popped suddenly open. And still they kept firing.

"Come on, Chief," Cannaday said. "Let's move while they're still occupied with destroying everything in sight." Even at that distance, he practically had to shout to be heard above the roar of the gunfire.

"Okay," Tony responded, "I'll go first. You stay about a hundred feet back and keep me covered." He reached out for Matt's hand and squeezed it hard. "Hang tight, Matthew," he said.

"Be careful," Matt told him. A terrible premonition made him want to say something else, but he probably couldn't have made himself heard, and there was no time left for that now, anyway. Whatever he wanted to say to Tony Canales should have been said earlier. He would never have another opportunity.

An instant later, Tony was flitting away through the trees, showing remarkable agility for someone of his age and girth, and about ten seconds later Cannaday moved off after him. Matt was able to follow their progress for the first 40 or 50 yards, but then their camouflage suits blended in so well with the trees and brush that he couldn't see them anymore, even through the binoculars.

The heaviest of the shooting seemed to be over now, and except for an occasional random burst, the automatic weapons were silent. If there had ever been any question about the possibility of salvaging the old homeplace, it was settled now, once and for all. The house was a ravaged ruin, its exterior walls and roof pockmarked by hundreds of bulletholes. From what Matt could see, scarcely a square foot of the place was unmarred by a fresh scar of raw wood, where a bullet had entered or exited.

Were these guys really so angry at being duped, he wondered, or did they just enjoy their work a lot?

Where the hell had these mercenaries come from? How the hell did Tommy Van Zandt find such murderous bastards? Or had somebody else actually sent them? In spite of all their precautions, had somebody else known they were there, after all?

And where was Sarah? Where in God's name was Sarah?

Oh, Jesus, he thought, Matthew Eastman was such a clever fellow. He had had everything so neatly figured out, and now everything had gone so completely to hell. If anything happened to Sarah, he didn't want to live. If Sarah was lying dead somewhere down there, he only wanted to die, too. And if she'd been anywhere around the house when the shooting started . . .

He tried to clamp his mind shut on the idea and deny its existence, but it kept wriggling free and nagging at him. For the first time in days, he found himself thinking about the bottle of poisoned amaretto in his kitchen pantry.

"Goddamn it, get hold of yourself," he whispered aloud. "What you've got to do is think, not panic."

Maybe he could find her with the binoculars. She had been wearing jeans and a dark blue jacket, nothing that would really stand out at a distance, but colors that were at least distinctively different from the predominant browns, yellows and greens of the countryside.

First, though, he took another look toward the house.

The raiding party seemed to be regrouping now and trying to decide what to do next. But as he watched, it became apparent that they were not in the mood simply to abandon their mission, march back down the road to their cars and drive away. Instead—curse the luck!—Matt saw them split up into groups of two and prepare for a systematic search of the whole area. They conferred briefly, reloaded their weapons, then set out in pairs, moving in all four general directions and traveling about 50 feet apart.

Now, he realized, Sarah was in more danger than ever.

Meanwhile, up the road to the north, he could make out part of the tin roof and one side of the ramshackle shed where Tony's unmarked squad car was hidden, but there was no sign of Tony or Cannaday yet. They hadn't been gone much more than ten minutes and undoubtedly hadn't had time to get that far yet.

"Hurry, Tony," he whispered. "For God's sake, hurry."

From the vicinity of the old shed, he slowly worked his way back with the glasses to the backyard of the house. His visual journey brought him in contact with two of the armed men who were moving rapidly northward toward the shed. In a few more minutes, they might be close enough to spot either the concealed squad car or Tony and Cannaday themselves, and that was yet another reason to worry.

"Hurry, damn it," he said again.

As his field of vision moved to the area between his observation post and the house, Matt saw two more of the gunmen. These two were heading in his general direction and he was startled to discover they had already approached to within 150 yards and were still advancing stealthily. He felt his already pounding heart jump in his chest, and he reached for the long-barreled pistol with his free hand, finding the safety catch with his forefinger and clicking it into the "off" position. If the two intruders continued on their present course, they would pass within a dozen yards of him and could hardly miss seeing the cluttered campsite. There was always the possibility that they would alter their course and pass at a safe distance, but then they would be in the dense woods to his rear and able to come within a few feet of him without being seen.

Despite Tony's assurances, it was growing more obvious by the second that Matt was in grave danger of being discovered. The question was no longer one of staying or going. Going was the only choice he had left. All he had to decide now was how long he dared to wait before he made a break for it.

He pushed himself up to a kneeling position and grabbed the briefcase—the damned, omnipresent briefcase—out of the folds of the sleeping bag, still gripping the Magnum in his sweating right fist. His adrenal glands were going wild and every muscle in his body was tensed and coiled for flight, but he forced himself to make one final pass with the binoculars over the area between himself and the house.

And that was when he saw Sarah.

She was about 200 yards behind and slightly to the left (or south) of the two men threatening his hiding place. She was scurrying along on all fours, half-running, half-crawling, and making pretty good time. As nearly as Matt could tell, she was apparently trying to reach the shelter of the house. That wasn't a bad idea, he realized, since the house was most likely the safest place on the farm, at least temporarily, with the execution squad occupied elsewhere and moving further away from it by the second.

But on the heels of this slightly comforting thought came a sudden, sobering realization. Sarah was perilously close to the old cistern, the same old cistern into which Matt himself had nearly fallen while searching for the buried box of evidence a couple of days ago. He had never told her about it, because at the time there had seemed no reason. If she should stumble into it, the fall alone might break her neck. And even if she survived the fall, she would surely scream.

And if she screamed, the two AK-47s would chew her to pulp as she lay helpless at the bottom of the hole.

Like shooting fish in a barrel, he thought, and the thought made him ill.

To hell with it, he told himself fiercely. It was now or never.

He threw down the binoculars, hugged the briefcase tightly against his chest, and picked his way north along the edge of the woods in the same direction that Tony and Cannaday had gone, staying low and holding the Magnum out in front of him. He was unable to move very fast, but within a minute or two, he had managed to cover 50 yards or so, and he crept to the edge of the woods and looked back, breathing heavily.

The two gunmen were coming up hard on the hidden campsite. They were no more than 75 yards away now and advancing steadily but cautiously. Barring some unlikely change in their path or rate of progress, they were going to walk right into the campsite within the next three or four minutes. When they did, the abandoned observation post was almost certain to capture their full attention, at least for a short time.

And that was when Matt would have to make his move into the open meadow and try to reach Sarah. If they saw him, he and Sarah were probably both dead, but it was the only thing he could think to do.

He ducked back into the brush and waited, trying to catch his breath and trying to hold it, all at the same time. He waited while the second hand on his watch made one complete circuit, then two. He was easing forward to take another look when he heard a sudden, low shout and froze in his tracks.

The shout was followed immediately by a short burst of gunfire, and he was sure he was dead.

The instant he realized he wasn't, he also realized it was the campsite they were shooting at. He broke from the woods, running at a crouch as hard as he could go until he reached the shelter of a small clump of bushes. Then he stopped momentarily and glanced back toward the spot where he had been sleeping a little more than 20 minutes earlier. He caught a glimpse of the two men poking at the empty sleeping bags with their weapons, and he could even hear the sound of their voices, although he couldn't distinguish any of the words.

Then he was moving again, crouching and running, trying to plot a mental course toward the last spot where he had seen Sarah. He came into a large open area where there was nothing growing but high grass, and he dropped to his hands and knees and started to crawl, pausing now and then to listen. He looked behind him once and saw that he was leaving a perfect trail in the grass, but there was nothing he could do about it.

By his calculations, he should have been very close to where he had last seen her. Of course, she had been moving basically away from him and traveling pretty fast, too, from what he could tell. But maybe she had stopped when she heard the gunfire.

He could only hope so.

A minute later, he reached another clump of bushes and

got back to his feet. He recognized his location now, and, in fact, saw some of his own footprints from two days ago as he crossed a bare patch of earth. The cistern was just to his right, still well-concealed by the high grass and weeds. As he hurried past it, he paused long enough to direct a fearful glance into its muddy depths and heaved a sigh of relief to find it still empty.

He pushed on. The gunmen would be past the initial shock of discovery by now. So what would they do next? Would they venture deeper into the woods or retrace their steps back across the meadow? Or would they, perhaps, signal the others somehow about what they had found and bring them all converging back into this area?

Abruptly, another burst of gunfire erupted, further away this time and well to the north. This time the sound of automatic weapons was punctuated by the sharp crack of pistol shots.

Tony, he thought, with a queasy feeling in his gut. Tony and Cannaday were into it with the two guys he had seen heading in their direction.

In the deep, forbidding silence that followed, Matt knew the confrontation was over, but he could only guess at how it had turned out, only hope Tony was okay, only pray he had reached the car and the radio in time.

He lunged forward, catching a glimpse of the roof of the house through the trees.

"Sarah!" he hissed in a loud whisper. "Sarah, where are you?"

He listened intently for a moment and thought he heard something, but maybe it was only the breeze in the grass.

"Sarah!" he said again, daring to let his voice rise a decibel louder this time.

He saw her running toward him then, her hair disheveled, her mouth quivering, tears streaming down her face. At first, he thought she was a trick of his imagination. If you wanted to see something badly enough, you would make yourself see it, right?

But she was real. He knew she was real when he threw his

arms around her and felt her shaking and struggling for breath.

"Oh, Matt," she gasped. "Oh, God, Matt, I thought I'd never see you again."

He held her frantically to him for a second. "Come on," he said then. "There's no time to talk. There's no time for anything. Lets get the hell out of here."

"But where?"

"That way," he panted, pointing north. "We've got to get to Tony's car."

"But I heard shooting over there."

"Doesn't matter," he said. "They're all around us. At least I know Tony and Cannaday went that way. We'll stand a better chance together than we do like this."

Ten minutes later, without seeing or hearing anything else of the gunmen, they came cautiously around a small patch of young trees and within sight of the old shed. Tony's white Dodge was still sitting there where they had left it yesterday, except that the door on the driver's side was standing open. Matt could see a vague figure behind the steering wheel, and for an instant his heart jumped with exhilaration.

Tony had made it, after all, he thought. Help was on the way. Thank God.

He sprinted toward the car, pulling Sarah along behind him, but when he was halfway there, he stopped with a start, sensing that something was wrong. He noticed that one of the tires on the squad car was flat and water was pouring out from under the radiator. Then he saw the line of bullet holes that started at the front fender and ran down one whole side of the car.

When he realized that the line passed squarely across the open door where Tony was sitting, he felt himself go sick inside.

He handed the briefcase to Sarah, pushed her behind him, and inched forward, holding the pistol out in front of him with both hands.

A dead man in green military fatigues was sprawled on the ground in a puddle of blood ten feet from the side of the car, and an automatic rifle was lying beside him. The man had been shot several times at close range. He was lying on his back with a surprised expression on what was left of his face. Most of the right side of his head was blown away.

Matt leaned past the open car door and looked inside at Tony. The stream of bullets from the AK-47 had cut him almost in half. They had gouged holes in the upholstery, and some of them had chewed all the way through the car and exited out the other side. Spatters of blood were everywhere —on the windows, the front seat, the dashboard, even the roof. Tony was still clutching his service revolver in his right hand, but his head was flopped back against the seat with blood pouring from his nose and mouth. He was trying his best to say something, but he seemed to be choking on his own blood.

"Oh, my God," Sarah said brokenly and turned away.

Matt reached out and tried to lift Tony's head. When he did, he saw Tony's eyes move toward him and realized he was still conscious.

"Did you get through, Tony?" he asked. "Did you get to use the radio?"

Tony's lips moved, but no sound came out, only more blood.

"What happened to Cannaday?" Matt asked. "Do you know?"

He thought Tony shook his head, or tried to, but he couldn't be sure. Then he heard Tony saying something in a horrible, gurgling voice.

"Call Benedict . . . FBI . . ."

There was one final spasmodic movement, then Tony's eyes glazed over and his neck went limp. He was dead.

Matt had no time to feel grief or sorrow. Those would come later—if there was a later. So would the stabbing, accusing daggers of guilt and self-blame. None of it would ever have happened if it hadn't been for him and his oh-so-clever little plan. If he had let Tony handle it his way, Tony would still be alive and they would all be safe and sound somewhere. How could he ever have convinced himself that such a stupid scheme would work?

He whirled away, his head reeling, and saw Sarah, her face

white and stricken, reeling and gagging against the back fender of the car.

Suddenly, he heard the sound of voices from somewhere across the meadow behind him. There was one distinct shout, then another, the second one closer than the first. Somebody was coming, and he didn't think it was anyone they wanted to see. Whoever it was wasn't very far away, either.

Clumsily and with hands that felt as though all the strength had drained out of them, he grabbed Sarah and dragged her away from the car and the ramshackle shed. He at least had to try to get her out of this alive. He was really past caring about himself, but he couldn't let them get Sarah.

"Come on," he said. "Come on, or we're dead, too."

There was a creek back in the woods, if they could get that far. As a boy, he had memorized every inch of that creek, every bend in its sandy bed, every cave in its red clay banks, every tree that towered above it. The creek eventually wound its way to within a few hundred feet of the isolated crossroads community of Prairieville. There was a store there—at least there used to be. There would also be people, a telephone, a mailbox, and a highway to somewhere else—connections to a world where everything was still sane and ordinary.

That other world *was* still out there, wasn't it?

It would be a long, arduous hike to Prairieville through the deep sand and occasional thigh-deep pools of the creek, but it was the only escape route open to them. The road was out of the question.

The creek was their last chance to keep from ending up like Tony.

No sight Matt could remember had ever been more welcome than the little white store with the two red gasoline pumps in front, which constituted the bulk of "downtown" Prairieville.

It was approaching noon, and he was sure they had traveled at least six or seven miles along the mostly dry stream bed, although it could have been even further. The last time he had traveled that meandering route, he had been about

13 years old and it had been a big adventure to go all the way to Prairieville by way of the creek. Now, though, he felt about 100 years old, and he was fearful, demoralized, exhausted and worried about Sarah. She was not only dead on her feet but also seemed to be in a mild state of shock, and they had to stop at frequent intervals to let her rest.

He had still managed to feel a faint hint of elation, however, as he clamored up the steep ten-foot creek bank, while Sarah stayed below to catch her breath, and found himself within sight of the farm-to-market highway. He knew then they were within a half-mile of where the store should be.

Once they had reached the creek, they had neither seen nor heard anything more of the assassination squad that had invaded the old farm. Matt had no idea what had happened to Cannaday. The sergeant had done a miserable job of covering Tony, but Matt was pretty sure by now that Tony had managed to make radio contact with police headquarters before he was shot, anyway. About an hour after they had begun their trek along the creek bed, they saw a low-flying police helicopter circling slowly overhead, and later on, they either caught sight of it or heard the sound of its engine two or three more times.

Beyond that, however, they were totally in the dark about what was going on. In a sense, their ignorance may have been the most distressing part of the whole tragedy. As the morning wore on, Matt could feel it feeding his fear and uncertainty until a kind of paranoia grew up inside him. With Tony dead, there seemed to be nobody left to trust. Tony's dying words had seemed to be a plea to contact somebody named Benedict with the FBI. Did this mean that Tony had already told the FBI something about the case? Was it possible that the assault team at the farm hadn't been sent by Tommy Van Zandt at all, but by some clandestine agency of the federal government—or maybe even the Soviets? Tony had said the two hitmen in Arkansas were KGB agents, and if this were true, maybe the human killing machines at the farm were Red Army shock troops. And what about Cannaday? Was it possible that he was actually a spy for the other side, who had been planted in their midst strictly to set them up for the kill? Was it all some giant, interwoven international conspiracy to get rid of him and Sarah and anyone else who might know anything about the damnable evidence, once and for all.

Even as they echoed through his brain, the questions sounded insane. But he couldn't make them stop, and he had no answers for them. All he knew was that he was through trusting cops and other so-called authorities. He was through trying to deal or reason or do the right thing. He had one final ace up his sleeve, and he was going to play it. Then, when that was done, he and Sarah were going to run for cover. Somehow, they had to buy themselves some time—time to get over the shock and try to sort things out, time to think

Somehow, they had to get away. That was all he knew.

It was 11:45 when they trudged up to the wooden portico in front of the country store. He made Sarah sit down on the worn bench in front while he went inside to buy two Cokes and inquire about the availability of a telephone.

"Yes, sir, it's right over there on the wall," said the middle-aged woman behind the counter, indicating a pay phone. "That'll be ninety cents. You-all having car trouble?"

"Uh, yeah," Matt said. "I've got to call somebody to come get us."

"You see some kind of excitement going on down the road?" the woman asked.

"Not that I noticed," Matt said guardedly. "Why?"

"Just wondered," she said. "I saw a helicopter circling around a while ago. We don't see many helicopters around here."

He took Sarah her Coke, then went back inside, dialed information and asked for the main number of the *Dallas Times Herald*. What he had in mind was a complete shot in the dark, but it was the only thing he could think of to try at this point.

"Sam Garrett, please," he said when the *Times Herald* switchboard operator answered.

There was a long, vacant pause. Sweet Jesus, let Sam be there, he prayed silently. Let him be working on a Saturday morning, even if he's the head honcho in charge of everything these days.

"City desk," a male voice said.

"Is Sam Garrett around?" Matt asked, trying to keep the desperation out of his voice.

"Hang on a second," the voice said, and Matt felt himself being put on hold.

A few seconds later, he heard Sam's unmistakable drawl on the line.

"This is Garrett. Can I help you?"

"Oh, Christ, I hope so, Sam," he said. "This is Matt Eastman."

It took a minute or two to persuade Sam to stop trying to catch up on everything that had taken place over the past 18 years and just listen. But when Matt finally succeeded, he told Sam as quickly and succinctly as possible what was happening: A deputy Dallas police chief and his murderer were both dead; a second officer was missing; seven other hired gunmen were at large in the area with an undetermined number of police out looking for them.

And, most importantly, the whole bizarre chain of events had a direct relationship to Tom Van Zandt, the man who would be governor of Texas, and the 24-year-old events surrounding the assassination of John F. Kennedy.

Matt realized it was a little much for anybody to digest on such short notice, but Sam Garrett did an admirable job of it.

"Listen, Sam," Matt said, "I'm going to leave an envelope for you at the store in Prairieville. I don't trust the mails, and even if I did mail it, you wouldn't get it until Monday or Tuesday, and I want to get it into your hands as fast as I can. This envelope is full of dynamite, Sam, believe me."

"I believe you," Sam said, "but where's Prairieville?"

"It's in Kaufman County, about five miles by farm-to-market road from the old farm where all the action's going on. The envelope's got some pictures in it that show Van Zandt hobnobbing with Lee Harvey Oswald a few weeks before the assassination, plus a written explanation of where the pictures were taken and what they mean. At this point, nothing would make me happier than to see one or two of those pictures on the front page of the *Times Herald* tomorrow.''

"I'll send somebody by to pick the envelope up, Matt," Sam said. "I've already got two reporters and a photographer heading that way, and they should be there in thirty or forty minutes.

"I'll be gone by then," Matt said. "I've got to get away from here."

"Where can I get in touch with you later?"

"You can't," Matt said, "but I'll get back to you when I can."

"I hope so," Sam said. "I guess you know if I got a call like this from anybody but you, I'd be pretty sure I was dealing with a nut."

"I wouldn't blame you," Matt said, "but I guarantee you this is on the level."

"Okay," Sam said. "In the meantime, I won't make any promises about front page pictures, but I'll damned sure take a look at what you've got."

As soon as he hung up, Matt opened the briefcase, took out a manila envelope he had prepared for Sam several days earlier and handed it to the woman storekeeper with instructions that it would be picked up shortly by a *Times Herald* reporter.

He laid a $20 bill on top of the envelope. "Promise me you'll put it in his hands, no matter what happens between now and then," he said, "and make him show you some identification first, okay?"

"Sure, mister," she said, gingerly picking up the bill and tucking it into her apron. Then she frowned at him. "I'll bet you've got something to do with that excitement down the road, after all, don't you?" she asked.

He smiled blankly at her. "What excitement?" he said.

About five minutes later, an old blue Chevy pickup chugged up to the gas pumps in front of the store, and a strawhatted farmer in overalls climbed out and went inside.

Matt was sitting on the bench under the portico with Sarah and wondering what they were going to do next, when he looked over at the truck and felt a peculiar tingling sensation inside his skull. At first, he thought maybe he was having a stroke of some kind. God knows, he had been under enough pressure for the past few hours to have a physical malfunction of some kind. But then he decided the sensation was merely an idea trying to form in his almost paralyzed brain.

Slowly at first, then faster and faster the idea took shape. He saw that the keys were still in the ignition of the pickup. From the position of the truck, the farmer had obviously stopped to buy gas, but the gas tank probably wasn't completely empty. Most likely, there was enough gas in it to get 20 or 30 miles down the road, maybe even further. Enough to get someplace where they might be safe for a few hours.

He put his arm gently around Sarah's shoulders and felt her lean limply against him.

"Sarah, baby," he asked with his lips close to her ear, "have you got enough energy left to run over and jump in that truck?"

She nodded vaguely, not seeming to comprehend the question.

"And can you do it in a real big hurry when I say 'go'?"

"I guess so," she said. "But why?"

He stood up, pulling her to her feet as he did. He glanced once toward the dark interior of the store, then guided her quickly toward the blue pickup.

"Because," he said, reaching for the door handle on the driver's side, "I think we're about to add car theft to our growing list of crimes."

CHAPTER TWENTY-TWO

November 8, 1987

Despite the small, distinguished patches of gray at his temples, Tom Van Zandt was still almost hurtfully handsome. His clean-cut, all-American good looks were so flawless, in fact, that virtually no retouching had been necessary on the photographs for his campaign billboards, 500 of which had been positioned on major highways across the state. And even for his TV appearances, the makeup people scarcely had to do anything at all with his face.

As Jerry Barnhill, his press aide, often said, if Tom Van Zandt had been an actor, he would have been in constant demand to portray a governor or senator or even the President of the United States. He looked exactly like what most people thought a political leader ought to look like, and he reveled in that fact, especially since his chief opponent in the Republican primary was a squatty, balding state senator from Lubbock.

Tommy Van Zandt's physical attributes didn't stop with a pretty face, either. He was also still as trim, virile and athletic-looking as most men half his age. And his looks were only the start. They were merely among the most obvious on a long list of advantages that had made him the odds-on favorite to win the governor's mansion in Austin in next year's election from the moment he had announced.

For one thing, he was enormously wealthy, with a personal fortune now in excess of $200 million. And in a state as populous and geographically vast as Texas, the ability to spend the most money in a campaign was often tantamount to election. He also had many powerful and influential friends in government, both at the state and federal level, and hundreds of people in key positions who owed him one type of favor or another.

His only real drawback was a lack of political experience, but he had good name-identification, Barnhill said, as a result of his high-profile job as CEO of one of the state's largest defense contractors (not to mention a carefully orchestrated series of large financial donations to various good causes over the past five years). Being the head man at Conlan Universal Aerospace since 1983 had firmly established his management credentials, but he had never run for any kind of political office before. Except for a brief stint as a deputy secretary of defense during the early years of the Reagan administration, he had never held any sort of governmental job, but that appointment should prove to be enough of a springboard. After all, John Connally had never been anything but a deputy Navy secretary before he won the governorship, and Tommy Van Zandt was every bit as handsome as "Big John" had been in his political prime.

In short, just about everything was going his way—so much so that he could actually see himself as a serious candidate for the White House in another six or eight years—until the goddamned envelope had arrived in the mail three days ago.

The goddamned envelope had changed the whole scenario. It had been the biggest shock of his life. It had also been the beginning of the end of all his dreams.

Still, he might have been able to head off the crisis of the envelope if he had been allowed to handle it his own way, if Alex Sutton hadn't had to interfere. It was Alex, even more than Matt Eastman, who had finally—irrevocably and irreparably—fucked up the whole works. By the time Alex and his goddamned storm troopers got through, there was nothing left to do but sit and stare out the window and think about what might have been.

Which was precisely what Tommy Van Zandt was doing right now, at 6 o'clock on a Sunday evening, as he sat alone in his private office on the second floor of his Denton County ranch house, brooding and drinking Scotch with a vengeance. A glass sat on the desk before him with an inch of Chivas Regal remaining in the bottom of it. On the wall behind the desk, draped carefully between the head of an elk he had killed in Colorado and the rack of antlers from a 12-point buck deer he had felled in New Mexico, was a huge red, white and blue banner.

"VICTORY WITH VAN ZANDT," it said.

Goddamn Alex Sutton, he thought, and he could feel the heat of his anger burning his face as he sipped his drink.

He never should have given Alex as much rein as he had, never allowed him to assume such a vital role in CUA management, and certainly never told him about Eastman and the envelope. Alex was extremely useful, and almost mechnically efficient when any type of violent unpleasantness was in order, but he had become far, far too dangerous in the past few years. Tommy knew he should have arranged a funeral for Alex right after they got rid of Dee Conlan, but the problem was, he had never been able to find anyone he trusted to do the job. Alex had turned CUA's security corps into his own private army—an army whose loyalty to its "general" was beyond any question. And outside of this collection of vicious hoodlums, ruthless ex-cops and hardened killers, Tommy didn't know anyone who was even remotely capable of getting the best of Alex.

And so, instead of being eliminated, the problem had grown. And the closer Tommy had sensed himself coming to the governor's mansion, the more acute it had become.

"You murderous sonofabitch," he snarled, slamming his empty glass down and reaching for the decanter on the credenza. "You just never get enough, do you?"

Tony knew he could have struck a deal with Matt Eastman if Alex had just stayed out of it. Tommy had always had Matt figured as a reasonable sort of guy. That was why he had offered him the job at CUA so many years ago. Tommy was convinced that both Matt Eastman's evidence and his permanent silence could have been bought for $540,000, and he would hardly even have missed the money. The money would have been nothing to get excited about. He had been ready and willing to pay it and forget it, but then he had made the terminally stupid mistake of telling Alex about it, and Alex had gone totally bonkers.

"I've chased that damned weasel all over this country, and somehow he's always managed to get away," Alex had said, "but I promise you he won't get away this time. This time I'm going to make sure."

Only he hadn't.

Tommy took a gulp of his fresh drink and listened to the muted sounds of telephones ringing down the hallway in Jerry Barnhill's office. The fucking phones had been ringing incessantly ever since before noon, keeping three staff people busy constantly repeating the same phrase over and over.

"Mr. Van Vandt will have no comment on the matter until Monday."

For all the good it was doing, he might as well have just taken the phones off the hook and sent the people home, but he couldn't quite bring himself to do that. He kept thinking that there must be an out somewhere, somehow, but he hadn't been able to find it, even before beginning to dull his thought processes with Scotch.

He heard a soft knock at the door, and the door opened almost instantly, even before he could respond. It was Pendleton, his very proper, very English personal aide, and there was an expression of pained discomfort on his face.

"Damn it, Pendleton, I told you I didn't want to be disturbed," Tommy snapped.

"I'm sorry, sir," he said, "but there have been some developments I thought you would want to know about."

"Developments? What could possibly develop that hasn't already?"

"Apparently, the *Dallas Times Herald* is coming out with another, more detailed article in its Monday editions," Pendleton said, "and one of their editors is on the line. He says he wants to read you the story and give you an opportunity to comment on it before it's published. Also, the Dallas bureau chief of the Associated Press is on another line. He's apparently seen an advance copy of the *Times Herald* article and is also asking for comment."

"Tell the bastards I'm still not available," Tommy said sourly. "I won't have a goddamned thing to say to any of the fucking media until sometime tomorrow at the earliest. That's all."

"Very good, sir," Pendleton said. He turned, closing the door softly behind him.

Tommy drank some more of the Chivas Regal as a growing sense of panic filled his chest. He reached over and pulled the bulky Sunday edition of the *Times Herald* across the desk toward him. What good would it do to listen to tomorrow's story after what they had already done to him? They had gutted him, totally gutted him. He directed his whiskey-blurred gaze at the inch-high black headlines across the top of the front page and shuddered as he read the damning words over again:

OLD PHOTOS LINK VAN ZANDT
TO JFK ASSASSINATION PLOT

And just below the main headlines, a smaller subhead added:

Gubernatorial favorite also named as murder suspect following wild Saturday shootout in Kaufman County

Why the hell couldn't they have just given Matt Eastman his money? Why did it have to come to this?

Through the tears forming in his eyes, Tommy stared down at the small 24-year-old file photo of Mollie O'Connor beside the larger picture of himself grinning and talking with that imbecile Oswald, and he ground his teeth so hard that he made his head ache. Sometimes he hated all women, including Kimberly, the buxom blonde bimbo just four years out of SMU who was supposed to be his fiancée. But he hated this one on the newspaper page in front of more than all the others combined.

"I wish I could have been there to see you die, you bitch," he said. aloud.

He wadded up the newspaper and flung it furiously across the room. There was somebody else he hated, too, he thought, somebody who wasn't going to get away, by God, with what this heavy-handedness had caused to happen, somebody who was going to pay, one way or another, for wrecking Tommy Van Zandt's most cherished lifelong dream.

He pressed the button on the intercom and heard Pendleton's instantaneous well-modulated reply.

"Have you been able to locate Alex Sutton yet," Tommy demanded.

"No, sir," Pendleton said. "No one's seen him at his office since early this morning, and there's still no answer at his condominium. We tried both numbers again just ten minutes ago."

"Well, keep trying."

"Yes, sir. Incidentally, sir, we just received another call from the Dallas district attorney's office. It's the third time they've called in the past hour."

"What did they say?"

"Mr. William Danforth, the chief prosecutor, requests that you call him at your earliest convenience."

The panic in his chest grew abruptly larger, like a balloon being inflated with a sudden burst of air. Tommy sighed. "All right," he said heavily. "Get him on the line for me."

While he waited for Pendleton to make the call and ring him back, Tommy poured himself another generous portion of Scotch. He was getting very drunk, which was something he rarely did, but the whiskey was doing almost nothing to dull the pain in his head.

Will Danforth and Tommy knew each other fairly well. They were both graduates of SMU Law School, and once long ago, Tommy had been an assistant DA himself. Both of them also belonged to several of the same clubs and were nodding acquaintances who had many mutual friends, although they never moved in the same social circles and Danforth's salary as chief prosecutor was little more than pocket change for Tom Van Zandt. Danforth was a good lawyer and a tough one, but he was a nice enough guy, as far as Tommy could tell. He also had aspirations about running for DA on the Republican ticket—aspirations that Governor Tom Van Zandt would be able to aid considerably. Surely he wasn't going to stir up a bunch of shit over these ridiculous allegations in the *Times Herald*.

The phone on the desk rang, and Tommy picked it up.

"Mr. Danforth's on the line, sir," Pendleton said crisply.

"Hey there, Will," Tommy said, forcing hearty cordiality into a voice that felt as though it might collapse at any second, "what can I do for you, old friend?"

Danforth's voice was unpleasantly stiff. "There's no easy way to tell you this, Tom," he said, "but this office is in the process of preparing capital murder charges against you, and we expect those charges to be formally filed within the hour."

Tommy felt his jaw go slack. "Murder charges?" he said. "In this absurd business about President Kennedy? What the hell do you mean?"

"It doesn't have anything to do with the Kennedy matter," Danforth said. "We'll leave that up to the feds, but we're charging you with two counts of capital murder in the death of D. Wingo Conlan four years ago and the death of Deputy Chief Antonio Canales yesterday morning."

"That's bullshit, Will," Tommy slurred in a shaking voice. "It sounds to me like the DA's office was sold out to the goddamned Democrats. They put you up to this, didn't they?"

"This is no political stunt, Tom, I assure you," Danforth said. "Judge Stillwell's issuing an exhumation order on Conlan's body in the morning. If the medical examiner finds what I think he'll find, we can prove capital murder in any court in the state."

The incriminating words of blame flew out of Tommy's mouth before his aching, addled brain could clamp it shut. "But what about Alex Sutton? He was there, too. He was the one . . ." he finally managed to stop himself from saying any more, but he knew it was too late.

"There's a warrant out for Sutton, too," Danforth said coldly, "but we're talking about you now, Tom. If you'll agree to surrender yourself at the Dallas County Courthouse within the next two hours, I'll spare you the embarrassment of sending officers out there to arrest you."

"What about bail, Will?" Tommy asked grimly. "If I agree to come in, will you recommend bail?"

"I'll recommend $500,000," Danforth said, "but only if you surrender yourself by 8:30 tonight. After that, there's no deal. I may go for a million, or I may go for no bail at all on the grounds that your freedom constitutes a public menace."

Tommy was vaguely aware of mumbling something as he hung up the phone. Then all the panic and sorrow inside him welled up in an overwhelming flood tide. He laid his pounding head on the desk, and the huge tears that rolled down his cheeks soon formed a puddle under his face.

This, too, was all Alex Sutton's fault. They had never needed to kill a poor, pathetic fool like Conlan. They had already gotten everything he had that they wanted, and he had been too stupid and childish to hurt them, even if he had tried. But Alex had insisted on getting him out of the way. It had been Alex who had suggested the subtle poison that would make Dee's death look exactly like a heart attack. It had been Alex who had obtained the stuff, and Alex who had put it in Conlan's drink as the three of them sat in Conlan's office. But now Alex was gone. Probably he had gotten away clean, to Mexico or even overseas, and left Tommy to shoulder the blame for all the rotten things he had done, the bastard.

"I would've been such a good governor," Tommy cried aloud.

After about five minutes, some semblance of reality began to penetrate his broken-hearted stupor, and he managed to pull himself together slightly and try to think. He realized there were several things he had to do, and that all of them had to be done in a hurry.

Somehow, he forced himself to function. He picked up the phone and told Pendleton to have the Mercedes brought around to the front porch. He also instructed him to call

Carroll Winship, CUA's general counsel, with orders to meet Tommy at the courthouse by no later than 8:30 with a certified check for $500,000. Tommy didn't care how Winship got a check certified on a Sunday night or how much he had to pay a bail bondsman.

All he knew was that he couldn't stand the humiliation of spending the night in jail, the disgrace of being locked up like a common criminal. He thought he would almost rather die first.

"Before you do anything else, though, get me some valium" Tommy rasped at Pendleton as he hung up. "My goddamn head's killing me."

As unthinkable as it was, maybe it was time to forget about appearances and the governor's race and everything else except sheer survival. Maybe it was time to admit defeat and plan his escape before it was too late. There was plenty of money in Switzerland . . .

The door opened and Pendleton came in. He was carrying a small tray with two white tablets in a paper cup and a glass of water. Tommy eschewed the water and gulped the pills down with a mouthful of Scotch. Now maybe his head would stop hurting enough so that he could think.

As he set the glass back down on the desk, he felt a sudden, tight discomfort rise in his chest. It turned almost immediately into a sharp, stabbing pain directly beneath his sternum. He felt as if all the air were being squeezed out of his lungs, and when he tried to catch his breath, the stabbing pain came again, even sharper than before. It was followed by another, then another.

Tommy tried to stand, but the pain crushed him back into his chair. He clawed at his tie and shirt collar, fighting desperately for oxygen.

"Good God, I feel sick," he gasped. "What's . . . what's happening to me?"

His blurring, frantic eyes found Pendleton's impassive face for an instant. There was a peculiar, twisted smile on Pendleton's thin lips.

"I think you're having a heart attack, sir," Pendleton said quietly as the room went black.

*   *   *

Matt lay tense on the hard motel mattress and alternately watched the flickering image on the screen of the black-and-white TV and the faint reflections from the flashing sign outside that danced across the wall in front of him. Occasionally, he reached over for the can of half-warm beer on the nightstand beside the bed and took a small sip, not because he really wanted the beer but simply to have something to do with his fidgety hands for a moment. If he had still been a smoker, this was the kind of night when he could have gone through a whole pack of cigarettes in a matter of three or four hours.

It was a little before 10 p.m. on Sunday—well over 36 hours since the blitzkrieg at the farm—but the combination of shock and despair still lingered on, creating a kind of mental paralysis that he couldn't seem to shake. Sarah had drifted off to sleep a few minutes earlier. Sarah always managed to fall asleep, no matter what, but for Matt, such relief seemed out of the question. Even the night before, when he had felt as physically exhausted and psychologically defeated as he could ever remember feeling, sleep had come only in short, grudging catnaps, most of them separated by extended periods of wakefulness.

He had watched the TV news and had seen the Sunday *Times Herald*. Sam Garrett had done his job thoroughly and with obvious satisfaction. Matt doubted that he could have done a better job with the story if Sam had let him lay out the page and write the headlines himself. But even knowing the trauma that Tommy Van Zandt must be going through by now because of the story didn't help Matt's mood or improve his ability to fall asleep.

Neither did it alter the facts. Tony Canales was dead, and his death had been Matt Eastman's fault. It was just that simple. Even if Tommy Van Zandt and Alex Sutton both paid with their lives and rotted in hell for what they had done, nothing could change what had happened yesterday. And nothing could erase the dead, heavy feeling that rested like a bag of cement in Matt Eastman's gut.

He had purposely driven the stolen pickup until it ran out of gas, then ditched it on Interstate 20 east of the Wills Point exit, then walked and hitchhiked the 15 miles back to the small, nondescript motel near Terrell. Although he knew his thinking was rather muddled by this time, Matt hoped when the authorities found the pickup, they would assume whoever stole it had continued on east in the direction they had been heading, rather than doubling back to the west, as they had actually done.

After telling the owner of the motel that their car had broken down and was in a town garage until Monday, they had gone directly to their room and barricaded themselves behind the triple-locked door. They had ventured out only a few times since—once to buy the newspaper, once for sandwich fixings, chips and beer from a store down the way, and once for a miserable breakfast of underdone bacon, microwaved eggs and brackish coffee at the motel restaurant.

They were reluctant to talk to anyone for fear they might give themselves away as fugitives. In fact, they were almost afraid to talk to each other. It was as if verbalizing their situation would only make matters worse somehow. Although Sarah didn't say much about it, he knew they basically disagreed on what course of action to take next. As usual, Matt was inclined to run for cover, to sneak back to Arkansas and try to blot out everything that had happened, or even to go somewhere new and start a fresh chapter in the game of hide-and-seek. In fact, if it hadn't been for Sarah's quiet resistance, they might already have been gone by now. In spite of everything, she still quietly insisted they should turn the briefcase over to the cops and get the whole mess settled once and for all.

Tony's dying words also frequently haunted Matt. One part of his brain kept telling him to heed Tony's admonition and call the FBI, but another part suggested insinuatingly that even the FBI couldn't be trusted.

There was no one they could trust anymore, he thought. Everybody in the whole damned world was out to get them.

He took another sip from the can of beer and made a face. The stuff was bitter, almost flat and just barely cool. He had never understood how something that tasted so good ice-cold could taste so disgusting lukewarm. The beer was a hopeless case, he decided, and there was no sense in opening another can. Since they had no refrigeration in the room, the new beer would be almost as unpalatable as the old one. The old movie flickering on the TV was a lost cause, too. The story line, if there was one, was completely lost to him, and the movie was nothing more than background noise to keep him from thinking too much.

What he really needed to do was force himself to lose consciousness if he could. If he could get even four or five hours of deep, uninterrupted sleep, the world might not look so bleak in the morning. He might even be able to think things through.

He was getting up to turn the TV off when he heard the sound outside the door and froze in a sitting position on the edge of the mattress, listening.

It sounded like a key turning in the lock.

Maybe somebody's just got the wrong room, he thought.

Bullshit, an inner voice snapped.

His hand slipped under his pillow and found the .357 Magnum there. Then he waited, with his heart pounding in his ears.

The door flew open suddenly and with great force. He heard the cheap chain ripped from its moorings as the door crashed back against the wall. Almost simultaneously, someone hit the light switch just to the left of the doorway, flooding the room with light.

Out of the corner of his eye, Matt saw Sarah sit up and heard her muffled scream. He raised the heavy Magnum with both hands, but realized almost instantly that it was useless. The room was already overflowing with tense, hard-faced men in business suits, and no less than four pistols were leveled at him.

"Drop it," one of the intruders said thinly. "We don't want to shoot you. We're federal agents."

The hell you say, Matt thought, looking from face to face. He expected one of them to be Alex Sutton's, but none of them were. He lowered the gun slowly, then tossed it to the foot of the bed, feeling it bounce against the mattress.

One of the men leaned over quickly and retrieved the Magnum. He holstered his own weapon and handed the long-barreled pistol to one of the others.

"Are you Matthew Eastman and Sarah Archer?" he asked. He seemed to be in charge.

Matt just nodded, feeling his exhaustion and depression disintegrating into hopelessness. But Sarah hugged the sheet around herself and blinked defiantly at the man. "I don't think you really have to ask," she said.

The man held out a badge and an identification card in a leather case. "I'm Special Agent Peter Benedict of the FBI," he said. "You two led us one hell of a chase, and I'm still trying to figure out why."

"Why not?" Matt said. "For all we knew, we had another one of Tommy Van Zandt's murder squads chasing us."

"You won't have to worry about Tom Van Zandt anymore," Benedict said. "He died about three hours ago."

Matt felt neither grief nor relief at the news. In fact, he felt nothing. It was as though he were incapable of any further shock.

"What he'd die of?" Sarah asked.

"It had all the appearances of a heart attack," Benedict said, "but we're pretty sure it was poison. Probably the same chemical that killed D. Wingo Conlan. Right now, it looks like suicide."

"Where's Alex Sutton?" Matt asked.

"Nobody knows," Benedict said. "There are warrants out for him, though."

"Are *we* under arrest?" Sarah demanded. "You're supposed to read us our rights if we are."

"Let's just say you're under the protection of the federal government for the moment," Benedict told her. "How long you remain so depends to a large extent on how fully you cooperate. Now, if you'll both get dressed, we'll wait outside. Then we'll give you a ride to Dallas. We've got accommodations waiting for you there, so you can relax and get a good night's sleep."

Not likely, Matt thought, not likely at all. "And then what happens?"

"Then," said Benedict, "beginning tomorrow morning, we've got an awful lot of talking to do."

CHAPTER TWENTY-THREE

At precisely 9 a.m. on Tuesday morning, the two unsmiling, noncommittal FBI agents assigned to Matt and Sarah appeared outside their rooms to drive them the two blocks from their hotel to the Dallas Federal Building. Once there, the agents escorted them onto the elevator, then down the barren and now unpleasantly familiar corridor to the same impersonal interview room where they had spent more than ten hours the day before.

"Just make yourselves comfortable," one of the agents said, "and someone will be with you in a few minutes." Then the two agents closed the door firmly and left them there.

Inwardly, Matt was resigned to the idea that they would probably spend the bulk of today inside the drab little room, just as they had yesterday. For all he knew, they would keep them there all week, maybe for the rest of the month. Hell, maybe forever. They had already told everything they could possibly tell, not only to Special Agent Peter Benedict, but to a half-dozen other people who wandered in from time to time to participate in the interrogation, as well. The FBI referred to it as a debriefing session, but to Matt, it bore a close resemblance to the kind of seemingly endless grilling he had seen suspects undergo in the old days at the Dallas police station. It was a good deal more subtle and restrained, but it seemed just as endless—and, after a while, just as pointless.

But he kept telling himself that he didn't care, one way or the other. They could keep them there, repeating their inane questions over and over as long as he lived, for all he cared. Sometime during the past 72 hours, he had experienced an almost total emotional shutdown. He no longer felt fear or anger or even grief. In their place was only a hollow emptiness. He would have much preferred to be left alone, to withdraw to some dark, remote, quiet place and go to bed with Sarah for about a week. But he was also desensitized to the point that he thought he could endure just anything for any length of time, if it came to that.

Sarah, on the other hand, was uptight, irritable and on the brink of rebellion.

"Comfortable, hell," she growled between clenched teeth at the closed door. "How could anybody be comfortable in a place like this? These chairs belong in a medieval torture chamber. I'd rather sit on the floor."

The echo of her pronouncement had scarcely died when the door opened again and Peter Benedict came into the room, accompanied by another man. Where Benedict was tall, impeccably groomed and thin-faced, the other man was short, stocky and heavy-jowled. He was also a stranger, whom Matt was certain had not been there before.

"Good morning," Benedict said coolly but amiably. "I hope you had a good night's sleep. You both looked like you could use it when we finished up yesterday." He turned and indicated the stocky man. "This is Jonas Moorhead of the Central Intelligence Agency," he said. "He'd like to talk to you for a few minutes, maybe ask you some questions."

"Why not?" Sarah said sourly. "Everybody else has."

Moorhead stared silently at her for a moment, then glanced at Matt, and finally sat down at the opposite end of the table from them without offering any greeting or making any effort to shake hands. Matt wondered if Moorhead always wore such a pissed-off expression or if it were especially for their benefit.

"Things will go a lot better all the way around if you'll just take a cooperative attitude, Miss Archer," Benedict told her. "This is a necessary procedure, believe me." He nodded at Moorhead. "I'll be down the hall when you're done," he said.

The three of them sat at the table facing each other for a long minute after Benedict's departure. When Moorhead finally spoke, Matt wasn't surprised that his unpleasant tone of voice exactly matched the expression on his face. What did surprise him was the meaning of Moorhead's words as it gradually sunk in.

"You people are living examples of why the media in this country needs to be controlled," he said testily. "I hope you know you've come about this close"—he held up a thumb and forefinger spaced approximately a half-inch apart—"to causing the United States government one hell of a lot of trouble and embarrassment. Do you realize that?"

Matt saw Sarah's cheeks flush bright red, but she managed to keep her mouth shut—at least for the moment—when he knew she wanted to scream.

"We've had a little trouble ourselves lately, Mr. Moorhead," Matt said blandly.

"Nothing at all compared to what you'd have if I had my way, Mr. Eastman, I assure you," Moorhead said. "This is the FBI's case, so it's up to Benedict and his people to decide what to do with you, but if they left it up to me, I'd make damned sure you were put out of circulation for a good long while."

"For what?" Sarah demanded, no longer able to contain herself. "I'm still trying to figure out what we did that was so godawful wrong—except for stealing some old farmer's pickup truck, I mean."

When Moorhead replied, it was the exaggerated patience of a man trying to explain nuclear fission to a three-year-old. "The only thing you did, Miss Archer," he said, "was damned near touch off the worst international incident of the decade, that's all. What you did could have put Soviet-American relations right back in the dark ages. You could have screwed up any chance for a super-power summit or meaningful disarmament talks for the next five years, all because of this witch-hunt of yours.''

"I don't have the vaguest idea what you're talking about,'' Matt said.

"I'm talking about Alexander Sutton,'' said Moorhead, "only we're certain now that his name isn't Alexander Sutton at all. The real Alexander Sutton was apparently kidnapped and killed in Germany in 1957. We're pretty sure the man who's been using his name for the past thirty years is actually a crack KGB agent named Igor Kaminsky.''

Even in his emotionally drained state, Matt felt his jaw drop with surprise. Then it was true. As much as Matt had thought about it and pondered over the possibility after seeing and hearing what had been in the briefcase, the shock of realizing it was true hit him with the force of a punch in the stomach. "Good Old Alex" had never been "Good Old Alex" at all. Jamie Cade's drinking buddy and Mollie O'Connor's boyfriend was an incredible, king-size imposter. The intrepid former lieutenant of homicide and chief of security for one of the nation's largest defense contractors was a goddamned Russian spy!

"But that's not the point,'' Moorhead continued. "The point is, we absolutely cannot—we *dare* not—give any official indication that we know this. If we accuse the Soviet government of complicity in the murder of an American President—if we even imply such a thing—we may not get Gorbachev to the negotiating table in this century, for godsake.''

There it went again, Matt thought. It seemed that every time he convinced himself he was totally beyond outrage, every time he was sure he was incapable of experiencing genuine fury anymore, he suddenly surprised himself by getting furious. It was happening again, and it was happening right now. It was happening because he couldn't believe his ears. A goddamned Russian agent masterminds the assassination of the President of the United States, or at least takes part in a conspiracy to assassinate him—almost certainly with the knowledge and approval of the Kremlin—and when that agent is finally exposed for what he is, the CIA's main reaction is to get pissed-off at the people who helped expose him. Somehow there was something terribly out of whack with this kind of reasoning.

"In other words, all you care about is covering for Alex Sutton, right? That's actually what you're saying, isn't it? You don't give a damn about what he did, do you?" Matt asked the questions evenly, already knowing what the answers were. "You figured out he's a Soviet spy by virtue of the evidence we brought in, but you don't want anybody else to figure it out. Isn't that the whole idea?"

"The point is, we can't prove he's a Soviet spy." Moorhead said. "We can't prove that he acted with the official sanction of the Soviet government to kill John F. Kennedy. Even if we could, it would still do us more harm than good, and if we accuse him publicly without ironclad proof—as you two have already encouraged the media to do—we might as well forget about normalizing relations with Moscow."

"Who the hell cares?" Matt exploded. "We haven't had normal relations with the bastards for the past fifty years, so what the hell difference does it make? All I know is, based on the evidence, Alex Sutton helped engineer the assassination of the President of the United States, for Christ's sake. I also know he wasn't the person he pretended to be."

"Could you swear to it in court?" Moorhead asked pointedly.

"On the first part, yes. On the last part, I don't know," Matt said. "Maybe I couldn't, but there's a certain Mary Cockrell in Van Wert, Ohio, who damned well could, I'll bet."

Moorhead shook his head. "No, she couldn't," he said. "The most she could have said was that he acted 'different' when he came home. That doesn't mean he wasn't the same person. If we ever tried to prove it, we'd just end up looking like bigger fools than we already do. It's just as well Mary Cockrell won't be giving any more testimony or depositions."

Amid the heat of his rekindled anger, Matt felt an abrupt chill. There was something about Moorhead's last statement that bothered him.

"What do you mean?" he asked. "Why won't she?"

Moorhead stared at him with hard, unrelenting eyes. For an instant, they made him think of Alex Sutton's eyes.

"Because Mary Cockrell's dead," Moorhead said bluntly. "She was killed yesterday morning in an explosion at her house."

"I know it's hard to accept," Peter Benedict was saying, with a trace of sympathy in his voice, "but you really don't have any choice in the matter. As far as the Justice Department is concerned, the Kennedy case has been closed ever since the Warren Commission Report of 1964, and it's going to remain closed."

It was an hour later and Jonas Moorhead of the CIA had taken his unpleasant voice and pissed-off expression elsewhere, but he had left a lingering pall over the drab little interview room.

"You've got to realize that today's world is a vastly different place from the world of 1963," Benedict said. "The personality of international politics has changed to an incredible extent, and so have the priorities of the U.S. government. The Cold War's over. We have no desire to heat it up again. It just wouldn't serve any purpose."

"But what about the evidence we brought in?" Sarah said. "Aren't you even going to do anything with it?"

"We're going to keep it in a safe place," Benedict said. "At some distant point in the future, we might have some use for it, but not now."

"If you're not going to use it," Sarah said insistently, "I think you ought to give it back to us."

Matt shuddered inwardly at the idea. He thought about all the hell they had been through, all the risks they had taken, all the people who had died horrible, meaningless deaths because of the evidence. And now it was going to gather dust in a file cabinet somewhere in the bowels of the Justice Department. It would probably be there somewhere, stuck away in some innocuous manila folders marked "Classified" long after they were all dead and buried. The unfairness of it all made him want to commit murder himself.

"I'm afraid there's no chance of that, Miss Archer," Benedict said. "The best thing for you to do is forget you ever saw it." He turned to Matt. "Look, I know you've been through a lot of grief," he said, "but let's be reasonable about this. There's nobody left to prosecute, even if we wanted to. Conlan's dead. Van Zandt's dead. And we're ninety-nine percent sure that Sutton—or Kaminski, if you prefer—is either dead, too, or safely back on Soviet-controlled soil by now."

"What makes you so sure?" Matt said. "As familiar as he is with this country after thirty years, why would he have to leave? And if he's dead, who would've killed him?"

"An agent with his experience would never risk being taken alive," Benedict said. "You can be sure that he had a vial of the same stuff that killed Conlan and Van Zandt. He may have swallowed it the minute he knew his cover was blown, or he may have made it out of the country, but I guarantee you it was one way or the other. We've had enough dealings with the KGB over the years to know he wouldn't have hung around.

Matt thought about Mary Cockrell, dead in an explosion at her home in Ohio. Dead in the same kind of explosion that had killed his own wife and child in Illinois. Dead like Mike Fisher in California, Jamie Cade in Dallas, Angel Garcia in Mexico, Little Lynn in Houston, Marilyn Moon in Nebraska, Mollie O'Connor in Arkansas. Dead like all the others, merely the latest in an endless chain.

"I think you're full of shit," he told Benedict.

The imperturbable agent smiled. "Maybe," he said mildly, "but I don't think so."

"What about that bunch of goons who came to the farm to kill us," Matt asked. "I know some of them are dead, but what're you going to do with the rest of them?"

"Four of them are dead," Benedict said. "Three were fatally shot by police and another one broke his neck falling into a old dry well out there. Two others are in federal custody, and two others are still at large."

"Will the ones you're holding ever be prosecuted for Tony Canales' murder?"

"I couldn't say," Benedict said vaguely.

"Do you know the identity of the two who escaped?"

"I couldn't say," the FBI agent repeated. "I can't discuss them at all at this point." He smiled again.

Matt shook his head. "I can't believe this," he said. "It makes you wonder if all those people who always claimed the FBI and the CIA were behind the whole thing in the first place weren't so far off base, after all."

Benedict's smile faded. "There's no point being ridiculous," he said.

"Is it ridiculous?" Matt demanded. "After all, you guys knew about Oswald months in advance. You knew he was here and you knew he was capable of assassinating a public figure, but you didn't do a goddamned thing about it. You didn't even tell the Dallas police. Hell, maybe you knew who Sutton really was even then. Christ, those crazy bastards at the farm may have all been on the federal payroll, for all I know."

"They weren't, I assure you," Benedict said. "I also assure you they'll be dealt with in accordance with what they did, but other than that, I'm simply not at liberty to say anything about them."

Matt started to say something else, something he might well have regretted, but Sarah put her hand on his arm and gave him a warning squeeze that said "Shut up while you're ahead."

"Are you done with us, then?" she asked hopefully, "Are you going to let us go?"

Benedict frowned for a second, then nodded. "Yes," he said. "Despite all the trouble you've caused, we've decided not to press any federal charges, and we've convinced the Texas and Arkansas authorities not to press any state charges either. So you'll be free to go in a little while, but before you do, I'd like to offer you a small piece of advice. I think you'd be wise to go back home, resume your normal lives, and try to forget the events of the past several days. I also think you'd be very wise to steer clear of the media from now on."

"But we're part of the media," Sarah said. "We both work for a weekly newspaper." She pointedly failed to add that copies of most of the really damning pieces of evidence from Mollie's briefcase, including the tapes, were safely stashed back in *The Jeffersonian* office, or that she was already mentally plotting the story line for a book on Matt's and Mollie's 24-year ordeal.

"Then I suggest you concentrate on local news and forget about murder, espionage, intrigue and international politics," Benedict said pointedly.

He stood up and turned toward the door, pausing almost as an afterthought to reach into his jacket pocket and pull out a packet of business cards.

"Here," he said, handing each of them a card. "If you should have anything you want to discuss, you can always call me." He paused in the doorway for a moment with his hand on the doorknob. "There'll be another agent and a stenographer along in a minute or two," he said. "Once we've taken a signed statement from each of you, you can go about your business. Goodbye and good luck."

Benedict closed the door quietly behind him and was gone.

It was 11:45 a.m. when they walked out the main entrance of the Federal Building and blinked in the bright sunshine of a November noon. They stood uncertainly at the corner of Commerce and Griffin Streets for a moment, and for the first time in days, Matt felt the heavy weight he had been carrying lighten a little.

It was over. It hadn't ended the way he wanted it to end, but it was over. The healing process was going to take a long time, but now it could at least begin. It was over.

He took Sarah's hand and pulled her close to him, relishing the warm, reassuring feel of her as he had never relished anything before.

Hundreds of people were rushing past them on hundreds of hurried errands as he put his arms around her, but he didn't care. He kissed her anyway.

"I love you," he said.

"I love you, too," she said.

A couple of passers-by giggled.

"There's a McDonald's across the street," she said. "Want to buy me a Big Mac?"

"Sure," he said, "but, hey, I've still got a couple hundred bucks left. We could go someplace a little fancier if you want to."

"Nah," she said, "a Big Mac's fine. Then I think we ought to take a short walk."

"You want to do some sightseeing?"

"Uh huh," she said, "I want to see every sight I can possibly see between here and the bus station. I spotted it yesterday, and it was the most welcome sight I'd seen since we got here. I think it's a couple of blocks that way." She pointed northwest. "Then the only way I want to see this town is through the back window of a Greyhound bus, headed east."

He grinned. "But I figured once you got here, you'd want to hang around for awhile."

"I always thought I would, too," she admitted, "but I changed my mind. You know what they say. You can take the girl out of the country, but . . ." She stretched up to kiss him again. "I just want to go home, Matt. Besides, we've got a newspaper to get out this week somehow."

"Oh, Jesus," he said, "did you have to bring that up?"

He felt almost normal as they walked toward McDonald's.

CHAPTER TWENTY-FOUR

November 22, 1987

They had been back for less than two weeks, but already
the trip to Dallas seemed far in the past to Sarah. Sometimes
it was almost as though it had all happened to somebody
else—somebody unrelated to her—and that she had only read
or heard about it, instead of experiencing it firsthand as she
had done. It was this very sense of detachment that made her
certain she could write a book about the whole affair, so
certain, in fact, that she had already roughed out the first
chapter, drafted a query letter and dropped by the public
library to get some publishers' addresses out of the current
Writer's Market.

In the meantime, her life had settled back into a pleasant,
predictable pattern for the first time since . . . when? Certainly since Matt's middle-of-the-night phone call of almost
a month ago, but probably since long before that, too. Ever
since her emergence from childhood, Sarah had always thought
of her situation at any given moment as being temporary.
From the moment she had finished high school, she had been
in a constant state of transition, if not physically, then at least

mentally. First it had been "after college," then "after I find a job and get settled," then "after I get married," then "after I find a better job somewhere else," and so on. Now, with Matt, she felt a sense of permanence for the first time, and that in itself might have struck some people as weird, since most of their time together had been so full of trauma, uncertainty and out-and-out craziness. But for reasons she couldn't explain and had no desire to try to explain, she felt more comfortable and restful with Matt than anybody else she had ever known. And yet, simultaneously she also felt more excited and stimulated and filled with creative energy than ever before. Within the past month, she had discovered what it was really like to be in love, and the discovery was indescribably reassuring. For a long time, she had feared that what she felt with Kyle was all there was to it. Thank God she had been wrong!

Two days after their return from Dallas, she had given up her furnished room at Mrs. Mitchell's house and hauled everything she owned out to Matt's place. The only reason she waited that long was because they both had to work practically around the clock to get *The Jeffersonian* out on time that week. She hadn't bothered to offer Mrs. Mitchell any explanation for leaving so abruptly, and for once the old biddy hadn't had the gall to ask for one. It was easy to tell what dire thoughts were running through her narrow little mind, though.

Sarah had even called her mother and told her straight out that she was moving in with Matt and they would probably get married sometime after the holidays. Her mother had taken it better than Sarah might have expected. She had cried a little, but she had only used the term "living in sin" once.

"If you're getting married that soon, though, it does look like you could have waited," her mother had sniffed.

"I've waited long enough for something I really want, Mother," Sarah had told her unyieldingly. "Sometimes I think I've spent my whole life waiting, and I'm not waiting anymore."

Now it was a clear, crisp Saturday morning, and Sarah was up early, as she usually was these days, and filled with exhilaration. She remembered that it was the 24th anniversary of the assassination, and there couldn't have been a more appropriate time to do some serious work on her book. She pulled down the hem of her knee-length flannel nightshirt, slipped on her terrycloth robe, and left Matt still sleeping among the disheveled bedclothes where they had made love the night before.

She had never realized until recently that she had such a capacity for enjoying sex. Sometimes it happened at midnight, sometimes at dawn, and occasionally even at midafternoon, but whenever it happened, it was always spontaneous, always good, always fulfilling—and she was always ready. She could feel a slight flush in her cheeks when she thought about how perpetually ready she seemed to be.

Hobo padded along behind her as she went to the kitchen, scooped coffee into the basket of the coffeemaker, filled the reservoir with water and flipped it on. As the machine started to hiss and gurgle and emit small spumes of steam, she went to the kitchen table and restarted the Mollie O'Connor tape she had been listening to at bedtime the night before. Sarah had been trying to spend at least an hour or two every day going back through the tapes and making extensive notes for the book. As she listened, she felt much more than mere sympathy for Mollie O'Connor. She felt a lot of genuine empathy, too. Matt's own ordeal had been long and excruciating, but in many respects, Mollie's had been a great deal worse. Sarah knew, with a certainty she had felt about very few things in her lifetime, that it was going to make a really tremendous book.

For a few minutes, she became totally engrossed in the tape and forgot about Hobo until she heard his low, patient whine from the back door, telling her he was ready to make his morning rounds. As she stopped the tape and got up to oblige him, she glanced at the clock on the wall. It was 6:20 a.m. and still quite dark outside, but she felt no need to turn on the porch light, since Hobo knew every inch of the backyard, both by smell and by heart.

She unbolted the wooden door, then pulled it back and pushed open the screen long enough for Hobo to slither through. She heard him clump down the steps, and then both he and his muffled footsteps evaporated silently into the damp grass of the backyard. Sarah knew from experience that it would take the old dog about seven or eight minutes to complete his routine and be back on the porch, waiting for someone to let him back inside and feed him.

As she was pouring herself a large cup of coffee and waiting for this procedure to run its course, she was suddenly struck with a burst of inspiration. She could actually hear the opening sentences of the next chapter of the book unfolding in her mind. They sounded so good that she was determined to try to retain them, but they were unfolding far too rapidly to be jotted down in note form. Excitedly, she picked up the recorder from the table and put it in the chair beside her. She punched the eject button, removed the Mollie O'Connor tape, quickly inserted a blank tape, and pushed down the red "Record" button.

"Notes for Chapter Two," she said softly when the red light came on. "At noon on November 24, 1963, Mollie O'Connor answered her telephone and learned that her employer, Jack Ruby, had just shot and killed Lee Harvey Oswald in the basement of the Dallas police station. In that instant, she knew that the killing had only just begun. In that instant, she knew she must run for her life. What she didn't know was that she would have to keep on running for the next twenty-four years, and even then she would never escape . . ."

Sarah paused abruptly, her train of thought derailed by a sharp, sudden, infinitely distressing sound. Above the husky vibrations of her own voice, she heard a single, agonized yelp from the backyard. She knew immediately and unquestionably that it was Hobo.

And she also knew—in the same instinctive way that Mollie O'Connor had known on that day so long ago—that something was desperately wrong.

To get it out of her path, Sarah shoved the chair with the recorder roughly under the table. Then she ran for the door, hitting the light switch as she got there and throwing a pale circle of light across the center of the backyard.

There was no sign of Hobo, at least not in the lighted area, but he often prowled in the unkempt shrubbery along the fence and in the dark corner behind the toolshed.

"Hobo!" she called. "Here, Hobo! Are you all right, boy?"

A blanket of absolute silence enfolded the yard.

She ran down the steps and onto the lawn, feeling the frosty grass chilling her bare feet.

"Hobo!" she called again. "Where are you?"

Then she spotted a dark shape lying very still on the ground behind a clump of privet hedge, and her heart skipped a beat. It was Hobo, all right, and she could tell there was something wrong, but she had no idea what it might be.

"Hobo?" she whispered, kneeling beside the old dog and reaching down to touch his shaggy form.

She pulled gently at Hobo's head, and she could tell by the limpness of his neck that he was dead. She turned his head and saw his eyes, open and sightless. Oh, God, she thought, the poor old guy must have had a heart attack. She felt tears burning her eyes, already dreading having to tell Matt. He would really be torn up.

She stroked Hobo's matted ears and the tousled hair along his neck. "Poor old baby," she said softly.

When she felt the wetness under Hobo's head, she drew her hand back in horror, staring at the bright-red blood on her fingers. This was no heart attack, she realized. The dog had been shot.

But there had been no sound at all, except for the one quick cry. She knew enough now to know that meant a silencer. And that meant premeditated murder. And that meant . . .

In the same split second, Sarah heard and saw the movement just behind her as something came out of the privet hedge. She gasped and tried to whirl away, but a hand with a crushing grip caught her wrist and jerked her back, twisting her arm tightly and painfully behind her. Then she felt the hard, cold barrel of the pistol pressing into her neck about an inch below her right ear.

"Make one sound or one funny move," a quiet male voice said, "and you'll be just as dead as the dog, I promise you."

She closed her mouth, clenched her teeth firmly together and felt herself propelled forcibly toward the back porch. At the foot of the steps, the man signaled her to stop.

"Where's Matt Eastman?" he said. "Is he in the house?"

"Yes," she said unsteadily, "he's still asleep."

"Good," the man said. "Let's you and I go wake him up. I always enjoy surprising old friends in the morning."

"What do you want?" Sarah asked. "Why are you doing this?"

"Because the people I sent to do it for me never could get the job done," he said. "You know the old saying: 'If you want something done right, you have to do it yourself.' Well, this time, that's what I'm doing—taking care of it myself. Now I want you to walk into the house very slowly and keep your hands where I can see them."

She moved carefully up the steps and opened the screen. The gun was still pressed against her, but now it was squarely in the middle of her back. Her mind was racing in all directions, searching frantically for some small shred of hope. Maybe Matt had heard them. Maybe he had had a chance to get his own large, ugly pistol out of the dresser drawer where he kept it. Maybe he was waiting at this very moment to turn the tables on the man behind her.

Possible, perhaps, but not probable. Matt was a sound sleeper, who took a long time to wake up fully in the morning. And this particular morning, he might never wake up at all.

"Turn around," the man said, once they were in the kitchen.

As she turned, Sarah had the illusion that she was moving in slow-motion. She saw the whole room revolve around her in infinite detail—Hobo's feeding dish on the floor, the coffeemaker with its almost-full carafe of hot coffee on the counter, her spiral notebook and empty coffee cup on the kitchen table, the chair where she had been sitting, left askew by her sudden departure, the other chair with the tape recorder . . .

From where she stood, she could see the tiny pinpoint of

red light that meant the recorder was still on. She hadn't stopped to turn it off when she had run outside a few minutes earlier, and now it was still silently doing its job, its twin spools slowly turning around and around. If no one disturbed it, it had at least an hour of time left on it.

She almost smiled at the thought—but not quite—as she raised her eyes to the man's face.

She had never so much as glimpsed this face in person before, and the only photos of it she had seen had been made many years ago, but she had no trouble recognizing it. It was older and wearier and the man who wore it was smaller and more frail than she had expected, but recognition came instantly.

Maybe Igor Kaminski was safely back in Russia today, just as the FBI and the CIA insisted he was, but Alex Sutton was nowhere near the U.S.S.R. this morning. Alex Sutton was right here in southeastern Arkansas.

He was, in fact, standing no more than six feet away from her, with his pistol trained on her left breast, somewhere below the nipple.

"What now, Mr. Sutton?" Sarah asked.

He smiled, perhaps at her perceptiveness, perhaps at something else.

"Now we're going to wake up Matt and have a short reunion," he told her. "Then, a little later, there's going to be a terrible explosion."

To a casual glance, Alex thought, they could have been playing a game of three-handed poker or getting ready for a quiet breakfast. They were seated around the table, facing each other, with Alex at one end and Matt Eastman and the girl named Sarah sitting across from each other at the opposite end. The difference, of course, was that Alex had the gun, and, as he pointedly reminded them now and then, they could both be dead in the space of two seconds flat if they were idiotic enough to try anything.

Alex had known he would relish this moment when it finally came, but he had underestimated the sheer pleasure and satisfaction it was actually bringing him. It had taken an incredibly long time to reach this point, and his failure to reach it sooner had cost him dearly, but now he was going to savor it to the utmost. In truth, he was enjoying this little tableau almost as much as he was going to enjoy blowing the house to splinters later on. First things first, he told himself. He felt completely entitled to drag it out a bit, too, if that was the way it was meant to be.

If anything was disappointing, though—even slightly perplexing—it was the fact that his two captives seemed calmer and more in control than the situation warranted. Waking Matt up with a pistol barrel under his nose had been amusing, but the only time Matt had really lost his composure was when he found out that his stupid dog was dead.

"One way or another, in this life or the next, you're going to pay for that one, you asshole," Matt had warned him.

Alex had only laughed. Considering how many humans he had killed in his lifetime, the idea of suffering divine retribution over a dog struck him as extremely amusing. He had killed the dog as a matter of course, to keep him from barking or otherwise alerting the occupants of the house, but it had been done with no particular malice or glee. As a point of fact, Alex was rather fond of dogs. Maybe one day he would own a dog himself when he was safe on some other continent. Perhaps a doberman pinscher or a pit bull. At any rate, he had disposed of the dog out of necessity, not for sport. But when he killed Matt Eastman, it would be an entirely different kettle of fish.

"Maybe it doesn't matter," Matt said, "but there are still some things I want to ask you, Alex. By the way, you don't mind me calling you 'Alex,' do you? I know it's not really your name, but somehow I still think of you as 'good old Alex.' "

"I don't care what you call me or what you ask me, Matt," Alex said. "Go right ahead. If I want to answer, I will. If I don't, I won't. It's that simple."

"Well, it seems pretty obvious how you got hooked up with Oswald, since he'd been in Russia and was known to the KGB and all," Matt said, "but I never could figure out how you and Tommy Van Zandt ended up as partners. I mean, here's Tommy, so damned conservative he won't drink pink lemonade, and here's Alex, a Soviet spy and a devout Marxist, and all of a sudden, you're conspiring together to kill the President. Politics make strange bedfellows, I know, but this always seemed pretty far-out to me.''

Alex smiled. It *had* been one of the history's more bizarre alliances, he mused, thinking back—not as bizarre as Stalin and Hitler, perhaps, but close to it. It had lasted a long time, too, until Tommy's problems outweighed any potential usefulness he might have had as governor of Texas, and he became too dangerous to remain alive. Now that it was over, though, Alex had no qualms about discussing their association. On the contrary, he liked talking about what he considered the grandest coup he had ever pulled.

''It was a simple coincidence,'' he said. ''It started with one of those drinking sessions we used to have once or twice a week. I'm sure you remember plenty of them yourself. It was . . .'' He paused and frowned for a moment, trying to remember. ''It was one afternoon in early September of '63. We were at the Patio Lounge, I think, and for some reason, everybody else left earlier than usual, and Tommy and I were left sitting there alone. As usual when he was pretty drunk, he started cursing the 'nigger-loving socialists' in Washington in general and Kennedy in particular. I just listened at first, but then I started tossing in a sympathetic comment here and there, and the next thing I knew, he was asking me if I could find somebody to shoot Kennedy when he came to Dallas.

''I said, 'Hey, Tommy, I'm a cop, remember? I'm supposed to catch killers, not hire them to shoot people.'

''And he said, 'Come on, Alex, I'm serious. Kennedy's leading this country down the path to hell, and somebody's got to stop him. With your connections, I know you could come up with the right man for the job, and if you did, you'd be a goddamned hero, and I'd see you got treated like one.'

''Then he told me about Dee Conlan and Conlan Universal Aerospace. He said he could get me a key position at CUA if I engineered a successful assassination. He said there'd be all kinds of big money and stock options involved, and that together we could control the company. With Kennedy gone and a hawk like Lyndon Johnson in the White House, he said defense spending was bound to increase and the more money CUA made, the more money we'd make.

"I told him he was talking sedition and high treason, but I was careful not to turn him down cold. A few days later, he called me aside and said he had sources in the Defense Department who were sure Kennedy was planning a total pullout in Vietnam before the end of the year. He said if that happened, all of Southeast Asia could probably go communist, and it would cost CUA billions in lost defense contracts in the bargain."

Alex chuckled to himself as he remembered what happened next. He routinely reported Van Zandt's overtures to his contact and asked for instructions, expecting his superiors to tell him in no uncertain terms to remove himself from the situation and have no further dealings with the man. But then his superiors completely surprised him, both by telling him to proceed, although with extreme caution, and by providing him with Lee Harvey Oswald as the fully expendable "assassin of record" for the mission, which the KGB nicknamed "Operation Trinity." Now, as Alex told him about it, Matt seemed almost as amazed as Alex had been then.

"Jesus, that's the most unbelievable part of all," Matt said. "It looks to me like the risk of having the Soviet government exposed as conspirators in the assassination would've outweighed anything they could've hoped to gain by killing Kennedy."

"That's what I thought at first," Alex said, "but when my superiors explained their thinking, I could see the logic behind it. Getting rid of Kennedy could have a lot of intangible benefits for the U.S.S.R. For one thing, he was a tremendously popular President abroad, and there was good reason to assume that Johnson would be less highly regarded and less adept at international politics. For another, our agents in Washington also came up with strong indications that Kennedy was, indeed, planning to withdraw American forces from Vietnam very soon, probably within a few days after returning to Washington from Dallas. But it was perceived that if Johnson were President, the withdrawal would never happen. So, since U.S. involvement in a long, debilitating land war in Southeast Asia could be construed as being highly advantageous to the U.S.S.R., this was another reason for removing Kennedy.

"Possibly the most important reason, though," Alex continued, "was that if 'Operation Trinity' were a success, it would guarantee me total access to the facilities of one of this country's largest defense contractors. I would be able to obtain valuable information on aircraft and rocket designs long before the craft were operational, and I could inflict incalculable damage to the U.S. military establishment. I assure you, my friend, you have no concept of how many unfortunate accidents I was able to cause over the years as chief of security at CUA."

"Oh, yes, I do," Matt said. "You've always been a specialist at unfortunate accidents, Alex, and not all of them involved the aerospace industry, either—not by a damned sight. But weren't you even a little bit worried about being caught?"

Alex snorted derisively. "I and my superiors both knew there was no possibility I'd ever be caught alive," he said. "Our only concern was Oswald. We knew he was almost as stubborn as he was stupid, and that it would take a lot to make him talk, but the consensus was that he *could* be broken, especially if the CIA got hold of him, so we knew he had to be eliminated."

"And that was your responsibility?" Matt asked.

"Yes, it was all carefully arranged, but when Oswald panicked and shot J. D. Tippit he screwed everything up and we had to go to an alternate plan. Putting too much faith in Oswald's ability to follow instructions could have been a very costly mistake on my part. Luckily, I was able to rectify it before any damage was done."

The girl had been sitting silently and listening for a long time when she suddenly spoke up. "But the damage came afterward, didn't it?" she said. "Because that's where Jack Ruby came in, and where all the spin-off killings began. Isn't that right?"

Alex nodded unsmilingly. "You could say that," he said, "but the important thing at the time was removing Oswald."

"That wasn't the only mistake you made, though," she insisted, "and it wasn't the worst one, either. If you hadn't taken Mollie O'Connor to Mexico when you went there to meet Oswald, a lot of things might've turned out differently."

"Yes," he admitted bluntly, "Mollie O'Connor was my biggest mistake."

There was no point in denying it, Alex thought. There would have been once, but not anymore. Mollie O'Connor had been a hundred fatal mistakes, all compacted into the most maddeningly desirable, infinitely sensual woman-child who ever breathed. Getting involved with her in the first place had been a monstrous enough blunder in itself, but taking her adoration for granted and letting her see and hear things that no one should have seen or heard had been an even more serious miscalculation. And not killing her when he had the chance had been the greatest error of all. He still dreamed of her often—more often lately than before, now that he finally knew she was dead—and she still taunted him and laughed at him from beyond his reach.

"Indulge me by telling me just a couple of other things, Alex," Matt said. "I've always wondered if you personally fired any of the shots that hit Kennedy, and, if you did, where you fired them from. I also can't figure how you managed to get Ruby to shoot Oswald for you. I know you did it, but I've never known how. If I have to die, at least let me die with my curiosity satisfied."

Alex held the pistol firmly in his right hand as he checked the watch on his left wrist. It was past 7:30 now, and the sun was high in the sky. He was allowing this matter to drag on far too long. He had not slept in almost 24 hours, and a deep exhaustion had seeped into his bones. He was 55 years old, after all, and the last two weeks had been very difficult, very draining.

"It's getting late," he said with a trace of reluctance. "I'm afraid we really ought to get this business over with."

"Oh, come on," Matt said. "After twenty-four years, you can surely spare another fifteen minutes, can't you?" It's not that much to ask."

Alex frowned thoughtfully. Going through it all again seemed pointless and futile in a way, and it was only postponing the inevitability of what had to be done. Still, if he were to be totally candid with himself, he would have to confess that he was as eager for one last opportunity to recount the details of the greatest accomplishment of his life as Matt Eastman was to hear them. He knew the recounting would summon forth vivid memories of Mollie, and as perverse and counterproductive as the memories were, he also knew how much he yearned for them. After all this time, he remained as hopelessly addicted to those haunting images of the past as he had ever been.

A wistful, faraway look softened the coldness in Alex's eyes as he began. How appropriate, he thought, that this was all happening exactly 24 years after his supreme triumph. There was a poetic irony in that, one that he fully appreciated. He knew that no other Soviet agent in history had ever carried out a more difficult or remarkable assignment. A surge of pure pride still made him tingle at the recollection of how skillfully he had done the job.

"I got up very early that morning," he said. "It was a day very much like this one, clear and chilly at first, but with a promise of pleasant warmth by afternoon. That meant the bulletproof plastic top on the presidential limousine would be down, just as we had anticipated . . ."

CHAPTER TWENTY-FIVE

November 22–23, 1963

By 6:45 a.m. that Friday, Lieutenant Alexander Sutton was showered, shaved, dressed and ready to go. As far as he could tell, Mollie was still sound asleep, her enticing nakedness clearly defined by the sheer silk sheet that covered her, as he started out of the bedroom. He paused for a moment to gaze appreciatively down at her and felt a brief but compulsive flurry of desire flood his loins. The smell of their love-making of a few hours ago was still in the air, and already he wanted her again, as fiercely as if he had never had her before.

But not now. Not today. Tonight, when it was over. That would be the time. Then she would melt the rigid coils of tension inside him and make him forget everything else but her, while she unwittingly helped him celebrate the success of his mission. He would live through today for that reason, if for no other, he thought.

Resolutely, he pulled the bedroom door shut behind him and tiptoed down the hall to the closet where he kept the rifle.

A moment later, he stepped out into the faint light of the

early morning and walked down the driveway to the car, where he opened the trunk, slid the rifle in beside the jack, put the small valise with his "working clothes" beside the spare tire and quickly slammed the trunk lid shut again. Then he climbed behind the steering wheel and the engine started with a soft, growling purr. As he he backed out the driveway into the street, he took one final look at the small, tidy brick house with its well-trimmed lawn and closely cropped hedges.

He liked looking at the house from the street. He drew pleasure from it in much the same way that he drew pleasure from looking at Mollie, although he hardly felt the same passion for the house that he felt for her. Next to Mollie, though, the house was his most prized possession. It was modest by North Dallas standards and located in a very ordinary neighborhood off Walnut Hill Lane, but it was the best he could manage on a homicide detective's salary, and he was proud of it. In Moscow—or any other Russian city, for that matter—a man could never hope to have a house like this. There simply weren't any houses like this; there were only the dismal flats where the workers lived, the better-built but rather stark apartment buildings occupied mainly by bureaucrats, and the opulent, secluded bungalows that housed the party elite. And even if there had been houses like this, Soviet citizens didn't own property; the state did.

This house was only the beginning, though. If things went well today and his situation at CUA became firmly established, he could soon afford a larger, finer house. Tommy Van Zandt implied that the salary for the part-time job would be $1,000 per month, or almost half again as much as he made from the police department for working full time. That kind of money could buy a lot of things, and the best part of all was that, according to Van Zandt, it was only the beginning. Although he thought of himself more often as Alex Sutton than Igor Kaminski these days, he was still a true socialist revolutionary at heart, he told himself, and completely faithful to the ideals expressed by Lenin and Marx. But if the decadent capitalists insisted on throwing money at him, he saw no harm in catching some of it—especially when what he did to earn it only enhanced the Soviet cause.

When he contemplated his new life ahead, he could find only one unfortunate flaw in the scheme of things, and that was that Mollie wouldn't be there. As important as she had been to him for the past six or seven months, and as much physical need as he had for her, he knew full well that Mollie had to die. It was going to be very difficult to kill her when the time came, but the time was drawing very close and there were no other options open to him. It was his responsibility, and he would fulfill it. It was just another dirty job that had to be done. There would undoubtedly be plenty of other women. He had never had any problem attracting women, but it would be hard, maybe even impossible, to find another one like Mollie. He would hate himself for doing away with her, but it was purely a matter of self-preservation now.

He had accepted the inevitability of it two or three weeks after they came back from Mexico. Many small factors had combined to whisper the truth to him, even as she slept unknowingly in his arms. He knew she had seen him and the others with Oswald, and since Oswald's picture would undoubtedly be in the newspapers after today, she would have enough sense to put two and two together. Alex also knew he had done any number of arrogant, idiotic things that had aroused her suspicions. On more than one occasion, thanks to his arrogance and carelessness, she had overheard him speaking Russian to his contact. He had been so cocksure, so certain that he had her completely under his control, that he convinced himself for a while it didn't matter. Now, though, he could tell by the look of fear and distrust in her eyes and by the distance he had sensed in her in recent weeks, that it *had* mattered. But it was done now and there was no undoing it.

There was nothing to do now but undo Mollie herself. The decision was made, and there could be no turning back. In all frankness, he should have done it before now, but since he had waited this long, he would just have to wait a little longer. It would have to be postponed until the Kennedy matter was taken care of.

But one evening soon, while Mollie's twin sister was spending the night away from the apartment they shared in

East Dallas, tragedy would strike. Already, four young women in Dallas had been sexually assaulted and strangled late at night in their bedrooms, apparently by the same killer. Alex Sutton had been assigned to the cases for the past three months, and he had studied the killer's trademarks and *modus operandi* until he knew them down to the last detail.

He had no doubt that he could duplicate them exactly when Mollie became the fifth victim of the "Sex Strangler," as the media was calling him. He had never strangled a woman during the act of intercourse, but it might prove interesting.

The very thought of it gave him an erection as he drove toward the downtown skyline.

Except for those on emergency leave, every police officer in Dallas was required to be on duty on November 22, 1963, and many were working double shifts. But the brunt of the load for the presidential visit fell on the Patrol Division, and in the Crimes Against Persons Division, of which the Homicide Bureau was part, the routine that Friday morning was pretty much business as usual.

At a few minutes before 11 a.m., Lieutenant Alexander Sutton told his commander, Captain Will Fritz, that he was leaving the station to interview two witnesses to a recent homicide. One, he said, lived in the Oak Lawn area just north of downtown, and the other was in a semiprivate room at Baylor University Medical Center, recovering from a gunshot wound in the abdomen.

"It'll probably take the rest of the morning," he said. "Anything happening so far on the Kennedy visit that I ought to be aware of?"

"He's due at Love Field within the next few minutes," Fritz said. "Just keep the dispatcher current on your position. If we need you for anything, we'll holler."

From the basement parking garage at City Hall, Sutton headed east on Main Street, then turned north on Central Expressway, then east again on Gaston Avenue toward Baylor Medical Center. Five blocks from the hospital, however, he pulled into a Texaco service station and stopped in a parking space beside the entrance to the men's room. There he awaited the message that would determine how he spent the rest of the morning—and perhaps the rest of his life.

The message came at 11:13 a.m., via the police radio.

"All units, stand by," the dispatcher said. "Full alert status is now in effect. Air Force One has landed. Units assigned to the motorcade route, take your positions."

And so the die was cast, Alex thought. Now if Oswald could just carry out his part of the scheme, the plan should work to perfection. In a way, Oswald was ideal for the scapegoat role. He was a high-profile lunatic with avowed Marxist leanings who had, without doubt, already earned a spot in the political suspect files of the CIA and FBI. But in another way, he was such a headstrong, erratic, unpredictable fool that it was impossible to trust him. Alex Sutton had had uneasy feelings about him from the beginning, but Igor Kaminski's superiors were convinced that Oswald represented the perfect pawn in this game of deceit. Sometimes Alex wished that Igor were more assertive with his superiors. Alex Sutton had trained himself over the past six and a half years to act, react and even feel exactly as an American would in any given situation. He didn't even think in Russian anymore, and sometimes he didn't understand Igor Kaminski at all. Alex had no use for Oswald, and he would be glad when his usefulness was at an end.

He went to the pay phone inside the service station, deposited a dime and dialed. The ringing at the other end of the line had a faint and distant sound to it, although the number he was calling was less than a mile away as the crow flies.

"School Book Depository," a voice answered.

"Lee Oswald, please," he said and waited.

It took Oswald almost four minutes to get to the phone from wherever he had been in the brown brick building at the corner of Houston and Elm Streets.

"Hello," he said. "This is Lee." There was a sharp edge to his voice but a dullness underneath.

"It's go all the way," Alex said. "Gee-Oh. Go."

"All right, I understand," Oswald said.

"I'll be at the theater at 1:45 p.m. sharp," Alex told him.

"I'll stay until 2:15 p.m. If you can't make it by then, we'll have to reschedule."

"I understand," Oswald said again.

Alex broke the connection and found that he was sweating profusely.

At 11:38 a.m., Lieutenant Sutton's unmarked Unit 719 turned into the sidestreet in front of the Texas School Book Depository, then veered right as the street dead-ended into a graveled area adjacent to a weed-overgrown embankment beside the railroad tracks that crossed over the Triple Underpass. The railroad was about 50 yards to the west and a wooden stockade fence stretched from the graveled area all the way to the edge of the grassy open space called Dealey Plaza. Below and 20 yards to the south, Elm Street made a curving descent toward the Triple Underpass. There was room for at least a dozen cars in the graveled area, but except for employees at the Book Depository, few people were even aware that it existed, and it was seldom used for anything. At the moment, the only other car parked there was an old Chevy sedan, which looked as if it might be abandoned.

The lieutenant made a hard right and pulled the car into the extreme southeast corner of the graveled area, stopping beside a large metal grate with a concrete storm sewer inlet beneath it. He carefully positioned the car so that it simultaneously faced the street and shielded the sewer grate from the view of anyone entering the area. This accomplished, he lifted the radio microphone off its hook below the dashboard and told the dispatcher he was at McKinney Avenue and Routh Street, preparing to interview a subject.

"Ten-four, Seven Nineteen," the dispatcher replied.

At 11:39 a.m., he checked out of service. By the time he would check back in again, just over an hour later, doctors would be wheeling President Kennedy into a trauma room at Parkland Hospital with half his head blown away.

Alex got out of the car and began a procedure which he had rehearsed and timed on a half-dozen occasions over the past month. Barring any unforeseen problems, he had at least twice as much time as he needed. The whole procedure took about 12 minutes and by his calculations the motorcade was still at least 25 minutes away. First, he took off his jacket and tie, folded them neatly and laid them in the back seat, being careful to remove the leather folder with his badge and ID from the inside pocket of the jacket and take it with him. As he moved to the rear of the car, he also unharnessed his shoulder holster and service revolver, then shed his starched white shirt, stripping down to the dark gray sweatshirt he wore underneath. He opened the trunk, placed the white shirt and shoulder rig inside and unzipped the valise containing his "working clothes"—short-sleeved khaki coveralls, long vinyl gloves of the type women wore to protect their hands while washing dishes, and a pair of rubber-soled canvas sneakers.

Inside the car, a message crackled over the radio.

"Three Seven-Six, headquarters. Kennedy motorcade clearing Cedar Springs and Inwood at this time and everything looks good. Three Seven-Six proceeding to Trade Mart for security deployment."

"Roger, Three Seven-Six. Ten-four."

At this snail's pace, Alex thought, it could take another half-hour for the motorcade to crawl through downtown. He didn't relish the thought of having to spend so much time in a cramped subterranean passage barely large enough for a human body, yet he dared not wait much longer to take his position. Small knots of curious people were already beginning to form down in the plaza below, and more were arriving every minute, as thousands of Dallasites utilized their normal lunch hour to catch a glimpse of the President.

Somewhere among the onlookers, Alex knew there would be two KGB regulars and at least three contract agents. Barton, the radical Bolshevik from Connecticut, would be there with a woman and small child, pretending to be a typical curious family. And Hamilton, a Britisher with an uncanny knack for looking like a policeman, would be circulating authoritatively through the crowd and maybe even giving occasional orders for people to move back. Alex didn't know who the other agents were, and it was just as well. They were all to be there merely in a passive role. They would use any opportunity to spread confusion and alarm among the crowd at the height of the crisis, but were under strict orders not to actively assist the assassins in any way.

He quickly removed his well-polished dress shoes and placed them in the trunk as he slipped his feet into the sneakers. He had just finished pulling on the coveralls over his trousers and sweatshirt when he saw a car come up the dead-end street and turn into the graveled area. His palms were suddenly wet and there was a fluttery feeling in his stomach, but this was no time to panic. This was a time to take the offensive and be assertive.

He threw up his left hand, signaling the driver to stop, and withdrew the folder with his badge from the pocket of his coveralls with his right hand.

"Hold it, mister," he said gruffly. "This is a secured area. You can't park here."

The car was a late-model Olds with a man and a woman in the front seat and a second man in the back seat. All were young, well-dressed and not particularly impressed.

"Who says we can't?" the driver demanded.

Alex flipped the folder open and gave him a good look at the badge. "Police officer," he said. "You'll have to park somewhere else. Sorry."

The man snorted. "I don't see why," he said. "You got no right to block off this area."

Alex leaned into the car through the driver's window until his cold, piercing eyes were a foot from the man's face.

"I'm not going to tell you again, mister," he said. "This is a secured area. Now you can either move along or I can call a squad up here and have all three of you taken to jail. Which is it going to be?"

"Oh, horseshit," the man said, jerking the car into reverse. "What is this, a goddamned police state?" He backed angrily out into the street and screeched his tires as he drove back the way he had come.

Alex watched the car until it was gone, then breathed a sigh of relief. Quickly, he pulled the vinyl gloves on, took the rifle out of the trunk and slammed the trunk lid shut. Then he knelt down and tugged at the sewer grate. It was heavy but a two-foot-square section of it came up with no problem, just as he knew it would, revealing an underground cubicle measuring about three-feet-wide by five-feet-long by four-feet-deep. At the bottom of the cubicle, at the end facing the slope overlooking Elm Street, a concrete drainpipe opened off into total darkness. The pipe was barely 18 inches in diameter, but Alex knew from queasy personal experience that he could crawl through it. He also knew that it led directly to a sewer opening in the north curb of Elm Street, an opening that would be no more than ten feet, at most, from the open-topped presidential limousine when it passed that way in a few minutes.

He took one last quick glance around, then lowered the rifle gently into the cubicle and dropped in after it, reaching up to pull the metal grate back into place, then sitting down on the concrete floor and taking a series of slow, deep breaths. He listened intently for a few seconds but heard nothing except the muffled hum of traffic on Elm Street.

In all likelihood, there would be other curious civilians in search of a vantage point who would try to park in the graveled area, but the closer the time came for the motorcade to appear, the more likely that police units assigned to crowd control would turn them away. At any rate, now that he was in the hole and out of sight, it didn't really matter, as far as Alex was concerned. He would have to take his chances of getting out of the cubicle unseen after it was all over, but in the confusion that was certain to follow the shots, he knew the odds would be in his favor.

He dreaded the thought of crawling the 60 feet or so through the pipe to the opening in the curb and especially the thought of crawling back. It would be dark and suffocating in the pipe, and there was a nagging fear in the back of his mind that he might hyperventilate and pass out before he was able to reach the cubicle again. He didn't want to think about what he was going to do; he only wanted it to be over. He had killed before, dispassionately and with no particular feeling, but he had never killed a President. He had never made history, and now he was going to.

To counteract the dread and the unwanted thoughts, he

used a kind of self-hypnosis that had proved effective before in other nerve-racking situations. He thought of the most pleasant sensation he could imagine. He thought of Mollie. He thought of her milky thighs and the curly, golden fleece between them. The pipe was the opening between Mollie's thighs. In entering the pipe, he was actually entering Mollie.

He felt himself stiffen with desire. There, that was better.

He looked at his watch in a shaft of sunlight from the grate over his head. It was 12:08. Time to move. He switched on his penlight and pushed his shoulders and torso into the pipe, thrusting the rifle before him.

"Here I come, Mollie," he whispered.

He heard the crowd cheering, and then he heard Oswald's first shot. The rifle barrel snaked out of the opening in the curb as he counted backward from five.

He was at four when the wheels of the lead car filled with Secret Servicemen flashed by, still proceeding at normal speed. The realization hadn't hit home yet.

". . . three . . ."

He heard the second shot and the motorcycles flanking the front fenders of the presidential Lincoln passed in a blur. Above him and to his left, a woman screamed . . .

". . . two . . ."

The limousine loomed directly over him, slowing almost imperceptibly as it passed from left to right. President Kennedy was standing in the rear seat, a look of confusion on his face, his hands moving toward his throat. Jacqueline Kennedy was a flash of pink, turning to stare at him. Governor Connally was falling . . .

". . . one!"

The rifle bucked, and the recoil slammed him backwards. The sound of the shot was deafening. It echoed like the crack of doom inside the narrow concrete cavern.

He saw a vivid splash of red against the glaring azure sky as Kennedy's skull exploded. Tiny droplets of blood sprinkled his extended left hand as he shrank backward into the primordial darkness.

In the fearsome, tomblike tunnel, he could feel Mollie's

thighs locked tightly around him. He could feel her rhythmic, writhing thrusts against him.

Above the wild ringing in his ears, he heard her moan with ecstasy as he reached a dizzying, thunderous orgasm.

Not a single person saw him when Alex pushed the grate back and poked his head up out of the hole. It was 12:41 p.m. and hundreds of people were pointing, staring and milling mindlessly on the grassy plaza below, but the area around the car was deserted. As a precaution, however, he left the rifle inside the drain pipe to be picked up later, at a less conspicuous time after the chaos was over. He quickly peeled off the coveralls, with the vinyl gloves already stuffed into one pocket of them, and threw them into the trunk, along with the sneakers. He retrieved his good shoes and stepped into them while he pulled his white shirt on over the gray sweatshirt, the sleeves and elbows of which were now very much the worse for wear from their contact with the walls of the pipe.

The radio inside the car was going crazy as he opened the door and slipped the key into the ignition. He had never heard such confusion on a police frequency.

As soon as he had his tie knotted, he snatched up the microphone. "Seven Nineteen on Elm approaching Triple Underpass," he said, cutting into the cacophony of transmissions. "Do you have descriptions of any suspects?"

"Negative, Seven Nineteen," the dispatcher rasped. "Just keep your eyes open and stand by."

Good, Alex thought. Oswald was a gullible, temperamental fool, but at least he apparently hadn't been caught in the act. The next step was for both of them to get out of the immediate area and keep their rendezvous at the Texas Theater in Oak Cliff. From there, Oswald believed he would soon be sprinted out of the country and into Soviet territory, where he would receive a top-secret but very glamorous hero's welcome and, eventually, privileged status as a political refugee in the U.S.S.R.

It was never going to happen, of course. In an hour or two, if Alex's luck continued to hold, Oswald would be clearly identified as the lone assassin of President Kennedy—and he would also be every bit as dead as Kennedy was.

The traffic was predictably heavy and slow-moving, but Alex was able to extricate himself from the jam of grieving, stricken humanity around Dealey Plaza with surprising ease. Instead of trying to negotiate the melee on Elm, he drove due south on Houston Street past the *Dallas Morning News* Building, then onto the dogleg of the Houston Street Viaduct, which carried him across the Trinity River to Oak Cliff.

At 1:22 p.m., Unit 719 was parked on Jefferson Avenue five blocks from the Texas Theater. Alex was smoking a cigarette and counting the minutes until his scheduled rendezvous with Oswald when an unnerving message came over the police radio.

"Attention all units vicinity Tenth and Patton. Signal Thirty-Two. Code Three with ambulance. An officer is down. Repeat, an officer is down."

Tenth and Patton was only a few blocks away, Alex realized, and if Oswald had gone by his rooming house for any reason, it was squarely on the route he would be taking to the Texas Theater. He thought of going on to the theater now, but it was still far too early, so he lit another cigarette and squirmed.

Minutes later, the dispatcher's voice crackled over the radio again.

"All Oak Cliff units, stand by. Be on lookout for suspect in shooting of officer at Tenth and Patton. Description follows: White male, 25 to 30, five-eleven, 165 pounds, brown hair, wearing light colored Eisenhower jacket. Approach with caution. Subject is armed and dangerous.

Alex dropped his cigarette out the car window and cursed. It was still over ten minutes until his rendezvous time. He waited, biting his nails, until 1:43 exactly, when he backed out into the street and drove slowly toward the theater marquee in the distance.

"Attention, all units," the radio suddenly blared. "Shooting suspect reported in Texas Theater."

Alex felt as if the bottom had just dropped out of his stomach.

He was still a block away when two black-and-white squads loomed up in his rearview mirror and tore around him with red lights flashing. When they screamed to a halt in front of the theater, four uniformed cops jumped out and ran toward the box office with service revolvers drawn. Just then a third patrol car careened around the corner from the opposite direction, closely followed by an unmarked unit.

"Goddamn you, Oswald, you trigger-happy idiot," Alex snarled aloud.

He brought the car to a skidding halt behind one of the black-and-whites and ran for the theater as hard as he could go, fumbling for his service revolver as he went.

He could hear sirens behind him now and see another unmarked unit streaking down Jefferson toward him. The other officers were already inside the theater.

Alex and the plainclothesmen in the arriving unmarked unit reached the theater entrance almost simultaneously. He recognized them as homicide detectives.

"Let's get the sonofabitch," Alex hissed. "Let's put him down right here!"

"Easy, Alex," one of the other detectives said. "We got a potential presidential assassin here. We got to go easy."

He felt his heart sink. He was so close, he thought, yet so far away. If only he had gotten there three minutes earlier, it would all have worked out so perfectly—more perfectly than he could ever have hoped for. But now it was all fucked up and bent out of shape.

The shit had hit the fan, as the Americans liked to say.

They were going to take the bastard alive, and there was nothing he could do about it.

Alex stayed late at the police station that night, along with everybody else. He was nervous, frustrated and distraught, but in spite of everything, he was also fascinated by the situation in which he found himself. Somehow, he told himself, he would still be the master of it. All he had to do was think it through.

He started trying to reach Mollie by phone early the next morning, unseemingly early. There was no answer at the apartment she shared with Hollie, but he was certain someone was there and simply refusing to answer. He continued trying all that morning and well into the afternoon, but still without success. Oswald's photograph was in both the *Dallas News* and the *Times Herald* that Saturday, and he had no doubt that she had seen it. He knew he had to think of something to tell her, some explanation that would satisfy her until he could solve the problem permanently, but first he had to find her.

About 7:30 that night, he went to the Carousel Club. Mollie had shows at 8:30 and 10, and he knew she wouldn't miss work, no matter what. He had reached the point where he had to see her or explode, and he wanted to see Jack Ruby, too.

A plan was beginning to take shape in Alex's mind. He had been interested in hypnosis for years and had received special training in it as part of his KGB instruction. Over the years, he had become very adept at it and had used it with varying degrees of effectiveness on dozens of people, but he had never encountered a subject as susceptible to it as Ruby. Several months earlier, he had put Ruby into a deep trance without trying. Strictly as a diversion, he had done it innumerable times since and had conditioned Ruby to the point that he could induce a state in which Ruby would do almost anything he suggested, simply by saying one word: "Chicago."

There was no need to hunt for Ruby. He came rushing right over as soon as Alex walked in.

"Can you believe the things that're happening in this town?" Ruby demanded. "I'm ashamed to say I live here. Poor Jackie Kennedy!"

"Come on, Jack," Alex said, "they've had assassinations in Chicago, too."

Ruby smiled vaguely. He seemed to have forgotten what he was saying. "Yes, I guess that's true," he muttered.

"This guy Oswald is a real shit, though, Jack," Alex said. "He really hates Jews, you know. He claims that's one reason he shot Kennedy, because he was sucking up to Jews all the time. At least that's the way he put it."

"The sonofabitch!" Jack said.

Conditioning, Alex thought, conditioning.

"Have you seen Mollie," he asked.

"Sure," Ruby said, "she's in her dressing room."

"Good," Alex said pointedly. "I was beginning to think she'd gone to Chicago."

When he opened the door and she saw him, Mollie refused to meet his eyes at first. She declined to offer her lips when he leaned over her, so he kissed her on the cheek, smiling his most disarming smile. But even after he sweet-talked her for a while, she remained distant and evasive.

"Come on, sweetheart," he said finally. "What's eating you?"

For the briefest instant, her eyes met his in the mirror above her dressing table, but then she looked away again.

"I don't think I want to see you anymore, Alex," she said.

He put his hands on her bare shoulders and massaged the tenseness he felt there. "I can't believe that, Mollie," he said evenly, "but if you mean it, I think you at least owe me an explanation."

She forced herself to look at him, and her eyes brimmed suddenly with tears she couldn't hold back. "I saw that man in the newspaper," she said. "The one who shot the President. That Lee Harvey Oswald. I know he was the same man you and Dee and Tommy met in Mexico. I don't want to know anything else about him or you or anybody else, Alex. I just want you to leave me alone."

He laughed and did his best to make it sound convincing. "You actually think I had something to do with what happened yesterday?" he asked.

"I didn't say that," she said. "I don't think anything."

"Listen to me," he said urgently. "What happened in Mexico was official police business. We were trying to put Oswald out of circulation before he did something terrible, something exactly like what he did yesterday. We just didn't move fast enough, that's all. You've got to believe me, Mollie."

She shook convulsively, and her tears left a muddy trail of mascara down her cheeks. "I want to believe you," she said, "but I don't know what to believe anymore. Damn it, I've messed up my mascara."

He stroked her neck and bent down to kiss her tenderly on the temple. "Look," he said, "come home with me tonight, and I'll explain the whole thing to you, right down to the last detail, I promise. Then you'll see. My testimony against this Oswald character is going to be the key to convicting him of murder."

She blew her nose and managed to get herself under control. "Okay," she said, "but not tonight, Alex. I just can't. I haven't had any sleep, and I'm all worn out." Her mouth smiled at him, but her eyes were somewhere else again. "Let's make it tomorrow night, okay?"

"Sure," he said. "Tomorrow night."

After the first show, she sat with him at a big table along with her sister, Hollie, and Hollie's boyfriend, reporter Jamie Cade, and some other people. When she and Hollie finished their second show, they came back for a while, but it was clear that Mollie wanted to leave.

Right after Tommy Van Zandt came in and started making tasteless jokes about the Kennedy assassination, Mollie and Hollie excused themselves and said they had to go. Alex could have strangled Tommy.

"I'll drive you home," Alex said. "Hollie probably wants to go somewhere with Jamie, anyway."

"No," Mollie said stiffly. "Hollie's tired, too. We've already called a cab."

He wanted to shake her, but he didn't. He would take care of her soon enough. After tomorrow night, he would never have to worry about her again.

She allowed him to kiss her as the taxi pulled in front of the club, but her lips felt strangely cold.

"We'll have a great time tomorrow night," he said softly, "and I'll set your mind at ease about everything, once and for all. Okay?"

"Okay," she said and pulled away from him.

He stared after the taxi until its taillights were swallowed up in the late evening traffic. He could still feel the touch of her on his fingers, the wetness of her mouth on his face, the smell of her perfume on his jacket. He wanted her so fiercely that he could have screamed, could have beaten his head bloody against the wall of a building, could have thrown himself down on the sidewalk and pounded it with his fists.

Tomorrow night, though, he would have her, goddamn it. He would have her in all the ways he wanted to have her. He would have her one last, glorious time—and then he would kill her. The idea had been repulsive to him at first, but now he was almost looking forward to it.

He never saw her again.

CHAPTER TWENTY-SIX

November 22, 1987

Sarah stared incredulously at the man who had called himself Alexander Sutton for more than 30 years. Along with the outrage she felt at what he had just calmly recounted, and the terror at what was about to happen next, she felt in almost total awe of him. Here in the kitchen of this old Arkansas farmhouse, sitting no more than seven or eight feet from her, was a man who had changed the entire history of Western civilization. Somehow, he looked too small and frail and physically insignificant to have done it—everything about him except his eyes, that is. His eyes left no doubt that he had done it—and could do it again today if it was absolutely necessary. She had never seen such eyes, such magnetic power, such malice.

She had lost track of time for a while—she thought all three of them had while the story was unfolding—but now saw that it was past 8 a.m. by the clock on the wall. That meant the tape on the recorder under the table had run out some time ago. It was a pity it hadn't lasted long enough to contain the whole fantastic story, but it had captured a substantial part of it. And, God willing, the tape could still be her ace in the hole. Its presence offered a wispy, miniscule fragment of hope, as a wild, impulsive idea began to jell in her mind. And it was really their only hope, as far as Sarah could see.

"You still haven't explained what happened with Ruby," she said, trying to stretch it out just a little further, to give her brain time to process the wild idea. "Do you mean all you had to do was say 'Chicago' and he went right out and shot Oswald?"

Alex smiled again. He had smiled often during the story, but it had never been a pleasant smile.

"It wasn't quite that easy," he said, "but almost."

"Let me guess," Matt said. "You called Ruby on the phone that Sunday morning, two or three hours before he showed up at the police station, right?"

Alex nodded. "It's a good thing I did, too," he said. "Mollie had been to see him, damn her. She'd showed him one of those pictures she took in Mexico, one of the ones I didn't know about that showed me with Oswald. That was the first I knew about those pictures, but they almost blew my whole plan out of the water right there."

It was strange, Sarah thought, considering that it had happened so long ago (she had been barely three years old at the time), but as she watched Alex's eyes, she could almost visualize Ruby's face as Alex described his mood that morning.

"Ruby was upset, but he seemed more confused than angry," Alex went on. "I knew he liked me and didn't want to believe I'd had anything to do with the Kennedy assassination or Oswald, but I also knew I had to get control of him quickly or there might be hell to pay. I'd never put Ruby in a trance over the phone before, but I decided it was worth a try. I told him the picture was a fake, forgery. I told him Mollie was crazy with jealousy because I'd been seeing another woman. Then I said, 'I want you to meet my other girlfriend, Jack. You'll like her. She's from Chicago.' "

"Obviously it worked," Sarah said. "What did you tell him to do?"

"First I told him to tear up the picture and forget it. Then I started in on Oswald and the Jews again. Ruby was totally bonkers on the subject. I told him Oswald thought all Jews were chickenshits and cowards. I told him how Oswald was bragging about making Jackie Kennedy a widow and Kennedy's children orphans. Then I told him about the transfer to the county jail that was coming up about eleven o'clock that morning.

" 'You don't want to miss that, Jack,' I said. 'Come to the Main Street ramp and I'll let you into the basement. Be sure and bring your gun along, too. I hear the commies are going to try to help the sonofabitch escape when we bring him down. You don't want a rotten sonofabitch like him running around loose and killing people, do you?' "

Matt laughed suddenly. "What you don't realize, Alex," he said, "was that Jack was making notes all during this conversation. At least, you might call it that. He didn't know what he was doing, I'm sure, but all the time you were talking, he was doodling on a scratch pad. Jamie and I found the sheet from the pad that night, along with the picture Jack tore up. Unfortunately, though, he tore the picture so that nobody could tell you were in it."

"I always wondered what you found," Alex said. "I discovered you were there a day or two later while I was questioning Ruby's roommate and one of the lawyers who went with you. Griggs, I think it was. At the time, Mollie had disappeared and I was more worried about her than anything else. I should have gone to Ruby's place immediately after the shooting to make sure there was nothing incriminating lying around, but the only thing on my mind that afternoon was Mollie. It's ironic, isn't it? If I'd been thinking straight, I could have saved you a lot of grief, Matt."

"You could have saved Jamie Cade a lot of grief, too," Matt said bitterly. "You wouldn't have had to kill him."

Alex shrugged. "At that point, he was just one more," he said, "but Cade brought his problems on himself, just as you did later. I guess I underestimated you and Cade, because I first thought Mike Fisher was the likeliest of the three of you to have found anything incriminating. Once he was out of the picture, I relaxed a little, especially when the months passed and neither you nor Cade came forward with anything. Then I found out Cade was nosing around at the police station and asking a lot of questions about me and my connections with Conlan and Van Zandt. I decided he had to be eliminated, so I took care of the matter personally."

"You killed him yourself?" Matt asked.

Alex nodded. "It was the logical thing to do, since I knew him well and was familiar with his habits. I followed him around from bar to bar that night while he was in the process of getting soused. I'd put a tap on his phone, so I knew he and his girlfriend had had a fight. She wanted to leave town and he didn't, or something like that. Anyway, I waited until he went home and then I called him and told him I needed to talk to him. I told him I'd only taken the job at CUA to find out more about Conlan and that I knew Conlan was mixed up in an assassination conspiracy. Naturally, he invited me up to his place.

"When I got there, it was a piece of cake. Cade was extremely drunk, sitting on the living room couch in his underwear, listening to records. I talked to him for a minute or two, and then I came up behind him. We were using Karate in the KGB long before it became popular in this country. One blow was all it took. He never made a sound."

"What about all the others?" Matt asked.

"I did some of them, and some of them were contracted out," Alex said. "We used two main criteria in deciding who to eliminate. The first was close association with Mollie. We didn't know who else she might have shown those pictures to. The second was close association with Ruby, especially anyone who might have noticed the 'Chicago' thing and the hypnotic hold I had on him. All the time, of course, we were trying desperately to find Mollie, but we never did, not until last month."

"Did you kill Mary Cockrell two weeks ago in Ohio?" Sarah asked.

"Yes," Alex said bluntly. "That was another bad oversight on my part, but over the years, I'd totally forgotten about her."

"I don't understand why you didn't just leave the country," Matt said. "Your cover's been totally blown. Your usefulness as an agent is over, at least in this country, but you accomplished your mission. You accomplished it in spades, I'd say. Why take the risk of hanging around and losing everything when you could be safe and sound halfway around the world?"

"Two reasons, really," Alex said. "First off, I don't want to go back to the U.S.S.R. What would be there for me, except a boring, bureaucratic job and a sterile apartment and a drab existence? I'll never go back to that kind of life again. I've learned to enjoy living in style and comfort, even elegance, if you will. I love all the things money can buy, and I've got enough money in Swiss banks to buy a lot of those things, I assure you. If it hadn't been for you and Mollie, I could have spent the rest of my days as a wealthy, powerful American executive and still do the job I was sent here to do. Until two weeks ago, it was my dream to live out my life in this country."

Matt looked mildly amused. "Are you trying to say you've been corrupted by us decadent capitalists?" he said.

When Alex replied, Sarah noticed that his voice was still calm and even, but his eyes were blazing furiously and his face was twitching with emotion.

"Yes," he said bluntly, "but you completely spoiled that dream for me, Matt. And that brings me to the second reason I stayed. It's very unprofessional of me, I know, but I stayed for revenge. I stayed for retribution and repayment. I stayed specifically to kill you."

He leveled the pistol at Matt's head. "This has been a most enlightening talk," he said, "but the time for talking's over now. You've used up all your nine lives, my catlike friend, and it's finally time for you to die."

Sarah tensed on the edge of her chair and jerked herself forcibly back to reality, away from the mesmerizing force of Alex Sutton's eyes.

They were mere moments—perhaps only seconds—away from ultimate disaster. The wild idea flitting around in her brain wasn't much to work with, but it was all she had.

"You can't mean you're just going to shoot us," she said. "I thought you always made it look like an accident."

"It won't matter," he said. "When this place blows up in two or three hours, enough gas will have accumulated in here to disintegrate everything into tiny little fragments. There won't be enough left of you to tell if you were shot or even to perform an autopsy on, not even if some ignorant backwoods medical examiner had enough sense to try."

You shouldn't talk that way about Arkansas, she thought, you smug, godless, rabid animal.

She let her eyes wander slowly from the chair that held the hidden tape recorder to the almost-full pot of hot coffee still steaming on the kitchen counter. They were both integral parts of her wild idea. Maybe she was merely grasping at straws, but it was better than dying with her hands folded in her lap.

Perhaps her hole card was only a deuce, but then again, maybe it was a joker.

"In that case," she said, "I guess you don't have to worry about the tape I've been making of this conversation. It'll probably be blown into a million pieces, too."

Alex's incredible eyes studied her. They were as flat and blank as ball bearings. Her own eyes met Matt's for a split second, and she could read the recognition in them. Matt could tell she was going to try something; he just didn't know what.

"I'm not playing any more games," Alex said quietly, shifting the gun toward her. "What the hell are you talking about?"

"The tape recorder," she said, returning his gaze with wide, guileless eyes. "It was on when you came in, and it's been on ever since. Every word you've said is on it."

The incredible eyes bored into her. "You're lying," Alex said. "You're making this up."

"No, I'm not," she said innocently. 'It's right here under the table." The muscles in her legs were as taut as steel bands as she leaned forward and reached toward the chair. "Here, I'll show you."

"Stop!" Alex yelled. "Don't move!"

He sprang out of his chair and came toward her in a crouch, the pistol held rigidly in front of him, the fat cylinder of its silencer aimed directly at her face.

"Maybe it's a tape recorder, and maybe it's something else," Alex said between his teeth. "Whatever it is, I'll see for myself." He motioned at her with the gun barrel. "Get up and stand aside," he ordered.

As she stood, she noticed a slight, almost invisible tremor in the hand that held the gun, and the tremor fanned the faint spark of hope within her.

Maybe it was fatigue or nervousness or simply the years catching up with him, but she thought Alex was just a hair less sharp than he should have been this morning. His perception was just a millisecond slow, his reactions just an eyelash out of synch, the steel trap of his brain just ever so slightly flecked with rust.

And when he stepped between her and Matt—into a position where he could no longer shoot them both in one unbroken, virtually instantaneous motion—she knew she was right.

As Alex reached for the chair to pull it out from under the table, he kept the gun pointed at her, but he shifted his gaze away for the smallest fraction of an instant.

Sarah heard his sharply indrawn breath as he saw the tape recorder. It slid out of the chair and fell clattering to the floor.

In a blind reflex action, Alex lunged to catch it. And when he did, Sarah lunged in the opposite direction, her hand clutching desperately for the handle of the coffeepot on the counter.

"You bitch!" Alex howled, but it was too late.

The next thing he saw—if, indeed, he saw it at all—was a sea of brown liquid engulfing him, as Sarah snatched up the coffeepot and hurled a quart of blazing-hot coffee full into his face.

Alex didn't see much after that.

He screamed in agony and fired two spasmodic shots with the pistol. One of them missed her by inches. The other crashed into the dishdrainer by the sink, sending fragments of china plates and coffee mugs flying in all directions.

As Alex stumbled blindly backwards, clawing at his scalded face, she smashed the empty coffeepot over his head.

"Run. Matt," she shrieked. "Run!"

Dimly, she saw Matt plunging toward the back door. She instinctively started to follow him, then caught herself. If they ran in opposite directions, she thought with cold, clear logic, Alex's chances of killing them both would be greatly diminished.

One of them had to get away. she told herself fiercely. One of them had to live to see this story told.

So she whirled back past the blundering, moaning Alex and ran as hard as she could go toward the front of the house.

Matt was all the way down the back steps and into the yard before he realized that Sarah wasn't with him. Once the realization struck him, he understood immediately what had happened, but understanding it didn't make him feel any better about it.

Sarah had used her head and hands while he had sat paralyzed, and she had saved both their lives, at least temporarily. Then she had used her head again while he had thought of nothing but getting away from Alex's blind fury. Once she had seen him head for the back door, she had gone in the opposite direction, knowing that Alex couldn't pursue them both at once.

Undoubtedly, it had been the smartest thing to do under the circumstances, but if anything happened to Sarah because of it, Matt Eastman could just forget about living and go ahead and die anyway.

He knew instinctively, though, that if Alex were able to go after either one of them, he would come after him first, even at the risk of letting Sarah escape unscathed. That was because, wounded or otherwise, Alex wanted to kill Matt more than he wanted anything else in the world. Matt was firmly convinced of that.

The thought had no sooner formed in his brain than he heard the screen door open, then bang shut again. He half-turned and saw Alex crash into the low porch railing and tumble down the steps. Alex hit the ground and rolled, but he was up again almost immediately, gasping for breath, waving the pistol, and appearing to sniff at the air like a bloodhound on the scent.

From his hairline to his lower jaw, Alex's face was as red and raw as an irritated hemorrhoid, and Matt doubted that he could see much more than a blur of light. There was no way to be sure, though, and Alex just kept coming on, not much more than a dozen long strides behind Matt in spite of everything and driven to superhuman effort by a mindless killing rage.

Matt pounded across the yard, forcing his legs to work harder than ever before. As he streaked past Hobo's lifeless, inert form, he felt sorrow tug at him, slowing him down for an instant, then shook it off and kept running.

But where the hell was he running to? The six-foot chain link fence was coming up fast, blocking his path, and he had grave doubts about his ability to scale it, especially since he was barefoot. The back gate was in almost the exact center of the fence, and there wasn't a sprig of cover for 20 yards in either direction, so if Alex could see anything at all, he would have an excellent chance of killing Matt before he made it through. And, hell, even if he managed to get out of the fenced-in yard, he would be shoeless in a field of burrs and greenbriar and only be putting himself that much further from Sarah, to boot.

His best chance was to hide someplace, then try to get behind Alex and go for the gun. Nothing was going to be solved as long as Alex had the gun and Matt had nothing in his hands but sweaty palms. The shrubbery along the fence was sparse and scraggly and in the process of losing its leaves for the winter. There still might be enough foliage to conceal him, but he doubted it.

If only he had something to fight back with, Matt thought, something to help tip the balance a little more in his favor. Matt's own pistol was lying in the bedroom, where Alex had found and unloaded it, but it was useless without bullets, and Alex had flushed all the bullets down the toilet. Still, there ought to be something.

As his feet and mind raced on together, his desperate eyes